DIE SMILING

ALSO BY LINDA LADD

Dark Places

Head to Head

DIE SMILING

LINDA LADD

PINNACLE BOOKS
Kensington Publishing Corp.
www.kensingtonbooks.com

PINNACLE BOOKS are published by

Kensington Publishing Corp.
850 Third Avenue
New York, NY 10022

All Kensington titles, imprints, and distributed lines are available at special quantity discounts for bulk purchases for sales promotions, premiums, fund-raising, educational, or institutional use. Special book excerpts or customized printings can also be created to fit specific needs. For details, write or phone the office of the Kensington special sales manager: Kensington Publishing Corp., 850 Third Avenue, New York, NY 10022, attn: Special Sales Department; phone: 1-800-221-2647.

ISBN-13: 978-0-7860-1887-1
ISBN-10: 0-7860-1887-9

First printing: August 2008

10 9 8 7 6 5 4 3 2 1

Printed in the United States of America

Prologue: *Sisterly Love*

One icy December morning the older daughter found out for sure that her mother didn't really love her. She was not even eleven yet when she opened her eyes that day. Light crept through the slat blinds on the dormer window beside her, gray and misty, slithering like ghosts. The attic was freezing this early in the morning, and she shivered and snuggled deeper under the thick quilted blankets.

Oblivious that Christmas day had finally dawned, her little half sister slept peacefully beside her, snoring softly from a stuffy nose. Sissy was eight years old, and everybody agreed that she was the prettiest little thing, so much prettier than her brother or older half sister. Oh, yeah, *dear little Sissy* was beautiful, all right, and it made the older one sick to her stomach the way people fussed over Sissy as if she were something so special. And it happened no matter where Momma took them, Wal-Mart or McDonald's or Pizza Hut, just about anywhere they went was exactly the same. Everybody wanted to reach out and touch Sissy's hair. The older one hated Sissy's stupid silky yellow hair. She hated every single other thing about Sissy, too, especially that little innocent smile that really wasn't innocent at all. Nobody ever seemed to notice it wasn't, except for the older one, and she always did.

The older one turned her back on her *oh-so-perfect* little sister and raised up on one elbow. She reached for the window cord, pulled the blinds up about a foot, and then gazed outside in awe at a winter wonderland. Snow was falling gently, and she watched it spiral down, then suddenly flutter this way and that when the wind swirled. She had watched it last night, too, at bedtime in the glow of the dusk-to-dawn lamp beside the old barn. Sometimes she didn't like so much cold, though, when she remembered the place where she'd lived with Momma and her real daddy, where it had been warm all year long. Now she lived in this colder place, ever since Momma had remarried and had two more children named Sissy and Bubby. No one here had an accent, like the one she'd gotten from her daddy who came from another country, either, and sometimes the other kids made fun of her, so she was trying to get rid of it.

It had snowed nearly every day since school let out for the holidays, and great drifts made her yard look like a giant birthday cake covered with smooth, shiny vanilla icing. She could barely make out the snowman they'd built yesterday. It had a carrot nose and two red apples for eyes, but Momma's pink-checkered apron around its waist was covered with white.

Snow piled on the windowsill, too, and the panes were etched with ice crystals that looked like the white lace Momma tucked around the bottom of Sissy's miniature Christmas tree. The older one turned from the window and looked at the little tree sitting on Sissy's bedside table. Tiny white lights twinkled in the gloomy morning, making the rhinestone tiaras hanging on the branches sparkle like real diamonds. Sissy'd gotten them at baby beauty pageants, eleven crowns in all, and the truth was that Sissy always got first prize, every single time she entered. She got trophies when she won, too, and colorful sashes made out of red and blue and yellow and green satin, but mostly red. Sissy's daddy had built special shelves downstairs in the living room to hold all Sissy's gifts and prizes. Sissy was his favorite, too.

One time, after the older one had screwed up her nerve enough to ask Momma if she could have her own little tree, too, Momma told her she could look at Sissy's tree and quit whining and maybe if she had won some contests when she was a toddler, she'd have some crowns to hang on a tree, too. After that, the older one had crawled underneath the back porch and cried for a long time but real quietly, so no one would hear.

Now, just thinking about that day made her angry all over again. She frowned darkly and leaned close to Sissy's ear, then she whispered through gritted teeth. "I hate you worse than poison, you stupid little thing, and I hate your dumb tree, too, and I hate your hair, and I wish you were as ugly as me."

Sissy didn't awaken, just burrowed deeper beneath the red-and-green patchwork quilt her Grandma Violet had hand-stitched for Christmas two years ago before she'd had a stroke and died. Strands of Sissy's long blond hair fanned out across the pillow, the exact color as summer sun. The older one picked up a curl and caressed the softness between her thumb and forefinger. Momma said her own hair was too coarse and mousy to be pretty. Nobody had ever asked to touch it, either.

Deep down inside her heart where she kept all her bad thoughts, the familiar rage rose from its low, controlled simmer, black and fast and furious. She grabbed a handful of Sissy's stupid, sunshiny hair and jerked it as hard as she could. Sissy cried out, and the older one smiled at her sister's pain, then tossed off her covers and sprang out of bed. She pulled off Sissy's quilts. "Sissy, c'mon! Santa's been here!"

Sissy bolted upright in bed, shivering and rubbing where her hair had been pulled. She looked around, her big china-blue eyes sleepy, her heart-shaped face confused. She looked beautiful, even all messed up. She'd worn her latest glittery crown to bed last night, the one she'd gotten last week when she'd won the Little Miss Snowflake contest, and she searched under the covers until she found it, then set it back atop her head.

"Sissy! Hurry up, let's see what he brought us!"

Sissy forgot her new prize and jumped out of bed. The hardwood floor felt cold against their bare feet, but neither noticed as they jerked on their fleecy robes and fluffy Disney World house shoes and raced out into the hall. Bounding down the narrow attic stairs to the second floor, they found their three-year-old brother already awake. His pull ups were probably soaking wet because he had lots of accidents at night, but the older one didn't care. She pounded on her Momma's door until her Momma and Stepdaddy opened it, all sleepy-eyed and tousled in matching red-and-blue plaid bathrobes.

Her stepdaddy's name was Russell, and he went to get his son, but the two excited little girls rushed downstairs. They paused at the turn in the staircase and gazed at the scene below in the living room. The big Christmas tree was all lit up, almost reaching the ceiling with its blinking and twinkling colored lights and a big white silk angel on top. In its warm glow, the older one could see the toys Santa had left them—two dolls—new Barbies still in the boxes!—and a bicycle with training wheels, and a baseball bat and glove for Bubby, all propped in a row on the brown couch! And there it was! The Barbie Dream House she'd wanted ever since she'd seen it at Wal-Mart last summer—all put together now and sitting by the fireplace!

She clamored down the rest of the way, Sissy close at her heels, both squealing with delight. Before she could reach the coveted dollhouse, her Momma grabbed her arm and pulled her away from the treasure trove awaiting her in the living room and into the front foyer. She could hear Sissy exclaiming over the Barbies, and Stepdaddy laughing as he carried Bubby downstairs. She tried to pull away to see what they were doing, but Momma held her arm too tightly.

"Now, listen to me, you."

At Momma's harsh whisper, the older one looked up, quickly filled with cold, hard dread. She knew that tone of voice only too well, when Momma turned a little crazy and her eyes got all black and scary, the one she only used when Stepdaddy wasn't around to hear.

"I couldn't get you anything this year, and I don't want to hear any hateful back talk about it. You know good and well that your cheapskate daddy doesn't send me a damn dime for you since he ran off and left us, and Russell said he's not gonna buy extras for you, not when you have a real daddy with tons of money somewhere."

The older one was so shocked that she could only stare at her mother.

Momma frowned. "You know how Russell made me quit working down at the Dollar Store. I don't have the money I used to have to spend on you. I only have what he gives me for food and clothes. And you ought to just be grateful that he feeds you and buys you the same kind of nice clothes he does for his own kids." She glanced into the living room and lowered her voice some more. "It won't be so bad anyway, you just ask Sissy and Bubby if you can play with their stuff. That's just the way it is now. You have to accept things the way they are. Nothing can be done. Life isn't easy, you got to learn that some time."

Momma's fingers tightened around the older one's forearm. "But you ask 'em nice, you hear, and don't let Russell hear you. And don't start that silly crybaby business, either, I'm warning you. I won't have it, not on Christmas! You aren't gonna ruin Christmas for Russell and the other kids."

"But I was good. I was good more than Sissy and Bubby! They're the ones that act naughty!"

"Your daddy doesn't love you, or he would've sent me some money for you because I wrote and asked him to. You sure can't fault me there. Russell loves his kids and that's why they got the toys. And your real daddy's the reason you never won any beauty pageants, too. Because you look just like him. It's a shame that you got all those freckles and didn't get my good looks. You best be satisfied that Russell even lets you live here with us. Your daddy sure doesn't want you. He hasn't come to see you since he left us for that slut he's shacked up with now. They're probably gonna have some kids together, and that's who he'll care about. His brats with her'll get plenty of toys for Christmas. Probably yours, too."

The older one sobbed, and her Momma turned her around and gave her a hard whack on the bottom. "Just look how ungrateful you are. You're lucky Russell doesn't cart you off to that foster home over on the south side, like he threatened."

Momma shoved her toward the steps. "If you're gonna bawl and carry on, you just get upstairs now, you hear me? Stop it, or you won't get Christmas stuffing and pecan pie for dinner, either."

But the older one couldn't stop crying, and she ran upstairs and threw herself onto her bed. She pulled the covers up over her head, but she could still hear Sissy's happy laughter floating up the stairs. After a while, though, she crept back downstairs and peeked through the banister.

Sissy and Bubby were still opening presents. Momma and Russell were laughing and hugging them, and she squeezed her cold fingers around the banister railing until her knuckles turned white. And then she knew that she hated them all. She hated Russell and she hated her real daddy, and she hated Momma. But most of all, she hated Sissy because Sissy got her Barbie Dream House. She wished she could kill her, kill her and throw her in the big river that wound through the cat-tle pastures where Momma and Russell would never find her.

Maybe she would. Maybe she'd think of a way to kill Sissy like they killed people in that movie Russell watched last night. It was called *Nightmare on Elm Street*. She would hide on the steps tonight when he watched another one he'd rented called *Friday the 13th*, because she'd heard him tell Momma that it was even bloodier and scarier than the one on Elm Street. Then she'd know how to kill Sissy. She was bigger than Sissy, stronger and taller, too. She could do it. She could take Sissy off someplace where nobody would see, kill her somehow, and nobody would ever know what happened to her. The idea that she could actually get rid of Sissy forever had never occurred to her before, and it made her smile and feel good and powerful and happy.

She went back upstairs and lay down on her bed, but now she was composed and quiet and still thinking about how she'd kill Sissy. She turned her head when Russell and Sissy came into the room. He was snuggling his dear little Sissy in one arm and carrying the Barbie Dream House in the other. He glanced over to where she lay on the bed, but he just smiled and talked to Sissy as he set up the dollhouse near the heat vent so precious Sissy wouldn't get cold.

Pure hatred lurched up the back of her throat. When Russell left, she waited until he was all the way downstairs, then rose from the bed and closed the door.

"Sissy, I wanna play with the Barbie Dream House. You'll let me, won't you?" She glanced at the door, not wanting Russell or Momma to hear. She had to be careful. Sissy was their favorite, even more than Bubby was, and he was the cutest little boy in the world with all those blond ringlets. She did like Bubby pretty good; she wouldn't kill Bubby because he was the only one she liked in the whole family. Maybe someday when she got older and bigger and smarter, she could kill Momma and Russell, too. But if they found out she was going to kill Sissy, they would send her off to that mean foster home.

Her little sister looked up, eyes so innocent and pretty and blue. There were designs in her eyes that looked like tiny little roses, all the way around in the blue part.

"Daddy said I don't have to let you play with my new toys if I don't want to. They said you tear stuff up and lose stuff, like you did Bubby's teddy bear."

"I didn't either! You threw it in the garbage can 'cause Bubby broke your tangerine crayon! I saw you!" The older one glanced at the door, wishing she could put her hands around Sissy's throat and squeeze and squeeze and squeeze. But she didn't. She grit her teeth so hard she thought they'd break and felt her fists clenching up, too. "Please, Sissy, please, just for a few minutes."

The younger one stared at her a moment, and then she smiled that beautiful smile that the Wal-Mart photographer said made her look like a perfect little angel. "I'll let you play with it but you have to let me hit you."

"Hit me? Why?"

"Because I want to, that's why. I want to slap you in the face like Momma does."

The older one looked at the Barbie Dream House with its pink-and-lavender striped curtains and its miniature white chairs and tables and bedroom suites. Sissy had gotten both the Barbies, too. One was dressed like a princess with a pink sequined gown and a teensy diamond tiara, and the other was dressed like a fashion model in a short denim skirt and a halter top made of red satin. They were both beautiful, with little heart-shaped faces like Sissy's. The older one had never had her own Barbie, but her nice teacher, Mrs. Dale, let her play with some at school.

"How hard you gonna slap me?"

"Real hard. You can't cry neither. If you do, it don't count."

"Momma won't like you hitting me."

The cherubic smile spread across Sissy's face again, but her eyes weren't smiling. They looked downright cruel. "Momma lets me do whatever I want, and you know it, 'cause I'm pretty and you're ugly. She told me so, lots of times. She says everyone's gonna love me all my life because I'm so pretty and blond. You got ugly hair and crooked teeth like your dumb old real daddy, and nobody's never gonna love you like they do Bubby and me, so there."

The older one knew what Sissy said was true. One time when Momma was very mad at her she picked up the gold hand mirror off the dresser and made the older one look in it and admit how ugly she was. Momma said she was ashamed of her and the way she looked. Momma said she was embarrassed to have to drag her around with her two other adorable children.

"Okay, you can hit me. But someday I'm gonna get you back for this. You just wait and see." And then she thought, Oh, yes, you'll see. Someday I'll get you good, and you'll be the star in a *Halloween* movie.

"Uh uh, better not or you'll get sent off to that awful foster home where people beat kids and make them eat Friskies cat food."

Sissy put down the Barbie she was dressing in a beautiful white lace wedding gown. Smiling, she got up and sat on her heels. She raised her arm and swung her palm against the older one's cheek so hard the older one was knocked off balance. She fell to one side and grabbed her stinging cheek. She fought back tears.

"You aren't cryin', are ya? You can't cry, 'member?"

"I'm not cryin', I'm not!"

"Okay. You can play with my Barbie Dream House until I say to give it back. But you better not tear it up, neither."

Still rubbing her reddened cheek, the older one crawled on hands and knees to the big dollhouse and carefully picked up a miniature couch. It was covered with purple silk and had tiny black tassels along the back. It even had itsy, bitsy black pillows on either end. Her face still burned like fire, but it had been worth it. She hated Sissy. Sissy never, ever got into trouble. Even Bubby sometimes got yelled at and smacked on the bottom, just because he wasn't Sissy. Someday Sissy would pay for slapping her face, someday Momma would pay and Russell would pay, and most of all her ugly real daddy would pay for not sending Momma money to buy her Christmas presents. Just wait and see. She would kill them all with sharp knives like the ones on Freddy's gloves when he was killing those older teenage kids down on Elm Street.

One

Twisting the ignition key, I fired up my black Ford Explorer and backed out of my parking space at the Canton County Sheriff's Department. It was a dull, uneventful, but beautiful early April day at Lake of the Ozarks, here in mid-Missouri, so my partner and I decided we'd stir up some excitement with one of our famous competitive shooting matches. We're headed now for the department's target range out in the boonies north of the lake, the winner buying the loser the most extravagant meal on the McDonald's drive-up menu on the way back into town. That's because we're both such big spenders.

Not that I'm complaining about the lack of excitement around here. Almost four months ago, we'd had a case straight out of hell, a pretty hairy affair with a couple of deadly psycho types fond of various and sundry poisonous creatures. Bud had nearly died in that one, and I was sporting a rather distinctive scar on my leg from a brown recluse spider bite that gives me the heebie jeebies to this very day.

But Orkin men visit my place regularly, and a can of Raid visits my Explorer regularly, and I haven't seen a single creepy, crawly critter since last Christmas. I don't think often of last summer either, when another case got pretty damn ugly in its own right, or at least, I try not to think about it. Unfortunately, my dreams don't always cooperate. Nightmares I do have, often and awful. And to think I thought this rural beat was going to give me some peace and quiet after my stint with the LAPD. Ha ha, joke's on me.

"Say, Morgan, how's the .38 Harve got you shootin'? Pretty good?"

That came from my aforementioned partner, Detective Budweiser D. Davis, Bud to everybody who knows him, on threat of death, at that. He was slouched in the passenger's seat, dressed down in a plain black departmental T-shirt and boot-cut Levi's. Usually he was all gussied up in designer suits and crisp, starched shirts, à la Armani and that ilk. The sleeves of his T-shirt did have ironed creases, though, of course, the guy was anal that way. I glanced at him as I swung right, took the SUV onto Highway 54, and accelerated toward the nearest bridge span. Atlanta born, handsome as Rhett Butler, with a killer Georgia drawl and intense gray eyes, Bud wowed the ladies like all get-out. He knew it, too.

I said, "Shoots good. Never take it off. Learned not to the hard way." I could feel the heft of the .38 now, strapped to my right ankle under my own boot-cut Levi's, just above my trusty black-and-orange high-top Nikes.

See, my best friend and former partner out in LA, Harve Lester, gave me this sweet little .38 Smith and Wesson for Christmas, one sporting its own brown leather ankle holster, and one that had come in pretty damn handy right off the bat. In fact, it saved my life when I was in a particularly vulnerable situation way down in a very creepy, dark place, so I don't take it off anymore, except to shower and sleep, and believe you me, it stays close at hand, even then. I rarely take off my trusty Glock 9 mm semiautomatic, either. It's snug in its shoulder holster under my left arm, just waiting for trouble to find it. Today, it didn't have long to wait.

Bud's cell phone started up, an annoying chimed rendition of Beethoven's Fifth Symphony; he's pretentious sometimes that way, but I betcha he keyed it in place of his former selection, "Friends in Low Places," which I totally preferred, only to please his girlfriend, Brianna Swensen. He fished the phone out of the pocket of his black windbreaker, checked caller ID, and I ascertained who was on the line immediately from his cheesy, pleased-as-a-monkey-in-a-banana-tree expression.

"Ah, looks like Brianna misses me, poor girl."

Brianna was his newest squeeze, and he was squeezing her long and often. I used to call her Finn because she looks like she could've been Miss Finland in the Miss Universe Pageant, actually could've won that galactic contest hands down, if you ask me. You know the type—long, silky legs, flowing natural blond hair, a face like a Rodeo Drive window mannequin modeled after a taller, willowier Jessica Simpson. Yep, Bud loitered in the halls of Valhalla most of the time now, grinning and beating his chest with doubled fists.

He answered the phone like a true goner. "Hi, babe, I miss you, too."

Yuck. And more *yuck*. So I busied myself with driving. Actually, I knew how he felt, I mean that silly grin and stuff. I was doing some rather inane smiling around myself of late, ever since I'd hooked up with the famous Nicholas Black, a rather fabulous-looking psychiatrist to the stars, who had begun to spend a lot of time ringing my bells. In fact, when we jumped into bed together, it sounded a lot like the Hallelujah Chorus on speed.

I passed over a bridge, admiring the spectacular view of Lake of the Ozarks off to my left. The water sparkled and glittered like a blanket of diamonds under a cloudless blue sky. It was a lovely, sunshiny morning, and fairly warm but still with a bite to the air. Flowers sprung up everywhere, azaleas, daffodils, tulips, dogwood trees. Made me want to go out and buy a trowel. But no one had killed anyone in our vicinity since the New Year, and we, the two ranking homicide detectives, were feeling pretty good about our little orderly corner of the world. Domestics and burglaries and shoplifting we could handle, armed to the teeth as we were. No problemo.

Bud said, "What?"

His concerned tone made me shoot him an inquiring glance. He was frowning. Uh-oh. Trouble in paradise. Maybe I had spoken too soon.

Then he said, "You gotta be kiddin' me." Not that I was eavesdropping or anything—but then he laughed, but sobered pretty damn quick. "Okay, got ya. I'm with Claire. We'll head over there right now. Keep everybody calm."

"What?" I said, not one to waste time idly wondering about things and truly hoping for a bit of mundane excitement to rev us up a bit. "And what'd you mean '*keep everybody calm*'?"

"There's an incident goin' on over at Mr. Race's Beauty Salon. And Bri's caught right in the middle of it."

I gave him a look, you probably know the kind I mean. I said, "What's up over there? Somebody get the wrong color nail polish and shoot up the place?"

"Hey, Morgan, give me a break here, would ya? This is serious. Bri's real upset."

"That's the place you gave me that twelve-month gift certificate to for Christmas before last, right? You know for hair styling and facials and pedicures, stuff like that?" The one I only used once. Couldn't abide being called *girlfriend* fifteen times during one haircut.

"Yeah. Mr. Race cuts my hair. He's the best around here."

Yeah, right. I remember the guy well. Mr. Race was not

one you easily forgot. A bit sissified, if you get my drift, gelled blond spikes, black silk shirt artfully undone to mid-chest. But Bud had discerning tastes and impeccable grooming. I could learn something from him, if I cared how I looked. "Okay, Bud, I'll bite. What's going on?"

"You'll laugh."

"No, I won't."

"He's bein' held hostage by an irate customer, and Brianna doesn't know what to do."

A gut laugh did tickle my innards, but I made myself not give in to it. A promise is a promise. But I had a rip-roaring good time inside myself for a second or two. "So it *was* a nail polish thing? What, somebody got fire-engine red instead of tomato bisque and freaked out?"

Bud shook his head as I pulled into the next blacktopped lake road, backed up, and then headed back the way we'd come. Hey, a call was a call. We were getting bored with all the law-abidingness in the land.

"Apparently this girl's a contestant in that Spring Dogwood Beauty Pageant that Nick's hosting over at Cedar Bend Lodge, and Mr. Race burned her hair with his new flatiron. She's goin' all ballistic and raisin' hell."

"Oh, for Pete's sake, Bud, you can't be serious."

"Just bear with me here, Claire. He's supposed to color Bri's sister's hair for the pageant rehearsal, and this is runnin' all his other clients late."

"Oh, now I get the urgency. We better call in backup for this one. Kansas City SWAT, too, maybe. Glad I've got both my weapons loaded and ready."

"Very funny."

Jeez, what some male detectives were willing to do for beautiful, leggy girlfriends who looked like they hailed from Scandinavia. Go figure. But, I have to admit, the call did sound rather interesting, more so than anything else we've tackled in the last few months. And as long as it doesn't include nests of spiders or severed heads, I'm good to go. I shuddered at those dark thoughts and then shoved some extremely ugly mental images out of my mind.

I made a beeline for MR. RACE'S WINNING LOCKS, THE SALON AND SPA FOR THE DISCERNING. Yes, that really is the name of the place. Yes, cockamamie it truly is. But it is also the premier beauty shop on the lake, located in its own luxurious digs in downtown Camdenton, less than a block down the street from the Sheriff's Department. As we drove past our office, I hoped the other guys didn't find out where we were going and why. I could already hear them laughing and fast-drawing combs out of their holsters.

I pulled into the parking lot, which was jam-packed with flashy little sports cars and big shiny SUVs, most of which were filled with sequiny evening gowns draped artfully across backseats and sparkly tiaras hanging from rearview mirrors. Mr. Race must have garnered a corner on the *Girls with Glittery Crowns* market. No wonder Bud liked to get his hair cut there. I patronized Cecil's Barber Shop for Men in Osage Beach. Cecil deemed me an honorary member despite my female gender, the thought of which reminded me that if my hair was long enough to pull back in a ponytail, I needed to cut it off ASAP. Black wouldn't like that, but he didn't like the T-shirts and jeans with ripped knees I wore much, either. It didn't seem to keep his hands off me, though.

Winning Locks was an ultramodern establishment with lots of silken drapes of varying shades of turquoise, green, and cobalt hanging in two gigantic front windows. Mr. Race hid rotating fans around inside that kept the fabric flowing in continuous motion and gave the effect of an underwater seascape. Big tanks of tropical fish finished the illusion. The front door was made of mahogany and beveled glass that blurred the interior. As we pulled it open, loud, and I mean headache-inducing, cringing-to-the-knees loud, feminine screeching quivered our goose bumps into marching order.

Crystal stemware beware. Eardrums brace yourself. Even Celine Dion couldn't hold a candle to this pitch range. Actually, the racket was coming from Mr. Race himself. Yes, inside was a scene straight out of Dante's Inferno, salon style.

Bud took charge with his usual official aplomb. "Hey, cut out that shrill crap, Race. You sound worse than a stuck pig."

The girly squeals stopped abruptly, followed by sobs that sounded a bit more manly, but didn't exactly rise to the machismo level. I decided that this altercation was Bud's baby and he could handle it. I'd stand around and be his backup and pull both my weapons if anybody started throwing brushes and pomade at us.

Mr. Race was breathing hard, chest heaving under his signature black satin shirt, and yes, it hung open, revealing his manly chest. Not a single hair was visible there, but it could've been hidden behind the big silver medallion he wore, one about the size of an IHOP pancake. His thin lips were trembling like crazy. I observed and analyzed the situation as I had been trained to do. His irate client had him bound to the swivel chair at his own red velvet–draped, thronelike styling station. One of his personalized black plastic smocks with Mr. Race's scribbled, hard-to-read signature emblazoned in silver script bound him bodily to the back. He seemed most relieved to see that armed law enforcement officers had arrived on the scene.

"Bud, Bud, oh, thank gawd, it's you. Corkie says she's gonna throw hair bleach right in my face. And she dumped in some permanent solution, some real potent stuff! You gotta stop her, Bud. It'll damage my skin for sure, and look, my nine and nine-thirty are both here waiting. This is really putting me behind."

I edged around Mr. Race's plump manicurist, a lady I hadn't been introduced to, but whose name tag identified her as Flash. She was dressed in a purple-and-pink tie-dyed shirt and bright yellow Capris and was calmly buffing the nails of a bouffanted, blue-haired octogenarian wearing a coral-and-gold lamé jogging suit. The old lady had chosen to polish her long clawlike nails the color of a very ripe eggplant. All ten nails were also adorned with little red stickers shaped like hats, identifying her at once as a member of the famous Red Hat Society, a group notorious at the lake for their wild monthly dinners at Applebee's, during which they all wore red or purple feather boas and took lots of pictures of each other. A good, wholesome group, however, who rarely caused trouble for the police.

Flash and the old lady were ignoring the commotion with Mr. Race and Corkie. But no wonder. *The Young and the Restless* was playing on a big-screen plasma TV hanging on the opposite wall. It was festooned in red velvet, too. Mr. Race's clients were obviously immune to dangerous hostage situations. On the other hand, some very amorous bedroom gymnastics were going on between Victor and some blonde young enough to be his great-granddaughter, maybe even great-great-granddaughter. And she looked pretty great, too. Not that I watch that soap, but I remember being titillated a time or two during my college days at LSU. I watched for a moment, in spite of myself. Victor was quite the Casanova, bending the gal backward over a couch and trying to kiss her. She was responding and all, but then again, he was holding a gun to her temple as incentive, so there you go.

Bud decided to take time to kiss Brianna's cheek and comfort her with a full-fledged body hug. Seemed like everyone was taking Race's dilemma in stride. Bud didn't seem particularly intent on letting go of Finn any time soon, so I decided that was my cue to get involved.

I said, "Okay, now, let's all get a grip here. Bring it down a notch." I addressed the irate red-haired young twenty-something holding the weapon. "What seems to be the problem, ma'am? Surely whatever it is, it's not worth all this commotion."

"Maybe not to you." She commenced with a severe blinking thing going on, holding back a flood of distraught tears, I presumed. I inched toward her, watching the white plastic bowl of caustic-smelling liquid she gripped in one hand. I sure as hell didn't want that stuff on my favorite black Remington T-shirt. She sobbed a couple of times then said to me, "Just look at it, my hair. Look what he did to me! There's no way I can compete now, and the pageant's getting ready to start! I've been rehearsing my baton-twirling routine for a good six weeks." More boo-hooing commenced.

I observed her hair. True, it was extremely frizzy on one side, and all broken off, and not a shade of red that was easy on the eyes. Maybe more like a bright shade of orangey pumpkin. Actually, she was sporting a do and hue closely akin to a Halloween Ronald McDonald after a drunken binge.

Always the diplomat, I said, "I think you look just fine, ma'am."

"Are you freakin' serious? It looks like a freakin' jack-o'-lantern and he burned the hell out of one side of it. It's not even two inches long!"

True, alas, all true. While I tried to come up with a comforting word or two, Bud managed to get over Brianna's lush curves long enough to join the negotiations. "It doesn't look that bad to me, either, uh, what's your name again, miss?"

"Corkie."

"Corkie? Seriously?" To give Bud credit, he didn't even grin.

"Yeah, so what?"

I knew a Corkie once, but he was a dog. I didn't mention that observation, either. I said, "Know what? I think you might be overreacting just a tad, Corkie. Put down that stinky stuff, whatever it is, and let's talk about this in a calm, adult manner. That smell's making people nauseous."

Corkie hesitated, thought about things a second or two. She said, "You just don't get it, do you? Just look at you. You look pretty without a dab of makeup on, and you obviously didn't take time to do a thing with your hair either." She eyed me critically with fierce beauty contestant acumen. "You'd look a lot better if you got some highlights, you know. Probably not ash, but not too gold, either, though. It'd really bring out that honey color. Really, you oughta consider it." Then she remembered her plight. Her grip tightened on her weapon. "But not here. Not with him doing it. Look at me, I'm ruined!"

"Maybe Mr. Race can fix your hair. Bud told me on the way over that he's a genius with hair and nails."

"Evil genius, you mean."

I considered that. Didn't know for sure, so I just shrugged.

"I am *not* an evil genius. Girl, *really*, how dare you?" Mr. Race was sputtering with full-fledged indignation as he glared at me. Hey, I didn't say it. I ignored him. He couldn't get at me. He was tied up nice and tight.

I remembered my LAPD hostage training and negotiation techniques. "Okay, Corkie, all you're doing right now is getting yourself in trouble. You don't wanna go to jail, do you? This is false imprisonment and threat of bodily harm. Assault, possibly. We'll have to add battery if you throw that stuff on him. Sitting all night in a cell with a bunch of drunks and hookers isn't going to help you get ready for the competition, now is it? This mistake can be fixed. Have you thought of just cutting it very short? That's what I'm going to do with mine."

Corkie let out a discouraged wail, almost equal in pitch to Mr. Race's, but not quite there before she gave it up. "But judges at the Lake never choose contestants with short hair to win! They like French twists and French braids! And sometimes big eighties hair!"

"Well, there's always a first time. Be different, think outside the box this year. Nick Black's one of the judges, isn't he? He told me himself that he liked my hair short, the shorter the better, he said." That wasn't exactly true, in fact, he said he liked it long enough to tangle both hands in, but luckily, he knew where to put his hands when it was short, too.

"You know Nick Black personally? My God, he is so freakin' hot."

I nodded, tried not to look smug about my choice of guys.

"You mean it? He likes short hair? He's hot, and I mean, *whoa, get the ice water* hot. Oh, my God, those blue eyes and that black hair, and all that money. He's so freakin' hot."

Corkie had suddenly turned into Paris Hilton sans the orange jumpsuit, at least not yet, but that might be coming later today. A terrible plight, to be sure.

I said, "Yes ma'am, that's the gospel truth. And he told me just the other day that New York and Milan models were cutting their hair ultra short this year. And what's her name? Petra, maybe, something like that? She's gone short, and I saw Keira Knightley on TV the other night and she had a pixie cut. You can be the first around here to buck the old long-hair trend. You'll stand out, Corkie, you'll be noticed."

Bud said, "Yeah. I'm a man, and I like short hair. And that color orange is good, too. Cyndi Lauper had orange hair once in one of her videos, right? And so does Carrot Top."

I gave Bud my best *are-you-friggin'-nuts* look.

Corkie said, "I know who Carrot Top is and I like his hair okay, but who's Cyndi Lauper?"

Bud looked startled that she didn't know about girls who just wanted to have fun, and I wondered if I was in a particularly asinine dream. Brianna joined our deep, insightful conversation.

"Oh, Corkie, please, be reasonable, now. Mr. Race can recut and recolor it, and I'm sure he'll do it all free of charge. He'll work on you until you're completely satisfied, won't you, Mr. Race?" She didn't give him time to refuse. "And tell you what, I'll do your makeup down at Swank's Couture myself. No charge. That's a $150 value."

Corkie perked up big-time. She lowered the perm solution a bit. Yes, we were good police negotiators. Trained to handle anything, even.

But Corkie wasn't done. She hadn't pouted yet. "Race hasn't even apologized. He just said I was having a bad hair day."

We all looked at Mr. Race. He did not look repentant.

Bud said, "Mr. Race, now is a good time to say something nice to Corkie. After all, you did burn off one side of her hair and make it orange."

"Okay, okay. Corkie, sweetie, I'm sorry, okay? I just misjudged the ingredients, or maybe I did get the wrong color, but it's been so hectic around here this week with all the contestants demanding extras. I'll fix you up, just like they said, no charge, anything you want. We can do hair extensions, if you want it long for the festivities."

Now Corkie looked delighted. She put down the bowl. She untied the stylist. They embraced like old lovers, kissed cheeks even, both sides, Continental style. Crisis over. Everybody could go back to watching soap operas. God was good. God save the Queen.

After everyone was friends again and thank-yous were exchanged all around, Brianna walked us to the door. She took both Bud's hands at the door and breathed out. "Bud, you were wonderful."

I couldn't quite figure where she got that, since she and I were the ones who talked Corkie down from her chemical crime spree, and Bud screwed up by mentioning Lauper and Carrot Top. Maybe the wonderful she was referencing was Bud's groping. One thing I did know. I was ready for more important things.

Bud said, "I'm glad to be of help. We're still on for tonight, right?"

Brianna nodded and snuggled in close for a second go-round. She'd probably been watching *The Young and the*

Restless, too, and Bud did have his .45 to turn her on with. I tried to look nonchalant instead of irked as they enjoyed a couple of minutes of a really good time, during which I began to wish Black would get back to town. He was in San Francisco, hosting a seminar at Berkeley on personality disorders, several clinical examples of which I might've just witnessed. He was due in later today. Maybe we could find an episode of *The Young and the Restless* to get us all hot and bothered.

Bud and Finn finally came up for air. Good thing, my patience was running thin. She said, "I don't know, Bud. My sister's here, you remember. I want you to meet her."

"Yeah, I want to. Bet she's not nearly as pretty as you." Bud, a.k.a. Charm Meister.

Finn laughed. "Oh, my goodness, Hilde's always been the pretty one. I'm the smart one."

Uh-oh, I thought. Brianna looked like a triple cross between Heidi Klum, Nicole Kidman, and the aforementioned Jessica Simpson. There wasn't anybody on God's green earth prettier than that. Except maybe Rob Lowe in *St. Elmo's Fire*. The smart part was iffy, too, but Finn did seem to have pretty much on the ball upstairs, a lot more than most models, a caste about which I knew very little, truth be told. She is really nice, too. I know that firsthand, but she'd won a bunch of beauty pageants in the past and that usually didn't score so high in the gray-matter department. But maybe I was biased against inhumanly attractive women.

Brianna looked at me as if she'd heard what I'd been thinking. I smiled brightly to hide my guilt. She looked troubled. "Actually, Claire, I'm really concerned about Hilde. She got down here a week ago from Kansas City and took a place up at Royal Bungalows."

That was one of the rental places Black owned on the lake, I recalled, but what didn't he own around here? He just loved buying things, especially hotels. All over the world, too. He wasn't too shabby in the gift-buying department, either. I found that out last Christmas just before all hell broke loose around the lake.

Bud said, "S'matter, Bri? You said the two of you had a good long visit the night she got here."

"I know, but that was several days ago. I haven't seen Sis since she moved up to the Royal. She told me she was exhausted and wanted to take a couple of days off to rest so I've pretty much left her alone. But now I'm worried. I couldn't get through on her cell last night, and she's not answering this morning, either. She's over an hour late for Mr. Race, and she never shows up late for hair appointments, especially right before a pageant's dress rehearsal."

Bud said, "Maybe she went shoppin' up in Jeff City at the Mall? Or maybe she's just outside on her deck, enjoying the warm weather."

"I don't know. I have bad vibes about all this, Bud. She's had stalkers in the past, and she always picks up on her cell, you know, in case it's her agent with a job offer. I'm half an hour late for work or I'd run up there myself. Pageant alterations and makeup appointments are keeping us so busy down at the boutique. I've been working late every night this week."

Bud said, "Well, how 'bout Claire and I checkin' out her place? I wanna meet her anyway."

Yeah, I wanted to get a load of her, too, but if she looked better than Finn, I wasn't sure I could take the shock.

"You mind, Claire?"

"Nope. It's right on the way to the target range. No problem."

"Okay, Bri. Don't worry 'bout a thing. I'll call you as soon as I talk to her."

We headed to our car, leaving Mr. Race happily snipping away on Corkie's pumpkin hair and gossiping about the other contestants, just like old times. High Noon at the Winning Locks was over. Bud walked Brianna to her red Corvette, the one she'd won in the Miss Miami Pageant a few years ago, and to think, she's just the smart one. I watched the two of them smooching their good-byes and looked away. Bud was a goner, all right. He might as well turn in his bachelor badge and buy the ring.

Two

The Royal Bungalows were built high atop some pretty impressive limestone cliffs that overlooked panoramic views of the lake in three, count 'em, three directions. There were six upscale individual apartments, each set into the craggy, windswept bluffs with utter privacy in mind. Hilde Swensen's was at the highest point, overlooking the rooftops of her sister bungalows scattered down the hillside. Far below lay one of the lake's quietest and most coveted coves, its olive green water rippling in the spring breeze and lapping at verdant banks. The view was really something, and Bud and I both admired it as we eased up the blacktop road toward Hilde's hideaway.

A cardinal-red Ford Fusion sat in the driveway, and we pulled up behind it and killed the motor. An Avis license plate was affixed to the rear bumper. We stopped in front of the low-slung, white concrete structure. A really nice place, designed with ultramodern lines and a green metal roof that probably sounded great in rainstorms, and lots of huge plate-glass windows. Extremely sleek, it looked a lot like something you'd see perched over a sunny beach in Malibu. It sat high up, but in a clearing with woods separating it from the bungalows below. The oak trees had just begun to bud out within the last week so the place was not as secluded as it would be in a few more weeks. The dogwoods were blooming everywhere, patches of pristine white in all the emerald hues. In summer the foliage would be thick and green and lush and give the tenant complete privacy.

Bud and I got out of the car. The stillness was striking. We stood with our doors open and looked at the bungalow. Far away we could hear the low, sporadic murmur of traffic on the bridge, and somewhere out on the water, a speedboat buzzed like an angry bumblebee. Otherwise it was unnaturally quiet. The place looked deserted. Slatted white wood shutters closed off every single window. Something cold and unsavory crawled across the floor of my stomach, and I knew what it was. Unease. Fear. My gut was telling me *uh-oh, watch your back, something wicked this way comes.* It's a sixth sense, true, pure instinct, but I'd learned to trust it. At the moment, it was standing on its hind legs and pawing the air like crazy. Visitors to the lake didn't usually close up a place this tight, not in this kind of weather and not with this kind of view.

Bud looked across the roof of the Explorer and said, "You feel it, too, right?"

"Yeah. Big-time."

"Maybe it's a good thing Bri didn't come up here."

"Yeah, maybe."

I searched the windows for any sign of life, hoping we were wrong. "Brianna give you a key to this place?"

"No. But she told me Hilde always keeps her doors locked 'cause of some kind of stalker problem a few years back. Said she learned to be careful about things like that."

"Well, that bodes well for her. Maybe that explains the locked-down shutters."

Bud and I moved cautiously toward the house. I told you

we'd had some pretty bizarre cases lately. We didn't take anything lightly. We didn't trust anybody, anywhere, any time. Nothing surprised us anymore. And maybe that's what this was. Nothing. Yeah, maybe it was quiet because the beauteous Hilde was asleep in her princess bed inside with Vaseline and cuçumber slices on top of her eyes. Maybe she always had quiet time when mentally preparing to strut her stuff on a pageant runway. My gut, however, was saying, *Yeah, right, and pigs could fly, too.*

I pulled out my Glock when we reached the wood steps that led up to the front door. I like the feel of it against my palm when I feel creeped out, unnerved, and about to be attacked. Bud had his weapon out, too. We were ready. Hopefully, all we'd do is scare the hell out of a sleeping beauty. We climbed to the porch without making a sound and stood on each side of the substantial dark green metal front door. Bud rapped with one knuckle and called out Hilde's name. No answer. Just silence and a rustling noise when a squirrel took off for home in a towering oak tree behind my Explorer, no doubt expecting gunplay. Spring had sprung, all right. So had my nerve endings.

I took the end of my T-shirt and tried the door handle. It turned easily.

Bud said, "Uh-oh. She always locks her doors."

"Yeah."

I pushed the door inward and called out her name again. Identified us as sheriff detectives. No answer.

We stepped inside. Bud tried calling her name a couple more times. Nobody answered. Nobody home. We were getting the picture. The living room and kitchen were beyond messy. Clothes were thrown around, and half-empty bottles of Evian littered the tables and chairs and kitchen counter. Cigarette butts overflowed a couple of glass ashtrays. Lots of stuff on the floor.

Bud said, "Most models are slobs at home, you know."

I didn't know that, but he had a helluva lot more experience with models than I did, so I believed him. We stepped cautiously through the living room. There was a folded newspaper on the bar, the *Kansas City Star* dated six days ago. I picked it up. Hilde Swensen smiled back at me out of a professionally done head shot. She was one beautiful lady, all right; Bri was right about that much. She had a killer smile and was wearing a three-tiered, glittering crown. Her name was below the picture, and the headline above the article read "Miss Spring Time Reigns Supreme."

"Look, Bud, here's a close-up of her. You didn't tell me she won Miss Spring Time. That's the one held down at the Plaza, right?"

"Oh, yeah, Bri says she wins more than she loses."

A black patent leather Gucci shoulder bag sat on the table next to the paper. It was standing open, and I saw Hilde's matching black Gucci wallet and key chain inside. There were a couple of photo albums there, too. I didn't touch anything.

"Her purse and keys are here."

"Maybe she's out on the back deck and didn't hear us come in."

A short hall led to the rear of the bungalow. There were two bedrooms, each with its own bath. We checked them out and found them clean and untouched. The master suite was a different story. Messy as the front of the house, clothes strewn around, dressers and bedside table littered with cosmetics, hair spray, and hot rollers, curling iron, all the paraphernalia of someone obsessed with their appearance. A big leather rolling suitcase sat open on the floor and fancy floor-length evening dresses were displayed on padded hangers on the back of every door. A one-piece red bathing suit had been tossed on the bed alongside a short black silk kimono. There was a pair of black fringed house slippers beside the bed. The burgundy-and-blue coverlet was flung back nearly off the bed, as if Hilde had gotten up in a hurry.

Bud said, "The place is clear. Back deck, too. Looks like she's not home. Must've gone off with a friend." He sounded relieved as he opened the French door that led onto the rear deck. Fresh air swirled in and smelled good in the stuffy room.

I walked to the bathroom door. It was closed. I felt the chill of dread as I knocked. I called Hilde's name, but knew she wouldn't answer. Standing to one side and holding my weapon pointed down, I pushed the door ajar a little and darted a quick peek inside. A strong smell of bleach nearly choked me. Bad sign. The bathroom was deserted, but my reflection flashed in a big white-framed mirror on the opposite wall. A second French door led out to what I assumed was the back deck, but burgundy drapes were drawn tightly across it. Identical curtains hid the shower enclosure, but there was a corner Jacuzzi tub designed to enjoy the spectacular view while bathing.

The bathroom was spotless. No towels on the racks; no face cream or hair spray on the sink; no trace of habitation. Weapon still ready in my hand, I moved to the shower enclosure, stood to one side, and jerked back the curtain. The metal rings screeched, but not as loud as I did when I saw what was sitting inside. I backed up as far as I could as fast as I could, until I hit the wall and had to stop. "Bud, in here!"

Oh God, it was Hilde Swensen, all right. The same curly blond hair, the same beautiful features, now waxen and white and wasted in death. She had been posed on the bench at the back of the shower. She had on a black one-piece bathing suit with a Miss Spring Time crimson sash draped diagonally across her chest. It had been stapled to the bare flesh of her left shoulder and right thigh. The three-tiered diamond tiara I'd just seen in the newspaper article was secured with bobby pins in the thick bun piled on top of her head.

Her hands were bound together at the wrist with black electrician's tape, waist high, forcing her fingers to hold on to a large bouquet of wilted red roses and white baby's breath. Their scent was funeral-parlor sweet, the smell thick inside the shower stall. Her large blue eyes stared back at me, wide open and glazed over, a look of shock and fear and horror forever imprinted into their depths. But it was her mouth that brought up the caustic burn at the back of my throat and made me want to gag.

Hilde Swensen's lips were missing, completely cut off, and I stared at her straight, ultra-white, movie star teeth frozen forever in the most horrible, grotesque skeleton's smile that I'd ever seen. Rivulets of blood had poured down her chin and long graceful neck in shiny dark red streaks that ran into the top of her bathing suit, lots of it, which meant she'd still been alive, heart pumping, when her mouth was mutilated. I fixed my gaze on the white rectangular welcome tag stuck on the bare skin of her right shoulder. Someone had left a message on it for us, printed in big box letters with a black Sharpie.

SMILE, AND SMILE, AND BE A VILLAIN.

The words triggered a memory, from Shakespeare, I thought, but then Bud was there beside me. He sucked in air then sagged against the door frame. "Oh, my God, my God, my God . . ."

He kept saying it as he backed into the bedroom, and I couldn't say anything, so I swallowed down my revulsion, but it took me a couple of minutes to get hold of my heartbeat. I moved forward, squatted down, and examined the woman the killer had arranged so meticulously on the bench inside the shower stall. It was Hilde Swensen, there was no doubt about it. I examined the floor of the tub for blood evidence. Completely cleaned out with bleach. Damn those CSI shows running nonstop on television with their how-to lessons on getting away with murder. Then I noticed the small pool of water still trapped in the drain hole. I bent closer, examined it, and did not like what I saw.

I leaned back and wiped my hand over my mouth. Bud had returned and calmed down some, and I looked up at him. He was still shaken, tanned face a bit ashen, and I had a feeling that was more now from anger than the initial shock of finding the body. I knew exactly how he felt. And I knew what he was probably thinking. He'd have to tell Brianna that her sister was not out shopping or getting her nails done but stone-cold dead, her mouth cut off, her eyes still filled with unbridled horror. It was happening again, just like it always did, and I felt the rage rise up inside me, too, hard, lethal, all-encompassing.

I set my jaw and got a firm grip on my own nerves, then jerked my cell phone off my belt and hit speed dial for Buckeye Boyd. He was the Canton County coroner and medical examiner and in charge of a crack crime scene team. He picked up on the second ring.

"Buck, it's me."

"Well, this can't be good, not by the sound of your voice."

"We need you up here at the Royal ASAP. We got a body."

"Homicide?"

"Yeah. Another sicko. Worse, you remember Brianna Swensen, Bud's girlfriend? It's her sister, but keep that under wraps because we don't have a positive yet. But I'm ninety-nine percent certain it's her."

"Oh, jeez, that's awful. Bud there, too?"

"Yeah. How soon can you get here?"

"Ten, fifteen at the most. Everybody's already down here for our staff meeting."

I flipped my phone shut. Bud kept rubbing his palms over his face. He was still sucking air, steadying himself with some major deep breaths. "This is gonna kill Bri, it's just gonna kill her."

"Yeah."

"Oh, man, Bri can't ever see Hilde like this. Not with her mouth carved up and all that blood."

"You wanna stay here with her or go string the tape?"

"I'll stay with her."

I said, "Smell all that bleach?"

"Yeah."

"The killer knows how to clean up after himself."

Bud was in control now and he came up behind me as I leaned down again to look at the water standing at the drain.

"Something's clogging the drain. See it?"

"What the hell is that?"

"I hate to say this, Bud, but I think it's her lips."

"Oh, God. Shit."

"Yeah, we better back off and leave things alone, until Buck gets here to process the scene. Let's see if we can find anything out on the deck."

As I stood up, I took a good look at the black-and-white tiled floor, searching for any trace of blood spatter. My guess was that's where the perp had scrubbed with the bleach, there and in the shower. I found nothing but a floor clean enough to eat off of. Bud jerked open the drapes on the door that led onto the deck, then stepped outside. I could hear him taking some more cleansing gulps of the lake-fresh air, and I followed and did the same thing. The morning sunlight nearly blinded me, and my spring fever and joy of the season was pretty much DOA now. I placed my gaze on the long vista that opened up across the horizon. Far away, I could just make out the glitter and flash of the lake and Nicholas Black's five-star resort, Cedar Bend Lodge, where it shone like a beacon, its myriad windows ablaze in the sun. All around us sat dark green cushioned deck furniture, six chairs, two chaises, and a matching table. Nothing else. No blood. No gore. No murderer's trail.

Bud and I moved over to the railing and stood looking out over the drop. Sometimes when perpetrators used knives to cut their victims, they cut themselves, too, especially if they killed in a rage. I knelt down, hoping the perp had left some of his blood behind for us, and that's when I saw it, on the rim of the deck outside the rail.

"We got blood, Bud. He went out this way, all right."

Bud shook his head, his jaw working underneath his skin. I knew he was still thinking about Brianna. "Why would he leave blood out here in plain sight when he went to that much trouble cleaning up the bathroom?"

"Good question. Maybe he didn't see it." I looked up at Bud. "Or maybe he was just in a hurry to get outta here."

"She's not cold yet and in full rigor, so she hasn't been dead too long. Half a day, maybe less."

"Yeah. And he'd have to've stuck around awhile to clean up this much. Maybe we surprised him when we drove up and he took off back here."

The back deck was about twenty-five feet square and hung out over the sheer plunge of the cliff. Heavily wooded, even now, this early in the spring, the trees obscured the lakeshore below and there were plenty of thick bushes and brambles to help hide somebody trying to flee the scene. Rooflines of the other bungalows were visible both to our left and right but none were directly below the deck, just trees and tangled undergrowth. We both peered over the railing and searched the ground about ten feet below.

Bud said, "Is that blood down there on those rocks? See it?"

I said, "Go ahead and string the tape. I'm going down and see what I can find. Maybe we'll get lucky this time."

"I'll give you a hand down."

I sheathed my gun and swung a leg over the top rail, then pulled my other leg over. I stood poised on the narrow outside ledge for a second, and Bud grabbed my hand to lower me to the ground below. We both froze as a sharp crack shattered the stillness. Sure as hell recognizing the retort of a gunshot when we heard it, we both instinctively ducked, but not before I felt the burn of hot metal as a slug ripped a shallow path across the top of my arm. The impact knocked me off balance, and I half-jumped, half-fell, landing hard on my wounded arm and rolling about three yards down the incline until a small stand of hickory saplings broke my descent.

Above me, Bud dropped flat on his belly on the deck and propped the nose of his .45 on top of the bottom rail. Another shot rang out from somewhere far below and to our right, and Bud returned fire with four quick, deafening blams while I lay low and fingered the wound through my torn T-shirt. It burned like hell, but was little more than a flesh wound, so I scrambled up onto my knees behind the steel brace that bolted the deck into the limestone rocks and tried to get a visual on the shooter.

Bud already had his cell phone out and was calling for backup, then he yelled down to me. "You hit bad?"

"No, it just grazed me. You see him?"

I peered around the metal beam. Halfway down the slope, I got a brief glimpse of a figure dressed in dark clothing half running, half sliding down the hillside.

"I got him. Let's go!"

I took off down the steep hillside, zigzagging and using the trees for cover. I couldn't see him anymore but I could hear him well enough, crashing through the thick undergrowth below us, causing rock slides. He wasn't far ahead of me. I could get him. Bud was right behind me now, I could hear him, too, slipping and causing his own avalanches as he barreled down the hill at full speed.

About thirty yards down, I fought my way out of a blackberry thicket, sharp thorns catching my clothes and scratching my face and hands; then I stumbled headlong over a log that sent me down hard, falling head over heels until I rammed up against another tree trunk. Before I was back on my feet, Bud burst through the brambles, caught hold of a sapling, and swung himself to a stop.

We both took off downhill again, but we couldn't hear the

perp anymore, and I knew he might be hidden somewhere ahead, in ambush, waiting to pick us off. I discounted that theory when I heard the roar of a boat's motor firing up and shattering the quiet. He had come in off the lake, and we had shown up as he was finishing up his kill. Still using trees to break our speed, we both managed to reach the bottom, but way too late to stop him. He was gone, and as I scanned the calm waters of the inlet I saw only the dissipating waves of his wake as his boat made the main lake channel. There, I could see at least half a dozen runabouts speeding in every direction. The closest was red and white, a runabout, but it disappeared around the forested curve of the cove within seconds.

I swore, sheathed my weapon, called dispatch, and told them to get the water patrol out looking for all watercraft in this branch of the lake, especially those with a single person aboard.

"Damn it, we almost had him," Bud ground out furiously, panting from the pursuit. "You sure you're okay?"

I pressed my fingers hard against the shallow wound to control the bleeding. It really wasn't bad, barely a nick. I'd seen worse. I'd live.

Bud started his climb back up the hill, still swearing under his breath, and I turned and labored my way behind him. My arm was beginning to throb pretty good now and was bleeding heavily, but I bound it up with my sleeve enough not to drip blood on the crime scene. When we reached the bungalow, I retrieved latex gloves and paper booties for both of us to put on before we entered the house again and enough yellow crime scene tape to cover both the house and the hillside where the perp had made his escape.

Bud took the hill, and as I taped off the front of the bungalow, I found myself gritting my teeth, fury at letting him get away rising by the minute. After working homicide at LAPD, I should've been used to this kind of thing. Mutilation murders weren't as rare as they should be. Out there I'd seen plenty of awful acts perpetrated on innocent people, and my last couple of cases here on the lake hadn't exactly been butterflies and roses.

Rural Missouri was spewing out its fair share of psychos, too. Yeah, lately Lake of the Ozarks was giving California crazies a real run for their money. I was trying to figure what sick reason would have driven a killer to remove a woman's lips. He was a psychopath, no doubt, but we'd have to figure out his motive to butcher up her mouth like that. And the note. That was pretty damn specific, too. I sure as hell wasn't looking forward to it. Anger flashed back across me, anger that something like this had happened, anger that it had happened to a loved one of a friend, anger that I'd had him in my sights and let him get away.

After I finished securing the house, a couple of deputies showed up and I set them out scouring the wooded area below the house for the bullet casing. I sat down in the front seat of the Explorer, got out the first-aid kit from the side pocket, then cleaned and doctored my wound. The bullet had blown a shallow, inch-long groove of flesh off the side of my arm that hurt really, really bad at the moment, but it wasn't deep and it wasn't serious. I had gotten lucky again. A helluva lot luckier than Hilde had been. I stripped the protective papers off a couple of giant-sized Band-Aids and pressed them into place. It was a mere scratch compared to what it could've been if I hadn't moved when I did, or to what I'd suffered before on other cases. I leaned my head back against the headrest, shut my eyes, and waited for the coroner's team to show up.

Sisterly Love

Little Miss New Year was the next pageant Momma made them attend. The older one didn't want to, but her momma always made her help Sissy get dressed in her fancy, sparkly clothes. Stepdaddy Russell was going to take Bubby to the sale barn, where they sold all kinds of horses and cows and rabbits and other neat things. It was a fun place, but the older one was never invited to go along. Momma always dragged her to the stupid contests, so she had to watch everybody make over Sissy.

Right now they were just waking up in their room at the Holiday Inn where the pageant was being held. It had taken them forty-five minutes to drive there from their house. Stepdaddy didn't like it because it cost money, but Sissy had begged and he had said okay. Momma always got them up so early so she'd have plenty of time to make Sissy look perfect. Sissy was frowning and complaining as usual, and Momma was coddling her. When she turned to the older one, she wasn't nearly so gentle.

"You, get out of that bed and get dressed. And try to look

halfway decent for a change. No need in you embarrassing us again."

The older one dragged herself up and padded barefoot into the bathroom. She got a washcloth, wet it with cold water, then held it against her sleepy eyes. She was so tired. Sissy had tossed and turned and complained to Momma about the three of them having to share a king-size bed until Momma made the older one get down on the floor with a blanket. It had been really cold and drafty down there, and the traffic outside on the highway kept her awake most of the night.

Yawning, she found a T-shirt and jeans and for the next hour or so, she sat and watched Momma part off and roll up Sissy's hair in hot rollers so it would hang down her back in lots of loose golden curls. Later, after Sissy got a bath in her special bath oil, scented sweet like gardenias, Momma would put lots of makeup on Sissy's face until she looked like a real, live movie star. Once she had even bought Sissy some false teeth inserts called flippers that hid Sissy's front teeth when she had lost baby teeth. Sometimes the older one wondered what it would be like to put on all that stuff. Maybe it might even make her look less ugly. Someday when Momma was gone somewhere, she was going to try it.

"Can I watch cartoons while you get Sissy ready, Momma?" she asked after a while.

"No, you cannot. You know all that noise makes Sissy nervous right before she goes on stage. What's the matter with you? Go run Sissy's bathwater. And don't get it too hot like you did last time."

Anger boiled up inside the older one, but she didn't dare say a word, not now. But someday she would get them both, kill them in horrible, painful ways, just like Freddy Krueger liked to do. She got up from the end of the bed and walked into the adjoining bathroom. On pageant days, Momma always yelled at the older one when Sissy was grouchy or obstinate because she didn't want Sissy to get upset and cry because her big blue eyes would get all bloodshot and the judges would notice and lower her scores.

Yawning some more, the older one turned on the taps and made sure the water was just the way Sissy liked it, then she got a washcloth and lay it folded on the edge of the tub exactly the way Sissy demanded. The special bath oil was in a pretty bottle shaped like blue dolphin and the older one picked it up off the counter, opened the cap, and dribbled it into the running water. The water foamed and the most heavenly flowery smell wafted up all around her. It smelled so good. Someday she would buy some sweet-smelling oil to use in her own bath, but not gardenias. She never wanted to smell like her sister.

Sissy suddenly appeared in the doorway and cried, "Momma! She's in the bathroom and won't get out. I need to take my bath! Make her get out!"

Momma yelled at the older one from the other room. "Get outta there right now and let Sissy get ready! What's the matter with you today? My God, you are just rotten to the core."

The older one stood aside, and Sissy walked in, curling her pretty little mouth into her meanest smile. "You better quit doin' stuff to make me lose this crown, or you're gonna get a whippin'."

"I'm not doing anything to you, Sissy," the older one whispered because she knew if Sissy got mad, she'd scream and cry and say the older one hit her or some other big lie to get Momma mad at her. And Momma always believed Sissy, too, but now, when Stepdaddy wasn't here to see, the older one had to be very careful because Momma would hit her on the back with a coat hanger if Sissy got her in trouble. Her fingers clenched up and her fingernails dug into her palms and she hated her sister so much she felt a little sick to her stomach.

After Sissy sat down in the silky, soapy water that smelled so good, Momma came to the door and said she was going downstairs to get some breakfast. She asked Sissy what sounded good to her, then left, telling them not to dare go outside the room or open the door to any strangers.

While Sissy washed herself in the scented water, the older one stood at the sink and looked down inside Sissy's pink plastic makeup case. It had lots of little trays for lipsticks and blush and mascara and every size of cosmetic brush. All the different kinds of makeup fascinated the older one, because after Momma put it on Sissy's face, she didn't look anything like a little girl anymore, but rather a tiny, glamorous movie star like the actresses they saw on TV walking down that red carpet to the Academy Awards. It always seemed sort of miraculous to the older one, and she stared at her own ugly face in the mirror, wondering for the thousandth time how she would look if she put all that magic stuff on her face. She fingered a small bottle of what Momma called foundation makeup, one called L'Oreal that cost almost ten dollars at Wal-Mart, wishing she could try it.

Behind her, Sissy stood up and watched her in the mirror while she dried off with a big white towel. "Go ahead. Put some of that on your face," she said. "Momma won't know."

"Yes, she will. You'll tell her."

"No, I won't. I promise. Let's see if we can hide all those ugly freckles."

The older one was tempted, really, truly tempted, but she wasn't stupid, either, and she wasn't going to fall for Sissy's lies. She didn't trust Sissy for one minute. "No, I'll get in trouble if I do, and that's what you want."

"Uh-uh, I just wanna see how you'd look."

Sissy had on her fluffy white terry cloth robe now, the one with her name embroidered on the pocket, and she moved up beside the older one. They stared at each other in the mirror.

"C'mon, you big chicken, try some on."

* * *

"No, you're gonna get me in trouble again."

Then Sissy smiled. "You better do what I say, or I'm gonna empty all that foundation makeup in the sink and tell Momma you did it."

The older one felt a stab of fear because she knew how angry that would make Momma. The foundation was the most expensive thing in Sissy's cosmetics box. And she knew Sissy'd do it, too. She'd done lots of things in the past to get the older one in trouble. "You can't do that, or you won't have any foundation for today."

Sissy smiled and slowly unscrewed the cap. "I'm pretty enough to go without it. Everybody says so. Here, put this on or I'll empty it down the sink."

Really afraid now, the older one begged, "No, Sissy, please, Momma will kill us."

"She won't kill me, not right before the pageant. She'll kill you." Sissy giggled as she tilted the bottle and the older one watched the precious makeup drip into the sink.

"Stop, stop, Sissy, please, she'll be back any minute!"

"Then put in on, right now. I want to see if it makes you look better. Do it, or I'll throw it on the floor and break it!"

Sissy raised her arm and held the precious bottle up high, and the older one swallowed hard, but Sissy'd do it. Sissy loved to get her and Bubby in trouble. Terror clutched the older one's heart, and she quickly scooped her fingers through the makeup in the sink and rubbed it on her cheeks. It did hide some of her freckles, and she stared at herself in awe, always having imagined that maybe someday she could look as pretty as Sissy.

When she heard Momma's key in the lock, she grabbed a towel and tried to rub it off, then froze in utter horror when Sissy suddenly hurled the expensive bottle of makeup onto the floor. It broke into a million pieces and spattered tan liquid everywhere, just as Momma appeared at the bathroom door.

"Momma, look what she did!" cried Sissy. "She said she didn't want me to look pretty today because she didn't! She said she wanted me to be ugly like her!"

Momma's eyes went to the mess on the floor and then back up to the older one's face. Rage overtook her, black and terrible and violent. She dropped a sack of powdered doughnuts on the counter and grabbed the older one by the hair. "You stupid, destructive little brat, I'm gonna teach you to leave Sissy alone! Sissy, you get in there on the bed and stay there."

Sissy ran from the bathroom, but she turned in the doorway and stuck out her tongue at the older one, just before Momma slammed the door and trapped the older one inside. Sputtering with fury, she grabbed her by the throat and pressed her back against the sink, and then she jerked the older one up bodily and threw her down into the bathwater. The older one choked and clawed against the terrible grip on her throat, but Momma was gone away inside one of her furies, and she held her too tightly for her to get loose. She thrust her head down under the water and held it there.

The older one struggled desperately, but couldn't fight free, and she stared up through soapy water that burned her eyes like fire and saw Momma's face, red with wrath and effort, as she held her submerged. This was the look that was the worst, this was when Momma did awful things. She held her breath and twisted desperately until Momma jerked her up again, and she coughed and sucked in air, but Momma forced her down under again, despite how she cried and begged her to stop. She fought hard, but Momma was too strong, especially when she was so mad. When the older one thought she could not hold her breath any longer, when she thought she was going to drown and maybe it would be better than having to live with Momma, her Momma jerked her out, and she gasped and choked for breath.

Momma ground her words out between clenched teeth. "Don't you ever touch Sissy's makeup again, you hear me? Don't touch it, don't even look at it, or you'll get a lot worse than this, you understand me?"

"I won't, Momma, I promise I won't," the older one said weakly, but she didn't cry until after Momma had stalked outside and slammed the door. Then she sat up in the cold water and cried hard into a towel, so Momma wouldn't hear and come back and punish her again.

Three

Sixteen minutes after I'd put in the call, Buckeye's white crime scene van nosed up the driveway and pulled in behind my Explorer and two other sheriff's vehicles. Buck asked me if I was okay and wanted to take a look at my arm, but I told him it could wait. So as they donned protective gear and removed a couple of aluminum equipment cases from the back, I filled them in about what had happened. When I described Hilde's body, they all turned and stared at me as if I'd made the whole thing up.

Unfortunately, I pretty much knew what they were thinking. Nothing remotely resembling this kind of gruesome murder had happened at the lake before I moved here from LA. It began last summer with one sicko nightmare from my past, happened again last Christmas, and now here we go, number three. I was probably what was attracting killers to this rural, tranquil, beautiful setting, just as I had attracted death to those around me all my life. They knew it. I knew it. Everybody knew it.

Buckeye snapped on his gloves and slammed the rear door of the van. I watched him pick up his case and look at me. He had a white beard and mustache that was usually trimmed close to his jaw but was a little long at the moment. He resembled the guy on that old Captain Kangaroo children's show with his white hair and rotund body. Mr. Greenjeans had been the Captain's sidekick, and there was a running *Where's Mr. Greenjeans?* gag circulating around the coroner's office. He wasn't joking now, however; he was dead serious when he said, "So you're sayin' this guy cut off the vic's lips and left them in the shower drain?"

I nodded. "That's what we think. He was still in the area and took a coupla shots at us, but he got away in a boat before we could get to him."

"God Almighty. Was she mutilated any other way?"

I shook my head, shrugged. "Not that we could tell. Body looked clean of visible wounds. Strangulation, maybe, but there's a lot of blood at the mouth. You'll have to tell us. Bud's stringing tape down behind the house where the perp shot at us, then ran." It was then I realized one of Buck's primary team members was missing. "Where's Shaggy?"

Shaggy's real name was John Becker, and he was undeniably one of the best forensics technicians in the state of Missouri, albeit a long-haired, hippie, nine-earrings-in-each-ear kind of guy. We called him Shaggy after the character in *Scooby-Doo*. He lived for his job and was always on time and ready to process a crime scene at the drop of a hat. His absence at the morgue was an unheard-of event.

"He called in sick today. Yesterday, too."

"You gotta be kidding me? Shaggy did?"

"Yeah, we're all in shock. He didn't say what the problem was, but I know he's got allergies that act up this time of year if he's not takin' Claritin. Or could be a Bruce Willis marathon runnin' on TBS."

Shag's obsession with the ex–Mr. Demi was legend, but nobody smiled at Buck's remark. Not with this kind of crime scene facing us.

Buck said, "Vicky, get all your stills of the victim, then do both the inside and outside up here, then let Bud show you where the perp went down the hill. You'll have to do the videos, too, till Shag gets back."

Vicky Jackson was our crime scene photographer, in her forties with three kids who drove her crazy with soccer practice and swimming meets and a husband who adored the ground she walked on. She was a charter member in good standing of the renowned, prestigious Red Hat Society of Camdenton fame and wore her purple boa well.

I said, "Vicky, take special care with this one, but I warn you, this guy spent a lot of time cleaning up after himself, so you're gonna have your work cut out for you."

Buckeye said, "Until Vicky gets done inside the house, we'll process the vic's car. That it over there?" He pointed at the red Fusion.

"Yeah. It's a rental, so I doubt if you'll find anything inside. I'm pretty sure everything went down inside that bathroom."

Two of Buck's people walked up the driveway to Hilde's vehicle as Vicky ducked under the yellow tape and climbed the front steps.

Buck and I watched her for a moment, then he looked down at the bloodstained sleeve of my torn T-shirt. He shook his head. "You sure that's not too bad?"

"Yeah. I got lucky and ducked the right way."

"Lucky, huh? Lemme see."

I stood still, trying not to grimace as he carefully stripped off the already blood-soaked Band-Aids and probed at the wound with a gloved forefinger.

"This's more'n any nick. Hurts pretty bad, I reckon. You probably oughta get some stitches."

I shrugged. "Sure, it hurts. So what? We almost had him, Buck. If he hadn't had a boat stowed down at the cove, we would've nailed him cold in the act."

"Hold still and let me clean this properly so it won't get infected. Hell, Claire, this is getting to be a real bad habit with you."

Yeah, as if I invited people to take potshots at me. Impatient to get started inside the house, I didn't want to wait for him to retrieve his medical bag and fix my arm, but I did. He was right, and I knew it. I wasn't Batman, not even Robin. I'd figured that out a long time and a couple of major surgeries ago. Too bad I wasn't. If I wore a cape and could fly, I bet I would've gotten the perp before he reached that boat. I watched Buckeye squeeze a long ooze of antibiotic goop into the wound and close the gash with four butterfly bandages. Then he handed me a bottle of water and a couple of Extra-Strength Tylenols. "These oughta do the trick. Trust me, you're gonna need them before the day's done. You find the shell casings from the gun that got you?"

"The guys are down there now. I don't think he had time to pick up after himself, and we got a pretty good lock on his position."

I took the capsules, swallowed both at once, then chugged down about half the bottle of water. Buck picked up his case and headed for the porch as soon as Vicky finished up inside and came back out the front door. Buckeye assigned a new young guy with red hair named Kenny Porter to head down with Vicky to process the hillside. Buck yelled for one of the techs working the Fusion to assist him inside.

Rubbing my aching arm, I watched them trot off to their assigned tasks. They were extremely good at their jobs, all of them. Buck didn't hire a tech who wasn't top of his class. If the killer had left trace evidence behind, they'd find it and not corrupt the scene while they did it. But I still wished Shaggy was on duty. He had my vote as the best of the best.

I leaned back against my SUV's front fender and waited for Bud. I wanted the people inside to get a good start before we nosed around. I hoped the time alone stringing the tape had helped Bud pull himself together. He was pretty blown away, but he'd have to get with it and quickly, too, or he'd be reassigned. The sheriff might do that anyway, once he found out Bud's close relationship with the vic's sister. Ten minutes later Bud walked around the back of the house and strode toward me. His face was set in hard, angry lines. He was all right now. My face looked like that, too.

I asked anyway. "You okay, Bud?"

"Yeah. I'm tryin' to figure out how to tell Bri. She called a few minutes ago, but I didn't pick up." He stared out into the distance where the lake water was now a polished silver mirror. "This sucks, Claire. Makes me sick."

"Yeah." His description was right on. I said, "Need another minute or are you ready to get started?"

"I'm ready."

I handed him the protective gear I had retrieved earlier, and we carried it to the porch, then donned the gloves and booties in order not to contaminate the crime scene. I put mine on in a hurry, eager to get to work, so I had to wait while he snapped on his latex gloves and slipped some paper booties over his shoes. He didn't seem as eager as me; he was probably still thinking about Brianna. We said nothing as we opened the door and entered the bungalow. Just inside the front door, we stopped and took in the place.

A female technician named Lana Foster was dusting for prints along the kitchen counters. She was a real cool lady I knew pretty well from Buck's Memorial Day fish fries at his place. She cropped her hair off almost to the scalp and wore jeans and peasant blouses under her protective suits. She loved guns as much as I did and was quite the expert on ballistics. She'd come aboard from the St. Louis PD and knew her stuff almost as well as Shaggy. She glanced at us without speaking, nodded, then concentrated her attention back on her work. Buck and the other tech were not in sight, but I could hear their voices in the back, where it sounded like they were processing the body in the bathroom. It was dusky inside the living room because of the closed shutters, so I reached over and switched on the black-shaded brass floor lamp beside the door.

"You done in here, Lana?"

"Yep. It's all yours."

Looking around, I decided the living room had most likely been ransacked. Not just a messy model's abode as we'd first thought. "Maybe the perp was desperate to find something, or he at least wanted us to think so."

Bud said, "Yeah, maybe he staged it to look like a robbery gone bad. Or maybe she put up a hell of a struggle before he dragged her into that bathroom."

I got a mental picture of the woman's mouth, lips gone, those rivers of blood staining her chin, and knew Bud was probably imagining the same sickening visual. I didn't look forward to my dreams tonight, not that I ever did.

"Let's hope she got some DNA under her fingernails before he subdued her."

Bud said, "Wonder why he dressed her up in that crown and stuff?"

"He's playing some sick game of his own. You know how psychopaths like to mess around, play God with their victims, you know, enjoy the vic's fear."

Bud shook his head. "He was tryin' to send a message to somebody with that sticker on her shoulder, but he had to know hangin' around here this long was pretty risky, in broad daylight, too. Anybody could've seen him. What I can't figure is why he lingered to take shots at us instead of getting the hell out of Dodge."

"If I hadn't ducked, I'd be dead now. Or you would be. Maybe he just didn't want us coming after him."

"Then why'd he pinpoint his position by shooting at us? Why not just do her and leave? He had her staged, the scene cleaned up. We hadn't seen him. Doesn't make sense."

"Maybe he wanted to see us find her. Make himself feel powerful to watch the police and crime scene investigators show up and admire his handiwork. Or like we said, we might've just surprised him and he panicked. Who knows what he's thinking? This guy's nuts."

Bud's phone started in with its stupid classical tune, and I knew by his expression that caller ID popped up Brianna's name. He didn't pick up. It rang until his voice mail picked up.

Carefully sidestepping the books, videotapes, dishes, and clothing strewn around on the shiny red oak floor, I made my way to the black leather bar that separated the living room from the kitchen. Four black iron bar stools were pushed in on the living room side. Hilde's Gucci purse was still there, and I saw a desk-size appointment calendar on the counter near where Lana was working.

"You done with the purse?" I asked her.

"Uh huh. Calendar, too. I'm wrapping up the kitchen now."

I sorted through the contents of the purse with a gloved finger. Billfold, still snapped shut, a glittery rhinestone key ring shaped like a big heart that held seven keys, a large clear plastic cosmetic case full of every conceivable kind of makeup and hair product. I pulled out a small red velvet address book tucked into a side pocket, and then I picked up the calendar and thumbed through the pages.

"This is gonna help, Bud. It's got a list of all her appointments and appearances for the last three months. Next month's, too."

"Good. I just found her portfolio."

Bud held up a book measuring about eight by ten inches and bound in fancy crocodile leather. Hilde's name was etched on the bottom right corner of the front cover, beautifully, in flowing gold script. Bud opened it and stared at the first photograph. "Man, this bites so bad. Why'd it have to be her?"

I moved closer and looked down at the picture. She had

been a beautiful woman, maybe even prettier than Finn, though I never would have believed that possible. I thumbed through the pages and found lots of poses, many of them after she'd won a pageant and was seated and holding a scepter, crown, and the obligatory roses. She always had a big, lovely smile on her face. I thought of the killer's quote, and my stomach turned. I put the book down on the counter. He considered her a villain. Why?

"You know that quote he left on her, Bud?"

"Nope."

"It's from *Hamlet*, I think."

"I dunno where the hell it's from, but it sounds pretty personal to me. What I wanna know is why he chose her. It's gotta be a some kind of betrayal thing. Otherwise, it's probably random. Hell, she's been here at the lake less than a week." Our eyes met and he shook his head. "Oh, God, this is gonna kill Bri. She talks about Hilde all the time, was real proud of her."

"Tell Brianna we're gonna nail this guy to the wall, that's what you can tell her. Look around, Bud. This guy was sloppy in here. Maybe he missed something in the bathroom or maybe that's his blood out there on the deck. If it's here, Buck's gonna find it. And my gut's telling me this isn't the least bit random, but personal, like you said. For some reason, this guy hated Hilde." I picked up the pocket calendar again. "I'm betting his name is right here in this book somewhere."

"I've gotta go tell Bri."

"Yeah. We'll finish up here and tell her together. You want me to do it?"

"No, I've gotta do it."

"Okay, let's get this over with."

There were lots of personal belongings to go through and we delved through a couple of scrapbooks she'd tucked into her luggage, bulging with pageant programs, pressed roses, and newspaper articles. There were a dozen or more videos of pageants, and I put them in evidence bags to check in and then view as soon as I had time.

I perked up considerably when I found a picture of Hilde sitting on the lap of some dark-haired, muscled-up, Hispanic-looking guy, who was holding on to her like he owned her and wanted everybody to know it. He was handsome in a swarthy, macho kinda way, and her boyfriend, no doubt. I memorized his face for future reference, then tucked the photograph in an evidence bag and stuck it in my purse. I'd ask Brianna to identify him as soon as she was up to it.

There were all kinds of photographs of Hilde and Brianna together, too, but most looked recent. They were always holding hands or posed with their arms around each other. They were obviously close in both age and friendship. I wondered about their background, where they came from, what kind of family they'd had.

I'd only met Brianna a few months back, actually the same day Bud had, when we'd gone into the fancy women's store where she worked to buy me a dress for a New Year's Eve gala. She and Bud hit it off big-time from the very beginning and had been an item ever since. I liked her right off the bat, too, but neither of us knew much about where she'd been before she'd landed here at the lake.

"You know much about Bri's past, Bud?"

"Not much. I know she lived in south Florida before she came here, some little beach place north of Miami. Said she competed on the pageant circuit with Hilde for a while, but didn't like it as much as Hilde did, so she dropped out."

"What about her family?"

"I don't know. We never discussed her family much."

"Did she seem reluctant to discuss them?"

"No, it just didn't come up."

I frowned when I heard a car pull up and stop out front. I wondered if Buckeye had called Shaggy in on this thing, and hoped so as I walked to the front door. But it wasn't Shag. It was Brianna, getting out of her red Corvette and staring wide-eyed at the crime scene tape. She looked terrified.

"Oh, crap, it's Bri, Bud. Better intercept her quick. You sure don't want her coming in here."

Bud wasted no time getting out the door and meeting Brianna before she had time to duck under the tape. I watched him take her arm and walk her away from the house and around to the back side of her car. He was holding her by her upper arms now, and she was trying to pull away and run toward the house. She probably already knew Hilde was in big trouble, but it was pretty damn clear when Bud told her Hilde's fate because her legs went rubbery and she collapsed to her knees. Bud went down with her and tried to hold her, but she kept fighting him. I could hear her screaming Hilde's name, but after a couple of seconds, those cries turned into a long, terrible, heartbroken wail. Lana looked over at me and shook her head.

Unable to listen any longer to Brianna's grief-stricken cries, I walked through the living room and into the back of the house. Because I knew exactly what she was going through. I had fallen on my knees once a long time ago, too, made the same kind of inhuman keening sound when I held my little boy's lifeless body in my arms. I still made those sounds sometimes, when no one was around to hear me.

Four

It was nearly half past three when I left Buck and his team to finish processing the crime scene and remove the body for autopsy. I wanted to talk to Brianna, find out what she knew—better yet, who she suspected could have hated Hilde enough to do something this godawful to her. I didn't want to push her too soon or too hard, or Bud, either, so I gave him an exploratory call as I pulled out of the Royal Bungalows, turned west onto the lake road, and headed back to Camdenton. It took him two rings to pick up.

"Yeah? Claire?"

"How's she doing?"

"Better than I expected her to, that's for damn sure. She's calmed down a little, anyway."

"Enough for me to ask her some questions?"

"Maybe. She's still pretty much in denial, I think, but she says she wants to help us, if she can."

"How about now?"

"Yeah, I guess so. Better to get it over with so she can take something that'll make her sleep."

Brianna Swensen lived in a house off Highway 54 in a little town with the unlikely and, yes, even unsavory name, of Roach, Missouri. It was about five miles southwest of Camdenton and I drove past the sheriff's department on my way there without stopping. I'd already reported in by phone to my boss, Sheriff Charlie Ramsay, and he was less than pleased that another sensational murder had come down at the lake so soon after the last one. He didn't blame me out loud but I wondered if that's what he was thinking. Hell, it was what I was thinking.

Brianna's house set atop a ridge about two miles down a winding blacktop road. Her Vette was parked out front. Bud had been at the wheel when they'd left Hilde's place, and he probably hadn't wanted to take time to put it in the garage. I pulled up beside it in the graveled semicircle driveway and killed my engine.

I sat there a couple of minutes, listening to the motor tick and watching leaves on the hedge along the house rustle in a gentle April breeze, not exactly eager to barge inside and torture Brianna some more, which pretty much was what I was going to do. It was imperative to interview her, however, and better me to question her than Bud. Let him hold her hand, put his arm around her, and be the good guy. Actually, he was the good guy. I climbed out, beeped my door locked, and walked up the L-shaped sidewalk to the front door, which was painted a cerulean blue. I knocked softly, ignoring the brass doorbell. Brianna's nerves were probably jangled enough. Seconds later, Bud opened the door, looking a little worse for wear. Actually, a lot worse for wear.

"Still okay to come in?"

"Yeah, she took a Darvocet a while ago. She wants to talk to you."

I followed him down a short entry hall, painted beige and hung with a black-and-white photograph of an old barn framed in white and then out into a living area that faced the back of the house. The whole place smelled good, like oranges and lemons. I wondered how Bri got it to do that. My house sure never smelled this good. A kitchen was visible off to the left with a short bar and ceiling-hung cabinets separating it from the living room. A pair of multipaned white French doors revealed an exceptional view of the wooded hills around Camdenton, but not quite as breathtaking a panorama as the one from Hilde's bungalow. I could just barely glimpse a little half-moon sliver of the lake on the distant horizon.

Brianna sat on a red-and-blue plaid couch facing a white brick fireplace alive with gas logs. They were dancing around and warming the room. Her face was unnaturally flushed, her eyes swollen from several hours of crying. She still looked beautiful, believe it or not. She was sniffling into a wadded-up pink Kleenex, almost as if she couldn't quite summon up the strength to wail any more.

I put down my leather handbag and squatted in front of her. I put my hand over hers. "Brianna, I am so sorry about your sister."

She nodded, and more tears leaked down her cheeks. She dabbed at them with the same soggy tissue that she nervously squeezed in her hand. I glanced at Bud, and he motioned with his head for me to sit down in the matching plaid chair that directly faced her. I did so while he took a seat on the couch close beside her and held her hand.

"Brianna, I really hate to put you through this right now, but we've got to ask you some questions, okay? I wish we didn't, I wish it could wait, but it really can't, not if you're up to it at all."

Brianna nodded, looked at Bud, and welled up again when he squeezed her shoulders. I waited a second or two, then started out as gently as I knew how. This was not going to be easy. I wondered if Bud had told her the grisly details yet. I had a feeling he hadn't. I wasn't going to, either.

"Do you have any idea why somebody might've done this to Hilde?"

Brianna sobbed aloud, jerked a fresh Kleenex from the box in front of her, and shook her head. She had pinned her long blond hair up into a bun like the one Hilde wore at the time of her death. Some strands had fallen around her face, too, just like Hilde's had, and she kept pushing them behind her ears. She licked her lips, and I made the mistake of thinking of Hilde's lips. I swallowed hard, tried not to show my revulsion at that image.

"No, oh, God, no, Hilde's really nice, you know, kind to people, just a good person, really. Even the other girls, the ones she competed against, didn't seem too awfully jealous that she won so much." She stopped talking, swallowed hard, dabbed some more tears, but all that mascara and eyeliner was not running in rampant manner down her cheeks. Actually, wasn't even smudged. Waterproof, I guess.

"And that's highly unusual around this kind of circuit, too," she continued, all muffled and weepy. "It's really cutthroat and intense, you know, every girl for herself. But Hilde made friends, and they all seemed to like her, respect her for her hard work, you know, and everything. And she did work hard, really hard. She's getting older now . . ."

Brianna remembered that Hilde wasn't getting older now and wouldn't ever get older again, and began to weep in earnest. While she recovered, I took my little notepad out of my handbag and wrote down the pertinent details of her remarks, but I was pretty sure that Bri was looking at all this and her sister through a pair of very rose-tinted glasses. I couldn't imagine the other contestants being quite so jolly about usually losing to Hilde Swensen. It didn't fit the stereotypical, bitchy beauty contestant profile entrenched in my mind, but maybe I was wrong about the beauties and bitches of the world. On the other hand, I'd never been within three hundred yards of a beauty pageant, made sure of it, in fact, so what did I know? That, however, and unfortunately, was about to change.

"Did she have any enemies that you know of? People who were jealous of her? Anybody who threatened her or accosted her verbally? I understand that sometimes happens to beautiful women. Other women don't give them a chance, you know, just decide to hate them at first sight?" Yeah, me, for instance, I plead guilty, 'fraid so.

Brianna nodded as if she knew exactly what I was talking about, as if it happened to her every day, and it probably did. My first impression when I'd seen her was that she was a haughty mannequin type with missing posters nailed up on bulletin boards concerning the frontal lobes of her brain. It turned out I was wrong about her, too, and me, a trained detective, at that. I guess it's true what they say about not judging a book, and all that rot.

Brianna said, "No, not that I'm aware of. She got some guys now and then who wanted to go out with her, date her and stuff like that, but she usually didn't go in for men who liked her just because she was cute and won a bunch of titles. You know, men who dated her so they'd have a trophy on their arm when they went into restaurants or clubs. If she got any hint that's what they were after, she'd drop them."

"Does she have a boyfriend right now that you know about? Somebody steady?"

"Well, kind of, I guess. Back in Florida. From when she lived at South Beach. His name is Carlos Vasquez. He owns this fancy gym down there, and he's a personal trainer, too. It's well known, a spa, where lots of celebrities go, you know, people like Gianni Versace. He was a regular there before that guy shot him."

I dug out the photo I'd found at Hilde's condo. "Is this him?"

Brianna took it. She nodded. "Yes, that's Carlos. I looks like it might've been taken a couple of months ago. He's sort of a camera buff."

"What's the name of Carlos's spa?"

"The Ocean Club."

"Did she live with this man?"

"She moved into his beach house for a while, but he ended up getting too possessive, so she moved out last Christmas. Actually, it was New Year's Eve. I remember because that's the day I met Bud."

Brianna smiled tearfully at Bud, and he smiled back, but when his eyes met mine, I knew he was thinking the same thing I was. "Was this Carlos guy ever violent with her, you know, slap her around, push her, yell at her?"

"I was pretty sure a couple of times that he might've slapped her around some and I know he used to yell at her, but Hilde said he didn't, that she never would've stood for anything like that. She's got a lot of pride and self-respect, and she's strong. She works out on weights every day and runs three miles." I was watching her face and saw the exact moment that the fact hit her that her sister hadn't been strong enough to fight off her killer. She burst into fresh tears and buried her face in her palms. This was not going well.

Bud draped an arm around her and pulled her head against his shoulder. I could barely stand the pained expression on his face. This was tearing him up. I went on, but tried to be gentle. "Do you have Carlos Vasquez's address and telephone number?"

"I think it's the same as it was when she lived with him. She's the one who packed up and moved out when they split. The two of us own a nice little beach house up the coast near Hollywood, pretty far away from all that stuff going on in South Beach. She's been living there alone since I moved up here."

"Okay." I thought about things for a minute or two. "Was she down there recently? Before the Kansas City gig, the last one she won?"

Brianna nodded. "She always scheduled a week or two off between pageants. She was in San Diego earlier this month, then spent a week at home in Florida, I think, before she flew to Kansas City. The only reason she entered the pageant here was so we could spend time together. We'd grown apart the last few years. She thought it was kind of rinky-dink after the big-city ones. I encouraged her to come early so she could meet Bud, so I guess this is all my fault!"

She dissolved into a torrent again and I sat mutely and watched Bud soothe her. He was doing a pretty good job of it, and I felt like an interloper in a private, intimate moment and wished I could get up and leave, but I couldn't. I hated interviewing friends, especially distraught friends. I gave her some more time to calm down, and she eventually did.

I said, "Did Hilde have any other boyfriends, other than this Carlos guy?"

"No. There were others in her past, of course, but I don't think she's kept in touch with any of them."

"Were they down in Florida, too?"

"Uh-huh, yeah. Some were. Hilde and I both moved down to Miami for college. You know, the beaches drew us. We both went to the University of Florida."

"Where did you live before moving to Florida?"

She hesitated. "Maine. A little bitty place near the Canadian border."

Bud seemed interested in this direction of questioning, so I suspected he was learning stuff he didn't know about Brianna's background.

"I understand that the two of you were close?"

"Oh, yes. We were always together, lived together and everything, until the last few years when I moved up here."

"Why did you move up here, Bri?"

Again, a bit of hesitancy. "I don't know, really. I didn't like the humidity in south Florida. It made my hair kink up. And it was too crowded for me, way too many people everywhere you went. I came up here once for a fashion seminar over at Cedar Bend Lodge and just fell in love with the lake. It was so quiet and peaceful with all these pretty views. It reminded me of the place where we were born."

"Why didn't you go back there if you missed it so much?"

Bud was frowning, like he didn't like where I was taking this, but Bri's past was pretty much Hilde's, too. And pretty murky, at that. I wanted to know who and why and what and where. I'm pushy that way.

"I guess because both my parents are gone now. Nobody's left up there on the farm. It's been closed up for years and is even more out in the sticks than this is." She stopped, coughed a little, and delicately moistened dry lips some more. "Bud, would you mind getting me a bottle of Evian? It's in the fridge."

"Sure, babe."

I watched him walk into the kitchen. He returned with the water and handed it to her, then I said, "Bud mentioned this morning that you said Hilde had a stalker a few years back. Do you remember his name?"

"Oh, no, she never found out who he was. The harassment just stopped one day, and he's left her alone ever since."

"What kinds of things did he do?"

"He left messages on her phone, and put gifts outside her door, stuff like that. I think he was a fan who'd seen her win a title somewhere, or something like that. I was living here when it happened so I don't know much else about it. Only what she told me in passing."

"Did he ever try to harm her?"

"No, I don't think he ever approached her in person. One day he just stopped bothering her. I guess he gave up."

"What can you tell me about Hilde's lifestyle?"

Brianna lowered her eyes and her voice became defensive. "Like what? What do you mean?"

Bud knew what I meant and didn't look happy with the question, either.

"I'm sorry, Bri, but I've got to ask. Was she a party girl?

You know as well as I do that South Beach's got that reputation, especially with all the beautiful people hanging around. I understand the party scene can get really wild with a lot of drugs and fast living going on."

I braced for a quick, indignant retort or a termination of the interview, but Brianna was only quiet a moment longer than usual. She finally said, "Hilde wasn't any angel, but she was a really good person. I swear it."

Uh-oh. Red flashing signals, siren wailing, and now we're getting somewhere. I chose my next words as carefully as I knew how. "What exactly do you mean when you say that she wasn't any angel?"

"She liked men, it's as plain as that. She liked to party, just like most girls our age. She liked to drink, too, but she wasn't an alcoholic, or anything, and she liked men paying attention to her."

Crap, that was something I wasn't thrilled out of my mind to hear. It wasn't something I wanted to follow up on, either. Bud didn't look ecstatic over this new insight about Hilde, to be sure, but he knew me well enough to know that I couldn't and wouldn't let it drop. Pursue it I must, friend or not. I tried to do so in a friendly fashion. "Liked to party as in . . ."

"As in she liked to party." Now Brianna sounded like a rearing mama bear, claws extended, daring me to come closer to little partying baby bear. I was sorry, but I wasn't going anywhere.

"You know, Brianna, I'd rather be anywhere than here at your house, asking you all these personal questions about your sister. I know she was a great person or she wouldn't've been related to you, but I've got to know these things if Bud and I are going to find out who did this terrible thing to her. I hope you understand that and don't think I'm enjoying this."

More tears, more agony, more comforting, during which I shifted uncomfortably in my chair, feeling like a jerk. Worse, an unfeeling jerk.

"I know, I know, I'm sorry, Claire, I just can't believe any of this has happened. She can't be gone, my God, why did this have to happen to her? That's what I don't get. She's not even from around here. And I don't care what she's done in the past, she didn't deserve to die."

"No, no, it's okay, don't feel bad. It's hard to answer all this stuff when you're this upset. I understand, believe me." And I did. I'd lost so many loved ones, I had no family left at all. I had buried those memories down so deep, slammed and bolted so many trapdoors that I never wanted to pry open again. Black said I needed to face some of that pain, work through it, take a crowbar to those locked places, but that was easy for him to say. Shrinks talked a good talk, but they didn't have to be the one to take the arrows in the heart, now did they? So I kept those memories buried in some very dark places in my psyche. Brianna would learn to do that, too, if she was lucky.

She cried some more. Bud and I waited some more.

In a little bit, Brianna sat up straighter, looked at me. Her eyes were not focusing so well anymore, but her makeup still looked good. I had a feeling the Darvocet was kicking in big time. She said, and her voice slurred on a couple of words. "Okay, I'm all right now. It's just this simple. Hilde liked the lifestyle at South Beach, and I didn't. I thought it was too slick and wild, and to be truthful, stupid, with all the emphasis on beauty and ultra-thin, muscular bodies. I mean everybody was anorexic or bulimic down there. It was more than appalling. You'd think that *South Beach Diet* book would've gotten through to some of those people about healthy eating, but it didn't. I couldn't wait to get away from all those shallow, self-centered types, but Hilde didn't feel that way. She thrived on excitement and important men in clubs who were always hitting on her. She especially liked celebrities."

"So, just that I understand you. Are you saying she's had lots of lovers in her life?" There it was, out in the open, hanging in the air between us like a big, ugly helium balloon filled with some kind of terrible odor, about to burst in a stinking explosion that would destroy our budding friendship.

Brianna heaved in a deep breath. "I am saying that she really liked to drink and dance and have fun, and when she got high, she liked to have sex, sometimes with men she hardly knew. She found that a big turn-on, not to know them, I mean. Sometimes she went home with them or to hotels, but she never took them to our place. She knew better than that, thank God. I tried to tell her that it was dangerous, that she was going to get herself in trouble, but she said she had a sixth sense when it came to guys. She said she could tell the crazies before she'd been with them five minutes."

Apparently she hadn't recognized the crazy who'd dressed her up in pageant regalia, severed her lips, and left a Shakespearean-inspired warning stuck to her bare skin. Not soon enough, anyway. This information complicated my investigation and could open it up to countless suspects hundreds of miles away, whose names I'd never know. I jotted down most of what Brianna said in my notepad, giving myself time to think. Bud and Brianna said nothing. I had a feeling Bud was shocked by what he'd heard. I know I was.

"Do you think she might've gone out partying this week after she got here and picked up somebody?" That was pretty ugly sounding, too. But necessary.

Brianna looked pained, but she was honest. "It's possible, I guess. She liked to meet new people, but it seemed to me she'd calmed down some since she broke it off with Carlos. She said she still cared about him." She looked at me. "Are you absolutely sure that person you found is her? Neither of you have met her. Maybe it's somebody that looks like her but isn't really her?"

"We found lots of pictures of her in the condo, Bri. One was recent, from her win in Kansas City. I'm sorry."

That pretty much extinguished any hope left inside her

eyes. She closed them. Her lashes were long and black and formed a half moon against her flushed cheeks.

"I brought along her calendar and address book. Do you think you might be up to taking a quick look and telling us how these people are associated with Hilde?"

"I'll try."

I handed her the appointment book first. She turned the pages slowly and touched each name in turn with an elegant French-manicured fingertip. "Most of these women are other models that she knows. Carole Lomberger runs a New York modeling agency. Carole's her personal agent, one of the best in the country, too. Eric Dixson is a top-notch photographer who follows the circuit around from city to city and contracts with pageant coordinators. He takes portfolio pictures for the regulars, too. He's really great. He did both our portfolios. He's here now to shoot the Cedar Bend thing."

I wrote that name down. I noticed Hilde had an appointment with him three days ago, and I was interested to see if she had kept it and what he thought of her behavior and state of mind when he shot her pictures.

"Mr. Race's number is in here. She's been to him before, too. He used to have a place in South Beach, did you know that?"

No, I didn't know that, but found it highly interesting, not to mention suspicious. Bud thought so, too, by his expression. He was saying very little, which was probably a good thing. Brianna wouldn't be able to blame him for dragging her sister's personal foibles through the proverbial mud hole.

"Were he and Hilde friends, or lovers, maybe, when he was in South Beach?"

That brought Brianna's head up, a startled expression on her face. "Oh, Claire, surely you had to notice that he's gay."

Yeah, I noticed. A blind person would notice. "Gay men kill, too. For all kinds of reasons."

That shocked her, probably just the realization again that

her sister was dead. More tears oozed and rolled, but she grabbed another tissue and somehow got through the appointment book before Bud decided Brianna had done enough.

"How about we end this for now, Claire? Finish up tomorrow after Bri's gotten some sleep?"

"Sure, fine. I'll say again, Brianna, I'm really sorry about what happened, and please know that Bud and I will do everything in our power to catch this guy. I promise you that. I will not stop until we get him."

Brianna looked grateful, and I gave her a brief hug, then skulked out, feeling about two inches tall for putting my friend through such a painful ordeal. But now I knew that Hilde Swensen had led a very dangerous lifestyle with very dangerous people, and that made my job solving this case a lot harder than I had expected it to be. But, hey, what's new about that?

Sisterly Love

When Momma went backstage with Sissy later that morning to await her turn to dance, the older one threaded her way unnoticed through a crowd of anxious mothers, grandmothers, and other relatives of the contestants. Some families had on T-shirts with pictures of their entrant on the front. She was glad Momma didn't make her wear a stupid shirt with Sissy's picture on it. She hoped she never had to. She wished she never had to see Sissy again.

Her hair was still damp from being dunked in the bathtub, the scent of gardenias clinging to her skin. She hated that fragrance now and hoped she'd never have to smell it again. The pageant was being held at a high school gymnasium, and she headed for the bleachers farthest away from the stage. She was going underneath the seats where she could hide and be alone and not have to watch Sissy win another stupid tiara.

When she reached the far end of the basketball court, she made sure no one was watching, then bent over and walked down underneath the bleachers almost to the half-court line. People sitting above her were talking and laughing, and she could see their feet, but none of them could see her. That's the way she liked it. She liked to be alone. She hated everybody.

When she found a dark place where she could lean her back up against the wall, she sat down and drew her legs up against her chest. She put her forehead on her knees and sobbed as loud as she wanted to because she knew the sounds of the crowd and music on stage would drown out her pain.

"What're you doin' under here?"

The older one jerked up her tear-streaked face. A boy had squatted down about a yard away. He was a couple of years older than she was. She knew him because he went to her school. Once or twice during the school year, he'd sat down beside her on the school bus.

She sniffed and quickly wiped her tears on the end of her T-shirt. "None of your business. Why don't you just get outta here?"

"Why're you crying?"

"None of your business, I said."

The boy had on one of those stupid T-shirts. His had a picture of two little girls that looked like twins, each with long curly blond hair. She remembered then that they were his little sisters. Their momma always alternated entering them in the kiddie pageants, but both girls always lost to Sissy.

"I want to sit under here with you. It's pretty neat."

"No, go away, I like being alone."

"Me, too. I hate everybody."

The older one examined him with more interest. She watched him move closer and sit down beside her. When he leaned his head back against the wall, she scooted away from him.

He said, "You smell good."

"No, I don't. This smell stinks. I hate it, and I always will."

He laughed at that, and then he said, "Why's your hair all wet? Your mom forget the hair dryer?"

"None of your business."

He said nothing else for a moment, just stared at her silently, then he said, "This T-shirt sucks. My mom makes me wear it."

"Yeah, it sure does."

He laughed again. "You're pretty funny."

"No, I'm not."

He kept up with the grinning, and she saw he had on braces, the clear kind that didn't show so much. She thought his front teeth looked pretty good and wished she could get braces because she had a crooked tooth right in front that Sissy said made her look like a goofy vampire.

The boy got himself comfortable, stretched out his legs and crossed his ankles. "Bet you're tired of these stupid pageants, aren't you? And all the crap goin' on around here, too. I've seen you hanging around at most of them. You always look sad. Did you know that?"

"I hate them."

"I do, too."

"I hate my little sister, even worse."

"I hate mine, too, both of 'em."

Surprised again, she stared at him out of narrowed eyes, and then she smiled. "Do you really? I thought I was the only one around here who hated my own sister."

"Nah, everybody who's got a sister in these stupid things hates them. They're all little spoiled brats."

"Yeah, brats. And I hate Sissy's smile, too. Everybody says it makes her look like an angel, but she's not, at all. She's really mean."

"Yeah, like 'Smile, and smile, and be a villain.'"

"What's that supposed to mean?"

"It means somebody's actin' real nice and smilin' all pretty, like nothing's wrong, but underneath that big smile they're planning to do you in. A guy named Shakespeare wrote that in one of his plays. *Hamlet*'s the name of it. My English teacher's husband's an actor and she had him come in and do a scene outta that play for us. It takes place in Denmark."

"Who's Shakespeare?"

"Just a guy who wrote up a bunch of plays and things back in the old days." The boy grinned some more. The older one watched him, and she couldn't help but think he was sort of cute with his dark hair that was long enough to curl up around his ears. He had a ring in his left ear, a tiny gold hoop with some kind of odd medallion hanging off it. She didn't get to have pierced ears, but Sissy got to, so she could wear Momma's dangling rhinestone earrings at competitions.

The older one leaned her head back against the wall like he was doing and thought about what the boy had said, and she felt a little better after that, knowing that everybody hated all those stupid, pretty little girls strutting around on the stage and pretending they were grown-ups, but she didn't say anything else to him. She felt strange being by herself with him. She had never been alone with a boy before. Momma hardly ever let them invite anyone else home to play.

Suddenly the boy said the most shocking thing. "How come your mom doesn't enter you in your age division? You're pretty, too."

Eyes wide, heart hammering, she fixed her eyes on him, far too stunned to say a word.

He frowned. "What? Why're you lookin' at me like that?"

"You said I'm pretty."

"So? You are. I heard some older guys talking about you once in the locker room. They said you're sexy already. They said you look a lot older than you are."

"Uh-uh." The thought of boys talking about her was frightening, but somehow exciting, too, but she knew the older boys looked at her breasts sometimes. She'd seen them doing it. Momma told her she'd developed way too early for her age, and Stepdaddy made Momma buy her a training bra so she wouldn't look so trampy. But the boy was surely lying about the pretty part.

"Yes, they did. I heard 'em plain as day," he insisted. He laughed softly. "They said you got some cute little titties."

"That's so gross, shut up."

"Well, that's what they said. I'm just telling you what I heard."

"Momma says my freckles make me ugly. And my hair's ugly, too. She says Sissy's the pretty one."

The boy nodded, gave a small shrug. "Yeah, Sissy looks pretty good, all right, but I like your hair the best. It's a prettier color. And hell, you can get rid of those freckles any time you want to."

Very interested now, but skeptical, too, she studied his face, thinking maybe he was making fun of her. "No way. I was born with them, and that's the way it's gonna be all my life."

"Yes, you can," he insisted. "My sisters had 'em, not as bad as you, but lots of 'em. My mom's a dermatologist and she's got all this bleaching stuff she uses on their skin. You should of seen it, their freckles just faded away and now it looks like they never did have any, ever. She uses it on my big sis, too, but she's gone off to college down in Florida now. You know, that's the state with the beaches way down south."

The older one wondered why his big sister hadn't stayed in her own state to go to school, but she stared at him, more interested in the bleaching stuff, but not sure she believed him. "Really? You telling me the truth or is this some big, fat lie so you can laugh at me later?"

"Aw, c'mon, why would I wanna make up something like that?"

Her heart began to thud, excited to think she could get rid of her freckles and be pretty like Sissy.

Beside her, the boy heaved a big sigh. "This sure as hell

sucks, havin' to go to these beauty pageants. My mom and sisters hate your mom and your sister. You know that?"

"No."

"Yep, they sure do. They take turns entering because they're the same age, but they don't ever win because your sister always does. I guess they're pretty jealous because they never get the tiaras. They usually just get third or fourth place, but sometimes they get second. I bet they'd like it just fine if Sissy dropped dead all of a sudden."

"I'd like that, too."

When he started laughing as if that was the funniest thing he'd ever heard, she began to laugh, too. She realized she rarely ever laughed, and it seemed sort of strange to be sitting down there in the dark and laughing with a boy. But she was beginning to like him.

"You hungry?" he asked when they finally stopped laughing. "I got a Kit Kat bar that I'll split with you."

"Okay."

They ate the candy and listened to the applause going on above them in the bleachers. When Sissy's music came on for her Little Bo Peep dance, the older one covered her ears so she wouldn't have to hear it. She'd heard it a million times at home, over and over, until she wanted to scream.

After Sissy's performance was done, the boy said, "You want some of that freckle-removin' stuff?"

"Yeah. Where do you get it?"

"Well, you have to get it from my mom at her office, you know, with a prescription, but mom keeps all kinds of it at home. She'd never know if I take some for you. Why don't you come over next Saturday, and we'll try some out on your face and see what happens?"

"I don't know if I can. Where do you live?"

"Just a couple of blocks over from your house, through that big patch of woods behind your barn. Remember how the bus picks me and my sisters up right in front of our front gate? Mom's taking them both to town Saturday afternoon at two for piano lessons. And Dad's going out of town to a doctors' conference this weekend. He's a plastic surgeon."

"Both your parents are doctors?"

"Yeah, but different kinds. So what'd you say? Come on over, and we'll try some of that cream out on you. And don't bring that stuck-up little sister of yours, either, or it's a no go. I can't stand her."

The older one smiled at that and thought that finally, finally somebody didn't like Sissy the best. "Okay, I will, but you gotta promise not to tell. Momma won't like me coming over there. She hates your mother. Says she's a stuck-up snob."

"Yeah, she is, sometimes, but all the moms around here hate each other."

They both laughed, and she said, "Promise you won't tell anybody that I'm coming?"

"Who am I gonna tell? But we can meet someplace else if it's gonna get you in trouble."

"No, no, there isn't anywhere else. I'll come over, but I'll sneak down that alley behind your house so nobody'll see me. Momma doesn't like me to go off our property."

"Just unlatch the gate and come in. It's the tall one that's painted red and has some fancy black hinges shaped like lions. I'll be waiting on the back porch for you."

Five

A glance at my trusty old Timex told me that I'd have just enough time to hightail it to Cedar Bend Lodge and nose around the pageant before Black's helicopter set down. The traffic was terrible and my rotten mood devolved in graduated stages from horrible to foul to mad as hell by the time I drove through the great stone gate that heralded my honey's resort for the rich and neurotic. It was beautiful, of course; everything Nick owned was rated in the stratospheres with more stars than Colin Powell's epaulets. I passed through the smooth, impossibly green golf courses, and admired the flowers, flowers, and more flowers. You name it—baskets, giant decorative urns, manicured beds, Black's domain made Epcot Center look like the Mojave Desert. But the place smelled great when everything was blooming. Couldn't knock that.

As soon as I drove under a portico constructed of stacked rock pillars and braked at the massive cut-glass doors of the gargantuan lobby, a valet in his black-and-gold uniform was at my window ready to serve/sustain my every whim. My intimate relationship with the good doctor had gotten around among his employees, no doubt, and was I ever treated like royalty around this place. A decided perk that I wasn't exactly used to, but probably could get used to fast. Love, even.

The valet was a young high school kid named Rob that I'd seen a couple of times around the resort. He was tall, with dark hair and big cocoa-colored eyes, nice looking, pleasant, and always had a wide smile lighting up his face.

He said, "Good afternoon, Detective Morgan. Would you like me to park your car?"

See what I mean about pleasant? The description of the afternoon was debatable, however, considering the pair of butchered lips I'd encountered earlier in a drain and couldn't erase from my mind no matter how hard I tried, but my smile was gracious. My life wasn't this kid's fault. "Has Doctor Black made it in from California yet?"

"No, ma'am, but they're expectin' him out at the heliport any time now. Everybody's sure all stressed out about this pageant that's goin' on."

"Yeah, must be bad for you, having to take care of all these gorgeous bathing beauties pulling their cars up out here."

"Yeah, breaks my heart. I dreaded this all week long." He grinned. Yep, he was a real hottie close up. He looked about sixteen or seventeen, and now I could see the waves in his hair and that his eyes were more the color of burnt cinnamon toast, which was the kind I usually make. He was still talking. "I skipped school today so I'd get to see these beauty contestants up close and personal. Some of them are models, too. I never did meet a real live model till today. They tip good, too."

I smiled and wished they all really were alive as I watched him drive off in my mud-splattered Explorer. Then I strode cross the lobby in search of the pageant-festive ballroom. It turned out the glorious festivities would be held in the Ozark Ballroom, the biggest and most crystal chandeliered of the three, all of which were magnificently appointed, of course. Ozark just won the glitz and glamour prize, is all.

Down long hallways, elegantly carpeted in black and tan, I trod until I finally saw half a dozen identical, black velvet–draped double doors, with workers scurrying in and out like ants on a honey spill. At one end of the gigantic room, a team of carpenters hammered like crazy on a stage and an attached fifty-foot runway, all under the screechy supervision of a young woman, tall and thin enough to be Twiggy's progeny. By her shrilly intoned instructions, however, I decided she was the pageant coordinator and made a beeline straight to her vicinity.

"Pardon me, ma'am. Are you Patricia Cardamon?"

The lady turned and looked me over with every intention of dismissing me pronto and ASAP; she had the haughty superiority that only a recently retired, ex-runway model could carry off. "Yes, I am she. May I help you?"

She might as well as tacked on at the end of her question, *You unworthy little pissant.* I had the time, so yeah, I looked her over, too. Up and down, even. She appeared to be mid-thirties, slender in an unhealthy, anorexic way but with good skin, good hair, good nails, good just about everything. Well, okay, good-looking seemed to be the word of the day. Sometimes I got downright suspicious that it couldn't be a coincidence that *all* Black's employees looked straight out of the pages of *GQ* and *Glamour*, all just as sleek and glossy, too. Maybe that was on Black's Cedar Bend employment application: *Please check the following that most describes your physical appearance: Drop-dead gorgeous, Beautiful, Pretty, Okay, Fair, Ugly, Butt-ugly. The last six need not apply.* Or maybe they just kept the ugly people in the basement.

"Yes, ma'am. My name is Claire Morgan, detective with the Canton County Sheriff's Department. We talked briefly on the telephone about twenty minutes ago."

"Oh, yes, now I think I remember."

Great. Patricia thought she remembered. One of the smart models. And she didn't seem pleased about it, either. I said, "As I told you on the telephone, I'm going to need a list of your contestants, as well as anyone else who has any kind of connection with this pageant."

"Well, I must say, Detective, that this will certainly be an inconvenience at the moment. You do realize that this contest will be held day after tomorrow, not to mention the full dress rehearsal tomorrow morning. Really, you are asking a lot."

Okay, the woman doesn't know about Hilde's terrible demise and can't know until I notify Black, so be nice, understanding, and benevolent. Coddle the nasty vixen. "Yes, ma'am, I understand that. However, you can rest assured that I do have a very good reason to inconvenience you this way. Official police business, in fact."

Ms. Cardamon gave me the slight raised-eyebrow treatment, designed to cower me, I suppose, or she had raised it as much as she could manage with at least thirty-five Botox injections keeping her all smoothed out and wrinkle-less. "What do you mean by official police business? I assume Dr. Black has been informed of this request." Did I mention the word haughty? Arrogant? Disdainful? Side effects of Botox poisoning? I do not know.

"That's precisely why I'm here today, Ms. Cardamon. To speak with Dr. Black about this situation. I understand he's due in about now."

"Perhaps if you tell me what police business you're talking about and exactly what you need from Dr. Black, I could pass the word along to him. He's a good friend of mine, and a very busy man, as well. You will probably need to make an appointment with his personal assistant."

Oookay, now Pattycakes was beginning to get on my

nerves. What few I had left. Apparently she didn't know I was a pretty good amiga of the good doctor, too, hot and heavy, well past the mutual groping level, in fact, and going on for almost a year now, to be precise. I made a note to watch her face crumple when he showed her how much he liked me, too, even more than her, I suspect. But hell, I could be polite until then. I wouldn't cuss or kick her off her pointy-toed high heels, or even sneer at her.

"I'm acquainted with Dr. Black as well, and I'm afraid this will require a private audience with him. Thank you for offering to intercede."

See how nice I can be when pushed to it? She nodded and somehow managed to re-arch that eyebrow into the frozen reaches of her forehead. I started to tell a joke to see if her face moved when she laughed, but decided I was behaving badly. Hateful, almost. "Now, if you could arrange to give me that list, I'd appreciate it. It would help as well if you would notify everybody involved that I'll be conducting interviews tomorrow, before, during and after the rehearsal. They need to schedule time to speak to me or to my partner, Bud Davis."

"Oh, dear, that will just wreck my time schedule. Couldn't you do it the day after the pageant?"

Sure. Or maybe next Christmas Eve would do. I gave her a dead, unblinking stare until I got her undivided, if superiority-tinged, attention. "I'm not playing games here, Ms. Cardamon. I'll repeat this again. I'm here on official police business, and we'll need your complete cooperation."

She made a sound closely akin to an old maid spinster's *harumph*. Couldn't say I'd ever heard anybody else do that, not to my face, anyway.

She said, "All right, Officer. I'll see what I can do."

"See what you can do right now, why don't you?"

Ms. Cardamon stalked off in a huff and yelled at one of her assistants, who looked downright startled. Displaced aggression, oh yeah. Can't yell at the pushy policewoman? Abuse your helper; it'll make you feel oh, so much better. Good thing her Chihuahua was safe at home.

I sidled around a while, remaining inconspicuous while I watched the people still laboring on the elaborate set and lighting created to make all the girls look ten years younger. That would put some of the competing tots back in the womb, no doubt. There weren't any contestants present that I could tell. Not unless they were disguised as overweight carpenters and various and sundry handymen dressed in denim overalls and wearing John Deere caps. Probably all still over at Mr. Race's fisticuffing it out with Corkie for appointments. It took about fifteen minutes for Ms. Prissy Pants to get back to me with copies of her lists. I thanked her politely. She flounced off, no doubt to check the red carpet's walkability in spike heels factor.

Sinking down in a chair on the back row, I went over the names, thinking it was going to take us a whole bunch of time to check out all the people involved in putting on a show of this magnitude. Bud and I might have to enlist help from our colleagues at the station. They probably wouldn't mind; most of them were males. The *thut-thut* of an approaching helicopter sent my heart all a-twitter at approximately the same rotation velocity of the rotor blades. Embarrassed at my eager anticipation of Black's return to the fold, meaning me, I didn't even deign to glance out the big plate-glass windows facing the lake as his chopper glided by in all its black-and-tan magnificence. Well, okay, I did give it a quick sidelong glance, but it was too far away to see if Nick was piloting. Double embarrassed at how much I had missed him, I forced myself to sit still. I'd give him time to disembark and get upstairs to his penthouse office/apartment/utopia. There would be titillating advantages in showing up there right after he got home from a lengthy absence. Even with some very bad news in tow.

It took me a while to wend my way through the huge, sprawling resort anyway, but I had a card key to his ultra private, exclusive elevator. See how special I am? Myself and room service was about it as far as extra keys to the master's penthouse were concerned. He wouldn't be expecting me to be here, either. I could surprise him for once. He sure as the devil had surprised me enough times, not that I was complaining, they were usually off-the-chart good surprises.

The elevator whisked me up with a quiet whisper and whoosh and opened with silent efficiency into a lushly carpeted hallway sporting another huge expanse of plate-glass windows overlooking a glittering lake vista, a view to die for, oh yeah. When Black got home, he usually headed straight for the office wing, so I turned in that direction. Imagine my surprise when I saw a tall, raven-haired woman standing at his guest room door, her Gucci luggage all around her like adoring subjects. She turned around and believe me, I knew at once that this was no bellhop dropping off the guru's luggage.

"Oh, hello there," she said.

Oh, hello there? That's when I recognized her. She looked just as good as she did on all her magazine covers, only ten times better. Bud had met her once in New York. He'd told me she was unbelievably gorgeous in person, with flawless skin and black-silk hair, but now I *really* believed him. Oh, yeah, it was Jude of the one name, all right. Black's famous ex-wife supermodel, a Venus de Milo blessed with both arms, and by the quizzical way she was looking at me, he hadn't mentioned me to her.

"Did I forget to tip you?"

Oh, man, did that ever smart. But I smiled, and real friendly like, too, not a grimace in sight.

"No need. Police officers aren't allowed."

Recognition flared then inside those big, expertly defined, mascara-drenched, almond-shaped green eyes. "Oh, my goodness. You're Claire Morgan, aren't you? I recognize you now from all the newspaper photos. Nicky didn't tell me you were going to be here."

No, I suspect he forgot to mention me at all. And *Nicky*, huh? Okay, Claire, be the adult you've always wanted to be. She's probably very nice or Black wouldn't have married her. Wouldn't have divorced her, either.

"Actually, I was at the hotel on official business and heard the chopper." I sure was using the word *official* a lot of late. Even I noticed it.

"Well, good. I was hoping I'd get to meet you this week. Nicky told me all about you. You must be quite a woman to have him so ga-ga over you."

Ga-ga? Now that made me want to gag-gag. And that's a hard question she posed, right? Let's see, should I say yes or no to being quite a woman? A quandary, to be sure. So I said, "It's nice to meet you, too, Jude." I stuck out my hand. I could be a real gent when called for.

We shook, and I made sure my grip meant business. She didn't wince too badly, so I stood there and breathed in her extremely expensive and delectable perfume for a while. It was flowery and sweet, not roses but something else, peonies, or gardenias, maybe. After a second, I ventured, "Black around?"

"He had to take a private phone call in his office."

"Well, please tell him I dropped by and that I need to talk to him. Police business. I'll be downstairs in the ballroom when he gets a minute."

She was looking me over pretty good, too, but trying not to appear to. Curious what ga-ga entailed, I guess. "He said he wouldn't be long."

"I don't have time to wait." I turned and pressed the elevator button, wanting to escape before she kissed me on both cheeks, NYC style.

"Claire? I just heard you were here."

That was Black's voice, and I turned and found him striding down the hall, grinning, looking really tall and hunky and very pleased to see me, if I say so myself. He was dressed in one of his dozens of six-thousand-dollar suits, no doubt hand tailored and hand delivered from some faraway hemisphere. This time it was black pinstripe with the snowiest white shirt ever laundered this side of Congress and a red tie that probably cost way too much for the scrap of material put into it. But he was all dimpled up with pleasure, his jet-black hair a little longish for him and slightly windblown from the rotors, and those pure blue eyes fastened on me, and me alone. So *ha ha*, Jude.

Unfortunately, I also felt that weakness in my knees he could bring out in me, so I locked them together and tried to be unaffected by his physical presence. After all, I hadn't seen him in two whole weeks, so give my hormones a break here. I felt rather awkward, especially when he grabbed me and gave me a big hug that brought me up on my toes, not that I didn't like it, but I put the brakes on before he could kiss me. After all, his former wife was inches away surrounded by her ritzy suitcases dripping their pricy logos and a cloud of Chanel.

"I should've called first," I said pointedly.

"No, I'm glad you're here. I missed you like hell."

Now Jude was the one looking awkward, but better her than me, I always say. I looked pointedly at Black to make him calm his engines, then pointedly at her for emphasis. Pointedly was getting a workout here lately, too.

"Jude, this is Claire. I'm glad you're finally getting to meet her."

"Yes, I recognized her. She's quite lovely."

Quite lovely? I bet she would've said tough, if my jacket wasn't covering up the big Glock 9 mm lodged under my arm in its shoulder holster and/or my most recent butterfly-bandaged gunshot wound. I said to Black, "Look, I didn't know you had company, and I don't want to interrupt. As I was telling Jude here, I have official business with you."

Black looked surprised. Imagine.

He frowned and said, "You're not interrupting anything. What do you mean official?"

Why was everybody saying that? "I hate to tell you this, but you've come home to a big problem concerning the pageant."

He looked relieved then, but that wouldn't last long. "Okay, let's talk about it in my office. Jude, make yourself at home. If you need anything, just call the concierge and he'll take care of it."

Black took my arm in a rather firm, no-nonsense grip as if he expected me to jerk away and take off at a sprint for the elevator, then led me down the hall and into the huge office wing. I didn't like it much because it felt proprietary, but I let it go. Poor guy was about to get hit with some very bad news. He deserved some consideration.

We entered his massive yet plushly appointed private office, tan and black, of course, and he shut the door behind us then trapped me against it, full body press. I didn't fight it when his mouth found mine, didn't resist for maybe four or five minutes of mutual heavy breathing, hot tongue kissing, and expert hand groping around under my T-shirt. And I didn't groan and complain, either, when he squeezed my recent gunshot wound against the door and sent a stab of pain coursing down to my fingertips. I told you already that I missed him.

After a couple more minutes of our hard-panting how do you dos, Black pulled back and muttered, and, yes, gasped out, I'm happy to say, "God, I'm turned on."

And he was, trust me. I could just feel it.

I said, "Ditto and back to you double, but we gotta talk."

Black stepped back and let go of me. "Okay, tell me what's up. And don't be mad about Jude. She signed on to be a judge, so I told her she could stay up here where the press couldn't get at her."

I righted my clothes and controlled my own machine-gun pulse. "How sweet."

"Mind if I stay at your place until she's gone?"

"My pleasure." Was that ever the truth. "Want me to pack up the toothbrush and T-shirt I left here until she's gone?"

Black laughed. "Why would I want you to do that?"

"I don't know. Just thought I'd ask."

"She knows I'm in love with you."

That was more than I knew. I tried not to look shocked. He hadn't said stuff like that much. "You told her that?"

"Of course. You find it so hard to believe?"

"Well, you haven't exactly mentioned it to me lately, or ever."

"Yes, I have. You just don't want to hear it. In fact, you change the subject if I get anywhere close to saying it."

"I do not."

"Then you're ready for me to say it out loud from now on?"

"This is a really stupid conversation. Listen, I've got something more important to talk to you about."

"See what I mean?"

"Forget us, damn it. This is serious. Listen to me."

He stepped back and jerked loose the knot in his silk tie. "Let me change clothes and pack a bag. You can tell me on the way to your place. I spent the entire flight looking forward to some downtime with you."

Wow, I did so like the sound of Jude being left coughing and wheezing in our romantic dust. Unfortunately, it wasn't going to happen. "We probably need to discuss it here and now. And you'll probably want to leave that tie on and take some time to think about how to direct your staff."

Black frowned. "This does not sound good."

"It's not good. One of your contestants has been murdered."

"Oh, my God. Who?"

"That's the worst part. The victim is Brianna Swensen's sister."

"Bud's girl? How did it happen? What's her name?"

"Hilde Swensen. She was slated to compete, and here's some more bad news. She was murdered up at the Royal Condos."

"Oh, God, I own that place. Why haven't I heard about this before now? Somebody should've called me." He sounded highly perturbed, looked that way, too.

"You're hearing it now. What's more, you've got to instruct your staff to let us interview everybody remotely connected with this thing. Your girl Friday downstairs is balking on me."

"Have you turned up any leads?"

"Not yet. Brianna says Hilde led a wild and crazy lifestyle in Florida, South Beach, no less, and it could have been somebody connected to that."

Black turned, paced a few steps away from me. Paced some more, while I leaned against the door and watched calmly. "I can't believe this. Not so soon. Good God—"

When he turned and faced me, I said, "Yeah. Nothing like this ever happened around here until I moved in from LA."

"That's not what I meant. And it's not your fault, if that's what you're thinking."

"Yeah, right. It's just another big coincidence."

"It could be a killer was drawn down here by the publicity of your last two cases, and there was a hell of a lot of it, too."

"Whatever. Right now, we've got to get things nailed down before tomorrow's rehearsal. I guess the pageant will still go on, or will it?"

Black shook his head. "I don't know. It'll be hard to cancel things this late. Let me think about it. Good God, this is awful."

"Let me know what you decide. I need to get back to the

office and brief Charlie in person. The newspapers haven't sniffed this out yet, but the minute they find out it's connected to you and this pageant, they'll be all over us."

"Yeah, what a surprise."

"I'm taking off pretty soon. Finish up here, and I'll tell you more of the particulars after I get the go-ahead from Charlie."

"I'll be over to your place later, as soon as I can get away."

"See you then."

"Well, be careful, for God's sake. Duck, weave, hide, whatever it takes."

Our private little joke, but unfortunately it was wearing a trifle thin. I wasn't ducking nearly enough, it appeared. Today I had ducked, all right, but still got myself a sore-as-the-devil shoulder. I decided to tell him about that little detail later so he wouldn't demand to examine and re-treat the wound before I left. I exited stage right in a big hurry, more than glad Jude had disappeared into the guest room and I wouldn't be forced to compare cheekbone structures with her.

Six

As it happened Charlie had been called to Jeff City, so I didn't get a personal sit-down with him. I elected not to go into detail about the case over the phone, either. He would be back in the morning, and I would brief him then. I left word with his teensy, sparrowlike secretary to fit me in as soon as he returned, and she promised to do so. I took time to check out the lakewide BOLO bulletin I'd put in on the boat, which was unlikely to draw a lead with such a sketchy description, but hey, maybe we'd get a break for a change. Maybe the guy's wife was suspicious of his bloody clothes and some extra lips lying around the house and would give us a call. On the other hand, the guy probably had battened down the boat far away and out of sight hours ago. Unfortunately, nobody had turned up a thing.

Maybe Black could help me figure out what kind of monster did this to Hilde when and if he could tear himself away from Jude. His insight could trigger something I hadn't thought of. He was a shrink, after all, and he definitely knew his stuff. He'd helped me on my cases before. Not that I depended on him or anything, but talking the case helped my imagination click. And all I could think about right now was catching this depraved pervert and the sooner the better.

After twenty minutes fighting five o'clock traffic, I hung a left into the private graveled road that led down to my little lakeside haven. I stopped at the security gate that my friend, Harve Lester, had installed last summer to keep the press off our backs. I used my trusty little remote, drove through, and watched to make sure the gate shut all the way and locked down behind me. When I passed Harve's place, I glanced at the house, missing him. He had gone to Michigan for a couple of weeks to visit relatives, but he'd be back soon. His Web site business had really taken off, and he had his hands full with design and implementation, not to mention his headhunting assignments. He was top-notch at his work and the word had gotten around. But he deserved time off, if anybody did. He'd been shot in the line of duty and suffered a life sentence in a wheelchair, but he never complained about his lot. He'd been my mentor and partner when I was a rookie at the LAPD, and the best detective I'd ever met. I loved the guy.

At the moment, however, all I could think about was Hilde Swensen. Every time I found myself alone, her butchered mouth kept popping up in my brain, and each time, my stomach flipped over like some kind of berserk gymnast. I didn't want to think about it anymore, and I didn't want to think about Black being cooped up at Cedar Bend with his really, really good-looking, impossibly gorgeous ex-wife, either. I wanted to find the guy who'd butchered up Hilde, and I didn't want to wait until tomorrow to get started. I wanted to follow people home tonight and demand that they tell me everything they knew. The need to catch the guy was eating its way through my gut, and I could feel the anger and strange excitement a homicide brought up inside me, excitement that was dark and disturbing but happened anyway. I wanted this guy so bad I could taste it. He'd been in my gunsight, for God's sake, and I'd let him get away clean.

I gripped the steering wheel until my knuckles turned white. This had never happened to me before. I'd never interrupted a murderer at the scene, much less let him escape. I stopped the car and went with the rage, taking deep, sucking breaths the way Black had told me to. I wanted to pummel the hell out of something, anything, maybe the first thing I laid eyes on would do. I took it out on the steering wheel with a doubled fist for a second or two, then spun some gravel as I took off around the last bend that would bring me to my little A-frame house, recently remodeled as a more than extravagant Christmas present from Black.

I realized with some personal disdain that I was hoping Black's big Cobalt 360 would already be moored at my pitiful little dock, but it wasn't there, and neither was he. I did notice, however, the big black Harley-Davidson motorcycle sitting at my front gate.

Well, well, whaddaya know, Mr. Joe McKay had come to pay me a visit and was making himself at home down on my private dock. Now this was a surprise, let me tell you, and not a guest I'd ever invited to drop by and have tea. The first thing I was going to ask him was how the devil he'd gotten by my security gate, then I remembered that he'd ridden onto my property unbidden before, last Christmas, to be exact.

I pulled into my new heated garage, another nifty little perk that dating Nicholas Black had provided, that, along with a number of awesome amenities inside my hitherto shabby little cabin. What can I say? Multimillionaire boyfriends, yep, they have a way of endearing themselves to us peons. Exwives not included.

I got out, slung off my jacket, fingered my wound, which had started to throb, while I debated whether or not I should take a stroll down to the water and make sure McKay wasn't trying to steal my old jon boat. Actually, McKay had helped me drop the hammer on a couple of bad guys once not so long ago, so I guess he deserved a quick howdy-do. Initially, I had hated the man's guts at first sight, but then again, I hated nearly everyone's guts at first sight. However, he had proved himself reliable in a particularly hairy situation and used his considerable expert demolition skills to my advantage, so I'd developed a new soft spot in my heart for him. I would definitely call him whenever I wanted anything blown to smithereens.

And, hey, did I mention he purports himself to be a real live psychic? A fact I still wasn't one hundred percent certain of to this very day, but it was hard to figure how he knew stuff before it happened. Maybe he'd come over today to tell me who killed Hilde Swensen. Great, now I could just drive over and arrest the freak and be done with it.

Oh, another thing, McKay was a helluva good-looking guy, Mr. Stereotypical Bad Boy Type, alive and well, and I found that irksome, too, for no particular reason. He waved me down to join him like he owned the place. That's when I realized he wasn't alone. Elizabeth, his little daughter, was with him.

I crunched a path across the rocky beach, then stepped onto my creaky gangplank that was built circa 1955. A couple of worn boards were loose again, and I made a mental note to fix them if I ever got the time. Or maybe Black could just build me a giant marina for my birthday.

McKay and Elizabeth were holding long cane poles, and a white pint container of worms sat between them on the dock. The contents writhed around like crazy, no doubt screaming, *Take him, take him, he's juicier than me.*

"Hey, McKay, feel free to come out here and fish anytime you like. No need to call first and ask permission."

McKay presented me with his own brand of lethal weapon, a smile so slow, so deadly, so potent with dimples and charm that some women would have dropped down and bruised their kneecaps on the spot. Alas, a swooner I am not. He was so typically the aforementioned bad boy material that he could've come straight out of a Hollywood casting call. You know, *Attention, please, all Colin Farrell lookalikes proceed up front ASAP*. He had that studied scruffy look, you know the one, sun-bleached blond hair, too long, too shaggy, just enough unshaven beard to be a scratchy turn-on, tight black Levi's, plain white T-shirt. The only thing he forgot to wear was his locket with Marlon Brando's picture inside it.

"Now, c'mon, Detective, I didn't figure you'd mind me comin' out here much since I saved your pretty little butt last Christmas."

"Not that I'm not entirely ungrateful for that, too, but if you'll remember, I'm the one who unlocked your handcuffs so you could."

"Yeah? You're the one who clamped them on me in the first place."

"Seemed the right thing to do at the moment."

He took a moment to examine me like I was a particularly succulent filet mignon that made his mouth water and his fingers itch for some A.1. Steak Sauce. That image made me hungry until I remembered Hilde and why I'd skipped lunch. Lipless corpses will do that to a person.

McKay said, "Change your mind about runnin' off with me, or you still got it goin' on with the shrink?"

"I'm still seeing Dr. Black, not that I ever considered running anywhere with you."

"You sure 'bout that? I've been sensin' some storm clouds might be brewin' between you and Nick. Thought maybe you got some trouble in paradise."

"Nope. Everything's sunny at the moment." I wondered, though, if he'd really seen my relationship with Black going belly-up in the near future, or if it was just another one of McKay's come-ons.

Actually McKay and I really are sort of friends now. I think we'd just gotten into the habit of this hateful verbal sparring and couldn't seem to let it go.

Little Elizabeth just stared at me. She didn't smile, didn't seem to recognize me at all. She was only two years old, and absolutely beautiful, blond hair, big blue eyes, and she made me think of my own child, Zachary. I'd lost him when he was two, and I looked away from her, blocking a swarm of dark memories before they could get started. I did that a lot nowadays.

I said, "Catchin' anything?"

McKay shook his head. "Hoped the bluegill would bite, but we haven't gotten a single nibble." He looked at the torn, blood-soaked sleeve of my T-shirt. "Got yourself shot again, I see."

"Just a nick, you know, like in the movies."

"Next time it might be 'Bang, Bang, you're dead, lady.' That happens in the movies, too."

"Thanks, McKay, make me feel better, why don't you? So enough of the small talk. Why'd you really come out here today?"

He searched my face the way he liked to do, the way he liked to do because it made me damn uncomfortable. Annoyed, even.

"Been dreamin' about you lately, detective."

"Oh, yeah? Who hasn't?"

He grinned, slow and affecting, but then he sobered and lowered his voice to show how serious he was. "You know that psychic thing I got? It's been actin' up lately, so I thought I'd come by and make sure you were alive and kickin'. By the looks of that arm, I'm right on, but maybe a mite late."

"Care to tell me what you're talking about in plain English instead of psychic mumbo jumbo?"

McKay decided to leave me in suspense. He squatted down beside his daughter, picked up a night crawler that had wriggled out of the paper container and thereby made itself way too conspicuous. Death wish, worm-style, I guess. McKay made a show of putting it on the hook, and I watched it wiggle like crazy, obviously aware of its impending doom.

"There you go, baby cakes." McKay smiled at Elizabeth as he dropped her line back into the water with a soft kerplunk. She said nothing, just stared at the water. Then he adjusted her straw hat to shield her face from the sun, and Zach's sunburned little face came barreling up from the depths of my heart again, with a backwash of pain so severe that I swallowed bile. The air was warm with a gentle breeze, the water smooth and green and serene, and I locked my eyes on the trees across the cove and gathered myself.

McKay's kid had been with us in our mutual nightmare in that godawful dark cave, and I hoped she had blocked out every detail of what had happened down there. I wished I could, too, but it hadn't happened yet, at least not in my dreamscapes.

When McKay decided to resume our conversation, he stood up and stepped away from the silent child. He stood very close and lowered his voice. I was not exactly unaware of his masculine appeal, but he was thinking about his daughter now. "Lizzie's gettin' a little better now, but still not so good. She won't say much and gets some real bad dreams about the bogeyman and his freak of a girlfriend."

"Yeah, I've spent a few nights with them myself."

"That makes three of us."

"Okay, McKay, I'll bite, what'd you dream about me?" I didn't really want to ask for specifics, specifics usually didn't bode well for me, but as mentioned, his visions sometimes turned out to be pretty dead-on. Better safe than sorry.

"I've been seeing these great big smiles. No faces, mind you, except for yours, and believe me, you're not smiling when I see you, just starin' all glazed eyes ahead, and darlin',

I think that means you're headed straight for some big, bad trouble."

I stared at him then, all glazed eyes ahead, creeped out, and fairly certain he was batting a thousand about my immediate future. On my last case, his knowledge of the crime scenes caused me to suspect him of major wrongdoing. Not this time. This time he was right on the money, and there was no way he could have known about the mutilation of Hilde's body. "Jeez, McKay, scare the crap outta me, why don't you?"

"So this smile thing makes sense to you?"

"Maybe. Anything else I might need to know?"

"Not yet."

"You see anybody else in these smiley-face dreams of yours?"

McKay shook his head. "One thing, though, that you ought to know."

"Yeah? What's that?"

"These smiles I see? They're dripping blood. So there you go. That's why I came out here. You know, knight in shined-up armor, trying to do the right thing, save your pretty little hide again."

I looked away, but I felt more than uneasy about my pretty little hide. He'd been on target enough in the past to make me want to believe him. Maybe having a psychic friend wasn't such a good thing. Maybe they should be avoided. "I appreciate your help, I truly do. How about taking a nice long nap, see if you can see the perp and get me his address like last time?"

"Maybe I should. Why don't you just lie down with me somewhere, you know, to get me started? That should get my dreams smokin' in no time."

He grinned again, one predominantly designed to rock me wildly about in my high-top Nikes, the same one that used to raise my hackles. Not anymore. I smiled back. He was growing on me, for sure.

"Is that really a smile I see, Detective? Hell, you didn't stalk off or pull your gun, or nothin'. That mean you're considering goin' out with me one of these days?"

"Nope. Not at all."

"Can't figure what you see in that Black guy. Doesn't seem your type."

Actually, McKay was ten on the accuracy scale again, even sans the dreams. Black and I were about as different as Nicole Kidman and Rosie O'Donnell. Truth was, I was probably a lot more like McKay, T-shirt, jeans, and smartass attitude. But Black rang all my bells and blew all my whistles, yep, created one helluva sexual cacophony. That was a hard thing to ignore.

"We're getting along just fine. Thanks for asking."

"Can't you give me one itty-bitty ray of hope?"

"You can hope all you want, but I'm with Black, period, and end of conversation."

"Oh, I'm gonna hope, all right. In the meantime, you take care, you hear me? And if it's all the same to you, Lizzie and I might hang out a while longer. She likes it down here on the water. Calms her down, know what I mean?"

His eyes were serious, and I could see how worried he was. I had a feeling the little girl wasn't doing so hot at all. "Yeah, that's why I live here, the peace and tranquility. Bring her out here any time you want. I was just kidding about the permission thing."

I watched Elizabeth for a moment, wondering if she really didn't remember me from that terrible cave of horrors. She'd been through a lot of very bad stuff, even before McKay brought her to Missouri, too much for a little kid, but it was clear McKay doted on her. He'd get her through it.

My cell phone started up with the Mexican Hat Dance song, and I said good-bye to McKay, turned, and headed back to the house. It was Black on the other end, and I actually got a bit of a sensual shiver when I heard his voice. Good thing McKay didn't notice or he'd make a wisecrack.

"I'm on my way."

"Did you get things taken care of?"

"Yes. I took time to check in on a couple of my patients staying here at the Lodge. Everybody's pretty shook up about the Swensen girl. Where are you?"

"Home." I picked up my jacket and purse, crossed the driveway, and entered the garage.

"I should be there in about ten minutes. How's that sound?"

"Sounds good. By the way, just so you know, McKay and Lizzie are fishing on my dock." Black has this little jealousy thing going on about McKay, so I thought I'd head that problem off at the bend.

"How sweet."

Sarcasm. I had to grin. "I didn't invite him. He just showed up."

"That's better."

Maybe I knew how he felt now. Jude was not exactly chopped liver when it came to competition. "Okay, see you then."

I flipped my phone closed, then stopped to punch in the code to disarm my alarm system and entered the house. Not that I needed a security system, after all I was armed with two lethal weapons and was more than adept at kickboxing my way out of trouble. My fingernails were longer than usual, too, which added ten more sharp weapons to my personal arsenal. But Black was more security conscious than Donald Trump and had me rigged up with this new state-of-the-art computer system that would probably even tie my sneakers if I asked it to. Too bad it didn't know how to cook.

Inside, my little pooch, Jules Verne, the French poodle, came barreling down the stairs, yapping like crazy. Black had brought him to me from his Christmas trip to Paris—see what I mean about the gift-giving thing? Jules jumped around on my legs, his tail like a windshield wiper in a downpour, and I picked him up and snuggled him close. I only did that when nobody was looking, but the truth was, I really liked the silly little mutt. He was always there to greet me when I dragged in all depressed and gunshot. Even Black took business leaves of absence from my mayhem.

Jules calmed down after a while, but his tail kept beating the floor as I stood at the window watching McKay with his little girl. Zach and I had gone fishing once, and he'd caught a little perch. He'd be eight now. I wondered what he'd look like now, if he'd lived to grow tall and be on Little League teams and in Cub Scouts, and then I determinedly pushed those pictures out of my mind. He was dead and gone, had been for almost six years, don't think about him, don't remember, don't make yourself want to die, too.

Instead, I let the anger come again, fast and furious, anger about my dead son, anger about my past life and all the death that came with it, anger about Hilde Swensen and the homicidal maniac running loose on my turf.

I needed to release some pent-up anger before Black came home or I'd probably take it out on the poor guy. I opened the back door, and Jules bounded out and ran around in circles as if he'd been locked in a box for thirty-six hours instead of sleeping on my very soft, luxurious, Black-bestowed, gold-and-black bedspread.

I'd work out a little, that's what I'd do, get the aggression out of my system. It always helped me think, that, and yoga, which acted to calm me down. I wasn't in the mood for calm now. I wanted the rage to roil up inside me, make me so angry that I'd think of nothing but solving this case. So I began my routine, protecting my wounded arm and jabbing my good fist into the punching bag I had hanging on the limb of a pecan tree outside my back door. Stopping, swiveling, kicking the absolute hell out of it. It made me feel good, it made me wish it was the guy who'd murdered Hilde, it made me feel like I was doing something to get him, but it didn't erase the fact that I'd had him in sight and let him get away.

The sound of Black's big Cobalt 360 thundered up out front, and Jules went absolutely berserk. He took off around the front of the house and down to the dock, and I followed until I could see Black stepping out of the big boat, my little poodle yipping and bouncing around him like a Mexican jumping bean. I watched Black secure the line, then rise and hold out his hand to McKay. They shook hands, then spoke together for a length of time that made me a trifle uncomfortable. A moment later, Black picked up the dog, then squatted down beside Lizzie, and to my surprise, she reached over and patted the dog's head. Stunned, I watched him talk to her, amazed the child had taken to him even that much.

McKay turned around and glanced up at me, almost as if he knew I was watching them, so I turned and entered the house. It wasn't long before Black came in the front door, carrying Jules Verne in one arm. He was smiling, and I realized then, with sinking heart, that I was beginning to need him with me more than I liked to admit. It was a weakness, true, and a vulnerability I wasn't at all sure I liked.

Grinning, he headed toward me with a look I knew pretty well by now, but his expression changed when he saw the bandage on my upper arm. "Oh, crap. Bullet or blade this time?"

"It's a minor bullet wound. Don't get all bent out of shape."

"Glad to hear it wasn't a serious bullet." Oooh, sarcasm from the good doctor.

"I don't know why everybody's making such a big deal out of this. It's just a scratch."

"Yeah? Well, you know how turned on I get when you're all weak and wounded."

"I'm not weak and wounded."

"I get turned on when you're not weak or wounded, too." He smiled at me and I actually quivered inside my belly because I knew what that look meant. He said, "Sit down and let me take a look at it."

I sat. He examined. We were avoiding talking about the homicide and how I'd gotten shot.

"At least this time you let somebody dress it who knew what they were doing."

"I put some Band-Aids on it, but Buck just had to do it over his way. He's always such a perfectionist."

"I suppose that's a good trait for a pathologist. Well, this time the wound doesn't look too bad. That's a change for the better." He stood looking down at me, his hands on his hips. He had changed into a soft black polo shirt with the Cedar Bend logo and khaki pants and boat shoes, all the best money could buy, but of course. He always wore the best. "Want to tell me how this happened?"

I told him briefly about being ambushed on the deck.

"So you surprised the killer at the scene?"

"I guess. He still got away."

"What's Charlie say?"

"He's outta town, so I talked to him on the phone. He said I could share the details if you keep your mouth shut. He trusts you."

Serious now, Black sat down across from me and propped his foot on one knee. Jules Verne jumped onto his lap, and Black stroked his soft white fur. Black was good at stroking, let me tell you. The dog still liked him better than me. Probably remembered their time alone together in Paris.

I stood up and paced, agitated, furious all over again that I let the killer get away and dreading describing Hilde's mutilation to Black.

"Okay, I see you're nervous. Let's hear it. How'd she die? A gunshot wound?"

"Buck hasn't given official cause. I suspect she was strangled."

"Where was she killed?"

"In the bathroom, we think. He left her posed in the shower stall."

"How's Brianna taking it?"

"Not so well. Bud's with her."

"Does she have any idea who might've done it?"

"No. But like I said, she told us that her sister lived it up a bit with the fast set down at South Beach."

"Do you have to go down there?"

"Probably."

"Tell Charlie I can fly you there on the Lear. I've got this whole week written off on my calendar for the pageant."

I heard the Harley fire up, and I turned and stared out the window. McKay and Elizabeth were heading home. I still hadn't gotten to the worst part and wasn't looking forward to it. "It was ugly, Black. He mutilated her."

"I see. What'd he do to her?"

"He cut off her lips and left us a note stuck on her shoulder with a cute little Shakespearean quote written on it." I told him what the message said, and he frowned.

"That's from *Hamlet*. You say the body was posed?"

"You bet it was. He left her sitting in the shower stall, on the bench, her hands taped to hold some roses. I guess he was placing her on some kind of throne. That would explain the crown, too. It doesn't make sense why he took a shot at me. We didn't even see him until he fired. Didn't have a clue he was still around."

"And all this happened in broad daylight? This morning?" He was silent a moment longer, then said, "He might've been drawn down here by last summer's press coverage. And the pageant would be the best place to get lots of media attention. Percentages don't support another sensational crime at the lake this soon."

"Tell me about it."

"This is not your fault, Claire. Don't blame yourself."

We were going into a rapid free fall into analysis mode,

and I wasn't in the mood for it. I changed the subject, not wanting to talk about myself anymore.

I said, "You and McKay looked pretty friendly down there."

"I asked him about Elizabeth."

"She took to you."

"You were watching?"

I didn't want to admit it, so I said, "She's not doing so good, is she?"

Black nodded. "I offered to work with her. Pro bono. I suggested we do it out here when she's fishing, so she doesn't get anxious."

I stared at him a moment, really, truly pleased, touched, to be truthful. "That's a pretty cool thing to do, Black."

"I can be cool when the occasion calls for it."

"Oh, I'm finding that out."

We smiled at each other.

He said, "Maybe you could help me with Elizabeth. You know, hang around when she's here, hold her on your lap, help her bait the hook so she'll be comfortable with me."

I stiffened because I knew where he was going with this. "Don't think I don't know what you're doing, Black. Killing two birds with one stone, right? Helping Elizabeth cope and forcing me to be around a toddler Zach's age."

"Nobody ever said you were stupid, Claire."

"Sorry, I can't do it. Not yet."

"Okay."

"I'm not ready."

"Okay."

"Is this reverse psychology again?"

"I'd never force you to do anything you don't want to do. I told you that from the beginning. I make the suggestions. You make the calls."

Black was good, oh, yeah, I'd give him that. Time for change the subject, part two. "You hungry?"

"I'll be starved afterward."

"After what?"

"After you give me the welcome I deserve."

"You got yourself a deal, Dr. Black."

"Tell me about it."

I was glad the talking was done for the moment, glad I didn't have to think about lifeless, staring eyes and smiles that dripped blood. Black could do that for me, just by his touch, and he was very good at it. Practiced, even, and at least for a little while, I didn't have to think about Hilde lying dead in the morgue, her mouth in a plastic evidence jar.

Sisterly Love

The older one couldn't wait for Saturday to come. She was so excited she could barely sleep. It didn't even bother her that Sissy was prissing around in the new tiara she'd won and talking about how pretty it was. The older one just tried to stay away from her and her stupid crown. Momma was taking Sissy to be photographed in her new blue sash and crown on Saturday, which would make it easier to slip away and meet the boy.

She waited until around two-thirty, then walked up the alley behind the houses, searching for the red gate. She found it without trouble, but there was no one outside on such a cold winter day to notice her entering the boy's yard anyway. She latched the gate behind her and picked her way carefully across the frozen grass. There was a pool house with lots of fogged-up plate-glass windows, and she stopped to look inside because she had never seen a heated indoor pool before. There was even a swirling hot tub and a great big TV to watch. She turned and headed for the back steps that led up into a large, glassed-in sunroom.

The boy had a really nice house, huge, and a lot newer

than their old farmhouse, and it was painted a really pretty yellow color, almost like canaries. The sunroom was long and furnished with wicker chairs and sofas with orange-and-blue floral prints, and the boy was sitting in a wicker rocker beside an orange fireplace shaped like a funnel. Logs were crackling and snapping inside the grate. He unlocked the door and let her in, and she stood by the fire a minute, warming her backside.

"Here, give me your coat. I'm glad you wore that white shirt in case any of that bleach stuff gets on it."

"You sure your mom won't come back and catch us?"

"Oh, yeah. She has double duty at the piano teacher's place so the twins can each get some practice in. And she wouldn't care, anyhow. She likes us to invite friends over. You wanna Coke, or something to eat? We've got some chips and onion dip, and stuff like that."

"No." Suddenly she felt a little nervous, and she looked around at all the expensive furniture and elaborate paintings with little lights attached to the frames and wondered what it would be like to have a momma who liked her to have friends over and took her to piano lessons.

"Dad's got some beer stashed down in the basement fridge. Wanna try some?"

"No. Momma'd kill me if she found out."

"Screw your Momma."

The older one liked the sound of that. "Yeah, screw Momma."

The boy took her hand and led her into a real big dining room with an elaborate crystal chandelier and lots of other crystal goblets and bowls sitting around on glass shelves, but he stopped halfway to the living room and looked into her face. "She beats you, doesn't she? I saw some bruises on your neck once when I sat behind you on the bus."

The older one nodded and was surprised when tears welled inside her eyes. She'd never told anyone that before; it was the deep, dark secret of their house. Even Stepdaddy didn't know what Momma did when he was at work. Somehow it felt good for someone else to know about it and look at her with sympathetic eyes.

"Don't feel so bad. My dad hit me once, too."

"Really? Why?"

"I got mad and slapped my mom once when I was about nine, and he walloped me good. I sure never did that again." He laughed. "I don't want to, anyhow, she and I get along a lot better now. I was just a stupid kid when I did it."

She couldn't quite bring herself to laugh about what her momma did to her.

"C'mon, Mom keeps the stuff upstairs in her bathroom."

The older one followed him through the house, looking around in awe at the wonderful place. It was really cool, beautiful, like rooms inside houses in the soaps she watched. Everything was all decorated pretty and everything was in its place, with lots of pretty plates sitting around on little wooden stands. The carpet was so deep that your shoes sank a little into it and was a creamy beige color, and she didn't see a spot of dust anywhere, not even between the banister rails. The house was completely silent, and something made her stop at the bottom of the steps and hesitate.

"Can't we do it down here somewhere?"

"Nope. Somebody might come to the door and see us."

Upstairs, he led her down a long hallway and into a huge master bedroom decorated in pale blues and browns. The bed had four posters and was so tall that it had little miniature matching steps just to climb up to the mattress on. She stopped at the footboard and admired it.

"Can I sit on the bed?" she asked.

"Sure, lay down on it, if you want to. It's all made up. Nobody'll know."

She climbed up the steps and sank down in the silky-soft brown satin bedspread. "This feels as soft as velvet."

"Yeah, it's made out of silk. It's got velvet on the other side, though."

The boy ran up the steps and took a big jump on the bed. It bounced her whole body right up off of it, and she laughed until he fell on top of her and held her hands imprisoned over her head.

"Hey, let go."

"Oh, c'mon, give me a little kiss. I'm gonna get rid of your freckles for you. You owe me."

"Uh-uh. Get off me, you're heavy!"

"Give me a kiss and I will."

"No."

"Then you'll just have to keep your freckles, won't you?

"That's mean."

"Hey, you want the bleach stuff, or not?"

She wanted it, really, really wanted it, and she was pretty sure she wanted to kiss him, too. Her body was feeling kind of funny now with the boy straddling her hips. His nose was nearly touching hers, and she could smell nacho cheese and potato chips on his breath.

"C'mon, all I want is one little bitty kiss. I've never kissed a girl before, and I wanna see what it's like. You ever kissed a boy before?"

"No, and I don't think I want to."

"Try it, you'll probably like it. You're old enough now. I bet you even got your period."

"What's that?"

He laughed and rolled off her. "Your Momma hasn't told you about periods, either?"

"No, what is it?"

"I know what it is because of my older sister. It's when you bleed down there a little. It comes once a month, I think."

"Uh-uh, you're lying."

"You'll see."

She sat up and looked down at him. He was lying on his

side with his head cupped in his palm. He was smiling and looking up at her. She decided then and there that he was really, really cute. Almost like the guys she looked at in the teen magazines in the school library.

"Let me touch you there." He pointed to the front of her shirt.

"Uh uh. You're being nasty."

"Just once. Not even under your shirt, and we'll get the stuff out of the bathroom."

She considered and decided it wouldn't hurt to do that. "Okay, I guess."

The boy reached out and put his forefinger on her nipple, and she felt a thrill course down through her body. He removed it at once and smiled, and then he said, "I guess we'll have to get married now, huh?"

Laughing, he jumped off the bed and she climbed down and followed him, wondering what his kiss would have felt like. She knew lots of girls kissed boys behind the hedges in the schoolyard, but she never had. She never thought any boys would want her to.

"Here it is. Put this towel around your neck. That's what Mom does with the girls."

She obeyed, and he took out a little applicator from the box and squeezed some blue gel onto it. "Okay, hold still. You got a few more than the girls, so we might have to do this a bunch of times."

She watched in the mirror as he gently spread it around on her face. "Is it gonna burn?"

"Not much. You got to let it get absorbed for a while, then you got to wear a baseball cap if you go out in the sun, or anything."

"I don't have a baseball cap."

"Well, I'll let you borrow one of mine. Dad brings me a ball cap from every place he goes on business. C'mon, I'll show you my collection."

They moved down the hall to his room, and when he opened the door, she gasped in surprise.

"Wow," was all she could think to say at first.

"Like it?"

"It's a little scary."

"Nah. It's just movie posters and stuff. I like this game, too, called Dungeons and Dragons. You heard about it?"

"Uh-uh."

"It's fun. You know you can be a knight or a wizard, or a princess, stuff like that, and go on missions, and things."

"Like King Arthur?"

"Sort of. Wanna play while that stuff gets absorbed in your skin?"

"Okay, I guess."

His bedroom was large and painted dark blue and had all sorts of posters and pictures of dragons and castles and sword-wielding knights hanging around everywhere. But there were even more posters advertising horror films, like *Nightmare on Elm Street* and *Friday the 13th* and *Halloween*. When she saw that he had a Freddy Krueger costume, she smiled and remembered her vow to kill Sissy.

"Did you dress up like Freddy at Halloween?"

"Yeah, Mom and Dad had a big Halloween party for all their friends, and they got that for me to wear. I love it. Here, look at the glove with the blades for fingers."

She picked it up. "These are real knives, aren't they?"

"Yeah. But I'm not going to use them on you."

They laughed together.

"Have you ever seen *Nightmare on Elm Street*?"

"Yeah. Sometimes my stepdad watches those kind of shows late at night, and I hide on the stairs and watch them, too."

"I've got all of them on tapes. We can watch them anytime you want. I love those slasher movies, you know, with all that blood and gore and stuff."

There was an IBM computer sitting on a big desk and a

large color TV that was on with the sound turned down. He also had a fancy stereo set and dozens of music cassettes. He had just about everything the older one had ever wanted.

"Man, your parents must have lots of money."

"Yeah, Mom and Dad get us pretty much whatever we want."

He walked over to a rack on the wall that held ball caps of every color. He tossed a green one to her that said FLORIDA GATORS in yellow letters. "Here, and you can just keep it. My sister brought me that last summer from Florida. She's gone over to Europe for a few months now to do some modeling. That's what Mom wants my little sisters to do, too. Be big supermodels."

"You're really rich, aren't you?"

"Yeah, my Dad inherited a lot of money from his grandparents down in Miami, and now he's a doctor and makes a fortune in stocks, and stuff, too. That's why my Mom married him, 'cause he's so rich. He married her because she's so pretty. I've heard them say so but they laugh afterward, so I guess they're just joking one another. I'm gonna be rich someday, too. Me and my sisters will inherit all this, like my dad did."

"We're not rich at all. My momma couldn't even buy me a Christmas present. Stepdaddy bought the other kids stuff, but not me."

That got his full attention. "Damn. That's a bummer. Not even at Christmas, huh? I got that Dungeons and Dragons game for Christmas. I haven't messed with it much yet. Want to learn how to play it with me?"

There was a round table by the windows with four swivel chairs, and he sat down in one of them and she pulled up the one next to him. He took out the board and explained a little about how to play, and she listened, but she was really more interested in how long it would take to get rid of her freckles.

"You think any of my freckles will go away today?"

"Who knows? I doubt if it'll work that fast, but Mom just kept applying it until my sisters' faded away. We can meet here every Saturday when Mom's gone with the girls until you got it just the way you want it. We'll play games and listen to music and then you have to let me kiss you once in a while, too. That's payment for me getting you this stuff free of charge, but it won't be so bad, you'll see. Maybe we can be friends, and everything. Maybe you'll even like kissing and stuff. Okay?"

She watched his fingers turning pages on the game's instruction book, and she thought about the strange, sweet stirring she had felt inside when he touched her chest. She wondered again if she'd be as pretty as Sissy when she got rid of her freckles and if other boys would want to touch her like he did. Then she said, "Okay, I'll come here, but you can't tell anyone. You have to swear."

"And you'll kiss me once in a while?"

She nodded, and he smiled and looked very pleased.

Seven

Early the next morning, Black and I got into his big, luxurious Cobalt 360 and sped across the lake toward Cedar Bend Lodge. He was in his element at the wheel, smiling at the sheer pleasure of operating such a big, massive machine, cold wind blowing his black hair, aviator shades deflecting the bright sun. He got that same look when he was piloting his helicopter or tooling around in his giant Humvee. I stood beside him and didn't share his chipper mood. Oh, yeah, birds were singing, sky was blue, flowers smelled good, but Hilde was still dead. When we hit the Lodge's private marina and Black eased the boat into its slip, Bud was waiting on the spotless planks of the dock.

"So how's Brianna?" I asked Bud as I stepped out.

"Sleepin'. She's got enough drugs in her to keep her conked out for a week."

"That's probably for the best."

Black spoke and strode off ahead of us, rested and ready for business and lookin' good, and for some reason, I elected not to accompany him upstairs to meet the Queen of the Runway a.k.a. Wife of the Before Me. Not that I thought anything was going on between them. I didn't. Black had made that a pretty nondebatable issue last night in bed in a myriad of inventive ways. Yes, he's quite the genius in the bedroom, I do have to admit. Even better, he's probably too exhausted to take on another woman this morning, even the perfect Ms. Jude. Do I sound jealous? Me? No way. It's just having all these perfect-looking women hanging around me all the time is beginning to grate on my nerves.

Back to Brianna. I said to Bud, "I hated to put her through that so soon. I really thought she wouldn't be able to talk to us."

"You and me both. She's a gutsy lady, more than people think. What about Buck? Does he know anything yet?"

"Nothing yet. Maybe today, hopefully this morning."

"Nick can't be thrilled the pageant's involved."

"Nope, he's not thrilled. He's trying to decide whether to postpone."

Bud nodded, stopped for a second at the entrance to the hotel, and took a deep breath. "Okay, let's just get this done."

"Black ordered the pageant coordinator to line up people for us to interview. The lady's name is Patricia Cardamon. Let's split up the girls and interview them separately. It takes longer, but we can probably eliminate most of them quick enough."

"Okay. Whatever."

Truth was, Bud was a little out of it, and who could blame him? His eyes were red rimmed, bleary, and bloodshot, and he had a little tiny wrinkle in the cuff of his crisp dress shirt. That just didn't happen. Otherwise, he was immaculate in the white shirt, navy slacks, and the yellow silk tie I'd gotten him for Christmas. Hey, but my T-shirt and jeans were clean and smelled like Bounce, so I didn't feel too bad. We were both relieved that Charlie hadn't ordered him off the case yet, and highly surprised, too. He'd done it before at the mere hint of a close relationship between one of his detectives and a suspect, even to me, when I got a little too close to a former suspect. Black, actually, a misstep I should regret but don't.

Inside the aforementioned massive and glittering Ozark Ballroom a great deal of shock and confusion reigned. Small knots of beauties sat together, hugged each other, and looked even more dazed than usual. Sniffling was rampant. Looked like Hilde really had been popular with the girls, after all.

Normally, Bud would be in hog heaven at the mere suggestion that he got to interview a bevy of beautiful women. However, he was not smiling at the prospect today, nor would he smile for some time to come, if I was any judge. Like me, visions of Hilde's butchered mouth popped into his mind every time anybody smiled. Most contestants, to their credit, had little desire to smile, either. None of them, however, were weeping openly and with the heartfelt urgency of Mr. Race. He approached us like a bleak and rumbling, runaway thunderstorm.

"Oh, Gawd, this's awful, unbelievable. Poor little Hil. Poor Bri. Both of them are so precious, absolutely they are, utter shining dears." I handed him a tissue from a industrial-sized box of Puffs, one treated with aloe so as not to damage the delicate skin around the eyes of said beauties, no doubt. One provided early on, and graciously, by my newly eager-to-please friend, Ms. Cardamon. She was truly helpful this morning and right off the bat, too. Probably had found out by now that Nicholas Black liked me better than her.

Bud and I took chairs from the row in front of Race and turned them around to face him. We sat. He cried some more. I handed him another tissue and said, "I understand that you had a shop in the South Beach area at one time. I didn't know that."

He nodded. Bud and I watched him mop up his tears. "Yes. That's where I met them both."

"How long ago was that?"

"I've had my shop here almost five years, this summer, in

August. I tried for a while to keep both shops up and running, but never could find anybody to manage the one down in Florida, not that I truly trusted, so I just shut it down and concentrated my energies here at the lake. It was exciting down there, and all that, but there were scads of crimes and break-ins, all that kind of stuff, so I liked it better here. But now look what happened. Nobody's safe, not anywhere, not anymore."

"So you were already settled at the lake before Brianna decided to move here."

He nodded, pretty much in control now, lucky for us. "She was a client in South Beach, too, the sweetheart." He turned to Bud. "She's just mad about you, Buddy. You're lucky, you know. She's a real catch. So was Hilde."

I'd never in my life heard anybody call Bud Buddy, not even his mom. I looked at Bud to see if he was going to belt him, but Bud just nodded and looked away. He was definitely not himself since the murder.

I said, "Women have a tendency to open up to their stylists, don't they, Mr. Race? Confide in them about their personal life and problems they're dealing with."

"Oh, sure, absolutely they do. I know things going on around here that you simply could not imagine."

Oh, yes, I could. After yesterday, I'd believe anything inhumanly possible could go down here at the lake. "Did Hilde ever give you any reason to think she was afraid of anyone? Or that she was being stalked or harassed?"

Race took a deep breath, then nodded. "She told me about a stalker once. A real nut job was bothering her. You think he came back and did this to her?"

"I don't know yet. What can you tell us about this guy?"

"Not much, really. I recall she never knew his name, but she did say he seemed to know her every movement, even before she did. She never even saw him, that was the real spooky thing, let me tell you. He'd send her all these gifts, too, that were actually sorta sweet, really, like pink stationery with her initial on it, an H, and once a nosegay of posies tied with a pink velvet ribbon. We decided then that he knew her favorite color was pink, well, it was mauve, actually."

Posies? Where the hell do you get posies? In fact, what the hell are posies?

Race wasn't finished. "And he sent her some notes, too, where he mentioned all these things about her, everything, and I mean everything, little things, like where she'd been for lunch, what she'd eaten, down to the salad dressing, even. He knew when she came in for me to do her hair, too. I tell you, I was creeped out and looking over my shoulder before he up and left her alone."

Bud said, "Did she file a police report?"

"Oh, yeah. With the Miami police. They questioned me, as if I was the one doing it, which was highly offensive to me, I will tell you. But Hilde told them right off that no way was I capable of such a thing. I believe they put a tap on her phone, too, but that didn't come to anything, either. They never caught the guy. He just quit messing with her. I don't know, maybe he found another girl to follow around."

"Do you remember how long this lasted and how it ended?"

"The last note he typed, and he always typed them, too, sometimes on sticky notes and name tags, believe it or not. You know, with those old kind of typewriters before they invented computers, the kind without cut and paste, I guess."

Bud and I looked at each other, as Race went on, "It just said stuff like this was good-bye and there was something to the effect that he might end it all, or take his life, or something like that. Hilde and I didn't believe he was going to do that for one second, of course. He was just working on her sympathy. She was a good person, and you know what? She did feel sorry for him. She told me so. Said she wished she could help him, that he must be a very sad, miserable person to resort to sending love notes to a stranger. I told her not to waste her sympathy on some psychopath like him."

"So she never responded to him in any way or did anything that might've encouraged him?"

"Certainly not that I know of. I told her to ignore it all and certainly not acknowledge anything, that it would just spur him on."

"Did this man contact her when she was out of town? I mean, when she was participating in pageants or modeling gigs in states other than Florida?"

Race thought for a moment, crossed and recrossed his legs, fiddled with his hair, fluffed the back of it with his fingertips. "I remember her getting notes and flowers and stuff at other pageants, yes."

"Which ones?"

"Some anonymous admirer sent her a bouquet of yellow daisies and white orchids when she competed in Houston. I remember that because I thought it was a strange choice of arrangements. Hilde wasn't a daisies kinda girl, know what I mean? She was elegant and poised, lilies or roses or gardenias, maybe, but daisies? Never."

Well, okay. "Can you think of anything else that might help us, Mr. Race?"

"No. I just know I'm going to miss her like crazy."

"Were you ever involved with her?"

"Oh, no, never. Just friends. Like with Brianna. Of course, I'm closer to Brianna now that we both live here. Before that, I knew Hilde better. She came in more often and I saw her out at the clubs more than Bri. Brianna likes the quiet life. She's a nature-loving kind of girl. I bet she even goes hiking and stuff like that. She told me once that she bought herself some of those hideously unattractive hiking boots with leather laces. Yuck. But she loves it here."

"Did you know Hilde's boyfriend down in South Beach?"

"Carlos Vasquez, you mean? What a jerk. A player, really. He used to push her around some, tried to control her until she got fed up and moved out. I mean, he told her what to eat, what to wear, what to think. Brianna and I were both relieved when Hilde dumped him."

"Do you know if he tried to contact her after she left?"

"I think so. I think it's fair to say he had a real obsession with her, especially after she left him. That's the way those kind are, you know. I had someone do that to me once, too, the tacky bastard."

"Right. Did she meet Vasquez before or after she had that stalker?"

"After, I believe. Yes, it wasn't long after, either, because I thought at the time that, good, he could protect her if the stalker came back. He's pretty buff. You should see his six-pack. I have to admit he's got a lovely body, but why wouldn't he? He's a personal trainer at his own club and works out all day every day with his clients. Too bad he's so possessive."

I hesitated, but I needed to know. "What kind of lifestyle would you say Hilde Swensen led?"

Race almost bristled, at least, shivered a bit. He donned an annoyed expression. "She was a good kid. Okay, she slept around some, but she usually only hooked up when she got high. And she was sober most of the time, you can believe that or not, but sometimes she just needed to vent, party a little, get rid of the stresses of the circuit for a while. Everybody always thinks these fabulous-looking women are so lucky, but they've got just as many problems as other people, just different kinds. I know, they tell me their woes all the time."

And I always thought it was just what color eye shadow to wear. "What sort of problems do you mean?"

"Guys went after them for their looks, tried to get them in bed, you get the picture, don't you? Notches on the belt. But

I know so many gorgeous girls, who just have zero self-esteem, and I mean, minus zero."

"How do you account for that?"

He shrugged one shoulder. "Who knows? I guess they thought beauty was all they had going for them. That was true, sure, for some of them, but others, like Hilde and Bri, they have brains, too. They just never needed them to get ahead. Why do you think I'm making money hand over fist? Looks are everything nowadays, look at Hollywood. Good looks and youth. You can't get a job out there if you're over twenty-five and weigh more than a hundred ten. Unless you're Diane Keaton and want to play the neurotic mother, of course. She's real good at that."

"Well, okay, Mr. Race, I guess that just about does it for now. Thank you for your time."

"No problem, honey. I want you to find the beast who did this."

"We will. If you think of anything else pertinent to this investigation, please give us a call."

"Okay. Do you guys think the pageant will go on? Has Dr. Black made a decision?" He looked at me, waxed eyebrows arched with questions.

"Don't know yet. He'll probably make a decision in the next few hours. Do you think it should?"

"Yes. Hilde would want it to. I know that for a fact."

"A fact? Why do you say that?"

"Because this other girl was killed once, just before a pageant, and everyone agreed it should go on. It did, and everyone dedicated it to her."

My ears perked. My heart raced a bit. Bud leaned forward, on the same wave length, and asked, "When was this?"

"About two years ago, I guess. I happened to be down in Miami, visiting some friends. They found her in her car near Okeechobee Swamp, nude and strangled. It happened about a week ahead of the pageant."

"Do you remember the victim's name?"

"Yes. She was a client of mine, too. Her name was Reesie Verdad. Cuban descent, gorgeous, with all this ebony hair and big glowing jet-black eyes. A nice girl. It was terrible, but they said she was into cocaine and messed with the wrong guys."

I made a notation of the name and year. It bore looking into, especially if Charlie sent me to South Beach to check out Vasquez, and I was pretty sure he would. I thanked Mr. Race and watched him move off toward the staging area where the dressing rooms were. Bud's phone rang, and he moved off by himself to take the call.

"Excuse me, Claire, I was hoping we could speak for a moment."

I turned and met the almond-shaped, green eyes of the ex-Jude-of-the-one-name and felt my insides cringe like I had to eat a worm. Whoa now, what was this all about? I had a feeling it was about one good-looking shrink with the bluest eyes this side of Frank Sinatra. And it seemed that Jude and I were already on a first-name basis. Not that she had any other names.

"Actually, I'm here today on official business." Here we go again. My old standby, *official*, used to stave off the unwanted, unnecessary, unsavory.

Jude's smooth brow dented with concern, but still looked damn good. "I know, Nicky told me you were conducting interviews down here, so I came down, hoping to get a word with you. What a terrible thing to happen to that young girl! I didn't know her well, but I did meet her at another pageant. I thought she was very special." She looked across the room at Bud. "I'd like to say hello to Detective Davis, too. He interviewed me last summer in New York, and Nicky said he had a close relationship with Hilde's sister. I lost my own sister when I was a child, so I know how she must feel."

"I'm sorry to hear that." I didn't want to think about losing family members, so I played nice.

"Well, I'm glad I got to see you again, Jude." See, I'm in a generous mood. As long as she didn't come on to Black in my presence, we'd probably get along just fine.

She smiled. I smiled. I was trying to get over the *Nicky* thing. I don't know why it bugged me for her to call him that. Okay, I'd called him that a couple of times myself, but I was usually being sarcastic. Nicky didn't fit my image of him, I guess. Sounded like something everybody called Steven Seagal in his dumb movies, except for that one I liked where he was in a coma for about a hundred years then got his muscles back overnight by lighting some incense candles on his body. Black, on the other hand, was a name that did my guy justice.

"Am I on the list for you to interview? Nicky wasn't sure. He said I should ask you."

"You were acquainted with Hilde Swensen, right?"

"Yes. But not well. She was active in the business and successful, so her name was well known around the circuit."

"I understand that she did some modeling as well as entering pageants."

"I believe she did, yes. Mainly in the Miami and South Beach areas, I think. I never saw her in New York, but she could have been there from time to time."

"Maybe I should ask you a few questions, if you've got a minute."

I got out my trusty pad and pencil. She sat down beside me and crossed some very long, shapely legs encased at the moment in some very stylish black silk pants. A black silk blouse was unbuttoned far enough down her throat to alert me that she didn't have on a bra and that *Nicky* had probably had a lot of fun in the cleavage arena when they were a marital duo.

"I hope we'll get to be friends, Claire. I can tell you, and you might be surprised at what I'm going to say, but I do wish you and Nicky well. This is the happiest I've seen him in a long, long time."

So what the devil was I supposed to say now? "Thanks, ma'am, for letting me know how I stand in your regard." or "Yeah, I make everyone happy like that." So I said, "Is that right?"

She laughed softly, and to my surprise, it sounded downright genuine. And I knew a genuine laugh when I heard it. "You bet. I tried but I just didn't have what it took to intrigue him the way you do."

Intrigue him, huh? I debated if that was sarcasm and decided to make light of it. "He's just impressed with all my bullet wounds."

She laughed again and didn't seem the least bit catty or two-faced, not that I could tell for sure yet. I haven't hung around with any of my lovers' ex-wives before, though, and in fact, I haven't had many lovers before, period. But I am pretty good at detecting phonies and snobs because I hate them worse than a mug full of arsenic. Jude wasn't snooty, either. But I wasn't really surprised that Black had chosen to wed a nice woman. He was pretty good at judging character and picking girlfriends, if I say so myself. However, our conversation was getting way too personal, so back to official business we go.

"Did you ever spend personal time with Hilde Swensen, Jude? For instance, did you ever go out to dinner together or to a movie? You know, just hang out together, girl talk, stuff like that?"

"Not really. We didn't know each other that well. We did have lunch once at the same table—at the Miami Four Seasons. It was the pageant mixer, but we never discussed anything remotely personal. She asked me questions about how to break into modeling in New York. I do remember that much." She gazed into my eyes. Hers were like, well, exotic, I guess you'd say, and the pupils were large and dark because of the dim lighting. I could almost see my reflection in them. She smiled again. "I do hope I haven't made you uncomfortable talking about Nicky."

So Jude was astute, too. "Don't worry, it takes a whole lot to make me uncomfortable."

"It's just that he speaks so highly of you. And I can't tell you how much I admire you."

"Me?"

"Yes. I've read all the newspaper accounts about your career. You're very good at your job. I always thought I'd like to be a police officer. Modeling can be so tedious. It's hard work, don't get me wrong, but we certainly don't help people in trouble the way you and Bud do."

Her whole spiel sounded just so sappy, but I forced myself not to agree out loud with wholehearted conviction. I envisioned her as Starsky to my Hutch. It didn't go down well. She'd probably wear a Moroccan leather holster lined in purple paisley silk by Prada and snap shiny, solid-gold, diamond-studded handcuffs on all her perps. Hell, perps would probably line up for her to run them in and want their mug shot taken with her.

Well, okay, hating her guts, which I'd expected I'd do, was out for the moment. She was being honest, I could tell, and she admired police officers. What more could I want? Shock of the universe, I couldn't find fault with the famous Jude, which was highly unlike me. We probably could've been friends if it weren't for that one tanned and muscular hunk thing we had in common.

Jude was not finished. "I'm sure there's no need for me to tell you this, because I can tell you're about as self-assured as they get, but I want you to know that Nicky is absolutely crazy about you. I mean, his eyes actually light up when he talks about you. He said you make him happy. He said his life didn't start until he met you."

Jeez, now I was really squirming in the saddle because

that life starting thing sure didn't reflect well on her, the first wife, now did it? But hey, was that a neat thing for him to say about me, or what? I glanced around, hoping Bud would get off the phone and come fawn over Jude. I didn't know what to say, so I returned to business. "Well, I guess that wraps up all the questions I have for you. If you think of anything else, please give us a call at the sheriff's office."

Black chose that time to enter the room, his entourage of highly attractive employees awash in his wake. When he caught sight of our little tête-à-tête, he came straight for us, no doubt concerned she was filling me in on all his syrupy compliments about me.

"I've decided to postpone the pageant until next week. I've offered the contestants a free stay at Cedar Bend until then. That way the girls who want can attend Hilde's services." He looked at me as if soliciting my approval.

So I said, "Okay."

Jude said, "I might have to reschedule an appearance in Los Angeles and go back to New York for a day or two, but I'll do my best to be back in time to judge."

Great, an extra week with an ex-wife living in Black's apartment. But then again, that would place Black in my house, at my disposal, which definitely had its perks.

"Claire and I have been getting to know each other," Jude said, smiling like that was true.

Black said, "That's good." His eyes were on me, however, saying, *Or is it?*

I said, "Jude knew Hilde. Did you know that?"

Black looked surprised. "Really? How?"

Jude shrugged a graceful shoulder. It made the great big, dime-size diamond studs on her ears wink and blink at me. "We met at a pageant mixer. I hardly knew her, actually."

One of Black's cell phones rang and he moved away to take the call, and I began to wish I was more popular with callers. I decided it was time to escape. "Well, nice talking with you, Jude. Bud and I need to wrap up these interviews and get back to the station."

"I hope we'll see each other again soon. Maybe the three of us can have dinner together one evening while I'm here."

Yeah, right, just what I'd been dreaming of. I said, "That would be very nice. Now, if you'll excuse me, I better get back to work."

Sisterly Love

After that first time, the older one met the boy often. Later, after his father returned home and wasn't playing golf on the weekends, they would meet secretly in a large Winnebago camper that his dad used for hunting and fishing trips. It was parked inside a specially made garage behind the pool house. These visits to the boy's house were like reprieves for the older one, and it was wonderful to be around somebody who liked her and was helping her look pretty. Nobody knew where she went after school and on weekends, and nobody seemed to care. Soon it would be summer vacation, and they could spend even more time together.

On one particular day they planned to play Dungeons and Dragons again because it had become their favorite game, but when she arrived, she was surprised to find that the boy's twin sisters were sitting at the Winnebago's dining table with him.

"It's okay, they won't tell Mom and Dad."

The boy frowned darkly at his little sisters as a warning, and they nodded solemnly. They were pretty little things, but it still didn't matter. They weren't as pretty as Sissy. "I'm

Sissy's sister, you know, the one who always beats you at the beauty contests. Did you know that?"

"Yes. We hate her." They spoke it together, almost in unison.

"I know. Everybody does. She's a horrible little brat."

The three of them smiled together, and then the boy said, "Okay, let's play. We'll figure out new characters for everybody. I'll be the Dungeon Master, of course. And I already have figured out some of the quests. It'll be fun, you'll see."

Instead of being wizards and dragons, they decided to be film characters. The boy insisted on being Freddy Krueger.

"He's my favorite character, and I've already got the costume. The rest of you can be Jason and the other bad guys, or whoever you want. We'll scare people we don't like."

They all agreed, and the older one found that the two little girls were not at all like Sissy. They were actually rather sweet, and they seemed to like her. They even admired the way her freckles were beginning to fade.

"Don't forget that you can't get out in the sun or they'll come back," one of them told her. "Mom always gives us sunblock to wear on our faces."

The boy smiled at the older one, in a way he did so often now. She felt her face grow hot and knew she was blushing. He said, "I've got an idea. Let's make a quest to scare Sissy. We all hate her, and she's an evil little bitch. Go ahead, tell my sisters what all she does to you."

So the older one began to tell them about the bathtub and the makeup and the Barbie dolls and the time Sissy pushed Bubby down the stairs and the older one got a terrible whipping from Stepdaddy. She told the boy and the twins things she had never told anybody, and their faces grew more and more sympathetic.

"She's really mean," said one twin.

"She deserves to be whipped," said the other.

The boy frowned and said, "Okay, let's think up a way to

scare her really bad, to make her think she's actually gonna die." He turned to the older one. "She's always making you feel bad and getting you in trouble. Let's see how she likes it."

They began to plan what they would do to Sissy, and the boy had lots of good ideas that he could make into quests for each girl. By the time the quests were decided upon, the older one felt happier than she had in a long, long time. She was finally going to get Sissy back for all the mean things she'd done. She couldn't wait.

The first quest was for the boy to complete, but the older one was going to have to help him get Sissy alone. So she listened carefully to his instructions and walked home smiling because Sissy was going to get hers very soon. .

The minute she got home Momma started yelling at her from upstairs. "Where have you been? You know Russell and I are going out to dinner tonight. You're supposed to watch Sissy and Bubby, so you get in there right now and watch them in the tub while I finish getting ready. Russell will be home soon to pick me up."

The older one went into the bathroom, and Sissy made a face at her. Both of the children were in the tub together, and the older one knelt beside the tub and began to lather Bubby's arms and back. He smiled at her, and she smiled back.

"Where've you been?" Sissy demanded. "I know you're sneakin' off all the time to do something bad and you better tell me what it is."

Still smiling at her brother, the older one ignored her. Soon it would be payback time, and Sissy would be sorry for all the things she'd done to Bubby and her.

"You better tell me, or I'll make up something and tell Momma and she'll lock you up in the barn."

"All right, I'll tell you. I go down to the river and read a book. I'm reading a Shakespearean play now. I'm sure you know what that is."

By the expression on Sissy's face, the older one knew Sissy didn't have a clue about the English playwright and that pleased her, too. The boy was teaching her a lot of things that she had never even dreamed existed. Things that her momma and stepdaddy didn't know, either.

"You're lying. Tell me the truth or you'll be sorry."

Ignoring her sister, the older one carefully rinsed the soap out of Bubby's strawberry-blond ringlets. He sat calmly and allowed it. He was a good kid and never caused trouble for anybody.

"That's a good boy, Bubby," she whispered softly. "You're a good boy. I love you, and you love me, don't you?"

The little boy nodded, but Sissy moved so fast that the older one barely had time to react. She had Bubby by his hair, pushing his head under the water. She was laughing at the way his legs were splashing, and the older one grabbed her and shoved Sissy until she let go and fell back into the water herself. Both kids came up sputtering and screaming, and then Momma was there and Sissy was screaming accusations.

"She's tryin' to drown me and Bubby. She hates us, she hates us!"

Momma grabbed the older one by the hair and dragged her down the steps and outside to the backyard. The older one screamed and fought, but Momma was too strong. Momma pushed her into the barn, slammed and bolted the door, then picked up Stepdaddy's rawhide riding crop hanging by the door.

"No, Momma, no, please . . . Sissy did it, she did it, I didn't . . ."

"Shut up, you little bitch."

Momma raised the crop and the girl felt it whip down on her bare thigh. She felt the agonizing pain, saw the blood oozing from a long thin cut and she scrambled away on her hands and knees, but her mother followed, striking her over and over again. Her white blouse was torn in back, and she could feel blood running down her back.

"Please, Momma, don't . . . I'll be good . . ."

Momma grabbed her by the hair and forced her up the steps to the loft. "You can just get in the punishment box and stay there, forever, for all I care."

The girl hurried to obey before the whip came down on her again, crawling quickly into the low wooden box. Momma snapped the padlock shut, and the girl peered out through the bars. She had been imprisoned here one other time, when Momma had found out that her real daddy didn't want her. But now she was glad to be there, safe from the whip and Momma's rage.

Momma climbed down the steps, and the older one could hear her locking the barn door. She began to cry as she tried to stop the bleeding on her thigh. She felt so bad that she began to wish she were dead. It would be better then, so Momma couldn't hurt her anymore.

Momma left her there all night and all the next day. She could hear Sissy and Bubby playing on the swings, and once Sissy yelled something ugly through the window at her, but she didn't care. She had finally wet herself, and she was hungry and her legs hurt from being bent and cramped up. When her Momma finally came after her, she walked slowly back to the house behind her, and Momma said, "I hope you've learned your lesson, girl. And don't be thinking to complain about your punishment to Russell when he comes home. He's already mad at you for making us miss dinner last night."

The older one didn't cry, didn't react to Sissy's gloating look, or Bubby's frightened one. She walked upstairs and shut the bathroom door and cleaned herself up. She stared at her dirty face in the mirror, and she vowed that she would kill Sissy and her Momma someday, in the worst way possible, and she would laugh while she did it.

* * *

The older one met the boy and his sisters about a week later. She hadn't dared get in trouble again. Even Stepdaddy was harsh with her, now that he thought she had tried to harm his precious son. He warned her to stay away from him and his children, or else. So she kept away and to herself.

When she finally could, she went to the boy's house and climbed into the Winnebago. The others were playing the game, and he was dressed in his Freddy costume. They were glad to see her and gathered around, and she was so touched by their friendship that tears welled up and she began to weep.

Then she told them everything, and the story spilled out in all its dirtiness and ugliness, and they sat staring at her, shocked, and then angry, when they saw the healing stripes on her legs and back.

"Your own Momma did that to you?" one of the twins said in disbelief. "She really did hit you with a whip?"

But it was the boy who was the most angry. He took her hand and held it and then he said, "We're gonna get Sissy for this. And your Momma, too. We'll make a quest right now, a way to hurt them back, to make them pay for what they did to you."

"Momma will tell your parents, and she'll whip me again. She's turned everyone in the family against me. They all hate me. And I hate all of them. I wish I could kill them."

The boy looked at her then at his sisters. "Okay, let me think of the best way to do it."

She stared at him, wondering if he truly meant it. "You mean kill them, really?"

"Yes, that's what you want, isn't it?"

She stared at him, a little shocked that he said it so casually. And then she thought how it would be without Sissy and Bubby and her Momma and Stepdaddy. "I would be all alone."

"No, you'd have us."

"How could we kill them?"

"We'd make it look like accidents. People get killed in accidents all the time. I read about it in the papers, and it's on the evening news, too."

"But how? We're just kids. I don't know how to kill anybody."

"Neither do I, but let me think on it. I don't make the A-plus honor roll every time for nothing, you know."

His little sisters laughed and clapped and said they'd like to see her Momma dead and gone forever. The older one frowned, not sure she really wanted to kill her mother, after all, even though she did hate her, sometimes she loved her, too, sometimes she just wanted Momma to love her back and be nice and tell her she was pretty.

"I don't think I want to kill them, but I want to pay Sissy back."

The boy looked disappointed for a moment, then he said, "Then let's scare the hell outta her. I just got a good idea. It can be our next quest—a quest of vengeance against your sister."

So the four of them sat there and planned it, and the more she heard about it the more excited she became. It could work. It really could, and so she walked home with the videocassette and a bundle of clothes in her backpack, and strange, dark joy in her heart.

That night when her parents went out to play bingo, the older one got out the videotape and took it into the den. She shut the door and told Sissy she couldn't watch it, and just as the boy had predicted Sissy barged in and said she could, too, or she was going to tell Momma on her.

"Okay, I guess I have to let you, but you're gonna be scared," she said. She pushed the cassette in, and *The Nightmare on Elm Street* began to play. By the end of it, Sissy was scared to death, her blue eyes round and terrified, and the older one smiled to herself, thinking that she hadn't seen anything yet.

"I told you not to watch it."

By bedtime, they were both drowsy and Bubby was already in his bed fast asleep. They went into their room and lay down, and it wasn't long before Sissy was snoring with her mouth open. But the older one stayed awake, waiting. At one o'clock her parents came home, and she could hear them downstairs for a while until Momma came upstairs to kiss Sissy good night. Then all got quiet but the older one lay there, grinning, and waiting for the hands on the clock to point to three.

"Nightmare time, dear little Sissy," she whispered. She rose from her bed and softly raised the window. She looked outside and could see the boy on the ground below. He waved, and she could see his teeth shining white in the moonlight. She quickly dressed in the boy's Freddy Krueger costume, pulled the orange-and-blue striped sweater down over her nightgown, put on the mask and then the horrible glove with blades for fingers. She tiptoed to the door, listened, but knew her parents were sleeping behind their closed door on the second floor.

Then she began to chant Freddy's little rhyme in a hoarse whisper, just like the boy had instructed. She waited until Sissy sat up in bed, and then she switched on the flashlight beam right under her chin. Sissy let out the most bloodcurdling scream imaginable, and the older one swiped down at her with the deadly glove. Sissy leapt from the bed and tore down the hallway, screaming bloody murder, and the older one laughed to herself, tore off the costume, and tossed it all out the window to the boy. She flung out the videocassette, too, shut the window, and climbed back into bed.

Sissy was back minutes later, in Stepdaddy's arms, trembling and bawling, and the older one sat up and rubbed her eyes as if half asleep. "What's the matter with Sissy?"

"She says you made her watch a Freddy Krueger movie and he came up here to get her."

"Huh? Who's Freddy Krueger?"

Momma looked at me. "Did you do that to your sister?"

"No. Where would I get a movie like that?"

They had no answer, and Stepdaddy finally said, "She just had a nightmare, is all. She'll be all right."

But after he'd taken Sissy downstairs to rock back to sleep, Momma frowned and searched through the older one's bureau drawers and under her bed. The older one pretended to sleep, but inside she was laughing so hard she could barely stand it.

Eight

I spent the next hour interviewing my share of the contestants. I got very little from them, except for a splitting headache. The wound on my arm was bothering me, too, a little, but not as much as the half a dozen shallow women vying for Black's glittery Diamonique crown and scepter. They all had airtight alibis, in fact, a lot of the girls spent their off times at the various competitions together, either shopping or dining out, probably on lettuce and ice water, judging from their string bean figures.

At the moment, my interviewee was a particularly spaced-out lovely by the name of Betina Long. She wasn't the usual blond goddess but a dark-haired little thing with big, luminous brown eyes and teeth as white as Santa's beard. She kept them on display throughout our interview as if I was a contestant judge asking her questions about her life's aspirations instead of a fellow dead beauty pageant queen.

"How well do you know the deceased, Ms. Long?"

"Pretty well, I guess. We sorta followed the same circuit. She won more than me, though. Judges pretty much like her type better, you know long legs and ash-blond hair." Any more wattage from her teeth and my headache was gonna go from ouch to banshee scream. I guess she'd just been programmed to smile widely after every sentence she uttered. Or maybe she was just practicing.

"Okay. Did she ever confide in you about a stalker or personal problems concerning other contestants?

Beaming at me, she said, "Oh, yes. She mentioned a stalker, and she told me once that she hated her sister worse than anybody in the whole wide world." More beam.

Uh-oh. "Her sister?"

"That's right. Her name is Brianna Swensen, and they lived together for a while until Hilde kicked her out because they fought all the time. Like cats and dogs, Hilde told me."

Smiling again, a long, sustained one. It made me want to frown, so I did. Maybe she'd get the hint.

"Did she say what they fought about?" I glowered at her, hoping to receive one in turn. She lit up like a particularly pleased lava lamp.

"She just said that Brianna got jealous when she won. Quit entering the pageants because she was tired of losing to Hilde. Hilde just had a more relaxed walk, and a much more natural smile. People say I do, too." She demonstrated.

I couldn't stand it, so I said, "I always heard that smiling constantly puts wrinkles in your cheeks."

Her smile went limp, and my headache thanked her.

"Did Hilde ever intimate that these fights with her sister became violent?"

"No. Well, she did say that Brianna had a temper and threw stuff at her sometimes. I think she said Brianna threw dinner plates and mugs, stuff that would break so Hilde was always buying new ones at Pier One." The smile was back, so much for antiaging fears. No wonder, this kid couldn't be much more than twenty-one. Aging was definitely on the back burner.

"Okay. Anything else you might deem pertinent?"

"Deem pertinent? You use some big words, don't you?"

I stared at her, considering how I could make my words short and succinct and preschool level. I spoke slowly in my inside voice. "Do you know anything else that would help me, Ms. Long? Like who killed Ms. Swensen?"

She showed me her teeth again, then laughed, a little trill, really, very melodious and Kelly Ripa. "You're pretty funny for a policeman."

I let the "man" part pass. I probably did look like a male to these girls. After all, I didn't have on lip gloss to make my lips all pouty. That alone might take away my claim to womanhood.

After a while, the cellular gods heard my plea for a ring tone to deliver me from this last smiling beauty goddess, and I left Ms. Long still chattering about the ramifications of the broken nail on her right forefinger and answered my phone. I could see Bud, where he conversed with a buxom, auburn-haired, short-shorted contestant across the room. He had a few more girls to talk to, and he looked all business. He *was* all business. He was intense, to be sure, but I had a feeling he wasn't going to last long on the case, especially after Charlie had time to figure out Bud was sleeping with the victim's sister.

I glanced behind me and watched Black stride off toward Ms. Cardamon while the beauteous Jude headed solo for the penthouse elevator. So far, so good. He was avoiding her snare. I tried to fathom if I felt threatened by the model and didn't care for the idea. Then I thought about last night. Nah. Black couldn't be that enthusiastic in bed if he was lusting after wife numero uno. My caller ID was flashing Buckeye Boyd's number, so I picked up in a hurry, eager to hear the autopsy results.

"Hi, Buck. Got a cause of death?"

"The victim was strangled. The only mutilation was to the mouth. And he didn't do the cutting with finesse. It appears he just hacked off her lips with a pair of scissors. From the jags on the edges, I'd say he used the little manicurist type and took his time doing it. I'm keeping the lips for evidence, so I'd highly recommend a closed casket."

"Did he leave trace?"

"We're not having much luck on that front so far. He's adept enough to use bleach and clean up after himself, so I doubt we'll find anything usable. Maybe down on the hillside when you were chasing him and hard on his heels. They haven't found any shell casings, though. My conjecture, for what it's worth, is that he's killed before and knows how to protect himself. There weren't prints or DNA on the shower curtain, no hairs, either."

"What about the blood on the deck?"

"It's the vic's."

"Was she sexually assaulted?"

"There was no trauma or vaginal bruising to indicate she was raped, but we've taken samples that might bear out sexual intercourse, consensual or otherwise, I don't know. Like I said, he washed her up pretty good. Probably destroyed any physical evidence he left. We're ready to release the body. Has Bud said yet where the sister wants it to go?"

"Hold on." I'd been watching Bud excuse himself from the woman he was interviewing and wend his way in my direction. When he reached me, I said, "Buck's ready to release the body. He wants to know if Bri's made her wishes known about the service."

"She wants to bury her here at the lake. That's all she's said, so far."

"Buck, we'll have to get back to you."

"Okay. We'll finish up the last of the tests as soon as Shaggy gets back."

"He's still out? You gotta be kidding me."

"Sounded sick as a dog on the phone this morning. Said he'd probably be in tomorrow."

"What's wrong with him?"

"Some kind of stomach bug, I think. I gotta 'nother call, see ya later."

We hung up, and I sat down next to Bud. Black was at the microphone now, announcing the pageant's postponement. The news was met by a low whisper of girlish dismay, at least until the moment he mentioned a free week for all of them at Cedar Bend Lodge. Mollified big-time, the models went back to their primping.

"What's the score with the girls, Bud? Any leads?"

"A couple of them knew the guy she used to live with, said he was a real asshole. Apparently, he came on to the majority of them, one time or another. They're sayin' that's why Hilde moved out. After a couple of the other girls told her he was cheating on her." He shook his head, sighed heavily. "Looks like we're gonna have to take that trip down to sunny Florida, after all."

"Black's offered his private plane for the trip, and I'm fairly sure Charlie'll give his okay, especially when it saves the department money. You thinkin' Charlie'll pull you off?"

"I can be objective, Claire."

"Yeah, I know that, but Charlie may not see it that way. And he'll jerk your badge if you don't back off, just like he did mine last year."

Bud frowned, his entire body set with tension. He was bummed out and exhausted and looked like he was going to explode if I said another word. So I didn't mention Betina Long's unflattering description of Brianna's relationship with her dead sister. I'd tell him later when he could handle it.

He said, "What's next?"

"I'm going downtown to interview the photographer. I expected him to be hanging around today, but Ms. Cardamon said he's only slated to show up on the day of the pageant."

"What's his name?"

"Eric Dixson. Cardamon says he owns a shop down on

that tourist strip near Bagnell Dam. I'm heading down there as soon as we finish up here."

"Want me to come?"

"I can handle it. Finish up with the girls you haven't interviewed and then go home and check on Bri. Maybe she's remembered something significant now that's she's had time to rest and think things through."

Bud nodded, and I watched him head back toward the knot of contestants still in line for interviews. Black was standing at the entrance watching me and talking on his cell phone. He hung up when I reached him.

He said, "Where you headed next?"

"I've gotta talk to Eric Dixson, the guy you hired to shoot the runway. You know him personally?"

"I met him last year when we contracted for his services. You don't have your car here. I'll take you in the Humvee."

"You just want an excuse to drive it."

"You bet. Patricia can handle the press release changing the date, so let's get out of here before any reporters turn up. I've got a feeling this is gonna turn out to be a public relations fiasco."

A few minutes later, we stood outside under the massive front portico, watching Rob the cute valet rumble up in Black's latest purchase, a massive black-and-chrome vehicle that looked straight off Iraqi battlefields. Black's newest fun toy. Actually, I loved it, too. It was as cool as hell. I'd hinted blatantly for my very own for Valentine's Day, but Black didn't take the bait. Probably afraid he'd never see me again. We climbed aboard, and Black took the driver's seat before I could beat him to it. Today I guess I get to be the navigator.

Black looked a bit incongruous at the wheel, all decked out in yet another expensive suit, navy blue this time, but his shirt was crisp and white and showed off his dark tan in a big way. He poked on a pair of designer sunshades probably worth the sum total of my entire wardrobe and then glanced over at me. "So, tell me, Claire, what's your honest impression of Jude?"

I wasn't exactly expecting that query, but I played along. "She's okay, I guess. Maybe I won't have to kill her after all."

Black laughed. He pulled out, and we drove down the entry road to Cedar Bend's massive stone entrance gate. He hung a left and headed toward downtown Camdenton. "She likes you, too. Couldn't wait to meet you, as a matter of fact. She wants us to have dinner with her."

"That's not gonna happen."

"That's what I told her."

Good answer, but the idea of breaking bread with Jude, or anything else, made me want to squirm. I changed the subject to something more pertinent. "Buck's ready to release the body."

"Yeah? I've been meaning to ask you, does Brianna know about the mutilated mouth?"

"No. I left that to Bud, and he says she can't handle that yet. He's going to try to convince Brianna to make it a closed casket."

"Good, maybe she'll never have to know the gory details."

"Hope so."

We were quiet for a while then, each thinking our own brand of morbid thoughts, the powerful engine a smooth purr underneath us. I did like this giant vehicle about as well as anything I'd seen in the last ten years. Maybe if we solved this case, Charlie would get one for all his deputies.

"Did the contestants give you anything useful?"

"Very little. I'm gonna have to take you up on the flight to South Beach."

"I'll order the Lear to stand by."

"You don't have to go with me, if you're too busy."

"I have the time. I have business to take care of down there, anyway."

"Okay, let me guess. You own a hotel on South Beach,

right? Five Star, six, maybe. On the ocean, fabulous views, top of the line, where Clintons and Bushes and other presidential types stay when they're in town."

Black turned and gave me *the* grin, the one that usually did me in. I did go into melt mode, I have to admit. "No, I don't own a hotel there. But I'm looking to buy one. This will give me a chance to stay there a few nights and see if it's worth the price they're asking."

"Mixing business with pleasure again, huh?"

"Don't we usually?"

We sure did, but right now I was thinking about the case and how he could help me solve it. "Have you come up with any thoughts on the perp yet?"

"I haven't had much time to think about it yet. Right now, with what I do know, I'd say he's not the usual psychopath, like the ones I've written about. I suspect the victim's body is his turn-on. That's why he picked a beautiful woman and dressed her in her crown and sash. He probably gets off on the corpse. I wouldn't be surprised if he took photos of the body to look at later. Maybe even a video. Or even the body itself to enjoy later."

A chill rippled over my skin like a cold wildfire. "You're not talking about necrophilia?"

He nodded. "Maybe. He's a sick son of a bitch. That's the kind of perpetrator who'd molest a corpse. The note he left is hard to explain. It doesn't seem like he's sending us a message. And he isn't asking for anything, either. The quote's well known enough, but I suspect it means something special to his twisted mind. It's pretty obvious he has some perverted fixation on the mouth, and smiles, too, by the sound of it. I've never run across another case with the lips removed. Have you run it through your data banks?"

"First thing I did. No hits yet. I talked to Harve up in Michigan earlier this morning, and he's gonna do a search for similar crimes and victims with severed lips, but hasn't gotten back to me with anything. This guy's MO's pretty specific. If a similar case pops up, it's probably the same perp." I glanced across the seat at Black "What about motive?"

"I'd say it's personal with him. The lips are something he equates with the victim. Could be he liked Hilde's smile or wanted her to smile at him or smiling triggers some traumatic event in his past. Who knows? Maybe this was just his way of forcing her to be pleasant toward him, acknowledge him positively in a way she wouldn't before. Or if you take the quote into account, it could be that she simply betrayed him and he's punishing her. I'm wondering why he murdered her at her place. It'd probably be easier to abduct her or lure her to his own lair and commit the murder there. It doesn't make a lot of sense, which again points to a crime of passion, something very personal."

"Who knows what makes a sicko tick." The truth is, though, I hope to hell Black's right about this being a personal crime. Another serial killer picking off victims here at the lake was the last thing I needed.

Black slowed for a traffic light and glanced over at me. "You didn't cause this, if you're still thinking that. Quit blaming yourself."

"And I thought McKay was the psychic around here."

"I know how you think. You always blame yourself if anybody close to you gets hurt."

"Well, my personal history pretty much supports that theory, wouldn't you say?"

Shrink or not, Black didn't have an answering quip for that one. Uh-uh, no glib answers this time. He knew my ugly personal history. He didn't have an alternate theory that would hold up.

Eric Dixson's place turned out to be touristy, all right. It was one of those trendy photography shops that catered to giddy tourists who wanted to memorialize their vacation at the lake forever and ever. Go figure. They stampeded in family flocks to our neck of the woods throughout the spring and summer months. There were also lots of state conventions held weekly in our fanciest resorts, Cedar Bend Lodge being the primo. Most of those attendees, however, were executive types who spent their time snapping pictures of themselves with colleagues holding expensive briefcases and/or recognition plaques with their names engraved on them.

As it turned out, Dixson had loads of colorful costumes for his clients to play dress up in. Black and I paused just inside the door, where a long rack of feather boas caught my eye. In rainbow hues, no less, purple and red being the predominant choice. Other racks held row after row of Union and Confederate uniforms replete with gold-fringed sashes and wicked sabers. Wannabe southern belles would feel right at home, too, frocks of every hue, every material, all designed to tie in the back over your clothes, one size fits all. About six thousand portraits of the aforementioned historically correct tourists hung about on the walls in the shop's trademark brown-and-gold paper frames. Eric obviously did a helluva good business.

We could see a man was working in a large gold velvet-draped alcove at the rear of the store. A group of a dozen or so ladies sat before his old-fashioned draped camera, all decked out in wide-brimmed straw hats and flowing antebellum gowns, a couple of gaudily bedecked saloon hall girls thrown in for good measure. They were giggling and teasing each other and having a rip-roaring good time. I briefly considered a citation for public intoxication, but decided they deserved a night out. One lady on the front row sat with both hands propped atop a closed ruffled parasol and looked quite the patrician matriarch.

Eric was egging them on, laughing with them, making sure they came back to immortalize their next vacation jaunt. I watched silently for a moment and wondered what it would be like to have that many friends to hang out with. I didn't make friends easily. For some reason, most of them turned out to be men—my partners and ex-partners, usually, and then there was Black, who had, against my better judgment, turned out to be much more than a friend. Maybe Jude could be my next best lady friend. I thought of her in that unbuttoned black silk outfit. Nope, nix that as a crummy idea.

Black and I stood silently and watched the fun. Hailing originally from the Big Easy, Black would go for the Confederacy uniform, I'd bet money on it. General Lee, probably so he could run everything and everybody like he did in real life. Moi? I would go floozy.

As I predicted, Black fingered the gold fringe epaulets on a gray Confederate general's uniform. "We might as well pose for him since we're already here. See that red saloon getup over there, it's got your name written all over it." So there you go. See how well we're getting to know each other?

"I've got a couple of those saloon outfits at home that I'll model for you tonight."

"Never mind. I'll stick with the shoulder holster and high heels from last night."

Some pretty sexy visuals danced around inside my head, until I heard Eric Dixson instruct the ladies to "Smile pretty now." Hilde's face welled up inside my head in its gruesome death mask, and I sobered back to reality pretty damn fast.

The chitchatting ladies took some time scraping together enough cash for each to have their very own, personal, eight-by-ten group portrait to treasure, a steal at just twenty-five dollars a pop. They left in a whirl of laughter and wafting expensive fragrances, and Mr. Dixson shut the cash register drawer, looking rather smug and satisfied as he headed toward us, his next pair of gullible, vacationing suckers.

"Sorry to make you wait. The more people in the shot, the longer it takes to get the lighting just right."

The camera angles in my line of work usually entailed only one dead body at a time, so I couldn't comment. "No problem. Are you Eric Dixson?"

His *looking-forward-to-shooting-you-nice-folks* expression faded to a *wary-as-hell-of-both-of-you* one. "Yes, ma'am, that's right. What can I do for you?"

I displayed to him the badge clipped to my belt. He displayed to me his startled face. I said, "I'm Detective Claire Morgan from the Canton County Sheriff's Department. I need to ask you a couple of questions, that is, if you've got a few minutes to spare."

He looked then as if he had a stash of weed hidden in his camera case. "I don't understand, Detective. I've got zoning permits to take these photographs, and my license is in good order. I made sure of that before I ever opened my doors."

"I'm afraid it's a little more serious than that, Mr. Dixson."

Dixson kept glancing at Black, who stood behind me, as tall, imperious, and sophisticated as ever, no doubt trying to look inconspicuous in his solid gold cufflinks and silk suit made by the finest tailor in Hong Kong proper. The giant Humvee sitting outside the plate-glass front window probably helped his image, too. Dixson was probably mentally rubbing his palms together, thinking Black had enough cash to order the Giant Deluxe Color Spring Package, double prints, one for each of us.

"Are you acquainted with a woman named Hilde Swensen, Mr. Dixson?"

"Sure. I've worked with her on several occasions. Actually I took her pageant portfolio for the Cedar Bend Dogwood Pageant a few days ago. Last Tuesday, I think. She asked me to come and set up at her place up at the Royal. Why do you ask?"

"So you're well acquainted with her?"

"Yeah, I guess you could say that. I mean, we're not romantically involved or anything like that. She's a nice kid.

I've known her a long time. You know, seen her around the circuit, and stuff."

Great, and he didn't have a clue that she was dead. So I was going to get to break it to him. Lucky me. "Mr. Dixson, I'm afraid I've got some bad news concerning Ms. Swensen."

"Oh, my God, Hil's okay, isn't she?"

"I'm afraid she isn't okay, sir. She was found dead in her condo yesterday, murdered, and we have reason to believe you might have been the last person to see her alive."

Dixson's face drained of color, and I mean drained as if somebody had pulled a plug in his jugular. Ghost white and trembling all over, he stumbled backward a step or two until a rack of Victorian white lace dresses brought him to a standstill. "Oh, my God, no way. What happened? Who could've done something like that? And why, why?"

"I'm sorry I had to break it to you like this, Mr. Dixson. I can see it's upsetting to you. Would you like to sit down? Maybe there's a more private place where we could talk for a few moments?"

Dixson had both hands over his mouth, and I had a sneaking suspicion he was about to lose his breakfast.

I said, "Take a couple of deep breaths, sir. I realize this is a shock."

"Oh, my God! I was just with her the other day! She was feeling so good, happy and smiling constantly, enjoying the spring weather."

I glanced at Black when Dixson mentioned the smile. "Let's sit down somewhere, Mr. Dixson. I have a few questions, but it shouldn't take long."

Using one hand to steady himself, Dixson moved on shaky legs through the narrow aisles crowded with racked costumes. I looked around at the displayed photographs we passed and marveled at how many families thought playing dress up was a fun souvenir for their trip to Lake of the Ozarks.

A maroon velvet curtain draped an archway at the rear

corner of the store, and Dixson parted it and led us into a large office. A huge, scarred, rolltop oak desk sat in one corner, and an oblong harvest table was positioned adjacent to a filthy window that looked out on a brick building across a narrow alley. The building was extremely old, at least a hundred years, I'd guess, and a single bare lightbulb dangled from the middle of the ceiling, giving the place a spooky, black-and-white, *Godfather II* kind of look.

Eric Dixson walked straight to a closed cupboard, opened one door, and pulled out a half-full bottle of Jack Daniel's. He unscrewed the cap and splashed a good portion into a short glass, a lot of it landing on the counter. "Sorry, I need a drink. Want one?"

Black shook his head.

I said, "No, thank you."

Dixson tossed it down like it was nothing stronger than grandma's root beer sarsaparilla, then gestured for Black and me to have a seat at the table. He poured himself number two straightaway, and I noticed his hands were still shaking. Maybe number three would do it.

Dixson sat holding the glass in one hand, the bottle in the other. He stared at Black for a moment. "It took me a couple of minutes, but you're that doctor, Nicholas Black, right?" He turned to me. "And you're the detective who's been in the newspaper for getting those serial killers."

I nodded, but did not want to rehash our well-documented notoriety. Black said his usual nothing and looked damn fine doing it.

Dixson sank down in the chair across from me and placed the bottle on the table in front of him. He tippled some more booze into his glass. I got out my trusty pad and pen. I better ask him what I wanted to know before he soused himself enough to pass out completely. He said, "How'd she die? Can you tell me that?"

I was surprised he craved the gory details, not after the

elaborate shock scene we'd witnessed a few seconds before. "I really can't get into that with you, sir. Right now, I need you to tell me about the last time you saw Ms. Swensen. How would you describe her demeanor on that day?"

Dixson tossed down another shot, poured some more, sighed some more, stared at me some more. Obviously he intended to drown his sorrows, right here, right now, not later, get it done with the detective watching.

"Maybe you should lay off the hooch until we get finished with our interview, Mr. Dixson."

When a bell rang at the front door, Black and I looked at the velvet curtain, then back at Dixson. Dixson didn't move.

Dixson finally said, "Ignore them. They'll go away if I don't go out."

"That can't be good for business." That was Black, ever the entrepreneur.

"Nothing I could do would hurt this business. Everybody wants to smile for the camera and take their own face home to look at."

Okay, enough about the joys of photography. "I asked you about Hilde Swensen, Mr. Dixson. Why don't we get on with this and then you can finish your drink there?"

Anger came up inside Dixson then, fast and furious, taking over his ruddy face like a flash of lightning. "Just give me a fuckin' minute, why don't you? For God's sake, she was my friend and now she's dead. You might be able to shove it aside and work your case, cold as ice, but I can't."

I looked at him. Black looked at me to see if I was going to shoot him.

Fortunately, Dixson got himself together real quick. "I'm sorry, Detective. None of this is your fault." He tossed down another glass of whiskey. He had to be feeling pretty good by now. Maybe it'd loosen his tongue. So I waited. The Patient but Cold as Ice Detective.

Dixson said, "Okay, okay. Hilde was fine, in a great mood.

We laughed, we played music while I shot her, the Beatles, can you believe it? Hilde loved the Beatles, especially the early albums. You know, *A Hard Day's Night* was the name of the one we listened to. God, we had a good time. She made a pitcher of margaritas, and we drank the whole thing."

Yeah? Well, surprise, surprise.

"Did Hilde drink often?"

Dixson shrugged. I was relieved to see him pick up the cap and screw it back on the bottle. "I really wish you'd tell me how she died. She didn't suffer, did she? She couldn't take much pain, ya know? Said she had a real low threshold for it. Even headaches sent her to the ER. And she just wasn't very brave, not when it came to pain, know what I mean?"

"Your relationship sounds like more than a run-of-the-mill photographer and client."

"We weren't lovers, if that's what you're gettin' at. But hell, I'm no different than most guys. I would've given my right arm to go out with her. One thing, though, she did trust me, even confided in me sometimes. She was a real unhappy woman most of the time."

"How do you mean?"

"She was terribly insecure, I guess. She had a tough childhood, she told me that a couple of times after she'd had too much to drink. A really bad scene when she was little, at least, that's what I got from it."

Black shifted slightly in the chair beside me, and I knew his shrink mind was analyzing in high gear and making all kinds of diagnoses. Mine was, too. He was probably dying to ask a few pertinent questions of his own. But this was my job, my turn to take charge. He wouldn't interfere, not yet, anyway.

"Hilde indicated to you that she was abused as a child?"

"That's what I took from it. I guess she never said that outright, but she used to tear up and cry when she got to thinkin' about it. I remember one time she sobbed like crazy, but like I said before, she was pretty damn drunk. We always drank when I was shooting her. Said it relaxed her. She was right, too, it did."

"Did she ever mention a sister?"

"You mean Brianna?"

"Yes, do you know her?"

"Oh, yeah. She's the smart one."

Well, here we go again with the Mensa Minnie versus Helen of Troy routine. "Smart one?"

"Bri's got a master's degree in psychology from U of Miami. That comes off as pretty smart to me."

Right. Me, too. Bud's gal was getting right up there with Black and all his psychiatrist diplomas.

Black couldn't resist that one, didn't hide his astonishment, either. "Brianna Swensen has a degree in psychology? She's never mentioned that to me."

"Yeah, well, she liked to play it down, because it used to make Hilde feel bad about herself."

I said, "So there was a significant sibling rivalry between the two sisters?"

Dixson barked a short laugh. It came out hard, almost contemptuous. "Hell, what'd you think? They're women, aren't they? They competed against each other for years. You think that won't wreck a relationship?"

"I don't know either of them well enough to make that kind of judgment. Other people have indicated to me that they were fairly close." Except Betina Long.

"Then these others, whoever the hell they are, didn't know a damn thing about them."

I looked down at my tablet, thought a moment, then took another tack. "What can you tell me about Carlos Vasquez?"

"Nothing much. He's Hilde's ex. But he doesn't like how she ran out on him. He's been using every trick in the book to get back with her, trust me. He's a real prick. Ask anybody who's had dealings with him."

"What kind of dealings have you had with him, Mr. Dixson?"

"I just knew him through Hilde. That was enough to know he was bad news, believe me. I heard he was mixed up somehow in the mob."

"Do you have any proof of that?"

"No. Just an idle rumor, but it wouldn't surprise me."

"Do you know when he last contacted Hilde Swensen?"

Dixson shook his head. "She didn't say much about him during the shoot."

"What did she talk about?"

"She kept saying she couldn't stop loving him, but that he cheated on her and she couldn't forgive that. I told her to give herself time and she'd get over him and find somebody worthy of her."

It seemed to be that he was speaking about Hilde as if she were still alive, but I didn't remark on it. "Do you know where I might find Mr. Vasquez?"

"I'd say your best bet is his spa. He used to be down there twenty-four/seven, at least when he's not out at the clubs trying to pick up somebody else's wife."

"It's clearly apparent that you don't care for this man. Did the two of you have difficulties?"

"We hate each other's guts, if that's what you call difficulties."

"Why is that?"

"He despises me because Hilde counted me as her friend. He didn't like her to have male friends, or female ones, either, as far as that goes. I hate him because he treats her like shit. Is that good enough?"

"I'm asking you questions because I have to, Mr. Dixson. I'm sorry if it makes you uncomfortable or makes you feel like I'm invading your privacy."

Dixson relaxed some, but only a little bit. "Yeah, I know.

Sorry. This hit me pretty hard. It's so sudden and nothing I ever expected. Like I said, Hilde and I are old friends."

"Did Hilde mention anything to you that you found odd or unlike her?"

Dixson considered a moment as he poured himself another drink. He didn't chug it this time, just sipped it, so I guess we were making progress there. "I remember her saying that she and Bri were getting along, said they weren't on the outs, for a change. She told me it wouldn't last, though, because Brianna had called up and jumped her ass again right before I showed up with my gear."

Black jumped on that. Butted in, couldn't help himself, I guess. "Did Hilde indicate what Brianna was upset about?"

I didn't glare at him or order him from the room. He'd verbalized my next question, anyway.

"Brianna was always on Hilde's back big-time about partying so much. Apparently, Bri's gotten to be a little prude since she moved up here and started dating that cop. Hilde didn't like Bri being in that kind of relationship."

Aha. Now we were getting down to some shiny brass tacks. "Why was that?"

"She didn't like cops, any of them. She got busted in Miami a couple of times on drug possession. By undercover guys who came on to her in the clubs, but most of it was bogus. Her lawyer always managed to get her off."

"What else did Hilde say about Brianna's relationship with the cop?"

"She said Bri was playing him along, that he wasn't her type at all and it wouldn't last."

"What made Hilde think Bri was playing this guy?"

"I don't know that. Hilde didn't elaborate. She just said Bri was using him and she couldn't figure out why."

"It sounds like Hilde and Brianna were two very different women."

"Not so much, really, if you knew them like I do. My

opinion? Bri's just playing at being a normal kinda girl with an upstanding boyfriend, white picket fence, and rosy future. Hilde said she'd get tired of that kinda boredom sooner or later and head back down to Florida where her real friends were."

This was definitely not going down well with me. In fact, it was making me highly annoyed. I didn't care for the idea of Brianna using Bud for any reason, much less to toy around with, and I didn't like the idea of the two sisters being cut out of the same sleazy cloth. Then again, I wasn't sure I believed everything Dixson was telling me. Something about the man bugged me. Actually, pretty much everything about him bugged me.

"What kind of relationship do you have with Brianna, Mr. Dixson?"

"I shot her portfolio three years ago, and it turned out great. She's a lot better subject than Hilde is, calmer, you know, more patient with what I want her to do. Hilde gets a little drunk in our sittings and quits too soon. Bri's a perfectionist and willing to do whatever it takes to get it right."

"I see." But I didn't see, and I had a hunch nudity was somehow involved in whatever it took to get it right. "Would you mind giving me a brief rundown of your whereabouts for the last two days, Mr. Dixson?"

The guy startled me by suddenly jumping up, rocketing his chair back against the wall. He glared at me, fists on his hips. Talk about a hair trigger. And I thought I was bad. "Hell, yes, I mind," he said. "I don't like being accused of murdering a friend."

Black stood up, too, all six three of him. Polite, I guess. Or maybe not, judging by the way he was clenching his jaw. He said, deadly calm, "The detective's not accusing you of anything, Dixson."

Did I mention that Black was unnecessarily protective?

And his cultured veneer was deceptive. Once I'd seen him so enraged that he'd nearly drowned somebody with his bare hands, and not so long ago, either. Of course, that somebody had been trying to kill us both, but that's beside the point. I can take care of myself. He knows that; he just forgets sometimes.

I was serene. I kept my seat. "Sit down, Dixson, and don't do something stupid."

Dixson tried to stare me down, but didn't get far with that, so he decided to sit. Black remained standing so he could look imposing, which he accomplished admirably. I took notes as if nothing had almost happened.

"All right. Is there anything you'd like for me to know, Mr. Dixson? Something you feel might be helpful to my investigation?"

"I didn't do anything wrong. I wouldn't touch a hair on Hilde's head." A small sob escaped him, but he stifled the emotion, looking embarrassed by the show of vulnerability. It looked fake, too, so he tried something else. "For God's sake, I loved her like a sister, I loved her face, her smile, her laugh, everything about her. I would never in my life ever think of hurting her."

Now he sounded like he was rehearsing a lame *Bold and the Beautiful* soap script, but I nodded as if his protestation had come off legit. "All right. Who do you think might have?"

"Might have what?"

I looked at him to see if he was kidding me. He wasn't, so I filled in the blanks. "Might have killed her."

"I think Brianna might have."

Black said, "That's absurd."

"Is it, Dr. Black? Maybe you'd change your mind if you knew them better."

These guys just didn't know how to be civil. "Where were you yesterday, Mr. Dixson?"

"Right here most of the day, working. I dropped in out at Cedar Bend part of the afternoon, too, just to see how things were going. Three to four, or so, I guess it was."

"Would you mind giving me a list of witnesses who might be able to verify your presence there, sir?"

"The pageant coordinator can, for one. Patricia Cardamon, I think she said her name was. She spoke to me at length about where and how she wanted me to shoot the runway. Ask her, if you don't believe me."

"Anybody else?"

"Some of the contestants and carpenters probably saw me speaking with her, but I don't know their names. And several tourist groups came in yesterday for portraits, but I can't tell you their names, either. They paid in cash, so I don't have a record."

"What about last night and the night before?"

"I was here both nights. That's when I process film in my darkroom."

"You did that all night on both nights?"

"Until I went to bed. I live upstairs over my studio."

"Alone?"

"Yes. I live alone."

"Okay, thank you, Mr. Dixson, I guess that'll do it for now. I might have more questions for you later."

"Any time, Detective. I have nothing to hide." He glanced at Black, who still didn't look particularly happy. "I apologize for getting angry and yelling at you. I guess I'm still a bit stunned by all this. That's the truth, I swear it."

"That's perfectly understandable, Mr. Dixson. No offense taken. You're not the first person who's been offended when I questioned them." I smiled so he'd believe it and shot a significant look at Black, so he'd remember that he'd been pretty irked by some questions I asked him once upon a time.

Outside, Black and I stopped for a moment and allowed

our eyes to adjust to the bright sunlight. Dixson definitely kept his studio a little on the dark side. Black slid on his shades. I squinted up at him. "If you can't behave, I'm not bringing you along next time."

"I don't like guys threatening you."

"I don't either. That's when I take it down a notch, one way or another. If I need you to beat anybody up for me, I'll let you know."

Black laughed. "Same back to you."

I smiled and watched a couple of tourists across the street picking through a rack of Lake of the Ozarks souvenir T-shirts while their children rode go-carts. "What was your take on Dixson?"

"I think he's probably been in love with Hilde as long as he can remember and that he's jealous of anybody remotely important in her life, including, and especially, Brianna."

"My, you sound like a shrink used to summing up aberrant personalities in a nutshell."

"What did you think?"

"Pretty much the same, but it's interesting to hear that Brianna and Hilde weren't exactly Mary-Kate and Ashley Olsen. Tell you something else, too, I'm more than interested in what this Vasquez guy has to say about the Swensen sisters."

"Me, too. Maybe we ought to surprise him down at South Beach and see how he reacts to news of Hilde's death."

"You're reading my mind."

"Wish I could. It would make things so much easier."

Black's cell phone chirped insistently and he retrieved it and took a look at caller ID. "It's the Lodge." He answered, listened, frowned, and I waited for him to hang up and give me the bad news. "The press is out at Cedar Bend, full force and demanding me to talk to them. I've gotta go back. How much you think Charlie's going to allow me to give them?"

"Not much, if I had to guess."

"Well, ask him as soon as you can and let me know. I'm heading back there right now. You coming with me?"

"No, drop me off at the station so I can talk to Charlie."

We got in the Humvee, both of us dreading what awaited us in the next hour or so. Even if Charlie was in a godawful mood when I ran the case for him, I still had the better end of the stick. Nothing sucks as much as facing the preening media morons and having to answer their stupid questions.

Sisterly Love

After they'd scared Sissy with the Freddy Krueger costume, nearly all their quests were revenge missions against Sissy. It was wonderful for the older one to have a crew of loyal allies to help her, and she felt good inside, powerful enough to make Sissy suffer for the first time in her life. Sissy still had trouble sleeping at nights, and the older one was glad she did. She felt utter gratitude for the boy, and his ingenious plans to hurt Sissy and make her feel threatened. The older one felt so much appreciation for him, in fact, that she began to let him kiss her and touch her, and she began to like it, and him, and the times when she was alone in the Winnebago with him.

Once when they were planning their next mission, one of the twins spoke up and said, "You know what I wanna do for my mission, Dungeon Master?"

"What's that, Princess Leia?"

"I wanna make Sissy lose the Fourth of July pageant so I can win it. I want you to think up a plan that'll make her lose."

"And I wanna win the one after that, too, when it's my turn to compete," said her twin sister.

They all watched the boy as he stood up and began to pace back and forth in front of where they sat at the dining table. He always did his best thinking when he walked around the room, and he was so brilliant that he always came up with good plans. This time, though, he left the Winnebago without a word and went inside the house, so they drank their sodas and watched a *Leave It to Beaver* rerun on the television set until he came back.

"Okay, guys, I got it. And there's no way they can catch us."

The older one smiled and thought how wonderful it would be for Sissy to actually lose a contest and not have a new crown to add to her collection. It would kill her! Momma would probably faint dead away!

"Tell me, quick," she said to the boy.

"Abracadabra, and here it is," he said, whisking a small round jar out of the back pocket of his Levi's.

"What's that?" she asked.

"It's a chemical mom uses on patients that peels the top layer of their skin off. We can sneak it into something Sissy uses on her face, and she'll look ugly the day of the pageant."

"What exactly does it do?"

"Like I said, it'll make her skin peel off, like she's got a bad sunburn, or it could make her face break out in pimples. I heard Mom say that happened sometimes. You know, as a side effect."

"Pimples! Oh, that'd be great," cried one of the twins.

They all laughed together because Sissy had the most beautiful skin in the world.

"Yes, she'd hate that, and so would Momma."

"Okay, raise your hand if you wanna do it."

The three girls raised their hands, and the boy grinned in triumph. "Okay, it's a go." He turned to the older one. "But you'll have to mix it in with something Sissy uses on her face, and you'll have to do it the night before the Fourth of July pageant."

"I could put it in her Oil of Olay. Momma always makes her rub it on at night. Or, we could use the foundation. She wears a lot of that when she goes on stage."

"Probably the night stuff would work better. Then she'd wake up the next morning and look in the mirror, and Pow! Ugly Sissy!"

They all hooted with laughter, and the older one took the jar of cream and put in her pocket. She felt the power rising up inside her, and it felt good, really, really good, and she couldn't wait for the day to come when she could see Sissy look hideous with her skin all peeling off.

She said, "I'll accept this quest and maim the cruel princess, and our own lovely Princess Leia will wear the crown."

The boy's little sisters jumped up and down with excitement, and the boy and the older one smiled at each other because Sissy was going down this time and they would get to watch.

The quest proceeded as planned, with no problems. The older one secretly mixed a little of the peeling chemical in Sissy's Oil of Olay the day before the pageant, and then she acted so sweet, so cooperative, so subservient to Sissy and Momma, that no one even suspected that she was getting ready to do such a terrible thing to Sissy. It was perfect. The boy was perfect, and the best friend the older one had ever had. He would be her best friend for the rest of her life. She would do anything for him, anything he asked. For the first time in her life, she was happy inside her soul.

She woke early and tiptoed across the room to see the results of their quest. She stared down at Sissy, at first dismayed at the red, blotchy patches peeling skin off her little sister's porcelain complexion. For a moment, she felt appalled by what she'd done and then she remembered all the lies Sissy had told about her, all the beatings she'd caused for her, and her guilt quickly evaporated. She climbed back in bed, pulled the covers up, and waited calmly for the fireworks to begin.

It didn't take long. Momma came up early, around seven, to wake Sissy so she could wash and roll her hair. This time it was Momma who let out the high-pitched shriek of horror, loud enough to nearly break everybody's eardrums. The older one sat up in bed and pretended to be half asleep when she mumbled about what was going on. She was becoming a pretty good actress now that she'd been playing the game. The boy and the twins would be very proud of her. If only they could see how innocent she looked!

Momma was bawling and screaming for Stepdaddy, and he thundered up the steps and ran into the room. He ground to an abrupt halt beside the bed and said in disbelief, "Oh, my God, what happened to her face?"

The older one kept saying, "What's going on? What's the matter?" until Momma turned to her and snapped, "Shut up. Sissy's sick."

They left Bubby for the older one to take care of and rushed Sissy to the emergency room. That's when the older one exchanged the jar of Oil of Olay in the bathroom for a new one the boy had bought at Wal-Mart. She took out just the same amount that was depleted from the other jar, then took the poisoned jar outside behind the barn and buried it in a six-inch-deep hole. The boy and his sisters were waiting there for her, and she told them excitedly that the quest was a complete success.

"A new princess will be crowned," she said and hugged the beaming little girl.

When Momma and Sissy returned from the hospital, Sissy was crying her eyes out because she looked so terrible. The older one frowned and put a sympathetic furrow in her forehead when Sissy complained that it burned and hurt really bad. The doctor didn't know what caused it, but thought it might be an allergic reaction to something she'd eaten or applied to her face, and Momma gathered up all the cosmetics and face creams and put them in a bag to be analyzed. The older one laughed and laughed inside and was so happy. Momma wasn't so smart, after all, not nearly as smart as the boy. There was no limit to what they could do to Sissy and Momma in the coming days. Oh, yes, the future was bright now.

Then the unexpected happened. Around noon, Momma came up to the bedroom where the older one was reading *Romeo and Juliet* and said, "Well, I tell you one thing. I'm not about to waste that fifty-dollar entry fee. You've been looking a little better lately. Get up and wash your hair. You're going to go on in Sissy's place. You'll just compete in the older division."

Stunned, the older one couldn't believe her ears.

"Get up, I said, and get yourself into that tub. It'll take me forever to tame that wild mop of hair you've got."

The older one obeyed, thinking she was surely inside a dream. And she loved it when Sissy stood outside the bathroom door and sobbed and whined and cried because the older one was going to be in the pageant instead of her. Momma opened the cosmetic case and carefully applied the foundation and blush with all the care she'd always used on Sissy, and when the older one looked into the mirror, she actually thought she looked a lot like Sissy.

"You don't look half as bad as I thought you would. And for the talent competition you can read one of those weird poems you're always reciting. It's not as good as Sissy's dance, but it'll have to do. The girls in your age division aren't nearly as pretty as the ones in Sissy's competition, but don't get your hopes up. You don't have a chance in hell to win. Believe me."

Stepdaddy stared at the older one when she walked down

the steps. He didn't say anything, but he had never looked at her that way before. His expression was like the boy's when they kissed, and she didn't like Stepdaddy looking at her that way. She didn't like it at all. Momma didn't, either, because she pushed the older one's back and told her to hurry up and get in the car. Upstairs, Sissy was yelling and crying and throwing her toys against the wall, but everybody ignored her.

At the pageant, the older one was scared to death to walk on the stage. But the boy sidled up to her when Momma was busy at the entry table and wouldn't see him.

"You look good enough to eat," he told her.

The older one smiled. "Sissy doesn't anymore. She'd give you heartburn."

"Told you your mom should enter you in these things. You'll win, wait and see."

The older one did win, and nearly fainted from shock when they called out her name. She walked out to the end of the runway, and she smiled at the boy where he sat in the audience below as they placed the most beautiful tiara atop her head. Momma ran up and hugged her in a way she had never hugged her before, and the older one was so overwhelmed that she almost forgot all the mean and horrible things her mother had done to her in the past. Her mother did love her, now that she was pretty, and that's all she had ever wanted.

The boy's little sister won her division, too, and they wore their tiaras together in the Winnebago and drank some beer that the boy had taken from his Dad's liquor cabinet. They toasted the success of their quest and the victories in the beauty pageant, and after the little sisters left, the boy made love to the older one in the back bedroom of the Winnebago for the first time ever, and she loved it. She loved it, she loved wearing the tiara when he took her virginity, and she loved him. He had changed her life from utter misery to a beautiful, fairy-tale world, bright and wonderful and happy.

She loved him. She would do anything in the world for him, forever and ever.

From that day on and for the next couple of years, the older one was as happy as she had ever been. Now it was so different between her and Momma. Now she was the one winning crowns, and even Stepdaddy was paying attention to her and giving her hugs. Sissy was the one now who was always in trouble with them. Her face had never fully recovered from the chemical in her Oil of Olay, and she bore some shallow scars that didn't look too bad, but that her foundation couldn't hide. So Momma wouldn't let her compete anymore, and when Momma got mad, now it was always Sissy who got the whippings. Stepdaddy still loved Bubby the best because he was a boy and now he could play baseball in the backyard and hit the ball with a bat.

Best of all, though, was the boy. He was devoted to the older one, and they loved each other deeply. They still played the game, too, and went on their secret quests. Once they even put a laxative in one contestant's food the day of the pageant, so she couldn't compete against one of his sisters. She got really sick and had to be admitted to the hospital. Sometimes the older one felt bad about hurting people, but the boy said they only performed their quests against evil, hateful people. So far he had been right. The girls they'd chosen to target were really mean and terrible and everybody who knew them hated them.

More than even playing the game, she liked making love to the boy. He was so brilliant, so smart, and he knew how to use a condom so he wouldn't get her pregnant. He had become very interested in photography and sometimes he took pictures of them together in bed. Once he had used the video camera that his parents had gotten him for Christmas. They watched their homemade porno over and over, and each time they did, they both got very excited and turned on. They spent every moment they could together, and they always made love and talked about the future they'd have together when the boy graduated from high school and college. He told her that someday she would be Miss America or even Miss Universe, and she believed him. She believed everything he said because his predictions always came true.

Nine

Bud's Ford Bronco was parked out in front at the station when Black dropped me off. Good, Bud could drive me home after I finished debriefing Charlie. I hadn't any more than gotten in the front door, however, when I heard Charlie bellowing my name. A minute later Bud came around the corner and strode toward me in a big hurry.

"Charlie saw Nick drop you off. Let's go. He called me in because he wants to talk to us together. I was about to call you. Hurry, he's on the warpath."

Yeah? No joke.

When we made Charlie's office, he was smoking his pipe, but it didn't look like he was sending up peace signals.

"Sit," he ordered, but he wasn't nearly as perturbed as I expected, so I quickly considered myself lucky.

We sat. Charlie took a moment to puff on his pipe until it was as inflamed as he was. "What the fuck is going on around here, might I ask?"

I braced myself for the F bomb times twenty, his usual total when frustrated, hoping he had addressed that question to Bud.

"Well, Detective Morgan, I'm waiting here."

"Yes, sir. We found the body yesterday morning after being sent to check on the victim by her sister, Brianna Swensen. She couldn't reach her by phone and asked Bud to check out her condo. We were on our way to the target range, so I went with him. That's when we discovered the murder victim."

"Well, that's quite a coincidence, wouldn't you say?" He turned his ire on Bud. "I take it by Morgan's statement that you're well acquainted with these two women, right, Davis?"

Bud went for Honest Abe. "I'm dating Brianna Swensen, sir. Have been since New Year's."

"Oh, is that right? You're dating the victim's sister? Well, so much for that. You're off the fuckin' case. Why am I the last fuckin' person to know what's going on around here?"

"I believe you were out of town until now, sir." I ventured as hesitantly as I knew how, since I wasn't exactly the hesitant type.

"Yes, I was fuckin' out of town, Detective, but I do have a cell phone that actually fuckin' rings in other places when I'm out of this county. Why the fuck wasn't I apprised of all of this before now?"

Let me explain. Charlie is a Southern Baptist who never takes the Lord's name in vain, but other words less offensive to his religious tenets are fair game. He uses certain obscenities often and enthusiastically and with a great deal of skill, I might add. Bud and I are used to it. We usually don't even flinch. Charlie was fuming, indeed, and he turned to the window and muttered some really unique and inventive versions of the same sentiments. I braced myself, set my shoulders. I wanted Bud back on the job, and I intended to plead his case and take the heat.

As it turned out, when Charlie spun to face us again, the F word was still alive and well, overused, and forceful even. I didn't have time to utter a single syllable because his face went from ruddy/infuriated to ash-white/shocked in about two seconds flat.

Charlie stared, in what appeared to be unbridled horror, at whatever stood in the doorway behind us. Bud and I twisted around in tandem to witness what could possibly have sent him into such a state of hangdog speechlessness. I felt my own face drain because there behind us, not three feet away, stood Charlie's sweet and gracious, born-again, lovely wife, Ellie Lynn Ramsay. Even worse, she had her equally virtuous, straitlaced, and godly minister in tow. I would describe their facial expressions way past startled, sliding in at third to stunned disbelief. The F word was rarely mentioned in their Sunday School lessons, if I had to guess.

Charlie swallowed hard. He looked sheepish. I have never in my life seen him in sheepish mode. It took me a few seconds to get over the sheer amazement of it. Finally, Charlie cleared his throat, gave a weak smile, and said, "Why, Ellie Lynn and Brother Arnold. I didn't see you standing there."

Yeah, I suspect he *definitely* did not. Brother Arnold was well known to be as kindhearted and generous as the day is long, but I was fairly certain that profanity was not on his to-do list. Bud and I had enough sense to avert our eyes and stare at the wall behind Charlie. I, for one, tried to appear invisible. Charlie now looked red faced and ashamed. Can't say I'd ever seen that in him before, either. He didn't wear it well.

Ellie Lynn Ramsay finally found her voice, but she sounded a bit shaken herself. "Yes, Charles, I can see that you were unaware of our presence. Apparently, we have caught you at a bad time. We'll go now and let you get back to work."

They went, leaving the door wide open, her prickly barbs no doubt still sticking in her husband's conscience. I didn't dare look at Charlie. Or Bud. Face rock sober, I refocused my eyes on the floor as Charlie sank down in his swivel chair and muttered something a little less obscene under his breath. It was still pretty graphic, nonetheless.

Finally, he said, "Well, I really stepped in that."

We refused to comment. Charlie got up, rounded his desk, looked down the hall after his retreating wife, then quietly closed his office door. "I guess you know I'm gonna catch hell when I get home tonight."

I considered that rhetorical and didn't comment. Neither did Bud.

The sheriff went on in a more normal tone of voice. "Okay, that's my problem, and I'll deal with it later. Go ahead. Tell me what you're doing to solve this case."

I told him. He listened, turning his ancient chair toward the windows. While I ran the case, he rocked back and forth and kept us entertained with screechy-springs music, his eyes glued on the blue sky outside.

"And, sir, I was recently apprised that reporters are now gathered at Cedar Bend demanding to know what happened. Dr. Black asked me to get your permission to hold a press conference. He wants to know exactly what he is permitted to reveal."

Charlie considered the request for a time, having calmed down considerably. His face was back to his normal reddish hue, his breathing fairly normal. "Hell, I already talked to them once today, and thought I'd given them enough to keep them satisfied for a few days, but I guess not. Let Nick give it a go, I guess. He's damn good at getting people's attention, I'll give him that. I saw him on Court TV the other night, talking about that case where that has-been actor what's his name shot his girlfriend. When does he want to do it? Soon?"

"Yes sir. ASAP. He asked me to call him as soon as you made a decision."

"Tell him to go ahead with it, but not to give any more than necessary, have him tell them as little as possible, in fact. Go ahead, call him. I bet you've got his private number on speed dial, don't you?"

I did, of course, but, well, bringing it up was uncalled for. "Yes sir, but he's number five. You and Bud are one and two."

Charlie frowned slightly. Bud grinned a little. It was good to see that he still could dredge up a pleasant expression. He hadn't displayed many lately. I punched the number in, and Black picked up almost immediately, obviously waiting for the okay. "Charlie just gave the go-ahead. He said not to overdo it with the gory details. Make the announcement short, sweet, and to the point."

"Got you. What time will you be home tonight?"

"Don't know yet. Not early."

"Why don't you come to my place this time?"

"Oh no, uh-uh. I think not."

"Jude doesn't bite."

"But I might."

"Yeah, I recall."

I smiled a little at that, remembering, until I caught a glimpse of Charlie's death glare. He didn't blink, either. "It kills me to interrupt your private chitchat, Detective, but we are discussing a freakin' case here."

Freakin'? Bud and I exchanged subtle glances, but didn't maintain any eye lock. It looked like Charlie had decided to turn over a new and less blasphemous leaf. I wondered how long he could carry on with such a drastic change of habit.

"Yes sir." I didn't take offense at his impatience. Charlie was a good man, excellent sheriff, even remained calm most of the time; he just got a tad testy when we had a bloody, horrendous, unsolved murder at the lake. Like now. I said, "Gotta go. We're debriefing Charlie. Call me later."

Ten minutes later I walked outside and got into the passenger's seat of Bud's Bronco, dreading what I was about to bring up to him. I didn't say anything until we were on the highway heading to my place then I took a deep breath.

"We need to talk, Bud."

"Yeah? What's up?"

Okay, maybe I'm going to put it off another minute. "How's Brianna feeling?"

"Pretty good, I guess. Except she thinks she wants to view the body."

"That would not be good."

"Oh, yeah, I'm discouraging it, big-time." He glanced across at me. "Okay, what's eatin' you? I know when you're stallin'. Hit me with it; get it over with. Hell, I'm off the case, anyway, what difference does it make?"

That's what happens when you work with somebody for a long time. They know your idiosyncracies and just about everything else about you, too. And this would make a difference to Bud. Irk him, even. "Okay, Bud, but you aren't gonna like it."

"Probably not. So what? I haven't liked anything that's happened today. Shit, my mood couldn't get worse."

Au contraire. "I'm getting some feedback on Brianna's relationship with Hilde, and it's not good."

Bud's frown dug even deeper vertical lines between his brows. I wasn't used to seeing him so angry and edgy. He was usually the good old boy from Atlanta, grinning and wisecracking and telling goofy stories. "What kind of feedback?"

"People are telling me they didn't get along. That they hated each other's guts, even."

Bud muttered something, and I duly noted how his fingers clenched tighter around the steering wheel. "Who the hell told you that?"

"Dixson, the photographer, seemed pretty sure of it, and a couple of the girls mentioned the sisters fought a lot."

"That's pure bullshit. Bri's never said one bad word to me about Hilde."

"But would she?"

Angry now, Bud jerked the wheel to the right, took us to

the curb, stopped, and stared straight ahead, the car still idling. "What the hell's this all about, Claire? Are you sayin' Bri's now a suspect?"

"I'm not saying she is. But I can't say she's not, either."

"I can."

"Yeah, well, that might be the reason Charlie pulled you off. No offense, but it's obvious you're not being objective when it comes to Brianna."

Bud was more than offended and didn't try to hide it. Jamming the gearshift into drive, he swerved out into traffic again. "Bri's incapable of hurting anybody. For God's sake, Claire, you know her, too, how sweet she is. Can you see her slicing off Hilde's mouth and taking shots at us? Get real. Hell, she sent us up there. She wouldn't have done that if she'd just murdered her sister."

"Maybe, maybe not. It's kinda convenient, don't you think, the way she sent us up there to find the victim? Gives her a pretty convenient alibi."

"Okay, think whatever you want. I say she didn't have time or opportunity."

"Maybe she had an accomplice."

"Oh, get real, Claire, this theory's crazy. It doesn't make sense. If somebody was in it with her, why would she send us up there before he got away?"

"Mixed signals? Or it took longer than he expected to clean up and pose the body?"

"Bullshit. I'm telling you she couldn't do it. You saw her after I told her, she was a basket case."

"Okay. All I'm saying is when you think about this, Bud, you've got to remain objective."

"You're tellin' me that? After you jumped into bed with Nick Black when he was number one on our suspect list."

Bud had me there. "Yeah, and I should never have done that. But I'd already been taken off the case by then, and that makes a big difference. C'mon, Bud, let's not argue about this. Just keep an open mind and keep an eye on her. If somebody else did it, and it was this personal, who knows, he might have it in for both sisters. He might come after Brianna, too."

"You think I haven't thought about that? Why do you think I'm staying nights at her place?"

"Okay. Give her my best. Tell her I'm thinking about her."

"Yeah? Just not what you're thinking, right?"

Bud was furious and drove to my house in complete, uncomfortable silence. He dropped me off without a word, backed up, and then spun gravel on the way out. Great. Just what I needed. But I wasn't overly worried. We'd had disagreements before. Deep down, he knew I was right about this. I probably shouldn't have mentioned it. Given the time, he would've come to the same conclusions on his own.

Sisterly Love

One lazy summer day when it was very hot outside and the bees were buzzing around in the pasture behind the barn, the older one and the boy lay naked and entwined in the hayloft behind some bales of hay. The boy had set up his camera on a shelf above them, and he was caressing her intimately, and she had her eyes closed, enjoying the sensation of his gentle fingers and thinking she couldn't be any happier than she felt at that moment. The spell was broken when somebody thrust open the barn door below them. The boy grabbed her, put his hand over her mouth, and pulled her deeper into the shadows.

Downstairs, they could hear Momma's voice. She was dragging Sissy by the back of her T-shirt, and Sissy was screaming to the top of her lungs for her daddy. But Stepdaddy had taken Bubby to a ball game, so she had no one to rescue her. They quickly grabbed their clothes and put them on, and the boy lifted down the video camera and turned it on Momma as she pulled Sissy bodily up the steps.

"This'll prove that she abuses you guys when her husband's gone," he whispered.

Momma had the riding crop in her hand, and she was saying awful things about Sissy. Terrible things, even worse than the things she used to say about the older one. Sissy was fighting not to be put into the punishment box, screaming that she was scared, that she couldn't stand to be locked up, but Momma began hitting her with the whip over and over, on the back and legs, until Sissy lay curled in a fetal position, moaning and sobbing.

"I can't let her beat on her like that, I can't," the boy whispered. Before the older one could stop him, he jumped up with the camera and shouted for Momma to stop. "You better quit hitting her. I got it on video now what you do to your kids!"

Momma whirled around in surprise, eyes still black with rage, and then she started toward them, slapping the crop on her palm. "What you doing up here, you nasty little shit? Screwin' my daughter? You think I don't know how you're always trying to get into her pants? Well, it's gonna stop right now. You're never gonna see her again, so get the hell off my property before I call your snooty doctor mommy and tell her what you've been up to."

The boy thrust the older one behind him as Momma advanced on them with the crop, ready to protect her, but before they could get away, Sissy was back on her feet, head down, charging Momma from behind. She hit her hard from the side, ramming her toward the edge of the loft. Sissy fell to her knees near the drop-off, but Momma couldn't grab hold of anything and she screamed as she went off the loft and fell to the barn floor twenty feet below.

"Oh, my God," the older one cried, running to the steps.

Below, Momma lay on her back on the concrete floor, her neck at an impossible angle, the riding crop still clutched in one hand. The older one started down, but the boy grabbed her by the arm and stopped her. "Don't go down there, she's already dead. Look at her head. The fall broke her neck."

The older one started to cry, but Sissy moved on her hands and knees and peered over the loft's edge at her mother's body. "Good. I hope she's dead. I hope I killed her. I hate her."

The older one stared at her, and the boy turned the older one's horrified face to make her look at him. He smiled. "Now we've got Sissy exactly where we want her, babe. She killed your Momma, and they'll put her away forever for that. You're free of both of them."

Sissy looked up, and the older one stared at the red, angry slash marks across her arms and legs, and then Sissy scrambled toward her and clutched her around the knees. "No, please, please, don't tell on me, please, I'll do anything you say. I'll be good. I'll wait on you and give you anything of mine you ever want. Please, please, don't tell Daddy I pushed her."

The older one cried harder because Momma was dead, and she did love her after all. Momma had been treating her nice for a long time now, but she understood why Sissy did it. How many times had she wanted to hurt Momma, kill her in awful, painful ways?

The boy grabbed up Sissy and shook her by the shoulders. "You better do what I say, every single thing I say, because I got you murdering your mom on tape. I filmed every bit of it. From now on, you're going to be our little slave girl, and you're going to do everything I say or this tape goes straight to the police."

Sissy stared up at them, her blue eyes huge, frightened. She nodded slowly, and the boy smiled. "That's a good little slave girl. Now all we have to do is make this look like an accident." He paced back and forth along the hay bales, thinking, and then he stopped in front of the older one. "When's Russell coming back with Bubby?"

"In a couple of hours, I guess."

"Okay, this's what we're gonna do. Sissy, get inside that box and we'll lock it. That'll make the cops think you couldn't have pushed her. I'm gonna fix the steps to look like the rail broke off and made her fall. Then the two of us will go back to my house and tell my parents we've been out in the Winnebago all afternoon playing games. My sisters will back that up. Then we'll hang around with them and my sisters in the house, so we'll have an airtight alibi. Your daddy will find her when he gets home and figure she accidentally fell down the steps, and then everyone will find out how she put Sissy in the punishment box and know how she used to abuse you. It's perfect."

"Yeah, perfect!" cried Sissy, and then she actually smiled as she crawled calmly into the box and let the boy set the padlock.

The older one burst into tears again and fell to her knees, overcome with emotion, but she wasn't quite sure why. The boy gathered her into his arms and comforted her and kissed her hair, and when he told her everything was going to be all right, she believed that, too.

Ten

Hilde Swensen's funeral was held at Lohman's Funeral Home several days after the murder, a little soon in my book, but that's the way Brianna wanted it. I couldn't figure exactly why the big hurry, unless she just wanted to get it over with. Black insisted on going along with me, and there was a surprisingly large crowd already gathered at the plush, Victorian-decorated funeral parlor. The first person we ran into was Jude, gee, just lucky I guess. She gave me a quick, unwarranted, unwanted hug, and I smiled the whole while and tried not to choke on her perfume, yes, probably straight out of Coco Chanel's Parisian beaker, the same stuff Black gave me for Christmas. I wondered if he got hers, too.

Jude said, "This is all so very sad, isn't it?"

"Right." I nodded, forcing a little concerned expression, but I wasn't sure Jude was really all that torn up. Black looked his usual uncomfortable self when the three of us were hobnobbing together. What did he think I was gonna do? Get her in a headlock or challenge her to a mud-wrestling duel? Both ideas sounded intriguing, I had to admit. Hey, I could take her down, no problem.

He said, "Let's sit down. The service is about ready to start."

I led the way into the chapel because I wanted to find a spot where I could surveil the pews to my heart's content and detect any false tears or half-hidden, smug, *I-got-away-with-murder* facial expressions. I saw Bud sitting on the front row on the left side of the aisle. Brianna sat beside him, dressed head to toe in black, a wide-brimmed black felt hat with a black lace veil obscuring her face. She was obviously a big fan of dreary Victorian funereal wear. Probably why she picked Lohman's with all its lace doilies on the furniture.

I guided the previously married duo to the other side where a row of short pews sat adjacent to the main room. I stood back in gentlemanly manner and let Black and Jude precede me, but I really just wanted a seat on the end of the pew so I could get out in a hurry, if need be. Even more than that, I didn't want to sit by Jude.

When I sat down, Black leaned close enough for me to smell his sexy aftershave. It reminded me of sweet things. "What exactly are you looking for?"

"Anything that will help me."

My gaze met Bud's from across the way, and he didn't smile, but gave a little short nod of acknowledgment. That meant he was over his miff. Good. Now, too, if I knew him, and I did, he would begin to watch Brianna for suspicious behavior, whether he liked the idea or not. He was a good cop. That's what good cops do. I wasn't so sure she had anything to do with it, probabilities were that she didn't, couldn't do anything so brutal to her own sister, even if she did secretly hate her guts. Like Bud, I couldn't really see Brianna whip out a pair of scissors and play snip-snip with her sister's lips.

However, stranger things had happened. Lots of times. Maybe she was some kind of split-personality psycho gal, Black would call that disassociative disorder, but he's a shrink, and I'll call it what I want. Those kinda crazies will always be split personalities in my book.

Now Bud was leaning down and whispering to Brianna, and looking mightily concerned about what she was saying back. Then he shot me his *Help!-get-over-here-right-now* look. I knew it well.

"Be back in a minute," I whispered to Black, but didn't give him time to object.

I crossed the room, feeling pretty conspicuous in my college-days black pantsuit and combat boots, but I had to hide my guns somehow. Everybody else in attendance looked like they'd walked straight off the pages of a last-rites fashion layout in *Mademoiselle*. I sat down on the other side of Brianna. She took my hand and squeezed my fingers, but I could barely discern her features through the intricate black lace.

"Thank you for coming, Claire. Your being here means a lot to me."

I kept squinting and trying to see her eyes through the veil but couldn't manage it. It makes me nervous when I can't see somebody's eyes.

"I'm really sorry, Bri. I know this is hard on you."

Then Brianna sobbed softly and lifted the black handkerchief in her hand up underneath the veil and dabbed at her tears. Where the hell do you get black hankies? I have never seen one in my life. Maybe you had to order them off eBay. Her shoulders shook with emotion, and so okay, I feel damn guilty suspecting her, especially with Bud leveling his *I-told-you-you're-barking-up-the-wrong-model* look.

Then Bud said, "Brianna wants to put something in the casket with her sister."

Oh, crap. I hadn't been expecting that. Now I understood his SOS signal.

"I really want to do it," Brianna told me, all throat-clogged and weepy. She opened the hand that wasn't holding the handkerchief and revealed the little gold locket shaped like a heart that was lying in her palm. "I want Hilde to wear this. I know she'd want to. We exchanged these hearts when we graduated from high school. Mine has her picture in it, and hers has mine. We always believed they were lucky, you know, we wore them on special occasions, times like that. You know, for good luck."

I figured it was a little too late for good luck in Hilde's case, but didn't say so. "How about letting Bud do that for you, Bri? I really think it would be a better idea. Just so she has it with her, that's the important thing."

"No, really, I feel like it's something I need to do myself. Just one last time. See her and say good-bye. You understand?"

Bud said, "Listen, Bri, believe me, you don't wanna remember her this way. It's better to think about how she looked the last time you were together."

"Bud's right, Bri. She's not going to look the same as she did in life."

Brianna suddenly stood up. "I'm sorry, but I have to. I'm stronger than you think, truly I am. I want her to wear this forever, and I'm going to put it around her neck myself."

"We need to tell her, Bud," I said.

"Tell me what?" Brianna looked at Bud. I guess she was, the damn veil was making it hard to tell.

Bud said, his voice very low. "Okay, Bri, I didn't want you to have to deal with this, but you're not leaving me much choice." He hesitated, looked around a second. "She won't look the same. The killer disfigured her face."

Brianna began to moan, a very low and terrible sound. Her fingers were clenched together, knuckles white. "I still want to see her one last time. I need to see her." Her voice was loud enough to quiet the low murmuring of the room.

Bud stood up and whispered, "Okay, ssh, Bri, then let's do it now before they bring the casket in here. It'll be more private back in the viewing room."

Bud took her elbow and led her out a side door into an adjoining room. I stayed where I was. I'd seen enough caskets and dead bodies inside them. In fact, I didn't ever want to see another one. I watched them walk to the closed white coffin, one that somebody should have locked up nice and tight and then thrown away the key. I thought of Hilde's hideous skeleton smile and knew that Brianna would regret this decision for the rest of her life.

Clarence Lohman, the funeral director and owner of the place, was standing guard at the coffin, waiting for the signal to roll it into the sanctuary. Short, thin, pointy features, pencil mustache à la Don Ameche in the *Cocoon* films, and about the same age, early eighties, maybe even older. He wore a somber suit and expression to match. He listened to Bud's whispered request, looked mightily concerned, and shook his head vehemently. He didn't want Brianna looking at her sister's body, either. Brianna stepped closer and spoke to Lohman for a moment, and he reluctantly nodded, then assumed that solemn, compassionate, bowed-head expression that they must teach in Funeral Parlor 101. I wondered what he really thought about when he was standing around at strangers' funerals looking concerned, maybe the Cardinals' baseball game on TV tonight or if his wife was having lasagna for dinner, or hey, maybe, he really was as sympathetic as he came off. The organ played on, softly, heartbreakingly, "In the Sweet By and By." God help me, I hated funerals.

I didn't want to see Brianna's face when she looked down upon Hilde's hideous lipless grimace, so I put my attention on Black and Jude and tried to think about them instead. They looked damn good together, too good, unfortunately. Instead of a crack shrink, Black could've been a male model and walked the runway, too. Spectators would probably pass out from his sheer sex appeal alone. At the moment, he was looking *what-the-hell's-going-on* at me. Jude was looking *you're-my-soul-and-my-life's-inspiration* at him. So I looked *back-off-lady-you-had-your-chance* at her. Uh-oh, love triangle brewing here, right?

Black must have noticed my interest because he got up, strode across the room, and sat down beside me. "What's going on, Claire?"

"She's insisting on viewing the body, even after Bud told her about the mutilation. I don't want to see her reaction. I wish I could just leave."

I kept waiting for some kind of horrified shriek, didn't hear it, but Black was watching Brianna and Bud. He frowned and said, "They've opened the casket, but Brianna doesn't seem all that upset."

A bit shocked at that notion, I turned around and found Brianna placing the locket down into the coffin with her sister but showing no shock or revulsion, none that was audible anyway. To my surprise, it was Bud and the funeral director who looked like they'd seen a ghost. I got up and walked into the viewing room with Black close behind me. Truth be told, the last thing on earth I wanted to see was Hilde's mutilated face again, but Brianna's nonchalant reaction to it was just a little too bizarre to ignore.

When I reached the casket, I understood right off why Brianna wasn't upset and why Bud and the funeral guy looked dumbfounded. I stared down at Hilde Swensen in her white satin-lined casket with its beautiful embroidered pillow and tufted silk lid. Only her mouth wasn't disfigured anymore. Her lips were sewn back in place and expertly painted with fire-engine red lipstick. She looked peaceful and lovely, as if no sicko maniac killer had gotten his jollies by hacking off her lips.

"Thank you, Mr. Lohman. She looks just like she's asleep," Brianna said to the funeral director, then took Bud's arm and slowly walked back into the chapel. Bud looked at me, frowning big-time.

"How did you get her mouth to look that good?" I asked Mr. Lohman.

His eyes locked on mine. "I didn't."

"What'd you mean, you didn't?"

He shrugged, seemed genuinely nonplussed. "It's a closed-casket service. We prepared and laid out the body, of course, but we didn't do any kind of facial reconstruction. We didn't have the lips to work with. I don't know how this happened. It's impossible."

Black said, "Sweet Mary."

I said, "Who could've done it?"

"I don't know," Mr. Lohman said. "But whoever it was knew what he was doing. You just don't know how difficult it is to reconstruct a mouth and have it look acceptable, especially when you're talking about shorn lips. That's why we always recommend closed caskets in these kinds of cases."

"Well, I wanna know what the hell's going on here and who tampered with this body."

"Yes, ma'am. Please, do investigate. Nobody should've had access to the body, not without my permission."

"Get the word out to your staff that I want to talk to them as soon as the funeral is over."

We stood there as a couple of Lohman's employees wheeled Hilde's coffin into the chapel, and Mr. Lohman kept telling Black and me that he was as shocked as everyone else that some phantom plastic surgeon wizard had performed such a miracle transformation on the corpse. Imagine. This funeral parlor had been in his family for seventy-five years and nothing had ever happened like this before. He knew for a fact, he insisted, that the client had been alone inside the casket, safe and sound the night before when they had locked it for the funeral service. Lord have mercy, nothing had ever happened like this before, he reiterated, but at least they'd done a good job, had eased the suffering of the family, but nobody had ever tampered with one of his clients before, never, ever, as God is my witness. Good thing, I thought. Sure wouldn't be good for the burial business.

Black and I returned to our seats, and the service began. We listened to lots of pretty girls tell pretty stories about the pretty murder victim, and one distraught hairdresser sob loudly in the back, that being Mr. Race, of course. When I glanced back to see who it was carrying on so, I saw that Corkie was comforting him, her hair long and dark red now. Brianna didn't stand and eulogize her sister, but continued to dab at tears that were apparently dripping like a faucet behind the dark veil.

I sat there with Black and Jude and thought about how Hilde's corpse could possibly have been tampered with, expertly so, at that, and without anybody knowing it. A pretty good trick, to be sure, and I wanted to know who had done it, and more important, why. The perp was the logical explanation of who might want to skulk around and re-desecrate his victim's body, but oh, yeah, in a good way this time. That didn't make a helluva lot of sense to me, actually none whatsoever. Why would some wacko hack off Hilde Swensen's lips while she was still alive, then sneak in and mysteriously reattach them so she'd look nice at the funeral? And if it wasn't the perp, then who the devil was it? The whole scenario was crazy, but I was going to find out if it killed me.

I watched Brianna stand at the front of the room and thank the people filing by for coming to pay their respects. Two granite-faced funeral home guys were rolling the casket outside to the waiting hearse. Bud finally got a minute and sought me out.

"What's up? Lohman looks as white as a sheet."

"Yeah, and for good reason. He says his people didn't reattach the lips, and he doesn't know who did or why."

"I don't get it."

"Me either, that's why I'm sticking around to question the staff. This happened for a reason, believe you me."

"Are you sayin' the perp broke in and did it?" Bud's frown was back. "Why would he do something like that?"

I shrugged. "Go on with Brianna, she needs you. At least, she doesn't have to remember her sister the way we do."

I told Black that he needed to accompany Jude to the cemetery and then take her back to Cedar Bend, and he argued a couple of minutes, wanting to stay with me, but finally agreed. I gave the chapel time to clear out, and then I sat down in a room chock full of red-faced, mortified morticians and gave them the third degree.

I started off at the top of the heap, Mr. Lohman, himself. So far, he'd pretty much given me the three monkeys/*Hogan's Heroes* routine, i.e., I know nothing, I see nothing, I hear nothing. He also looked on the verge of having a very serious nervous breakdown, probably because he was beginning to realize what kind of lawsuit could come out of this sort of thing. His hands shook as he got out a pack of Marlboros and a Bic lighter from the inside pocket of his suit coat. He held them ready, but didn't light up even though he sure did want to.

"All right, Mr. Lohman. I want you to think about this and tell me how it possibly could have happened. I take it you didn't check the body before the service?"

"No, ma'am, not when it's a closed casket funeral. We put the departed inside and lock it down right after they're prepared."

"When was the last time anybody opened that casket?"

"We finished her preparation yesterday morning. That's when we locked the casket and brought it in for today's service."

"Does anybody watch the building at night? A security guard? Night watchman?"

"We've got a night watchman. I called him in right after we found that Ms. Swensen's body had been . . ." He strove for the right words and came up with ". . . disturbed. There he is, sitting in the green chair beside the door. Walter Costin is his name." He motioned the man over. Costin had been watching us warily, like he thought he was in big trouble, and guess what, he was. He got up quickly and headed in our direction. He looked nervous, too.

Walter Costin was probably around thirty, but was dressed more like a sixteen-year-old. He had dark brown, curly hair, that almost reached his shoulders, and big, expressive eyes with long black eyelashes. About six feet tall and rather on the long and lanky side, he was wearing a black T-shirt, flared jeans, and a big silver swastika on a chain around his neck. Oooh, how cool can you get? I noticed that he also had a swastika tattooed on his right wrist.

"You a Hitler fan, Costin, or what?"

He smiled, and suddenly didn't seem so apprehensive any more. He started to talk in this deep, gravelly voice, sort of like Darth Vader's, except that Costin spoke rapid-fire with clipped-off, enunciated words. "No, ma'am. This . . ." he held up the swastika by its chain, "originated a long time before the Nazis ever came to power. Truth is, it's near three thousand years old and used mostly as a symbol for good. They've found coins and pottery with swastika symbols on them dating way back to ancient Troy, as far back as 1000 B.C., I think."

Okay, so the guy thought he was Indiana Jones. "Is that right? Troy, huh, the big wooden horse, and all that?"

"Yes, ma'am. Swastika comes from a Sanskrit word, *su*. It meant 'good.' Pretty ironic, huh?"

"Yeah, ironic. I take it you're a history major, something like that?"

"Yes, ma'am, that I am. I commute over to Missouri State in Springfield. I got a major in Ancient Civ and I'm working on my doctorate. I picked up this medallion on an archaeology dig last summer in Turkey. University sponsored it."

"Better watch where you wear that thing, Walter. Some

people are still sensitive to what it stood for in the 1940s, and I'm one of them."

"Yes, ma'am. I understand exactly what you're saying. And everybody calls me Walt." Big grin.

Walter was a real friendly sort, and not precisely what I was expecting for a mortuary night security man, nope, never would've guessed such a guy to be on familiar terms with Helen of Troy's spending money and drinking cups.

"How long have you worked here?"

"Just a couple of weeks. Wanted to earn some extra money for the next dig. It's in Greece."

"You're the one in charge here at night, right?"

"Yes, ma'am. I come in at eight o'clock in the evening and stay until around seven-thirty the next morning when Mr. Lohman gets here."

"And you were here last night?"

"Yes, ma'am."

"Alone?"

"Yes, ma'am."

"Did you see or hear anything out of the ordinary?"

"No. It was real quiet, just like normal, nothing going on."

"Where was the body when you got here yesterday?"

"It was locked down in the Swensen viewing room, ready for the service, just like all our other clients were. Nobody could've gotten access to any of those viewing rooms without the alarm going off."

"Well, it's pretty certain that somebody did just that, now isn't it?"

He gave a little shrug, nodded, didn't seem too overly concerned that somebody had a private sewing bee with one of their clients.

"Nothing unusual happened? No peculiar phone calls, unidentified noises, bad vibes?"

"No, ma'am."

"What about the outside doors? How do they lock?"

"They all have automatic latches. Once I get here, I can fix them to lock from the inside whenever they close. You can push the lever down to get out, but nobody can come in without a key."

"Who has keys?"

"Me and Mr. Lohman, is all. He always gets here early and unlocks the front door for everybody else. All the other doors always lock up behind anybody leaving the building."

"And you said nobody was here with you? You were alone the entire night."

When he hesitated, I knew I had him.

"Okay, Walt, you gotta tell me the truth. This is a very serious matter. Who was in here with you?"

Walter Costin gave a furtive sidelong glance at his boss, who had moved away and was speaking in low tones into a cell phone and by the expression on his face just barely holding back unbridled hysteria. Talk about bad publicity for a funeral parlor. Headline: "Free Casket Spray If Somebody Tampers with Corpse. Lost Lips Found at Lohman's."

Walter lowered his voice, finally looked concerned about our mutual problem. "I don't want to lie to you, Detective. I do have a friend who comes by here sometimes at night. We hook up my PlayStation 2, play all night long, sometimes. We don't hurt anything, but Mr. Lohman'll fire my ass, if he finds out I let somebody else in here after hours. Yeah, and my girlfriend came by last night, too, and we got together, you know what I mean." He wiggled his eyebrows in a suggestive manner, but I didn't bite.

"Got together? What does that mean?"

"Had sex."

But of course, they did. Probably in a closed casket, judging by the other things going on around this place. "Okay. Where did this interaction with your girlfriend occur?"

"Back in the back, in the storeroom. Don't tell Lohman,

but I keep an old cot back there for me to sleep on between my rounds. We didn't hurt a thing, I swear to God. Nobody was in here but us. See, it's like this, we don't get to spend much time together 'cause she dances out at one of the gentlemen's clubs at night and I go to classes in the daytime so we meet down here and do it, you know? It's the only time we've got to be together."

"What about the other guy? The one you said plays games with you. Where was he when you were in the back with your dancer friend?"

"He was playing in the lunchroom. He was getting close to breaking both our scores and didn't want to stop."

"So you're saying that both these individuals were here with you last night?"

"Yes, ma'am. I'm real sorry about what happened. I feel real bad somebody got in that lady's casket, but Mr. Lohman said whoever it was fixed her up real good, expert like. I sure can't figure why anybody'd do something like that, though."

"Yeah, it tweaked my curiosity, too. I'll need the names of both your friends. Somebody got in here last night and messed with the body, probably while you were busy humping your girlfriend."

Costin glanced around some more; now he was getting really jittery. "Okay, okay. I'm gonna tell you the truth now. Sometimes I forget to lock the back door, maybe, once in a while, I guess, but I never thought much about it. Hell, who wants to break into a funeral parlor?"

Yeah. Who, indeed?

"And I would've heard anybody coming in that rear door, I swear on a Bible. Pam and me were in the room right beside that door and we were just in there fifteen minutes, twenty tops."

Fifteen minutes wasn't exactly the six-hour tantric sex enjoyed at Sting's house, but still plenty of time to get the job done while some freak had his way with the nearest corpse.

"All right. I need to talk to Pam and your other friend. Give me their names and where I can find them."

"Oh, God, no, don't do that, please. Pam'll freak out."

"Too bad. You can call her and tell her to come down here. Or I guess I can talk to her at the sheriff's office. But I want to talk to her right now, got it?"

"Yes, ma'am. She's probably still asleep, but I'll call her."

"What about the other guy? The one playing the game?"

"Shit, he's not gonna like getting caught up in the middle of this, either. See, he works over at the coroner's office. Everyone around here calls him Shaggy, but his real name's John Becker."

I froze where I stood, absolutely stunned for a second or two. What? Shaggy? Here? I frowned. "How are you acquainted with John Becker, Mr. Costin?"

"We met after I got this job. He's been around at the medical examiner's morgue when I go pick up the bodies. We got to talkin' one day about PlayStation games and then started hangin' out some. You know Shaggy?"

"Yes, I know him. And I know where to find him. Get on the phone and get Pam down here right now."

I sat down while Walt called his girlfriend and tried to figure out what the hell Shaggy had to do with all of this. One thing I did know. I didn't like his involvement, not one bit.

Sisterly Love

The day they had her Momma's funeral was rainy and overcast with gusty winds whipping through the grave markers and shaking rain from the trees above the mourners' heads. Everyone was solemn and tiptoed around whispering things about poor little abused children and how no one knew what was really going on in that house, not even the daddy, that the mother seemed so interested in her girls, entering them in all those beauty pageants and working tirelessly on their costumes and dance lessons. Then the adults would come up and hug the girls and tell them that they were safe now, that nothing like that would happen ever again, and that they should be brave and think about a very good future.

After the burial when they returned home, the older one sat on the living room sofa, watching the mourners moving around and filling their plates with the food spread out on the dining room table. Her eyes remained mostly on the boy. He was talking to a friend of his from the high school, a girl, a really pretty and popular one. She was looking up at him, smiling and seeming to hang on his every word. The older one wondered what he was saying to her, and if he wanted to lift up the pretty girl's skirt and touch her in the private places like he did with her. She felt jealousy rise up inside her in a way she'd never felt before, but then her stepdaddy sat down beside her. He was holding Sissy on his lap, and he draped his arm around the older one and pulled her head down upon his shoulder.

"I'm so sorry, girls, that she hurt you like that. I didn't know how bad it was, I swear to you, I didn't know she used that whip on you, or any of the rest of it."

Sissy snuggled deeper into his arms, and he kissed her on top of her head, and then he kissed the older one on the temple. She did feel safer now that Momma was dead, and Stepdaddy had promised to take good care of them. He held them both for a long time, and when Bubby ran up, the older one pulled him onto her own lap, and they sat together, a regular family, at last.

In the days and months after Momma was in the ground, Stepdaddy was very nice to the older one. He said she was old enough now to have a room of her own, and he moved Sissy downstairs into Bubby's room. Sissy made no complaints, said nothing at all, just helped him move her things. She never said anything bad or unkind to the older one now, but obeyed every single thing they told her to do. The boy had the damning videocassette locked up in a footlocker in his bedroom and kept the key around his neck on a chain, and Sissy knew that all he had to do was take it to the police and she would be taken away forever for killing her own mother.

Sometimes they took Sissy with them into the Winnebago and let her play their game. She became a slave to all of them and had to do things in their quests they didn't want to do. Sissy always did what they said, especially the mean, secret things, and she seemed to like doing it. She said that being a slave wasn't so bad.

But things weren't perfect, either. Stepdaddy refused to let the older one date the boy, or anyone else, even though she had reached sixteen and all the other girls in the pageants had boyfriends. So she and the boy continued to sneak around and have sex wherever they could, and now that she had her own room, it was easy for the boy to climb up the tree at the back of the house and sneak across the roof to the window beside her bed. And the fact that Stepdaddy had started to drink more than he used to helped them a lot, too. He seemed lonely, and he often drank after the kids had gone to bed. He sat down in the den alone in the dark and drank a twelve-pack of Budweiser and watched horror movies. But it didn't matter; he always got up the next morning, fixed breakfast, and got them to school, so his drinking habit didn't hurt anything.

One night when the boy was in the older one's bed and filming their lovemaking, they finished, breathless and sated, and lay together afterward, whispering about him going off to college soon and how she could come with his parents to visit him. Then they heard the heavy footsteps coming up the stairs and knew it was her stepdaddy. As soon as the boy heard the doorknob turn, he slid down onto the floor beside the wall. The older one pretended to be asleep, and when her stepdaddy came close to the bed, she could smell the booze on him and knew by the way he was staggering that he was even drunker than usual.

"Hey, baby," he whispered, low, slurred. "You 'wake?"

The older one pretended to rouse from sleep. "Yes, Daddy. What's wrong?"

"Nothin', jus' thinkin' 'bout you bein' up here by yourself. You okay? Not lonesome, are you?"

"I'm fine. I like it up here."

"Good, I wan you to be happy. You know that? I wan you real happy."

"I'm happy, Daddy."

He sat down on the bed and put his hand on her thigh. "Gimme a hug, baby."

The older one sat up and put her arms around him, but he smelled awful, of Camel cigarettes and beer and the motor oil he used at work. He hugged her close, too tightly, and caught his fingers in her hair. "You sure got good lookin', know it? More'n Sissy now."

"Thank you, Daddy," she whispered.

Her stepdaddy held on, and she wished he'd go away. "You ain't my real kid, so you can kiss me and nothin'd be wrong with it."

She began to struggle. "No, I don't want to, please, Daddy, go away, you're drunk."

"Gimme a kiss g'night first."

Behind her stepdaddy's back, the older one saw the boy rise up on his knees beside the bed, but she thrust her stepdaddy away and grabbed the telephone on her bedside table. "Go away and leave me alone or I'm gonna call 911! I mean it! I will!"

When she started to punch in the numbers, he got up and staggered away. "I just wan love you, 's all," he said groggily from the door. "You'd like it, too. You'd like bein' with me."

Trembling, she ran to the door and listened to him stumble back down the steps, grumbling to himself and half falling in his drunken stupor. The boy came up behind her, and he was so angry that his voice shook. "That fucker. He was gonna rape you. I'll kill him if he ever touches you!"

"Ssh, or he'll hear you. He's just drunk. He doesn't know what he was doing. He won't even remember coming up here in the morning. If he wanted to rape me, he would've tried it."

"Like hell. He's gonna be up here every night now, and I can't always be here to protect you."

The older one liked that the boy wanted to protect her,

and she went into his arms and pulled him down on the floor. "Make love to me, I love you," she whispered.

They lay there, kissing and touching, until the girl stiffened in his arms when she heard a sound filtering up from downstairs. "Wait, wait a minute, I hear Bubby crying . . ."

The boy stopped kissing her, and they lay still a moment, still breathing hard. Downstairs, the younger boy's cries filtered up the stairwell. "Oh, my God, he's doing something to Bubby."

She grabbed her robe, and he pulled on his jeans and they ran downstairs and along the corridor to Bubby and Sissy's bedroom. Bubby was standing beside his bed, crying, but he was alone. Sissy's bed was empty.

"Where's Sissy?" she whispered.

Bubby sniffled. "He took her like he always does. I never get to sleep with him, and Sissy always gets to."

The older one's blood ran cold, and the boy cursed under his breath. They tiptoed down the hall to the master bedroom and threw open the door. Stepdaddy had Sissy spread-eagled on the bed, holding her legs down, one hand over her mouth, the other under her nightgown. They could hear her screaming muffled under his palm.

"Stop!" the older one cried, running toward him and trying to pull him off her little sister. The boy helped her, jerking the man off the bed with all his strength. Stepdaddy reeled under the unexpected attack, so wiped out that he fell to the floor and couldn't get up. He kept mumbling about how pretty his girls were before he grew still and lapsed into loud snores.

Sissy threw herself into the older one's arms, who held her tightly and tried to comfort her hysterical crying. "Has he done this before, Sissy?"

The younger girl nodded with her face hidden in the older one's nightgown, and the boy gave the man a hard kick in his side. Sissy sobbed out, "He says all daddies do this to daughters pretty as me."

"Oh, God, he's an animal," the boy muttered, furious.

The older one felt sick in the pit of her stomach. "Sissy, why didn't you tell us?"

"I was scared. He said he'd bring Bubby instead, if I didn't sleep in his bed."

The boy and the older one looked at each other, and she shivered with horror at what had been going on. Then Bubby ran into the room and clung to the boy, crying and saying his daddy had parked the car in the woods where nobody could see and done things to him, too. Anger rose in the older one, so hard and fast, she was afraid of herself. She said, "Let's kill him. Right now. While he's too drunk to fight back."

The other three kids stared at her.

Then the boy said, "Are you serious? You really want to kill him?"

"Yes."

"Me, too," said Sissy.

"Me, too," said Bubby.

"Let me think," said the boy. They all moved away from the snoring man on the floor and went out in the hall where a small night-light barely illuminated their faces. The boy paced around nervously, his fingers entwined and squeezing each other, the way he always did when he was thinking up interesting quests.

"Okay, but I'm not gonna do this by myself. You all have to help me. We're in this together, right? I'm not gonna take a murder rap for any of you, if anybody ever finds out what we've done. You understand that? You have to do it yourselves, and then you can never tell anyone, or we'll all get the electric chair."

All three nodded, and then all three began to cry. The older one grabbed the two younger ones against her and hugged them close while the boy continued to pace and think about what to do.

"I guess we could smother him with a pillow. He's too drunk to fight. That way there won't be any wounds or blood, or nothin' like that to clean up. And there won't be any marks on the body, either. Nobody will suspect any of you. Why would they? And nobody will ever know what happened. They'll probably just think he stopped breathing for some reason. You know, died in his sleep of indeterminate causes."

The boy sat them on the floor around him and told them exactly what they had to do and then exactly what they had to do and say the next morning. They would get up, and the older one would get the other two ready for school as if nothing had happened. She'd tell the police later that she thought her stepdaddy was just passed out again from drinking too much because that had happened every night since his wife died.

They all nodded in agreement, and the boy went upstairs and got his video camera. Then, together, they went back into the bedroom, struggled the drunken man off the floor, onto the bed, and under the covers. He groaned and moved his head slightly but did not fight them, so the boy filmed from the foot of the bed as the other three all took hold of a pillow, put it over his face, and pushed down as hard as they could until he stopped breathing. The boy turned off the camera, herded them outside, shut the door, and told them all to remember what to do in the morning. Then he sneaked out of the house and went home. The older one took Sissy and Bubby up to her bed and held them until they fell asleep. None of them cried. None of them woke up the next morning until the alarm went off for school.

Eleven

Unfortunately for me, Walter Costin's stripper girlfriend, Pam Letassy, or Smokin' Hot Wildcat, if you preferred stage names, turned out to be too young and too stupid to be much use to me. Said she didn't hear or see anything or think about anything or anybody but Walter, who was the love of her barely legal, young life. I tended to believe her, judging from the doe-eyed, zombie devotion she paid to his every word and deed. She was also quaking in her spike heels at the mere thought of her preacher daddy finding out she'd been having a sexual tryst in a funeral parlor, not to mention that she had a smokin' hot wildcat of a job dancing in a strip club, both of which would indeed be a big shockeroo for any red-blooded Midwestern clergyman.

Even more unfortunately, Shaggy was the next interviewee on my agenda, so I called the morgue to let him know I was on my way over to talk to him. Buck informed me that Shaggy still wasn't back to work, which revved up all kinds of terrible thought processes inside my head. It made him look guilty, that's what it did, and did I ever not like that.

I had to pay him a call to discount his involvement, and I

didn't care for that idea, either. Not that I truly thought Shaggy could ever hurt a fly; it just couldn't happen. He was a self-designated hippie peacenik, if there ever was one. Paying Shaggy a get-well visit wasn't exactly out of line, so I stopped at the nearest Quickstop, picked up a liter bottle of cold Mountain Dew and a package of strawberry Zingers, two of his favorite, if less than wholesome, foods.

Shaggy Becker lived in small white ranch house in the outskirts of Osage Beach, one I'd visited on any number of occasions, usually to watch a Bruce Willis flick or a Mizzou basketball game. He lived at the very end of a street that was pretty rural, actually, and tree-lined with big shady, spreading elms. It appeared deserted as I drove down its length, everybody still at work, I guess. His old mustard yellow Volkswagen bus sat in the driveway, the rear window plastered with surfboard decals. He'd never been on a surfboard in his life from what I'd been able to gather, but that didn't stop him from pretending he was dating Gabrielle Reece. His bass boat was sitting at the side of the house covered with a dark blue tarp.

I got out and looked around, all quiet on the western front. I waited for my sixth sense to quiver up a few danger signals as it had at the Royal, but nothing came to make me tense up and get an itchy trigger finger. I turned and looked to my right when I heard a slight bumping noise, but it was the wind knocking around a hanging bird feeder on the front porch of a house down the street. An old man was sitting near it in a rocking chair with his back to me, but he didn't move or look in my direction so I didn't pull my weapon.

Climbing the front steps to the uncovered stoop, I stepped around a big pot of geraniums that appeared to be gasping for breath but not having much luck. Shaggy didn't exactly have a green thumb, by the looks of his yard and the plethora of dead potted plants sitting around. I hesitated when I saw that Shaggy's ancient front door, the one I'd helped him paint bright red about six months ago, stood ajar. You know, it just usually doesn't bode well when you find somebody's door ajar. I had learned that many times in many hard ways. I opened my jacket, put my hand on the grip of the Glock, and hoped Shaggy was still in possession of all his mouthparts. I stood to one side and tapped a knuckle on the beat-up screen door. Shaggy's voice called out from inside, familiar and unterrified, and I felt distinctly relieved, even though he'd called out for me to go the hell away.

"It's me, Shag. Claire. I brought you some goodies."

I pushed the door open and found him lying facedown on his overstuffed brown sofa, the kind that you sank down to your elbows in. His giant sixty-inch television was the dominating feature in the room and was blaring with all the blams and thunderous sound effects of *Die Hard with a Vengeance.* There was another couch, this one pull-out and blue velour, two ancient, unmatched recliners, and a coffee table made out of a piece of glass balanced on one of those big wood spools for holding electrical wire. A couple of PlayStations sat atop it, some empty Wendy's sacks, and an opened and nearly empty bottle of Pepto-Bismol. I was pleased, though, to see that he looked as sick as the proverbial Irish setter, then felt guilty that I could even suspect such a good friend of breaking and entering somebody's coffin. What is the world coming to?

Apparently surprised to see me, Shaggy pushed himself up to sitting and gazed squinty eyed at me. Barefoot and bedraggled, he had on his usual gray T-shirt and baggy, faded-out biker shorts, and his reddish dreadlocks were mussed, to put it mildly. He took both hands and pushed his hair behind his ears, revealing twenty or so ear piercings. A Dude, he definitely was. "What're you doin' here, Claire? Something wrong downtown?"

I moved across the living room and placed the paper bag full of my exquisite culinary gifts on the coffee table in front of him. "Nope. Just came to see for myself if you were playing hooky."

"God, Claire, I'm sick as a dead dog."

If you ask me, that's pretty damn sick.

"Can't keep anything down at all. Some kinda bug, I guess, so better not get too close. What you got in the sack?"

"Mountain Dew and Zingers. Guess I should of gotten you Rolaids instead."

"The Mountain Dew's okay, but I'll save the Zingers for later. How're things comin' on that case with the dead beauty queen, anyways? Buck told me about it, but I haven't been able to help much. I went in once but didn't last long before I puked."

"We're still working it." I hesitated. I did not want to question him. He was too savvy about my motives for asking him questions, but then again, on the same side of that coin, he knew how investigations worked and that I was merely doing my job. Why would he be offended? As usual, I was dead wrong. "Hey, Shag, now that you mention it, believe it or not, your name came up in that very investigation. I guess I'm gonna have to ask you a coupla questions. You feel up to it at all?"

"Huh? Me? What'd you mean my name came up?"

"Well, first off, where were you last night?"

I grinned as if it was just so silly a question to have to ask, but my humor fell flat. Shaggy stared somberly at me, then looked down at the bottle as he twisted off the Mountain Dew's cap. Without speaking, he took a swig. I waited, definitely on edge now, and wondering against my will if he was trying to formulate the best way to answer without implicating himself. Man alive, I didn't like thinking the worst, not with a good friend like the Shagman. But my gut was telling me otherwise, that he was gearing up to tell me a bunch of lies. If that was true, I wanted to know why.

Finally, Shaggy turned his gaze on me. "What's really goin' down here, Claire? You and Bud makin' me your primary suspect? Is that it? Thanks a helluva lot."

I wasn't expecting him to go on so high the defensive this early on. I hadn't accused him of anything. Yet. I guess his reaction was understandable, though. I wouldn't like somebody coming into my house and insinuating I was a sicko scissors murderer.

"Hey, Shaggy, c'mon now, don't get all pissy with me. Like I said before, your name came up, so I'm here to find out what you know, no big deal."

"Maybe not to you. Sorry, but this doesn't feel cool to me, like you're accusing me of murder. If it's really no big deal, why didn't you call me up and ask me over the phone?"

Good question. Why didn't I? "I wanted to make sure you're all right. You never miss work. We're all sort of in shock about it." I put on another big cheesy smile that no doubt looked pretty lame. His expression told me I was right on about that.

"Yeah, or you're checkin' to make sure I really am sick, is that more like it? You think I don't know how you and Bud work your cases? I've seen how you think a million times, and right now, you're thinkin' I killed that woman." He stopped suddenly, shook his head. "Man, this sucks. What'd you think? I get off strangling ladies and slicing off their lips?"

"How'd you know the lips were severed, Shag?"

He gave me a look that made me want to cringe and apologize. I didn't do either.

"Because Buckeye filled me in and let me view the body when I went in that day, that's how. Ask him if you don't believe me. You gonna tell me how my name came up, or will that compromise your investigation?"

Oooh, sarcasm, alive and well. "The night security man

at Lohman's says you were over there last night playing on his PlayStation. I take it you're telling me that's not true?"

"That's bullshit is what I'm telling you. I was right here on this couch last night, sick as a dog like I just said, all night long. What kinda crap is this, Claire? I don't even know anybody at any funeral homes. Who said I was there anyways, I have a right to know, don't I?"

"A guy by the name of Walter Costin. Ring any bells?"

"Hell, no." Angry, Shaggy tipped up the soda again and drank a few gulps, and then I saw the name register in his eyes. He lowered the bottle and stared at me. "He's that guy that picks up for one of the mortuaries. Now I remember, but I sure as hell don't hang out with him. Why don't ya cut me some slack here?"

He lay down on his back and draped a forearm over his eyes. I took a seat on the black corduroy recliner and felt like a dirty, rotten, less than friendly cur. I believed him, of course. No way Shaggy could ever in his lifetime commit this kind of crime, but why would Costin finger him if they barely knew each other?

"Have any idea why Costin put you at the scene if you weren't there?"

"Maybe he just wanted to take the heat off himself, ever think of that? All I know is that I wasn't there. What the hell difference does it make, anyhow?"

"Because somebody broke into Hilde Swensen's casket last night and sewed her mouth back together and nobody knows who."

Shaggy bolted upright, looked at me for a minute, then to my shock, he burst into tears. Speechless, I stared at him while he wept into his palms for a minute or two, but he got himself under control pretty fast. He rubbed the tears off his face with the back of his hand and looked genuinely offended. "So you think I might've done it 'cause this guy said I was there? That what this's boilin' down to, huh?"

"No, of course not. I'd like to know why he wants to implicate you in this when you barely know him."

"Hell if I know. To save his butt and get you off his back, maybe? Or he could've been afraid he'd lose his job. All I can tell you is that I wasn't over there last night, period. And I'm sure as hell not into messing with dead girls's caskets. Jeez Louise, this is such major bullshit. Hell, I can't believe this." Shaggy leaned back and interlaced his fingers on top of his dreadlocks. Still upset, he stared at me in unfriendly fashion. "Thought we were friends, Claire, and look at you, comin' at me with this sick shit."

"Oh, c'mon, Shaggy, you know I've gotta check out every lead I get. Your name was mentioned by a primary suspect. I had to get your take on what he said. That's all there is to it. Why are you getting so bent outta shape?"

"Where's Bud? Downtown gettin' a search warrant signed out on me and my pad?

I smiled, and this one was for real. "Nah. You'd let me look around if I wanted to, wouldn't you?"

I watched the flush that ran up Shaggy's neck and darkened his face. He looked ready to grab me by the throat and have a good time squeezing the life out of me. "Snoop around in my stuff all you want, Claire. Sorry I don't feel like giving you the grand tour. I thought we were pals, but I guess not, huh?"

This was not going well, uh-uh, getting ugly, yes, indeedy. "Anybody here with you last night that could verify your story, Shaggy? Anybody call, come by?"

"*My story?*" He narrowed his eyes and set his lips in a thin, tight line. "Nope. No corroborating witnesses to give you for my *story*. Guess nobody wants to be around the stomach flu. I'm gonna bawl my eyes out, if you catch it."

Childish jab, yes, but very Shaggyesque. Especially when he's hot under the collar, anyway. Like now. I quit with the friendly, shucks-I-really-don't-like-doing-this routine. He was taking this seriously, so I got a bit annoyed myself. "Now, look, I had to do this and you know it. Sorry if I offended you, but I've got to follow leads wherever they take me."

"Yep, I see that. Thanks for your consideration."

Shaggy was royally pissed off, all right. "Okay, I get it. Just tell me what you know about this guy, Costin, and I'll get out of here and leave you alone."

"I hardly know him is what I know. I remember he's a real friendly kinda guy and always wants to talk when he comes in the morgue. He's new at it, and maybe we sat down in the break room once and had a coke, or something, after we got the body loaded. That's all I can tell you."

"Do you remember anything he talked about?"

"He talked about liking to play PlayStation. I think I said I did, too, and we compared notes on how far we'd gotten on some of the games, maybe, stuff like that. Truth is, I don't really remember. It wasn't important enough, just regular stuff."

"You remember if he told you anything about himself?"

"God, Claire, I feel like I'm gonna hurl, gimme a break here." He lay down again and put a towel over his face. After a few seconds, he spoke again, "He said he goes to school at Missouri State in Springfield, some kind of history, ancient history, I think, or maybe it was archaeology. I dunno."

"Anything else? Try to think. How about having a girlfriend? Did he say anything about that?"

"Yeah. He said she's a stripper and hot as lava, I remember him saying that, because I thought, wow, that's pretty damn hot, lava is. I think her name was Patsy or Pammy or something like that with a P. And he said her parents don't like her seeing him, so they have to sneak around."

"Why don't they like him?"

"I dunno. That's all I remember him sayin' about it. I'm tellin' you we didn't talk much."

"Did he say exactly when he started working at Lohman's?"

"Nope. Like I said, I think he's new around here, but who knows because I hardly know him. I still can't believe you actually drove out here to give me the third degree. Jeez, give me a break. Some friend."

Okay, now I was beginning to feel pretty low, guilty, even. "Well, I did bring you some Mountain Dew, didn't I?"

"Yeah, and that's supposed to make me feel better about gettin' my balls busted?"

"Hope so."

"Well, sorry, but I'm pissed. I would never think bad of you. And I sure as hell wouldn't accuse you of somethin' like this, either. Hey, you got what you came for, didn't ya, so why don't you just get the fuck out of here and leave me alone?"

"Okay." I stood up. "If you think of anything else about this Costin guy, give me a call. Please."

"Yeah, right. You'll be the first to know."

"Hey, Shag, don't you think you're overreacting here just a tad? I came out to check on you and ask for your help with my case. What's the big deal?"

"Because we're friends, Claire, but I guess you don't really know much about that kind of thing, do you? Everybody's fair game to you, Miss Hardass Super Detective of all time, friends or not, take 'em down, throw away the key, who cares that they're friends and neighbors and relatives. Take 'em down, solve the case, stomp on people who've never done anything to you. Hey, why don't you just go ahead and get outta here? Or do I need to call a lawyer first?"

"Cut it out, Shaggy, you're saying a lot of stupid things right now that you'll probably regret when you feel better."

"Leave. Don't let the door hit you in the ass on the way out."

I took him up on that pointed yet pleasant invitation and left, but I knew Shaggy's irate behavior was way out of character and way out of line. He was a very even-tempered kind of guy, even more so than Bud, and he'd been involved in most of my investigations in one way or another. He knew how things worked.

Unfortunately, I felt bad anyway, and his last words hit home in a big way. He was right, too. Having friends wasn't exactly a forte of mine, something I'd shied away from over the years, so keeping them hadn't happened a lot, either. Shaggy had been one of the exceptions. We'd always gotten along great. He was a good guy. I liked him about as much as anybody. I wondered if he could be hiding something and what it could be. His life had always been pretty much an open book. Maybe I should talk to Buck, find out if anything was going on with Shaggy that I didn't know about. Or maybe he was just sick and out of sorts.

Whatever the case, I felt almost two inches tall when I got back into my Explorer and backed out of Shaggy's driveway. Today was not turning out to be any better than yesterday or the day before, or the year before, actually. I was alienating all my buddies one right after another, so didn't feel particularly like Miss Congeniality as I headed back to the station to fill in Charlie and Bud. After that, I was going home to lick my wounds for a while. Maybe if Jude wasn't hanging all over Black, he could make me feel better about having to grill my good friend.

Twelve

When I got downtown, eased in my parking place, and made my way to the front entrance of the sheriff's office, Bud was right there, waiting at the front desk, impatiently, by the looks of it.

He said, "Charlie's already thinkin' about putting me back on. You gotta make sure he does. I'm goin' crazy sitting around doin' nothing while that psychopath runs free."

"Charlie changed his mind already?"

Bud nodded, excited about Charlie's possible decision to reinstate him, and I knew the feeling. When I'd been pulled off a case, Charlie had jerked my badge, and under similar circumstances. I hadn't liked it, either. In fact, I'd hated it. I'd felt naked.

"What about Brianna? Doing any better?"

"No. She's asleep now, but it finally hit her, I think, and she went off by herself for a while and when she came back, she got all hysterical and cried for two hours. Out of the blue, she just went to pieces. Man, and now she's tellin' me she wants to break up."

"What?"

"Says she doesn't want to see me anymore, that she wants me to stay away from her. I guess seeing Hilde at the funeral was too much for her. She's actin' weird, and I'm not sure what to do about it."

I frowned. Why on earth would Brianna turn her back on Bud now, as good as he'd been to her?

"She doesn't mean that. She's been through a lot. It's just pain talking. She's grieving." And I knew what I was talking about on that front.

"You think Nick might be willing to see her? I'm tellin' you she's in real bad shape all a sudden."

"Probably, you can ask him. But give her a little time, that's what she needs more than anything. She's still in shock. Hell, so am I."

Bud did not look convinced. "Yeah, I guess so. But she acts different now. Scared, almost, or something. God, I wish I knew what to do." He glanced away, shaking his head, then returned his gaze to me. "What about you? Anything new at your end?"

"Not much. I'll fill you in after I run the case for Charlie. I'll see if I can talk him into putting you back on."

Once summoned inside the inner sanctum, I sat down across the desk from Charlie and quickly launched into the details of my recent interviews before Charlie could start cussing. According to Bud, who'd been forced to hang around the station more than me of late, the sheriff had toned down his purple-tinged rants and raves since his wife had pulled the plug on his foul and profane but considerable cursing acumen. Actually, he appeared fairly calm at the moment, collected, even. Pretty good showing for him.

After my fast-talking spiel dwindled and dried up, the facts laid out, as inadequate as they were, he said, "So, in essence, you haven't found out one damn thing that's worth a plug penny?"

I sort of nodded, although I didn't know for sure what a

plug penny was. “Well, sir, I haven’t had much time to investigate yet. You know, I’m trying to handle this case on my own. It’s gonna take lots of footwork. I haven’t even interviewed my primary suspect, that being Hilde’s ex-lover. He’s the guy who runs a health club at South Beach.”

Charlie considered me. His face was not florid, no cuss words, no bulldog, Winston Churchillian glare. I began to suspect high doses of Xanax with a little dab of potent tranquilizer thrown in for good measure. Maybe I needed a swig of that elixir. “All right. You best get down there and see if he can alibi himself for the last few days. If you get a rap sheet on him, get ahold of the arrestin’ officers and see what they can tell you. Does this guy know Hilde’s dead?”

“No, sir. I plan to hit him with the news before he can manufacture a convenient alibi and have it waiting for me. Maybe if we’re lucky, the news won’t get to him before I do.”

“Okay, let me think about this for a sec.”

Charlie swiveled back to the window and stared outside a while. I waited. This was His Way. I was used to it and sometimes enjoyed the quiet. I was antsy today, though, and didn’t enjoy it for long. I fidgeted, waited not quite another minute, maybe two, before my patience hit a brick wall and collapsed writhing on its belly.

“I need Bud’s help on this, Sheriff, and as you know, Bud’s strictly a professional, a seasoned veteran. He’s not gonna go off half-cocked just because he’s involved with Bri. You know him better than that.”

Charlie turned to me, but didn’t say anything. I tried some more. “I can handle most of the interviews on my own, but he could check out the body-tampering thing while I’m down in Florida. I need some help on this, sir, and Bud’s just sitting on his hands, doing nothing.”

I paused again, waited hopefully for him to jump in and agree wholeheartedly. Nothing happened. Silence reigned. Valiantly, I did not give up. “Okay, my gut tells me that that

Walter Costin guy at the funeral home has a hand in all this, but I'm not sure how yet, or why. I think if we put a tail on him, he might get nervous and lead us to something pertinent. Should I give that top priority or head down to South Beach as originally planned?"

"Is Nick going with you?"

I nodded. "Black's offered me use of his private plane. Said he's got some kind of hotel business down there and I can hop a ride."

"Good. Get his take on the perp's psychology. He's proved himself useful in the past."

"I'll feel him out on the flight down." I realized belatedly how untoward that sounded, but also like something that would probably happen. Luckily, Charlie didn't attach the lustful connotation.

"Let him help us out, if he can. Like I said, I trust him."

"Yes, sir. So do I."

I sat waiting, foot-tapping edgy, and could almost hear Bud's boots tromping up and down the hall outside; chomping at the bit, he was, to be sure.

Charlie turned back to the street view and resumed his staring-into-space routine. I wondered how he did that without getting bored. Or falling asleep. "Okay, I'm gonna give Bud a chance and see if he can remain impartial. He can tail Costin, because I sure as fuck, I mean fudge, don't want Bud in Florida raising hell outside my jurisdiction."

Fudge? Coming out of Charlie's mouth? Oh, man, you gotta be kidding me.

Charlie was frowning. "Don't look at me like that, Claire. I promised Ellie Lynn I would tone down my language here at work."

"Yes, sir. I understand." I quickly changed the subject, but fudge, really? I couldn't believe it. "Reinstating Bud will be a tremendous help to me in this case, sir. Thank you."

"When do you leave?"

"Today, if possible. Tomorrow at the latest. As soon as Black can make the arrangements."

"Right, okay, get the hell out of here and keep me posted, dadgumit."

"Yes, sir."

Although I was summarily dismissed, there was still that one huge white elephant in the room that I hadn't mentioned, or at least, there soon would be. "One more thing, sir, and I do hate to bring this up." That got his attention and was it ever the truth.

"Yeah? What's that?"

I did not want to say this, but knew I had to. "Well, thing is, see, Shaggy's name turned up in one of my interviews."

At last, I had his undivided attention. The window gazing stopped; his chair swiveled and squeaked its way back to face me. "You mean, Shag from down at Buck's office? Johnny Becker?"

"Yes, sir. 'Fraid so."

"How's that?"

I cleared my throat, licked dry lips, braced myself for Unbridled Sheriff Rage. "Well, sir, I don't think Shaggy's involved in any of this, of course not, but Costin did place Shaggy at the funeral parlor the night the body was disturbed."

Dented brows, flushed face, the whole works. "What the fuck does that mean?"

Oops, and so much with the fudge substitutes. "Apparently they know each other a little bit. Costin said Shaggy went down there to play video games that night."

Oh, boy, was that ever a black scowl to behold.

"What the fudge do you mean?"

Glad Charlie was trudging down Ellie's straight and narrow again, I said, "I talked to Shag already, and he denies being there, but can't prove it. He's been home sick with stomach flu, so nobody can verify his story."

"Screw this fudge shit. You got to be fuckin' kiddin' me."

Relapse number two, and counting. "No, sir."

"Shit. That's just great. If the papers get hold of this, they'll go nuts. What's Buckeye have to say?"

"I haven't talked to Buck yet, Sheriff."

"Well, don't. I'm gonna call him myself. I can't believe Shaggy was stupid enough to get himself mixed up in shit like this."

"He's denied it, sir. He just can't prove he was home alone that night." I paused. "I believe him, sir. We both know Shaggy. He's incapable of messing with a dead body." I laughed. Weakly, though. The guy was a crime scene investigator, after all. He messed with corpses for a living.

"Yeah, but shit happens. Tell Bud to check it out and see if he can turn up anything dirty in Shaggy's background."

"Sir, do you really think that's necessary at this point? This is Shag we're talking about."

Scowl turned to ugly glower in a great big hurry. I turned to quivering jelly in the same space of time.

"Yes, I think it's fuckin' necessary, Detective. Any other questions?"

"No, sir. Thanks for putting Bud back on the case. You won't regret it."

"Well, we'll see about that, now won't we?"

I did not leave Charlie in a smilin' good mood. But I was about to put Bud into a great one, so it was sort of a tit for tat. Bud was waiting outside in the corridor. He stopped his pacing and gazed expectantly at me.

"You're back on. He wants you to tail Walter Costin and find out if he's hiding anything." I lowered my voice and told him about Shaggy's possible involvement. "He wants you to do a background check on Shag and see if anything crops up."

"Oh, man, this is bad. Shaggy's gonna be pissed at me."

"He's already pissed. Don't worry, you won't find anything. Shag'll check out clean. Listen, I gotta go to Miami and check out Hilde's ex-boyfriend." I glanced around, waited for a female clerk to pass by, then lowered my tone. "You can do this without losing your cool, right?"

"Yeah. I'm good. It just took me some time to accept all this is happenin'. Man, it seems so unreal."

"Okay, that's what I told Charlie. Well, keep me posted on what's going down with Costin. It shouldn't take me more than a couple of days at South Beach."

"Hey, by the way, Bri said we could search Hilde's beach house down there, if we think it might help. They used to live in it together, but Hilde stayed there alone after Bri moved up here. Both their names are on the deed, and she told me where to find the key. I can give you directions to the place. It's thirty, forty minutes up the coast from Miami. Maybe you'll get lucky and turn up a lead there."

"Yeah, maybe. How long's Hilde been living down there on her own?"

"Ever since she left that Vasquez guy. Bri says their place is kinda remote. She wants to make sure everything's all right down there. Maybe this'll ease her mind some."

"Sure. Tell me how you get there."

I listened to the directions, which turned out to be fairly simple and easy to remember, as was the location of the extra key. Behind the glass light fixture on the front porch. Not exactly security conscious, but easy for me to find.

"Bud, you sure it's okay with Bri for me to check out the place and see if I can turn up something?"

Bud nodded and said he was going to track down Walter Costin and see where that led. He was smiling, happy to be back on the job, and I was smiling as I finished up a couple of reports languishing on my desk. With Bri being the sole owner now and giving me permission, I could enter Hilde's residence legally and without the Miami PD tagging along for the ride. Yeah, that way I could take my own sweet time tossing the place for clues about what kind of ugly stuff Hilde had been into in the days and months before her death. Because, so far, dead ends were leading to dead ends.

Fifteen minutes later, I left my desktop in a relative clean state, for me, walked outside, got into my Explorer, and punched in Black's private cell number. He picked up on chirp two.

"It's a go on South Beach. How soon can you get away?"

"The plane's due in any time from JFK. Jude took it home for some kind of modeling commitment, but she's coming back in time for the pageant."

Well, that struck me as the best news I'd had since I'd found Hilde's mutilated mouth. Black had managed to cheer me up, after all. Except for the Jude coming back part. That rather sucked.

"Too bad, so sad. I'm gonna miss that purty little gal like crazy."

"She likes you, Claire. She told me you were very nice."

"Wow, now I'm so thrilled I can barely stand it, 'cause she's so world famous and skinny, and all that."

Black laughed. "I'll try to take your mind off her on the flight."

"Ditto, believe you me."

"I'm looking forward to having you to myself for a couple of hours. All I have to do is check the status of a couple of patients here at the Lodge and I'm good to go. Most of my schedule's cleared for the pageant, anyway. This is as good a time as any to check out that South Beach property I've got my eye on. I've got a couple of friends in the area, too."

"I can't be gone longer than a few days. Anyway, I gotta get back and do my income taxes before the fifteenth."

"Bring everything with you, and I'll send it over to Coffman and Company in Springfield. Bill, the guy running that office, is a genius at taxes. I'm taking all my business to him now, and he's saving me a ton of money."

"Just so I get a big refund check, that's all I care about. I also have that little issue of body tampering at a funeral home to worry about."

"Any progress there?"

"I think the killer played with her while the night security man and his girlfriend were getting it on in the back room. The guy's name is Walter Costin, and he's a weird bird, let me tell you. Strange thing is, though, Costin says Shaggy was there that night, too."

Black remained silent for a few seconds. "Shaggy, your crime scene friend?"

"The very one."

"Why would Shaggy be at a funeral home late at night? Or at all, for that matter?"

"He says he wasn't. Says he barely knows this Walter Costin guy, and definitely was at home sick in bed that whole night."

"My bet's on Shaggy. Why would he lie to you about it?"

"That's my take, too, but something's going on here."

"That might possibly be the understatement of the year."

Black was right on there. I told him I'd meet him at Cedar Bend heliport in one hour. I drove home, packed my duffel with a suitable supply of boot-cut jeans and black T-shirts, and a blue denim shirt baggy enough to hide my shoulder holster. I'd sleep in my T-shirt, but that usually didn't stay on long anyway, not with Black around. I stuck in my toothbrush and a big envelope stuffed with my tax stuff that I was extremely glad to get rid of, then scooped up Jules Verne to be babysat by Black's crack household staff while we were in the land of sunny beaches, and actually made it to Cedar Bend Lodge before the hour was up.

Twenty minutes later, Black and I settled ourselves in the comfortable black leather recliners inside his luxury Lear jet, surrounded by its sumptuous black-and-tan accoutrements and onboard staff. Black was dressed casually for him, in tan

Dockers and an immaculate white monogrammed shirt that showed off his tanned skin and white teeth and hard-packed muscles. He looked good to me, especially when he suggested we retire to his custom black-and-tan bedroom at the rear of the plane as soon as the flight attendant disappeared into the galley. We hadn't seen each other since earlier that morning, after all, so what can you expect?

We did wait for the seat belt light to go off, we were that much in control, then found our way to the aforementioned romantic tryst in a very large bed with his signature black satin sheets, at which time everything else came off, too, in titillating fashion, at that. Our carnal little freight train started the second Black's lips touched my bare flesh and roared through both of us with just as much clack and fury as an Amtrak locomotive flying through a Montana railroad crossing.

All in all, it was quite an adventurous and enjoyable two hours in the air. One thing for sure, it left us naked and entwined, breathless, satisfied, and more than a little dazed by the sheer fury of it all. After a sudsy shower together, we ended up happy and relaxed with matching damp hair and soothed muscles a good twenty-five minutes before set down, our mutual needs sated in a big way, which was always a good thing. Now we could get down to business and catch a few criminals and buy a few hotels.

Sisterly Love

In the aftermath of their daddy's death, the boy persuaded his parents to take in the three poor little homeless orphans. It didn't take a lot of encouragement. His mom and dad already liked the older one a lot, and his mom probably thought that now she had four pretty girls to dress up for pageants and live vicariously through. Stepdaddy's funeral was pretty much deserted. Child Protective Services searched for the children's other blood relatives without much luck. So far, Stepdaddy seemed to be alone in the world, and the social workers had not been able to locate the older one's real father. That was fine with the older one; she hated him, anyway.

The social workers jumped at the chance to place them with such a good family, two doctors for parents, no less, not to mention the wealth and prestige involved. So the decision was made, and the children were all as happy as they could possibly be. The boy's house was big, but the mom put Sissy in the boy's oldest sister's bedroom because she was still working in Europe and rarely came home and gave Bubby his own private room near the master bedroom. The boy insisted that he'd like to move out into the Winnebago, now that he was almost old enough for college. He needed his privacy, he said, with all these girls hanging around the house. So the parents agreed and gave his old room to the older one.

Everything progressed admirably, and none of the children ever mentioned again what had happened that night. Sissy was so grateful to be saved from the awful things her daddy had done to her that she willingly continued to be a slave to all of them, including the twins. Bubby grew shy and withdrawn, but the boy's parents really felt sorry for him and were always hugging and rocking him and trying to make him smile.

The older one loved it at the boy's house. Her new room had a little balcony that he could climb up whenever he wanted, and they made love every night before they went to bed. The boy had found porn sites on the Internet, and he got where he liked to watch them a lot and wanted her to, but she didn't like them much at all. But she loved him to distraction. He had saved her so many times from so many things. And now Sissy was different toward her, subservient and silent, and they could always make her do anything they wanted.

One night the boy said he wanted Sissy to join them in a threesome, but the older one said no, absolutely not, and he got mad and slapped her across the face. Shocked, she ran back to the house and cried in bed, but it wasn't long before he climbed in through the balcony and held her and begged her to forgive him. He said it was all the sex videos that made him think of the three of them together, and he didn't really want to do it, either.

The beauty pageants continued, but now the boy could drive the girls to them when his mother was on call at the clinic. Usually the older one and one of the boy's sisters won their divisions, but Sissy still had some scars that hurt her chances. She was losing now to the twins and one smartalecky girl from the next town, one who always turned up her nose when she saw any of them. So one night when they were gathered around the game board, planning their quests, Sissy said, "I wish that girl Kelly was dead. She always beats me when it's my turn to enter."

The boy stared at her, and the older one didn't like it much when he went up behind Sissy and rubbed her shoulders. Sissy leaned into him and closed her eyes like she really liked it.

The boy said, "Well, we can kill her, if you want."

Everybody froze and stared at him, but he didn't laugh like he did sometimes when he teased them.

"What're you starin' at? We did it before, didn't we? And nobody was the wiser. Why would we get caught this time?"

"We can't just kill her," the older one said cautiously.

"We can kill anybody we want to. We've already proven we can. We just have to stick together. Be a team. Anyway, Sissy hasn't won anything in a long time, and it makes her sad. She's part of our family, plays the game with us now, and we owe her a little consideration. Right, Sissy?"

"Right," said Sissy. She smiled up at him, adoration in her eyes.

"Then we'll get rid of Kelly, just for you. I'll design the best quest for us ever, one that won't fail. Something quick and easy that'll take her out of the picture."

"I don't want to," said the older one. "It's not right. It's too risky. It's a terrible idea."

The boy frowned at her, and something in the way he looked at her made her shiver a little bit. Lately, he was acting strangely, going off by himself and not telling her where he'd been. It alarmed her and made her feel like something terrible was going to happen, but she loved him so much. They all loved him so much.

"Okay, but just remember this. I've gotta tape now that'll

put all of you behind bars or in the electric chair. All I got to do is show it to the cops."

The older one looked down, but she was scared now, of what they were planning to do and of the boy, too. He had changed. He even looked different, and he took pictures of everything. He liked to take pictures of them with their clothes off and videos of him making love to her. She was growing more and more afraid of him, but then he would whisper in her ear and touch her so gently and she would melt and cling to him.

The boy planned the quest for a weeknight. He had found out that the girl had ballet practice at the high school on Tuesdays at seven P.M. and that she always walked home to her house just down the street. So on that night, he gathered all the kids together in his car, had them put on gloves, and drove down to the nearest Wal-Mart store. He had watched the store employees for a whole week and knew which employees came in at seven and worked all night. He parked a good distance away and walked around to the car he'd chosen in the back lot. Nobody was around so he got inside and quickly hot-wired the ignition. When he drove back around to the front and stopped beside his own car, the others scrambled inside and they took off, laughing and slapping high fives.

Then they lay in wait, just up the street from the girl's house. It was pretty much deserted there, but it was a good part of town with lots of expensive homes that sat far back off the street among trees. The boy's family lived just two streets over. When the pretty girl walked up to the intersection, he pulled out from the curb and headed toward her. She kept walking, her back to the car, and when he was almost to her, he floored the accelerator and drove straight into her. The car hit the girl with an awful thump, and she flew into the air and came down on the other side of the street. The older one looked back, but the girl lay where she had fallen and did not move.

"You killed her! Oh, my God, she's dead."

"No, she isn't. But even if she is, so what? She was a whore. She didn't deserve to live."

Sissy and his little sisters were clapping, and Bubby looked up at the older one and began to make a low moaning sound deep inside his throat. The boy drove to the corner up from their house and braked the car, "Okay, get out and stop that kid's crying, or Mom and Dad will suspect something. Hurry up, I've got to ditch the car, then go into Wal-Mart so I'll have an alibi on their security cameras! Hurry up, get out! And keep your mouths shut about this!"

As the other children ran down the sidewalk toward home, the older one stood on the street corner and watched the boy drive away. He was out of control. She had to think of a way to talk him out of evil quests, or they were all going to go to hell.

Thirteen

A limousine was waiting at the Miami International Airport, but, of course, it was, long and white and luxurious, pretentious, even. Did I ever mention that Black liked to travel in style? We left the muggy, humid heat of the tarmac and climbed inside air-conditioned, comfortable plushness. As Black answered his cell and spoke in rapid French to someone at his Paris clinic, I realized that I was getting used to his megabucks lifestyle. Me, who loves McDonald's cuisine and Kmart togs. Actually, I still do prefer them, but I'll eat and drink Black's four-star entrees now and again, if necessary. He does the same for me with Big Macs and fries.

The hotel Black was interested in was called the Hotel Imperial. It appeared he was drawn like a moth to names implying wealth and prestige and hoity-toity. It was a twenty-story high-rise, art deco, and exclusive to the max, but of course, again. He must have called ahead with the hint of a multimillion-dollar offer to buy because we were met at the end of the red carpet like the maharajah of Marrakech and his tagalong detective friend. I was surprised when the two suntanned young executives who met us didn't kowtow and back their way into the mirrored, chrome elevators. I made a point not to notice the groveling. But believe me, somebody in this hotel's boardroom really, and I mean, *really*, wanted Black to sign on that dotted line.

We were given the penthouse, of course, the Presidential Suite, in fact. Surprise, surprise. A regular George and Laura we were. With chocolate-dipped strawberries and a chilled bottle of Dom Perignon and a giant fruit basket, vegetable tray, and several dozen urns of red roses, but no cheeseburgers. And even a huge silver tray with Black's favorites, Oreos and chocolate chip cookies. Maybe there are harem slaves with bare midriffs and sponges waiting in the bathroom to bathe us, who knows?

"I think they want to impress you, Black, maybe even want you to buy this place."

"So far, so good. We'll see." Mr. Arrogance and throw them a few crumbs if they slither on their bellies and beg.

I said, "Wanna go shake down a creep with me?"

Black said, "I thought you'd never ask."

"Good, but first let's scope out Hilde's place. Bud gave me directions on how to get there."

Earlier while in the circling pattern, I had notified Miami PD by phone that I'd be hitting town and would be by later to pick up their help in interviewing one of their residents. I made sure my permit to carry concealed as an out-of-state law enforcement officer was kosher with them as well as the airport officials. Once I got the A-OK on that front, I made sure both guns were loaded, the Glock hidden under my baggy shirt, the .38 on my ankle, extra clips snug in my pockets.

Yes, ma'am, I felt pretty damn secure as we walked out the front doors of the burgundy-and-navy hotel lobby and into the blazing afternoon sunshine. I'm getting pretty paranoid about being attacked by bad guys, you see. Imagine that.

The beach stretched out just across the street from the front of the hotel, tan and sandy and warm and oh, man, did I ever want to lie down on it and soak up some rays. The day was perfect, the air balmy, the sun bright, the temperature a lovely 79 degrees. Paradise, uh-huh, you got that right. Too bad I was more intent on getting on the nerves of one Carlos Vasquez.

The same white stretch limousine was waiting at the curb. I stopped and looked at it a moment then dug in the heels of my orange-and-black Nikes. Black stopped alongside me.

"What?" he said.

I said, "Don't you think that thing's gonna make us look a wee bit conspicuous?"

"Could be."

"How about hailing a cab instead? Or renting some kind of low-key car for a couple of hours?"

"I'm sure they've got a hotel car we could use. I keep complimentary cars for VIPs at my resorts. Let me check."

What'd you know? One wave of his hand and let it be done.

Within minutes a white-vested valet drove up in a Lincoln Continental, black with tan leather interior. Okay, still a mite flashy, and not exactly as ominous a presence as a giant Humvee, but I'll make do. Black's cell rang for the umpteenth time since we'd left Missouri. He checked Caller ID, then said, "I have to take this. Hold on a minute."

Pacing a few steps away, he talked all serious-like in very low tones, so I enjoyed the scenery. The ocean was cobalt blue at the horizon, shaded with lighter bands of turquoise and aquamarine, large waves crashing and foaming against the beach. I loved that sound, always have. I was well acquainted with Miami, as a matter of fact had even lived here once for about six months, in one of the few foster homes I had not loathed and/or run away from.

Black snapped his phone shut and walked back to me. Uh-oh, he was frowning and shaking his head, storms incoming.

"Something's come up that I can't get out of. I'll get another driver and you can take the Lincoln. I'll go in the limo. Meet me back here in what? A couple of hours enough?"

I didn't ask what was up. It didn't matter; he had his life, I had mine. Sometimes the twain met; sometimes it didn't.

"It might take longer than that. How about three hours? And I can drive myself. I know my way around here, and I have directions to Hilde's place."

Black appeared surprised. "You know the Miami area?"

"Yeah, I lived here once upon a time. Doesn't look to me like it's changed much."

"Why didn't you tell me you'd lived down here?"

I shrugged. "I don't know. Why should I?"

"Last time you went out alone, remember what happened? Trouble follows you around like a goddamn shadow."

I started to take offense, but okay, it had happened on and off in the past, mostly on. I reassured him. "All I'm gonna do is poke around in Hilde's stuff, then pick up a couple of things for Brianna, then I'll head back here. Oh, yeah, I forgot, I'm armed to the teeth and a trained officer of the law, too."

"Wait till I get done with business before you go after Vasquez, okay?"

"Sure. I've gotta report in to the Miami PD and get an officer to accompany me, anyway. Relax, Black, do your thing. I can take care of myself."

Black gave me a quick good-bye kiss and an embrace that was pretty damn embarrassing in front of all the fawning hotel employees loitering around, then he walked me around to the driver's door. He is polite that way, despite all the big bucks. "See you later, Claire. Call me if you need me. And duck and weave, for God's sake."

"Right. You, too. Never know what might go down in serious hotel negotiations."

Black smiled and strode off toward the white limousine awaiting his pleasure underneath the hotel's canopy. I turned the key and listened to the engine kick over and purr like it knew how awesome it was. Not exactly the same tune my Explorer played, but I was particularly pleased about the dark tinted windows. I had left my sunshades on the plane and was already getting a glare headache from sun, sand, and water.

Hilde and Brianna's joint beach house was indeed located north of Miami proper, well away from South Beach and most other tourist traps, up around the city of Hollywood, as a matter of fact. I knew the general area pretty well, so I drove the scenic route north on Highway One where it edged the sparkling azure sea. It was cool and quiet inside the car and brilliantly beautiful outside, and nothing against Black, but it felt good to be alone with my thoughts for a while. I needed to think about the case and figure out the whos and whys and whats, so I spent the thirty-minute drive wrestling down a bunch of ugly demons roiling around inside my mind. Unfortunately, at the moment they had me pinned in a half nelson.

As it turned out, the place that Hilde and Brianna Swensen owned was indeed a sweet little slice of paradise. If Brianna decided to sell it, I tell you one thing, I sure wouldn't mind putting in a bid. I was pretty attached to my very private little A-frame house on the lake with all its peace and quiet, but this place just might give it a run for its money. The beach house sat just off the coastal highway, at one end of a wide and sweeping sheltered cove with a string of about seven or eight other private residences dotted fairly far apart along its curve. Sea grass and some low dunes separated the houses from the sea, many of which had boardwalks down to the water. Not top of the line in south Florida beach real estate, but not exactly sharecropper shack city, either. Hilde and Brianna had walked a fair amount of runways to afford this getaway, I can tell you.

There was a covered carport around back and some kind of big storage shed, but no garage, so I pulled underneath it and climbed out of the Lincoln. I left the car cooling in the shade and trudged through deep sand around to the front door, which faced the ocean. The sand was so warm, in fact, that it made me want to strip off my socks and Nikes and go barefoot. I resisted the urge. Business first, but later was a different story.

The structure was not too large and covered with planked siding stained a pale melon color. The shutters were painted white and not battened down. Windows were the old-fashioned louvered kind, circa Florida in the 1950s. It was an older place, recently updated by the looks of it. There was a wood deck on the front, but no furniture. Hilde probably stored it inside the shed when she was away. And she had definitely gone away this time.

I turned around and gazed up and down the beach at the other homes. There didn't seem to be anybody out enjoying the weather, and I found that hard to understand. I wondered who the neighbors were, though, and if the Swensen sisters knew them well, and if any of them were insane stalkers. I turned back to the water and stared at the incoming waves for a couple of minutes, allowing the sea breezes to ruffle my hair around and listening to the stiff palm fronds rustling above my head. I liked that sound, too, I liked the smell of the sea, I liked the heat on my face. Man, do I ever like Florida, and everything about it. Maybe I would move down here someday.

Truth was I'd buy this place for myself if I had a bank account like Black's, but he already had some beach properties here and there around the world, so probably wouldn't be interested in this little insignificant place. He'd probably buy it for me, if I asked him to, but I wouldn't and never wanted to be that beholden to anybody, anyway—tempting though it was.

It was a quiet stretch of beach, tranquil, just the way I liked it. No wonder poor Hilde hadn't wanted to move to Missouri with her sister. It was a wonder that Brianna had given up and left this slice of Eden. I felt behind the front porch light as instructed until my fingertips hit the key. I slid it in the lock and opened the door.

Inside, the house looked fairly neat, but very lived in and enjoyed, too. More so than did Brianna's spotless abode in Roach, Missouri. I'd guessed right about the fifties thing, judging by the roll-out handles on the louvered windows alone. I liked older beach houses better than the fancy new ones with all their plate-glass windows and multilevel decks. The old-timers had more character, I guess. Seemed more permanent, too.

The living room wasn't particularly big, but comfy enough, longer than it was wide, with a couple of matching turquoise-and-yellow floral couches and white tables with four white lamps and whitewashed walls, pretty typical Florida decor. The kitchen adjoined; white, too, with white countertops and black-and-white geometric tiled floor. Very clean and orderly. All the appliances were new and shiny stainless steel.

I didn't touch anything—habit, I guess. But this wasn't a crime scene and I had permission to be here. It seemed like I was trespassing, anyway. I moved down a short hall and passed a small bedroom being used as an office and then walked into a larger one that stretched the back width of the house. It looked as if two bedrooms might've been made into one with an added-on adjoining master bathroom. The drapes closed off the windows, and it smelled and felt stuffy, but the bed was neatly made. There were lots of photographs and envelopes strewn out over the burnt orange, blue, and sage striped bedspread. I bent and picked one up by the corner. It looked like a picture of Brianna and Hilde together, circa ages four and six, maybe. They were cute then, too.

I glanced around and felt unable to breathe in the close, warm air. The scent of Hilde's perfume lingered, barely perceptible, Fendi, I think. Then I remembered how it wafted up out of the shower curtain when Bud and I found her body and got a little sick nibble inside my gut. Deciding what I needed was some more of that sea-fresh air, I moved to the window and jerked back the white drapes.

The man came barreling out of them at me so swiftly and unexpectedly that I couldn't react fast enough. He charged head down into my shoulder and knocked me back onto the bed. I bounced back up fighting and sent the heel of my hand into his temple while I scratched frantically inside my shirt for my weapon. He hit me back, a hard punch to my left cheekbone, but not enough to stun me and not before I had my Glock out and jabbing hard against his groin.

"Don't move. You hear me, don't you move a muscle."

He must've valued his private parts because he froze. I got up, panting, a little dizzy from the blow but not enough to let down my guard. I recognized him now, even with that scared-as-hell expression on his face. Carlos Vasquez himself. Looked like I didn't have to go looking for him, after all.

"Down on the floor, Vasquez. On your belly." Unfortunately, I didn't have my handcuffs with me. Great.

He got down on his knees, back to me, then twisted around to look up at me. When he spoke, I detected a mild Hispanic accent. "Who the hell are you? You're trespassing."

"Wrong. I'm here with permission from the owner, and you're in deep shit because I'm turning you in to the Miami PD for breaking and entering, not to mention trespassing. You happen to know their number?"

"Wait, no, listen, please, don't do that. You don't understand. Please, wait just a second. I'm just out here to find out where Hilde is. She's supposed to be home by now, but hasn't shown up and I can't get ahold of her anywhere. I've been calling this condo up in Missouri where she's supposed to be staying, but can't get an answer. I called the hotel where they're having the pageant and tried to get ahold of her sister, but nobody's telling me anything. I'm worried out of my mind about her."

"Okay, just shut up a minute, and we'll sort this out. Get up. Slowly."

He struggled to his feet, then suddenly dodged right and knocked up my gun arm. A shot went off, the slug hit the ceiling, and then he was out of there, darting down the hall and out through the open front door. I gave chase up the beach, firing a warning shot in the air, which he didn't heed. I cursed and sprinted after him and was gaining ground when I heard heavy footfalls thudding on the packed sand behind me. I tried to turn, saw a huge black guy with long Jamaican dreadlocks, but before I could level my weapon on him, he tackled me around the waist. We went down hard together, him on top of me, and I wheezed for breath as the air was knocked out of my lungs. A second later I had my gun pressing into his cheekbone. Problem was, his .45 was pressed against my right breast. We stared into each other's eyes, then said together, "Police officer. Drop the gun."

The same breathless growl, almost in tandem, too. Quite a team we were already. His face looked almost as surprised as mine did, I'm sure.

"You first," I suggested politely.

"Don't think so. Ladies, first," he insisted. He spoke with some kind of accent, too, Jamaican maybe, had said *don't tink so* in a singsongy way, like in calypso ballads. He had on a black linen shirt with bloodred orchids all over it, like the kind steel drum band members wear, and the scowl on his face was the same color as the orchids.

"Take your left hand and slowly show me your badge, and maybe you could get the hell off me, too," I suggested, not quite so politely this time.

The guy kept me pinned in the sand with his chest while he pulled his badge case from the back pocket of his jeans and flipped it open right in front of my eyes. His gun didn't waver and neither did the intensity in his caramel-tan eyes.

"Okay, put the gun down, now," he said.

He pronounced that *de gun*, but since I was definitely at a disadvantage here, I put de gun down in the sand and felt for the badge hanging around my neck. I pulled it out of my T-shirt, and said, "Okay, I believe you. Here's mine." I held it up for him to see. He didn't sheath his gun and barely took a glance at the badge. Instead, he tossed my weapon a few feet away into the sand and kept his gun aligned with my head.

"Turn over, lady. I'm cuffin' you, then I'm takin' you in."

"I guess you didn't notice this badge I'm holding in front of your eyes?"

"Every pawnshop in Florida carries fake badges. Hit men make them look real au'tentic, too, just like yours."

"Hit men? Is that what you think?" I laughed, and yes, it was hale, hearty, and highly contemptuous. "Oh, that's brilliant, Officer. And thanks a lot, you just let my murder suspect get away. Job well done."

"Shut up and turn over. Put your hands behind your back, mon, and don't try anything stupid."

"Sorry, *mon*, but you've cornered the market on stupid, all by yourself. I can prove I'm a detective, down here from Missouri on a murder investigation. Check downtown, if you don't believe me."

"Oh, yeah? Long way from home, huh? Funny thing, nobody downtown told me you was droppin' by to visit. Sorry, you're just shit outta luck wit' that lame a story."

"Believe it, you asshole. And get the hell off me."

He moved slightly off me, until I could breathe again, then he said. "Turn over or I'll do it for you."

"Don't be stupid, I'm a cop." Yes, I am now repeating myself because I have run out of words any more descriptive than stupid. I started to turn over, mainly because of the weapon jammed into my face and the fact I wasn't in a position to get a good knee into his groin, but Jamaican Americans were impatient, I guess. He grabbed the front of my shirt and roughly jerked me up, then flipped me facedown. I groaned when his knee dug into my back and ground me roughly into the sand while he snapped cuffs on my wrists. So much for professional courtesy.

He jerked me up and onto my back again, frisked me, quickly and efficiently and in an ungentlemanly fashion, at which time he came across the .38 strapped to my ankle.

"Guess you have a coupla hand grenades in your bra, too," he muttered, tossing the second weapon toward the first. Satisfied that I was truly disarmed at last, he got to his feet slowly and glared down at me. I expected him to plant a hobnailed boot on my stomach and pose for pictures like some kind of safari hunter over a dead rhino, except that he had on size-nineteen leather sandals. He'd probably ride me around on the hood of his car, too, with a *hey-look-what-I-got-me-everybody-a-trussed-up-detective* sign. Instead, he stared down at me in unfriendly fashion, while he sheathed his weapon in a holster hidden underneath his loose, and yes, garish, tropical print shirt. He retrieved my two weapons and thrust them into the waistband of his black jeans. "Looks like Vasquez got in a few punches before he took off runnin'."

"We exchanged fists, yes."

I was truly hacked off, yes sir, I was. I knew because I was trying to talk while my teeth were clenched tighter than a oyster shell protecting its pearl. I inquired, "Where the hell did you come from? You're making one big mistake letting that guy get away."

"Yeah, sure, you can tell me all about it on the way downtown."

So he was a wise ass, too. I probably would've loved him any other time. Jeez, the guy had to be at least six-nine and two hundred fifty pounds, and he jerked me up like a rag doll and dragged me along, one fist caught in the back of my shirt like I was some recalcitrant kid held by the scruff of his neck all the way to detention hall. Humiliated and still spitting sand out of my teeth, I got my feet going in the deep sand and trudged beside him, up a grassy dune, then down the other side, where a red Jeep Cherokee was waiting. It sure as hell didn't have any police markings. I said, "Want to tell me why you're out here watching Vasquez on the sly?"

"Nope."

The giant idiot opened the passenger's door, thrust me inside, then rounded the front and got in the other side. He was so big and broad, his shoulders barely fit into the seat. He was built a lot like an NBA player, Shaq's younger brother, maybe. The Heat should've recruited him, believe you me. But he looked more like a larger, more ripped Denzel Washington, which I and most other women would agree wasn't exactly a bad thing. He turned the key and fired up the ignition, then glanced sidelong at me. His lilting singsong just sounded pissed now.

"You jus' screwed up an important surveillance, lady, and my boss ain't gonna like it one bit."

"Back at you, big time, mon."

He suddenly smiled and showed me some very big white teeth. "You think you're a tough little lady, don't you?"

Oh, God, please, not a macho man, that would be the last straw. "Yeah, I'm tough. That's why I carry all these weapons. A little lady I'm not."

"I'll give you that."

"Thanks."

"Your face is bleedin'."

"Thanks again, for your concern. Not to mention the big bruise on my back in the shape of your bony kneecap."

He grunted and started the engine, and then the ride downtown was pretty much along horrendously uncomfortable lines. I sat hunched in the seat, my arms bound behind me, my hands aching in too-tight cuffs, my previously wounded shoulder screaming, and blood oozing out of a cut on my left cheekbone. He didn't even put the seat belt on me. Needless to say, there wasn't much sociable chitchat going on. About three minutes into the drive, he switched on a blaring station straight out of the Bahamas, if I was any judge. Unfortunately he sang along with the calypso music like he was Harry Belafonte on a banana boat but without the mellow voice. I sat livid, listening to a helluva lot of off-key day-os, imagining ways to kill the Goliath Mon and counting all the horrible things I was going to do to this creep the minute he took off the cuffs.

Sisterly Love

Kelly, their hit-and-run victim and Sissy's competitor, did not die, but her spine was injured so badly that she had to use a wheelchair. The older one was sick about it, but Sissy was ecstatic because the boy said he wouldn't let his sisters enter so Sissy could win the next pageant. The boy's dad had decided to do some plastic surgery on Sissy's scars, some kind of new technique done with a laser beam. Soon the scars were invisible, and Sissy was beautiful again and she did win! But the older one felt sad, and she didn't like the way the boy was treating the others. He was calling them his slaves and minions now and telling them daily they'd do whatever he wanted or he'd show the murder video to the police.

Once, the older one searched and tried to find the incriminating tapes so she could burn them, but he'd hidden them too well. Every time she got angry and stood up to him, he would sweet-talk her and reach up under her blouse and then kiss her breasts until she could not think clearly. She loved him so much, and she couldn't stop, no matter how hard she tried.

Life went on in the boy's house for a long time. They all

were growing up and getting big, but the boy's quests continued and so did his threats. But then a catastrophe happened, one that no one had expected. The woman from the Child Protective Services showed up at the front door one morning and said that she'd found the older one's real father. That he lived in Florida and that he wanted custody of his daughter. The older one could only stare in disbelief, and the boy's parents said no and that they wanted to adopt her, adopt all three of the kids, but the social worker shook her head and said that was wonderful for Sissy and Bubby, but now impossible for the older one. She said that she was taking the older one in the morning and that she needed to pack what she wanted to carry on the plane and that the rest could be mailed.

That night the older one lay in the boy's arms and wept hard against his chest.

"But he hates me. Momma said he hates me and didn't ever want to see me again. I don't want to go."

"Ssh, sweetie, it's okay. I'll kill him and then you can come back to live with us."

The older one shook her head against his chest, but realized that maybe that was the only thing to do, after all. She didn't like the killing quests, but this was different. He was taking her away from the boy and all the people she loved. She was even fond of Sissy now, too.

They talked through the night, and the boy told her that he would tell his parents he'd changed his mind about Vanderbilt University and wanted to go to school in Miami. They had a beach house down there, anyway, he told her, one his grandparents had owned and he could live in it and so could she, after he'd killed her father and she was in college. It sounded good, but she cried when the boy's mom and dad hugged her good-bye and told her they'd come visit her often with the other children.

The social worker took her on a plane to Miami International, and the older one was terrified to meet her real dad. She had only seen a picture of him, that was all, but her Momma had told her terrible tales of his awful temper and drunken rages. She felt her hands shaking and her stomach quivering when she and the social worker left the plane tunnel and walked onto the concourse. Then she saw him. He looked a lot like she did, and he was standing with a blond-haired woman and little boy around eight years old. The little boy held a sign that read, WELCOME HOME. WE LOVE YOU. There was a rainbow and lots of smiley faces painted on it.

The man came forward and looked down at her. He smiled and said, "I've waited so many years for this moment. I'm so glad you're here."

The older one only stared at him, not sure what to say or what to think. "Thank you, I guess."

The man laughed, and then he introduced his wife and son. The social worker sat down and spoke to them a long time about the procedures, but she had to catch a flight back in one hour so she bid the older one good-bye. "You're going to be fine. I know you're probably scared to death, but we've checked them out completely and they'll both be good to you. But here's my card and cell phone number if you should ever need help or just want to talk. Are you going to be all right?"

"I guess so."

The girl took the card and listened as her father told her about where they lived and how she would have her own room. They all got into his Mercedes and drove to his house up the coast. She felt strange, as if she were in some kind of weird dream, but she wasn't afraid. She just didn't know what to do or say or how to act, and she missed the boy dreadfully.

They ate outside on a screened-in back patio they called a Florida room, which also had a swimming pool inside, but not one as big as the boy's was. She sat in a padded deck chair and watched her little half brother put on goggles and dive after dimes and nickels her daddy threw into the water. She smiled, but still felt overwhelmed and like crying, because she didn't know these people at all and she was going to have to live with them.

After a while the mother took the little boy to bed, and the older one sat in the chair and looked out over the long, grassy backyard. Her father came outside later and sat down in the chair beside her. He was very polite.

"Do you mind if I sit here with you?"

She shook her head. He brought her an ice-cold can of Pepsi, but he had a mixed drink in his hand, and she wondered if he would sit for hours and get dead drunk like her stepdaddy used to. But he only drank about half of it and then placed it on the table between them.

"I want you to know that I searched for you. For years I looked everywhere, but your mother took you so far away that I couldn't find you."

"Really?"

"Yes. I hired private detectives, everything, but you seemed to just vanish."

"Momma said you remarried and didn't want me."

"She was lying. I was awarded custody by the Florida courts, that's why she ran with you." He was quiet for a couple of minutes, then he said, "I know this is going to be hard on you. They told me you were happy with your foster parents."

"Yes. I love them, and their kids."

"I don't want you to be unhappy, but I need a chance to get to know you. I've missed all the years watching you grow up, and now look at you. You're a young woman now and a very beautiful one."

She looked at him and saw the tears in his eyes. He meant it, she could tell. She was shocked. "I always wondered why you didn't want me."

"I did want you. Please believe that. I can show you report after report from my investigators, but they never could turn up a lead on you. That's why I stayed here instead of going back to Europe. It's a miracle the social worker somehow put two and two together when they searched for your birth certificate. That's how they found my name. I feel like God finally heard my prayers."

The older one stared silently at him and realized his emotion was for real. She believed him, but he was still a stranger and she felt abandoned on some alien planet. "Will you let me call home and talk to my brothers and sisters sometimes?"

"Of course. I'll get you your own personal cell phone and you can call them anytime you want. I know how much you're going to miss them. And I'll take you up there to visit whenever I can."

He smiled, and she smiled back because she truly did believe him. That night he gave her his own cell phone, and she lay in bed and dialed the boy's number. He answered at once and said, "How is it? He hasn't hurt you, has he?"

"No, they're okay so far. I got a really nice room with its own bathroom."

The boy got quiet. "So you already like it there better than here, is that it?"

The older one was startled by his angry tone. "No, of course not. It's just not as bad as I thought it'd be. My daddy says he's always wanted me with him, that my mom was lying about him hating me."

"Don't believe him. He probably just wants to get in your pants like your stepdad."

"I don't think so. He and his wife are both really nice, and I've got another little brother."

"Don't be stupid. You belong here with me, and you know it."

"Yeah, I miss you."

His voice softened. "I miss you, too. That's all I've been thinking about since you left. And you should've seen my mom after you drove off. She bawled for an hour, and so did Bubby. He's taking it harder than anybody."

"I wish I was there in bed with you."

"Me, too. And you will be. I'll see to it."

"When?"

"I haven't figured it all out yet. I already told Dad I thought I'd go to college in Florida, so I could see you now and then, and he said that was okay with him. He said I could live in the beach house, too. See, that's just a few months away, and I'll be down there with you and we can be together again."

One day when the older one was particularly unhappy and missing the boy and his family, she walked down to the end of the backyard where there was a little goldfish pond. She sat there in a swing under an flower-covered arbor and wept into her palms. She had not started school yet, so she hadn't met anybody her own age, and although her daddy and his wife were very nice to her, she was lonely. Sometimes she couldn't get the boy on the phone when she called, and she was afraid he had forgotten all about her.

"I hate seeing you so unhappy," her father said from nearby.

Alarmed, she looked up at him, and he came and sat down beside her. "Is it that you're missing your other family?"

The older one nodded, unable to speak but was stunned by what he said next.

"I've been thinking about this and I've talked to my wife, and we realize it wasn't fair to drag you down here the way we did. I was just so anxious to have you back, sweetheart, and I'd looked for you so long. I was really afraid something would go wrong and I'd lose you again."

"I know. It's not you. You've been very good to me. It's just that, I'm, I guess, just sort of depressed. You know what I mean?"

"Yeah, I do." He glanced up at the house. "Like I said, I've been thinking about all this, and I thought, well, I thought I'd take you back there to visit, if you want. Just the two of us, we'll get a plane up there this weekend. We can make it a surprise, if you think that's a good idea. But I want you to come back here with me after you visit them. Will you do that?"

The older one smiled and for the first time, really, truly wanted to hug him. She did so, and she could hear how he let out a pleased breath. "Yes, I'll come back. Thank you, thank you. And I do want to surprise them. They'll like that."

"Okay, we'll go tomorrow, as soon as I can book a flight."

The plane trip seemed interminable, but she and her real father talked all the way and she told him about what it had been like with her mother and how she had been treated and tears had come into her daddy's eyes. He told her how sorry he was that he hadn't been able to find her, that she'd had to suffer and that she'd never, ever have to suffer like that in the future. Then they had hugged and he had kissed her forehead and she believed that he really did mean all of it.

They rented a white Toyota Camry at the airport and the closer they got to the boy's house, the more excited she became. When they arrived early that morning, she ran to the front door, and when the boy's mother greeted her with surprise and pleasure and hugged her warmly, she cried again and asked where the boy was.

"He's still asleep out in the Winnebago, but he'll be so excited. Let me call him."

"No, no, I want to surprise him."

"He's missed you so much these past few months. Hurry, he'll be so happy to see you."

The older one left her real daddy drinking coffee at the kitchen table with the boy's mother and ran down the backyard. The door to the camper was locked, but she still had her key, and she knew the boy would probably still be in bed this early on a Saturday morning. She sneaked inside, smiling, and headed for the back bedroom where he always slept. She threw open the door and cried, "Surprise!"

The boy sat up with a start, and she laughed happily, but then she saw that he wasn't alone, that Sissy was in bed with him. Both were naked, and the boy's face was so guilty, so shocked to see her that he only stared speechlessly at her.

"Wait, please," he cried, jumping out of the bed and grabbing his jeans. "You don't understand, let me explain."

The older one was so stunned herself that she just stood there, staring stupidly at them. Sissy held the sheets up over her breasts and looked scared. Somehow, the older one got out, "Go ahead then, explain."

"I just missed you so, that's all. And Sissy looks like you, and she said she wanted to, and I didn't think you'd mind . . ."

The older one had heard enough, and she ran out of the camper and up the backyard to where her daddy was chatting in the kitchen. She told him she wanted to leave, that she never wanted to come back again, and he looked relieved and said that was good, that he was glad she felt that way, and then they got into the car and went back to Florida. She cried the whole way, and her real daddy patted her hand and handed her tissues until she was finally exhausted and fell asleep on the plane.

Fourteen

Downtown, Calypso Mon led me through a crowded precinct station right out of *Miami Vice* reruns sans pastel T-shirts under white linen blazers with rolled-up sleeves, pushed me into an interrogation room, and handcuffed me to a hook welded onto a steel table. He took my badge and weapons and self-respect and left me sitting there alone to stew, which I did with a great deal of enthusiasm and internal nastiness and low-throated growling.

Almost an hour later, the giant jerk was back with his sheepish yet toothy Denzel smile.

"Okay, your story checked out. Your sheriff wants to talk to you. I warn you, he ain't so happy."

I rubbed my sore wrists as he unhooked me. "Me, either. Where's the damn phone?"

"Right this way."

He preceded me down the hall and through a large, spacious detective squad room. I looked around for all those built female forensic techs dressed like hookers with flowing blond hair and plunging necklines like on *CSI Miami*, but only saw a bunch of regular looking detectives having a good time staring mocking holes through me. They were smiling behind their hands, too, but I didn't get any verbal jeers or heckles. The phone was sitting on a desk beside some tinted windows that looked out over a wide, sunny street with lots of people in shorts and tank tops and sunglasses strolling around.

"Yeah, Sheriff?"

"What the hell do you think you're doing down there?"

I lowered my voice. "I was checking out Hilde's house when I was attacked by her ex-boyfriend, who was hiding inside. Vasquez took off, and when I gave chase, this asshole Miami police detective the size of Mount Everest tackled me and let the suspect get away."

No answer. Momentary silence. "They told me you got hurt. How bad is it?"

"Just a little bump on the head and a couple of cuts and bruises, sir. But you should see the size of this Miami PD guy, Sheriff."

"Get it doctored and get back to work. Now that they know you're legit, they said they'd fill you in and assist you in your investigation. Why the fuck didn't you check in with them like I told you to before you went looking for this guy? Dadgumit, you know procedure better than that."

"It didn't happen that way, sir. I called in and said I'd come down here later and pick up an MPD guy before I went to Vasquez's place. How was I supposed to know Vasquez would jump me at Hilde's house?"

"Bullshit, you should've requested an officer to go with you in the first place, but I suspect you wanted to toss Hilde's residence before they could beat you to it. I know one thing, Detective, I'm sick and tired of you and Bud bending rules and making this department look like amateurs. That crap's gonna stop, you got that? I've got enough to deal with now that the press is hounding me to release details on the Swensen woman, and Bud hasn't turned up a damn thing on Costin, either. I want you to get a move on, wrap it up down there, and get the hell back here."

"Yes, sir."

I hung up and turned around, trying to appear as if I had not just gotten a royal reaming out. The detectives were all working diligently now. No smiles. No taunts. I still felt like a fool. I also felt like punching a certain one of them in the steely muscles of his solar plexus, if I could just reach that high.

I watched him saunter over, all smiley and floral. "Guess what, Detective? We're 'posed to sit down together and compare notes, jus' the two of us, too. Fun, fun. First, though, I guess we oughta fix that cut on your face."

"Forget the cut on my face."

"Yeah? And be brought up on assaulting a fellow police officer." He grinned, Detective Friendly, all of a sudden. What was this comedian routine, anyway? The guy think he's Bernie Mac?

I glowered. "Okay, we've thrown each other to the ground and held our big weapons to each other's vital body parts. Now that that's out of the way, maybe we should get down to business."

"Let me clean that cut and it's a deal."

I sighed. Put upon. And I thought Black was bad about stitches and Band-Aids.

"Okay. Where can we talk? Someplace private."

"Follow me."

I followed him, and we walked together in gritty, unrelenting silence down a couple more gray carpeted corridors to a conference room furnished with a long white table surrounded by cushioned sea-green chairs and a couple of comfortable yellow-and-pink plaid couches lining the walls. Florida decor, and everything. I chose the nearest couch and sat down at one end and waited for the giant to fetch the departmental first-aid kit.

"Gee, you're really cool when you want to be," I said. Snide, yes, ma'am.

"Yeah, I am. I'm not so sure about you."

"Oh, no, now you've hurt my feelings and I'm just all torn up inside."

Calypso Denzel dribbled some antiseptic solution on a cotton pad and said, "Maybe we ought to introduce ourselves."

"That'd be polite. Why didn't I think of that when you were kicking my ass on the beach?"

He smiled, unperturbed, which perturbed me. "Detective Lieutenant Mario Ortega, goin' on twenty-two years here at Miami-Dade."

Damn, he outranked me. "Detective Claire Morgan, Canton County Sheriff's Department."

"You were at the LAPD before that, right? Highly decorated there, too, I hear."

"Now that's a lucky guess."

"I checked you out."

I hated to think what else he'd found out. None of it would be good, I can tell you that. "Okay, enough with the *this-is-your-life* crap. I'd like to know why you were skulking behind the sand dunes and thought it necessary to take me down like some kind of Miami Dolphin linebacker."

Mario dabbed a bunch of antiseptic on my open cut and waited for me to scream. It stung like hell, but I locked my lips and took it like a tough little lady. Probably disappointed I had a high threshold of pain, he said, "I was tailin' Vasquez. We were tipped that he's gotta contract hit out on him."

"You telling me that hit man line you used on me was for real?"

Ortega nodded. "It's supposed to go down this week. We got the word off a fairly dependable source, and we don't want it to happen."

"Why am I scared to ask why?"

"Because Vasquez's workin' an undercover sting for us,

and we gotta protect him till it goes down. The hit rumor might mean he's been made. We're tryin' to find out."

Not sure what to think, I watched him assiduously take the paper backings off a Band-Aid with fingers the size of ballpark franks. "Well, Ortega, I really hate to break this to you, but Vasquez is a primary suspect in my murder case. That's why I'm down here, to interview him and check out his alibi."

"You always hold a weapon on your suspect when you interview him?"

"I do if he jumps out from behind the curtains and slugs me in the face. You?"

Long, slow, white grin. "Okay, that's understandable enough. Why'd he jump you?"

"Maybe you should ask him. He's your snitch."

"There's more to it."

"Well, hit me with it."

"Carlos Vasquez is involved wit' the crime family that runs things down here. The Rangos family, ever heard of them?"

"Great. And, no, I haven't heard of them. Why would I?"

"The Rangos thinks Carlos is a street punk, but they got him doin' some money launderin' for them through his place called the Ocean Club."

"He's dirty into drugs, I take it."

Ortega nodded and lounged down in a chair and swiveled it around to face me. "That's how we got him to cooperate."

"What about his girlfriend, Hilde Swensen? She involved in any of this mess?"

"No. He's been tryin' to find her. Said he can't get hold of her and it's drivin' him crazy."

"He can't get hold of her because she's dead. Somebody murdered her, mutilation style. Cut off her lips, then strangled her."

Ortega sat straighter, frowned at me. "Did you say your perp cut off her lips?"

"That's right. Snipped them off with manicure scissors and left her all dolled up in the regalia she'd won in a beauty pageant. You have something similar?"

"A case a few years back had a similar MO."

I perked up considerably. "Same thing with the mouth?"

"Yep."

"When?"

"Two, three years back. Found the body over in the Everglades. Part of the face was bit off."

"Bit off?"

"That's what the medical examiner thought. The gators got him before we did so she didn't have much to work wit'. And guess who it turned out to be. One of Jose Rangos's own nephews. Young guy, not long outta Mexico. Name was Esteban Rangos. They claimed the body, had a private funeral, and didn't cooperate with us, in fact, they didn't seem to care if we found the perpetrator, or not, so it went cold."

"So they could get the guy themselves, I take it?"

"Exactly. And when they find him, whew, watch out. The Rangos don't mess around when they're after blood vengeance. Leave their own little personal calling card."

"I hate to ask."

"They cut off both earlobes and let them bleed down onto the chest, something to do with a Mayan symbol for bloodletting, I think."

"Nice little decorative touch. Kinda like that Sicilian dead fish thing?"

"Yep. Or the Colombian necktie. We see some of that, too, now and again."

"How about a vic named Reesie Verdad? That name ring a bell? A friend of our vic mentioned her."

"Yeah, I remember that one. A real young kid, Cuban, I think, pretty but a cokehead. Perp confessed. Turned out it was drug related. Jealous ex-boyfriend. He's doing life."

"Okay. I can mark her off, but the guy in the swamp sounds like the same perp."

"Wanna take a peek at the Esteban Rangos murder file?"

"You bet I do."

"Okay, let's go."

I took the time to swallow down a couple of the Excedrins he'd shaken out into my palm, then followed him outside and down into the basement where they kept the most recent cold cases. We checked in with the duty officer, then sat down at a table to wait while he meandered down the appropriate row looking for the right cardboard box among the hundreds stacked on metal shelves. I hated cold case storage. Every box meant a victim without justice, and that ate at me. Maybe someday I'd have my own personal crusade against unavenged victims. Nothing I'd like better than to snap handcuffs on some deviant who thought he'd gotten away with murder for years. It'd be like Christmas every day.

The young guy in charge had dark hair and an immaculate uniform. He looked fit and healthy with a natural blush in his cheeks and an apparent penchant for weightlifting. His short sleeves fit tight around some impressive biceps. They couldn't compete with Ortega's, though, but who could, other than Arnold Schwarzenegger in his *Conan the Barbarian* days. He walked back to us, carrying the box we'd requested, and I judged him to be a new recruit, biding his time here in the dusty dungeon until he could join the fun at gruesome murder scenes. It probably wouldn't take him long to wish he was back down here without blood spatter and bloated corpses and blowflies. He said, "Here, you go, Mario. Good luck."

The officer nodded an acknowledgment in my direction, but didn't question my credentials. I guess he trusted Mario's judgment about letting me take a look-see. Ortega lifted the lid off the box and took out everything inside. I picked up the autopsy pictures first, then wished I hadn't.

"Good God."

"Yep. The ME thinks he was mutilated and murdered first, then a gator got him after he got dumped in the swamp."

I spread out the pictures on the table and studied each one, looking for similarities. The man looked like he might have been young, strong, even features, long dark hair, what was left of it. I picked up a close-up of the man's mouth. The same jagged cut marks that I'd seen on Hilde. No finesse, just hacked off indiscriminately. I remembered the blood running down Hilde's throat and into her roses, which meant she'd been alive and suffered horribly when he'd severed her mouth. Chances were this one had suffered the same agony as Hilde had. I wondered if he'd still been alive when the alligator dragged him under.

Another picture showed the entire head. Part had been bitten off, including the left ear and one side of the throat. A full body shot revealed that the right leg was gone below the knee and the left foot was missing. Rough-edged gouges in the torso indicated there might have been more than one alligator tearing at the body. There was lots of decomposition.

"My gut's still telling me it's the same perp."

"Your vic dumped in water?" Ortega asked.

"No. She was decked out in beauty pageant crown and roses. Propped up in the shower stall. He was sending a message to us, or to somebody. He cleaned up the scene with bleach. What does that tell you?" I looked at Ortega.

"That he's gettin' better at it."

"Yeah. Any other cases have this kind of MO?"

"Nope. We got lots of floaters down in the swamp, but none wit' the lip thing. I gotta picture in here somewhere of the vic."

He searched among the reports and pictures until he found the photograph he was looking for. "Here you go."

I looked at Esteban Rangos's likeness. He was dark, handsome, even younger than I first thought. College kid, maybe.

He looked vaguely familiar, but I couldn't place why. "How old was he?"

"Just turned twenty-one. Our undercover guys said the Rangos were looking for the kid's murderer, purportedly had a big reward out for information on who did it and where he could be found. So far as I know, nothing ever came of it. Unless, of course, they found the perp, whacked him quietly, and nobody was ever any the wiser."

"How about letting me have a copy of this?" I held up the photograph.

"No problem. You really think these two are connected?"

"Yeah, maybe. Our victim's from this area, too. That's a bit too much of a coincidence for me to ignore."

"And you think Carlos might be the perp?"

"Never know. Maybe that's the reason for that hit man rumor. That's why I'm here, to check out his whereabouts. Were you on him twenty-four/seven?"

"Most of the week. Caught up and stayed on him since Thursday."

"So he might've been able to get to the lake and do her?"

"Maybe. Want me to check out the passenger lists for flights outta Miami since last week?"

"You know it."

Ortega picked up the photo. "This thing haunted me, and everybody else 'round here. It was strange that somebody had the guts to kill somebody that close to Jose Rangos. That's a death sentence, if there ever was one."

"Maybe you're right. Maybe they did catch up to him, sliced off an earlobe or two, and disposed of the body out in the ocean."

"Yeah, could've happened that way. We kept our ears to the ground, watched the Rangos pretty hard. Hear now and then they're still interested in buying information on the nephew's killer."

"What about motive?"

Ortega shrugged his massive shoulders.

"We think the Hilde Swensen murder might be some kind of revenge thing, going by the note the perp left on the body. Maybe yours is, too."

"What note?"

"A sticky note stuck to the vic's shoulder. Said, 'Smile, and smile, and be a villain.'"

"*Hamlet*," Ortega pointed out without hesitation.

Wow, it'd taken me a couple of seconds to remember which play the quote was from. "That's right. You a Shakespeare buff?"

"Yeah. Mel Gibson said it, right?" Then he laughed. "Just kiddin'. See, fact is, I'm in this amateur theater troupe. I always get cast as Othello."

Actually, I did remember *Othello* from high school literature. And Ortega was one helluva good Othello, even with *dat accent ting*. "I can see that."

"Maybe the perp's connected with theater in some way, actor, maybe? Or an English teacher."

"Could be. Do you mind if I make copies of some of this stuff? Officially. I'll sign for them. I want to read through the murder book and see if I can turn up anything pertinent."

"You got it."

"You're not so bad, Ortega. Unless you're planning to tackle me again any time soon."

"I guess I can refrain from that, if you behave."

We shared our very first grin. Buds for life. Besides that, I wanted him to help me get that copy of Esteban Rangos's file.

"Like me to have Jake over there run a copy for you?"

Oh, ask and you shall receive. "That'd be way cool, Mario."

He laughed. "You got it."

Ortega gathered up the materials and placed them back in the box and headed for Jake's desk. They spoke together a few seconds, then Jake took the box and headed for the back.

I watched Ortega turn when a heavyset, bearded man entered the room, then spend a few minutes whispering with him near the door. I didn't like the whispering much. Whispering usually meant bad news was a comin'. As usual, I was right on.

Ortega sat down across from me, and said, "We gotta problem."

Used to problems, I said nothing, but did know enough to brace myself.

"There's some guy upstairs demandin' to know where you are and what's goin' on. Wants to bail you out if you're charged wit' something."

I frowned. "Who?"

"Name's Black. Know him?"

Oh, that's my honey, always johnny on the spot with his big, huge pocketbook. No wonder I liked him so much. "He's okay. I flew down here with him. How'd he know I was here?"

"You got me, but that's not the bad news."

Crap. "What's the bad news?"

"Your friend, Black, up there? He's got Jose Rangos's personal sleazebag defense attorney with him."

I cringed down into my chair until I probably could've squeezed into a thimble. No wonder Black had jumped to attention when he'd gotten that last phone call at the hotel. I knew he had a few underworld connections in New Orleans, but I sure as hell hadn't heard him mention being chummy with anybody named Rangos.

"He's on the up and up, Ortega. I can vouch for him. He's a psychiatrist that my sheriff calls in sometimes to help with our cases."

Ortega looked at me and then his skeptical expression changed. "Hey, mon, he's not that guy, Nicholas Black, is he?"

Ah, Black and his famous face. I nodded. "You know him?"

"I've heard of him. I watched all the news accounts when that soap opera star got murdered at his resort last year."

Then I watched the truth dawn across his face. He was pretty readable for a homicide detective. "You're not telling me you're the detective who broke that case. Sylvie Somebody, the actress."

"Yep, that's me. I'm super famous now. That's why you recognized me right off for a hit man, cuffed me, and ran me in."

"Hell, I should've recognized you. Your picture's been out there enough, plastered all over the press, even down here. No kidding, that was some grisly shit."

"Yeah." Time to change the subject before he wanted to know some grisly shit details, so I asked, "How about arranging a meeting with me and Vasquez?"

"We can do that, but you gotta give me time to run him down again. I suspect he attacked you and bolted because he thought you'd come wit' orders from the Rangos to kill him."

"Maybe you should give some serious thought to inquiring about the Witness Protection program, Mario."

"As soon as this last sting goes down, that's exactly where he's goin'."

"What about him? He have any assaults on his rap sheet?"

"Nope. He's done lots of petty things, but nothin' as stupid as getting in over his head wit' the Rangos."

"People are telling me he liked to slap his girlfriend around."

"He might've. I haven't heard about it. No domestics on his record that I know of."

"Okay. I'm gonna give you my card. Call my cell as soon as you catch up to Vasquez. I'm not leaving here till I talk to him."

"You got it." He took out his own card and handed it to me. "Keep me informed about your case. And you might wanna tell that friend of yours up there, Black, that he doesn't need to be hangin' with the Rangos's attorney when he's in town. Might end up bein' hazardous to his health."

As if Black was afraid of anything, especially mob types like the ones he grew up with. "I'll surely pass that along. How about giving me back my weapons and badge? I feel naked, not to mention vulnerable. Miami's gotta rep for being dangerous."

Ortega smiled. "You got it."

We rode the elevator back upstairs, and within minutes I was in possession of my weapons again. Ortega stood back and watched me rearm myself. I felt a helluva lot better, too.

"I want to go back out to that beach house and look around. Do I need your department's permission? I have the okay from the owner."

"Want me to tag along to protect you from guys like me?"

I gave him a supercilious look that he could never misinterpret.

"Well, after the chief talked to your sheriff, he said you can search your vic's house on your own, but that you're not to go anywhere near Vasquez, not wit'out me along for the ride."

"Fine. Find him and give me a buzz."

"Pleasure meetin' you, Detective."

"Yeah, I just love the feel of Florida cuffs locked on my wrists."

He smiled and held out his giant paw, Mr. and Mrs. Cooperating Law Enforcement Officers shaking on it. It was like trying to shake hands with a catcher's mitt. His ring size must be 45 and a half.

Outside, in the darkening windows of the lobby, I found Black standing alongside the aforementioned lawyer, who looked like he'd climbed straight out of a Harvard Law School yearbook, tasseled loafers and all, and who apparently bought his dark suits from the same Hong Kong tailor that Black did. They could've been in one of those Doublemint gum commercials, representing the jet-setting, rich, and powerful tycoon kind of twins.

"You okay?" Black said as soon as I reached him. He eyed the bandage on my cheek with overt disapproval.

"I'm fine. Let's get out of here before one of us really does get arrested."

On the way out, Black introduced me to his nifty lawyer friend. Robert Bannington Sr., the best damn defense attorney in south Florida, of course, but I made sure we parted company just outside the front door and so fast that you'd think the guy had the chicken pox. He got into a black Rolls Royce Phantom with a liveried driver, obviously not a guy on assignment from Miami-Dade Legal Assistance. We headed to our own special little white stretch limousine, our getaway driver waiting for us with the motor idling. Oh, my, the high life. We climbed inside, shut the door, rolled up the window between us and the driver, and Black didn't mince words.

"For God's sake, Claire, what the hell happened this time?"

I matched his frown and perturbed tone with equal abandon. "What happened was that Vasquez was hiding in Hilde's house. He jumped me, but got away when an overzealous cop showed up and grabbed me."

"I should've gone out there with you."

"Yeah? Why don't you tell me what was so important that you couldn't?"

Black looked a trifle surprised at my pointed question and threatening frown. Then he metamorphosed into wary as hell. "I don't like your tone."

"Tough. I don't like your friends."

"How do you know where I've been?"

"Maybe because you waltzed into the Miami PD with a well-known, sleazy thug lawyer."

"He's the only attorney I know in Miami, so I gave him a call."

"Why does that make me feel nervous?"

"He represents lots of people in this town, important people. Sounds like you got pretty chummy with the guys who arrested you."

"Oh, yeah, we played footsies under the interrogation table I was handcuffed to, and they put Band-Aids on the wounds they inflicted, and everything. I think I'm in love with them now."

Black looked very slightly miffed by my sarcasm, but remained his usual unruffled shrink self. "Okay, where to, now that all the excitement's over? I take it you want to go back to Hilde's and finish what you started?"

"Oh, yeah, and I've got local permission this time. Want to go along, or do you have some other secret mob friends you're meeting for dinner?"

Over the last months spent in close proximity with me, Black had become quite adept at ignoring me when it suited him. "After what happened to you today? I think I'll tag along, just to bind up your injuries, if nothing else."

"Very funny." See, Black's pretty good with sarcasm himself.

Thirty minutes later, we turned off the ocean highway and on to the Swensen sisters' property. Darkness had swallowed up the view so we couldn't see the ocean, but we could hear the angry roar of the surf. Hilde's place was now as black as a tomb, and I suspected empty of desperate boyfriends, too. I felt better with my weapons back in their beds, and I had a feeling Black had a weapon or two hidden somewhere on his person. He usually did. But he was making me very uneasy with his associations, of late.

We paused at the front door, which still stood ajar from my hasty exit in pursuit of Vasquez hours earlier.

"Okay, Black, you know the drill. It's not a crime scene, except for me being attacked here, and nothing's gonna come of that. We have a legit right to be here, so we can snoop to our hearts' content."

I pushed open the door and hit the light switch just inside. A lamp in the corner came on.

Black stepped inside and said, "This place has been here for a while. Built as far back as the forties or fifties, I bet."

"Probably. You wanna help me search her stuff?"

"Oh, yeah. I was an MP for a while in the army. Did I ever tell you that?"

I was finding out there was a lot about Black I didn't know yet. He was pretty secretive with some of his background stuff, and for good reason, I now knew. I was irritated that he kept turning up close associations with criminal types, but tried not to show it. He couldn't help what family he was born into. "No, funniest thing, you must've forgotten. Was that before or after your Special Ops days?"

"Before. Long before."

"Then you know how to toss a room, I take it."

"Uh-huh. I'm fairly good at it."

"You take the living room and kitchen. I'll take the bedroom and office. Put everything back the way it was. Brianna's probably gonna have to come down here eventually and pack up Hilde's personal effects, and she doesn't need to find the place ransacked."

"Ransacking wasn't my intention."

I left him rifling through a bureau that had Hilde's cordless phone sitting on top. I stopped and waited when he pushed down the blinking red light on the black answering machine. Two seconds later, a man's voice broke the silence.

"Hey, girl, you back from Missouri yet? Call me as soon as you get in and I'll give you the latest scoop." No name, but maybe we could find that on Caller ID.

Two different male voices left similar messages but no names. The fourth call was from her estranged boyfriend, a.k.a. the moron who attacked me. I recognized his slight accent, even though we hadn't conversed much during our fisticuffs.

He sounded like a Latin lover, all right. He fought like one, too. More flight than fight.

Black and I locked eyes as his voice came through on a second call. "Okay, I give in. Please, Hilde. I want you back. Tell me what I have to do. I'll do anything you say, just come back home." There was a pause and Black and I stared at each other some more. "Please, Hil, I'm miserable without you. I'm sorry. I'll straighten up and fly right. Just call and let me come out there. I'll make everything up to you, I swear to God."

While the machine rewound, I clicked backward on the caller ID and wrote down names and numbers. Two of them were listed as unknown, one from a South Beach beauty salon. Carlos Vasquez had called from the Ocean Club, but I doubted he was holed up there at the moment, much too easy to find, especially for experienced hit men. We'd check it out later anyway. Not an official visit, just casually looking around, in case we ever wanted to join a fancy South Beach spa.

I walked to the large bedroom and stood in the doorway. It now looked as if somebody'd had a knock-down drag-out inside. Yes, that would be me. My head still felt like a knock-down drag-out inside, too. I thought of Hilde and how her face looked without her lips and how much I wanted to nab her killer. Dead or alive, didn't matter to me.

I was violating Hilde's privacy again by sifting through her personal belongings, but that secondary invasion of homicide victims was something I was used to. This room was ultrafeminine, more so than the rest of the house. Lots of lace, floral patterns, white wicker, even. I hate wicker, of course, white or any other color. There was an ornate wicker shelving unit, filled to overflowing with framed photographs and beauty pageant trophies and prize cups in every conceivable size and shape, all sitting on shiny mirrored shelves. I stood in front of the treasure trove and examined the pictures. Many were snapshots of Hilde and Brianna. I tried to figure which girl was the most beautiful, but they pretty much came out equal in my book. Every time I looked at Hilde's face, I saw a butchered, bloody mouth, however, so I guess I had to give Brianna the edge. I wondered where the crazy psychopath was and what he was doing. Then I wished I hadn't.

On the bedside table sat a silver frame with Hilde and a man I recognized as Vasquez. He looked better in the photo than he did in person, tanned very dark, virile and handsome in a white evening jacket. Arrogant, even. He was more muscular in person, and I knew for a fact that he didn't mind hitting a woman up the side of the head. I had a notion that he'd slap his own woman around if she didn't please him, too, and say stuff like "Just do it, bitch" and "You're lucky I even look at you." A far cry from the sniveling guy on the telephone or my scaredy-cat runner out on the beach.

In the photograph, he held Hilde on his lap, one fist caught in the back of her long blond hair, holding her head down against his shoulder, and I wondered why Hilde would want such a picture beside her bed. The guy was obviously manhandling her, unless she had been into a little hair pulling and S and M herself when caught in the throes of passion. Could that be it? He'd gotten a little too angry with her? A little too forceful in inflicting pain? That didn't fit the crime scene, though, or the shearing off of the lips.

Black walked into the room behind me and said, "Well, from the looks of things in here, you didn't go down easy when Vasquez came at you."

"I rarely go down easy." I noticed the book he was holding in his hands. "What'd you find?"

"Scrapbooks, about a dozen of them inside her cabinet. This one's the oldest and shows the place where Hilde and Brianna lived when they were little."

Black held up a letter. "And I found this from a law firm in Poplar Bluff. Bloodworth Law Office. They're one of the best firms in the state, bar none. And I happen to know that because they've done some work for me. John Booker's from that area and he put me on to them. The lawyers down there know their stuff."

John Booker was an old Special Ops buddy of Black's and currently Black's own personal private investigator. One time he dug up a whole bunch of ugly stuff on me that I didn't want known, but he ferreted it out anyway. But he was good. "Brianna never mentioned anything to us about living or working in that part of the state. What's the letter say?"

"The letter's gone, but you might want to give them a call and see what they can tell us. Ask for Scott Dale. He's Booker's contact and a helluva lawyer, and he'll help you, if he can."

"Yeah, I will."

We sat on the edge of the bed together, and I thumbed through the scrapbook. It had been put together a long time ago and had lots of newspaper clippings, old and yellowed, the pages crinkled and disintegrating on the outer edges.

"She's had this thing for years."

"It looks like they were in lots of kiddie pageants when they were little. No wonder they're so obsessed with competing."

"Yeah. Way too many, by the looks of it."

I turned some more pages and found a picture of an old house, Cape Cod style with dormer windows. Another faded photograph was a family shot. It looked like Mom, Dad, with three children gathered around. I wondered which one was Brianna. The girls looked amazingly alike when they were children, too. The third child looked like a younger boy. More photographs showed the farm had an old barn and lots of gnarled old trees in the yard. Other pages showed the children fishing off a riverbank with cane poles. Another had them standing in frilly dresses at the center of other exploited pageant toddlers, big, fake smiles plastered across their faces. What a weird life for little girls. JonBenet Ramsay and her fate came to mind.

"I'm going to take some of these books back to Brianna. I've got some questions to ask about her family and maybe these pictures will get her talking."

"You think Hilde's murderer goes back that far with her family?"

"Maybe. Who knows? It doesn't look like either girl grew up under normal circumstances. I'm surprised Brianna's got her head on as straight as she does."

"She probably won't, not after this kind of thing happened to her."

I finished checking out the bedrooms and found that Black did know his way around investigative search techniques. Maybe if I could ever get him to give up his multiple crime lord associations, we could be a team.

We were soon interrupted by Black's chirping red cellular phone, and I had a bad feeling about who it might be. He spoke for a few minutes in cryptic tones, then flipped the phone shut.

"Jose Rangos wants to meet you."

"Oh, no, no, no way. I know who he is, and I'm not going anywhere near him. I'm in enough trouble with the Miami PD."

"I'm afraid you'll have to."

I was not pleased. I showed it in my face. "Oh, really, I have to, you say? Why is that?"

"Because he wants to meet you."

"Too bad, so sad."

"I told him we were together now, and he insists on meeting you."

"Rangos is a crime boss, Black, and well you know it. I'm a police officer. The two don't mix. Especially where I'm concerned."

"He's a good friend to me and my family. Actually, I'm his favorite godson."

"Godson? Oh, please, Black, stop with this mafioso speak. I feel like I'm dating Tony Soprano."

"You know I'm clean. But Jose is determined to meet you. People around here don't say no to Jose."

"I'm not from around here. I say no and I mean no."

Black gave me a long look. "No, Claire, I'm sorry, but you don't say no to him, either. Besides, he's got a gift for you."

"Are you crazy? I can't take anything from him. I don't want anything from him."

"He says you'll want this. Please, Claire, I know this goes against your grain, but do it for me. I don't ask much from you, but this is important. We'll just stay a few minutes, and nobody will ever know we've been there."

Black didn't usually wax this serious, and he'd never before asked a favor from me. Unfortunately, I couldn't say the same. Like flying down here on his Lear jet. I thought of Ortega's warning. I thought of Charlie's warning. I thought of all the warning bells going off in my head. I know better than to agree to something like this, but okay, I am a curious sort. A gift's a gift. What people didn't know wouldn't hurt them, et cetera, et cetera. Rationalizations, all, yes, I know. Black should not have put me in this predicament.

We locked up the house nice and tight, and just before we got into the limo, Black leaned close, voice low, very clandestine and CIA-ish. "And try not to insult the driver. Felipe's one of Jose's personal bodyguards and takes care of people who are problematic to the family business, if you know what I mean."

"No, I don't know what you mean. Why don't you tell me?"

"Just don't insult him, okay?"

We got inside, and Black gave an address to Señor Felipe, he who was not to be insulted. Felipe looked over his shoulder at me, and I tried to memorize his features for future

Florida wanted dead or alive posters. He was middle aged, small and slender, balding on top with a neatly trimmed mustache and goatee and little black foxy eyes that watched people without doing much blinking. Jose's very favorite hit man, no doubt, who'd whack me if I refused to join his master for tacos. He grinned and showed me a couple of rows of sharp, foxlike teeth, so my analogy still held.

We rode in dead silence all the way there, which was fine by me. I was an officer of the law, remember? Visiting crime lords at their homes, not to mention accepting gifts from them, was a no-no, even frowned upon in cop circles. On the other hand, maybe I would find out something helpful to my case, or to Ortega's case. I doubted it, but stranger things had happened.

Fifteen

The Big Kahuna lived in the old and affluent community of Coconut Grove. Hey, why wasn't I surprised? The house was not as elaborate as I had expected, certainly not as much so as Black's godfather brother's estate way down yonder in New Orleans. And it was pastel pink, which I, understandably, felt was hard to stomach.

As we got out of the limo, I glanced around for a flock of flamingos flapping around. Didn't see a single one. Didn't see Sonny Crockett, either. Did see a swarthy looking thug dressed all in black holding a small but effective automatic machine gun. Jeez, Black and his friends, what's a girl to do?

"Well, tell me, Black, is he our welcoming committee? And I sure wish I'd remembered to wear my Kevlar vest."

"He's a welcoming committee, all right, but not ours."

"Okay. Now I feel better. Especially since Ortega gave me back my gun and badge."

"I'm armed, too. Not that we'll need weapons with Jose's men."

"Black, I declare, you're gonna get me in trouble one of these days."

"This gun is registered down here. Perfectly legal."

"Yeah, but who to?"

"To me."

"Oh, God."

"I told you, Jose's my godfather, the real one, who stood at my christening. He likes me to stay here when I visit Miami and provides me with whatever I need. I don't get to see him much, so it's nice I got to come along with you on this trip."

"Yeah? Let's just hope Charlie and my new friends downtown don't hear about who we're hanging out with."

"They won't. Let's go. Jose's waiting."

Inside, the house revealed big cavernous rooms, mostly done in aqua and gold and tan. Very south Florida with rotating ceiling fans with blades shaped like palm fronds, and everything. Air-conditioned, too, which I didn't mind.

Jose Rangos was sitting on a large flagstone terrace near the lighted backyard pool. It was surrounded by a screened-in pavilion and a bunch of flaming torches. He was dressed all in white, loose silk shirt and trousers, belt and deck shoes, big bushy white hair held back in a ponytail, probably impersonating an angel for my benefit. He looked more like Albert Einstein to me. He was smoking a thick cigar, which was not white and sort of ruined the illusion, not to mention the air quality. But there was a nice night breeze that warmed the skin and took the tobacco stench off to the next-door neighbor's house. No ocean in sight.

"So this is your famous detective that I've been hearing so much about."

I gave Black my best *I'll-get-you-for-this-if-it-takes-forever* glare, one that made him avert his eyes apologetically. Then I made nice.

"Nice to meet you, Mr. Rangos." I almost said señor because of all the Mexican decor hanging around, but stopped myself in time.

"And very nice to make your acquaintance, chica."

Chica? Where was I, anyway? Vera Cruz? I smiled as if I were having a good time. After all, he bought me a present. Maybe it was a new gun with the ID number filed off, something I could always use. Especially here and now.

"Nicky said you're down here working a case. Have you had any luck on it?"

I nodded, not about to fill him in on the details. I do draw the line sometimes.

"I think maybe I can help you, but first let me remember my manners. Would you care for a drink? A piña colada, perhaps?"

"I don't drink, but thank you just the same."

"Nicky?"

"Not right now."

"Well, then, sit down, *por favor*. Let us get to know one another."

We sat. He smoked. Nobody said anything. Some getting to know one another.

Rangos blew out a cloud of noxious smoke and studied me as if I was a rare specimen in the law enforcement phylum. "I understand, my dear, you were accosted by one of our people today."

Uh-oh. "What makes you think that, Mr. Rangos?"

He gazed at me, then focused undue attention on my Band-Aid and then threw back his hoary, leonine head and laughed uproariously, which made me a bit skittish, I must say.

"We keep an eye on all things that happen around here. And that bandage on your face and swollen eye verifies my information, no?"

"I don't mean to be rude, but I'm down here on a case and really can't divulge details to anyone." Despite my words to the contrary, I did sound rude, I know, so for Black's sake, I added the following, with a great big smile. "But I do appreciate your concern about my well-being. My headache's almost gone, too."

"I have a nice surprise for you."

Double uh-ohs. I had a couple of visions of my feet sunk into buckets of concrete and the roar of a speedboat heading to mid–Bermuda Triangle. "That's very thoughtful of you."

"I feel responsible about what happened to you today."

"You really shouldn't concern yourself." I glanced at Black for help. He sure had gotten quiet, all of a sudden. He smiled at me and took my hand. I frowned and took it back. I liked him a lot but I wasn't going to play lovers' lane with him to impress his "real" godfather.

"Come, I'll show you."

We all got up and Jose leaned heavily on a white cane with a silver head shaped like a lion, whose mane closely resembled Jose's own coiffure. We walked around the pool and out into a lush flower garden filled with geraniums and impatiens, with spicy scents galore, and Jose gave me a scientific overview of all his elephant ears and bougainvillea plants along the artistically lit pathways. He was a horticulturist in his spare time, he informed me, and I guess that meant when he wasn't offing people. Black appeared incredibly interested in gardening all of a sudden, and I wondered how many other crime lords he knew, up close and personal like. Maybe such associations were contained to southern climes, only tropical crime bosses appealing to him.

We strolled along for about five minutes on winding paths through lush vegetation that smelled good and tinkling fountains, our feet crunching on white shells. Along the way, I couldn't help but notice the seven-foot high stucco wall, pink, of course, with some kind of sharp spikes and coiled barbed wire on top, not to mention the seven Great Danes growling in their chain-link pen. I wondered how many unfortunate people had made this walk and if they were standing up on the bottom of the ocean with their hair waving in the Gulf Stream. Black was still smiling, so I guess we weren't on the hit list, or maybe he was smiling because he wasn't.

After a while I began to wonder if we were going to end up crossing a bridge into Key West territory, but then a stucco guesthouse loomed up from where it was hidden by lots of palm trees and more lush vines and manicured flowery vegetation. The lights inside the house were on, and once we had entered the front door, we were hit with very cool air and a very nice, beautifully decorated little bungalow that I assumed was reserved for Jose's special guests, a.k.a. godsons and their policewoman girlfriends. Maybe he was going to cede it over to me for future Florida investigations.

Jose finally turned to me and said, "I wish Nicky would have done me the honor of staying here at my home. I would have been honored to have you both as my guests."

"Thank you very much," I said. No thank you very much, I thought.

Then we moved down a short hallway that led to a large attached garage. "Inside here is my gift to you. Please accept it with my compliments." Jose beamed as he stood back, leaning on his cane, ever the gentleman, and allowed me to precede him into said garage.

Carlos Vasquez sat in a chair in the middle of the concrete floor. He had a gag in his mouth and blood running down his temple from a deep cut on his scalp and eyes that were bulging out of their sockets in a way that suggested terror. Two heavy hoods with guns and cheerful floral shirts were standing behind him. I had a feeling their knuckles were bruised up and bloody. All that working out and his sculpted six-pack abs hadn't done Vasquez much good when confronted by a couple of overweight, beer-and-tamale-swilling bad guys.

"Look, Mr. Rangos, I'm a police officer. I don't want any part of this."

Black didn't look pleased at the battered state of my murder suspect or my frank assessment of the situation, but Jose was quick to reassure us of his benevolent intentions. "You have nothing to worry about, chica. We aren't going to kill him. He just didn't want to come here, so we had to encourage him a bit."

Didn't want to come visiting, huh? Wonder why? But I did feel relieved. I'm sure Carlos felt even more relieved to hear he wasn't a dead man waiting. His eyeballs receded several degrees back into his head.

Always the diplomat, Black said, "Jose knew you wanted to interview him, so he provided you with a private opportunity."

Boy, did he ever. I looked around at all my new gun-toting, criminal friends and was afraid I was going to have to be rude again.

"I appreciate this, Mr. Rangos . . ."

"*Por favor*, call me Jose."

"Jose. But I'll need to talk to him alone. And I prefer that he isn't bleeding all over the place. You know how unsanitary that can be in this day and age."

Jose smiled. He had a nice smile, like a kindly old grandpa, eager to please his kith and kin. "I understand. Enrico, clean him up for the detective."

"Hey, maybe you can even untie him, take the gag out, you know, make him a little more comfortable during our chat?"

"Of course, if you're sure you'll be all right."

"Oh, I'll be fine. I'm a big girl and carry a gun, you know, the police detective kind."

He took a long look-see at me, then at my cheek, then at Black.

Black anticipated his question. "She can take care of herself, Jose. Don't worry about that."

That was surprising, coming from him, since he was always on my back about getting nicks and scrapes. Then Black said, "Maybe I'll take that drink now, Jose. Let Claire alone to do her job."

"Of course." Jose was just so dang gracious.

One of the big ugly armed thugs fetched a wet washcloth for Carlos to mop up his blood with, then departed with a friendly-like two-fingered salute to me. I waited for the door to close, then searched the ceiling and walls for hidden cameras and recording devices. I didn't see any, but I wasn't going to take a chance with the Rangos family, either.

"Okay, Carlos. What do you say we let bygones be bygones about this afternoon and just get down to brass tacks here?"

"Okay." His bottom lip was split and looked like it hurt like hell. He pressed the washcloth against it and watched me like I was a cobra in disguise. His eyes darted to the door every few seconds. He was scared to death and for good reason.

"I didn't know you knew the Rangos," he offered.

"I don't know the Rangos. I hadn't even heard of them until today. I came down here to talk to you about Hilde Swensen."

He sat up and licked some blood off his chin. He couldn't get it to stop bleeding, and both his eyes were beginning to swell shut. "Is she all right? I can't get hold of her anywhere."

I decided to give it to him straight. "Hilde's dead."

The shock was genuine, it had to be. His face went white under all the bruises and blood, blanched to the color of an onion, actually, and he began to shake and shiver all over. "No, no, how? Why?"

"I thought maybe you could tell me that."

"No, me? No, I've been worried to death about her. She didn't call when she said she would, and we were supposed to get back together when she got home." He began to cry, odd, silent tears that made tracks down the dried blood smears on his cheeks. Then he really began to grieve with loud heartbroken sobs and deep moans.

I didn't say anything, let him cry awhile. He'd had a hard day. I got up and made a slow circuit of the room, but still didn't see any hidden microphones and peepholes or blood-stained chainsaws and bags of cement, for that matter. That didn't mean they weren't there. Hey, I was a little paranoid, but who'd blame me?

"How did she die? A car wreck? She drives so fast, I warned her about speeding, especially when she's had a few drinks, and the lake has all those hills and cliffs . . ."

I perked up. "You've been to Lake of the Ozarks?"

"Yeah, once." He wiped up some tears and more blood with the washcloth. "We went up there to visit her sister. Didn't stay long, though, 'cause Brianna can't stand me." He stopped and bit down against the wet cloth. His next words were muffled and hard to understand. "She said I had to stay somewhere else, that she didn't have room for both of us. So I got a room at that big lodge place."

I retrieved and unfolded a matching lawn chair, one obviously intended for a second victim for those attending in pairs. I checked it out for blood spatter and other gore before I sat down. I'm fastidious that way. I gazed directly into Vasquez's puffy, bloodshot eyes. "Hilde was murdered. The killer cut off her lips, then strangled her to death."

The shocked expression that overtook his face could not be faked. "Oh, Dios, my God in heaven, who would do such a thing to her?"

"That's what I want to know. And yeah, it was a pretty bad scene, believe me. Where were you last Wednesday and Thursday, Carlos?"

"You think it's me? That I could do such a terrible thing to her? No, never, we loved each other, we were getting back together. I told her I'd do anything she wanted, be anything she wanted." His sobbing crescendoed into inconsolable blubbering, and I resisted the urge to pat his shoulder and tell him everything was going to be all right. It wasn't and never would be, not for him, apparently, or Brianna, and certainly not for Hilde. I gave him time to regain control. When he began to dab his tears with the bloody washcloth, I began again.

"Can you alibi yourself on those two days, or not?"

"Yeah, I worked at my gym both days, all day, and some of Wednesday night, all this week. My whole client list can verify my whereabouts."

"How deeply are you affiliated with Mr. Rangos?"

I wasn't specific and I couldn't be. I knew he was a police informant, but he didn't know I knew. He looked fearfully at the door. "I'm small potatoes. I launder some money for them, deal some coke in the clubs, but nothing else, I swear it. You can ask them. They had no beef with me, no hit out, or I'd already be dead. They probably wouldn't have roughed me up like this, if I hadn't jumped you today."

"Why did you jump me?"

"I panicked. Word was out that somebody wanted me dead. I thought then that somebody'd sent you to get me."

That somebody being Rangos. And that word wasn't from the street but straight from the Miami PD, Ortega, to be precise. He might be thinking everything was gonna be all hunky dory and coming up roses now with Rangos and his goons because he wasn't dead yet, but I wasn't so sure. If they ever found out he'd been talking to the police, much less snitching, he'd be wearing concrete buckets in his shoe size before he could blink.

"You're playing a dangerous game here, Carlos," I said, very low. "You're gonna get yourself killed."

He swabbed off more blood and nodded, but his eyes were wary and guarded. "They asked me a lot of questions about why you're down here snooping around at Hilde's. You know, where she was, what happened to her. They wanted to know what I knew about your case and what Hilde had to do with it. But I didn't know anything. I didn't even know she was dead." Carlos buried his face in the washcloth and wept like a baby.

But this little tidbit of news caught my attention big time. Maybe the Rangos shared our theory that Hilde's death was connected to Esteban Rangos's murder, but how would they know Hilde was dead, much less the victim of a gruesome mutilation? Ortega was the only one I'd told and he'd no doubt filled in his chief, but rumors ripped like wildfire through the corridors in police departments. The Rangos could have a dirty MPD cop on the payroll. Or maybe their sleazebag lawyer got them the information somehow? Or maybe it was Black who spilled the beans; I'd told him everything. Nuh-uh, no way. I discounted that right off as ridiculous. He might insist on my paying a social call on his favorite godfather now and again, but he'd never, ever give up the particulars of my case. No way. I'd bet my life on it. But I'd ask him anyway.

"Okay, we're gonna go down to the Ocean Club and check out the people you say can alibi you. Have any problem with that?"

He shook his head, and I knew he was just glad somebody was getting him out of this combination garage/torture chamber. "Is there anyone else you think might want to murder Hilde?"

He wept again, and I almost felt sorry for him until I remembered that Brianna had witnessed him pushing Hilde around. Psychopathic killers were good criers, too, when they needed to be.

"Lots of the other girls were jealous of her, and lots of guys wanted her, that's what made me so crazy. Everywhere she went, they hung around us and tried to get her to notice them. Some of them were freaks, too, perverts. Especially one of them."

"Who was that?"

"I don't know his name. I just caught her with him once, and she said he was a relative."

"Is your jealousy the reason you broke up?"

"Yeah. She moved out, way up there on the coast where she wouldn't have to run into me."

"And started dating other men?"

"Yeah, and that nearly killed me. I love her, I swear."

"Maybe if you couldn't have her, nobody could. Is that what you were thinking?"

"No, Dios, please believe me. I missed her. I fucked up, hurt her a couple of times when I was drunk, pushed her around a little, but I wasn't going to do it anymore. I just wanted things back the way they were."

I wasn't sure I believed much of what he was saying. He slugged me pretty hard out at the beach. The little thuds and Excedrin-resistant vibrations inside my skull vouched for it. He wasn't exactly trustworthy, either. Even thuggish gangster types had their doubts about him.

"One more thing, Hilde's sister said Hilde had a stalker for a while. Said it went on just before the two of you hooked up. Know anything about that?"

His gaze darted away. Oh, yeah, he knew something about that. I waited to see if he'd lie to me.

"Okay, it was me. I just wanted to go out with her, is all. I thought I'd give her some neat gifts and stuff, and then invite her out and tell her it was me all along."

"Not such a good idea, Vasquez. You scared her."

"I know. That's when I stopped it. I just asked her out then and she said yes." He put his hands over his face and wept a boatload of genuine tears. Could be for love of Hilde like he wanted me to think, or maybe because Rangos's henchmen had beaten him to a pulp. I'd just have to figure out which was the case.

"Okay, Carlos, now all I have to do is get you out of here

alive. Just come with me, do exactly what I say, and don't try anything stupid, you got that?"

I found Black and Jose still having drinks on the terrace. All very civilized and sophisticated. They both stood up, polite to the bone, when I dragged bleeding Carlos up to them. Such gentlemen, why, I never.

"We're going down to the Ocean Club and check out Vasquez's alibis, then I'm taking him to the Miami PD and finish questioning him there."

Silence. I hesitate to describe it as dead, but it was. Goons stood straighter everywhere, fingers tightened on tommy guns, shovels were thrown into the trunks of sedans, hellfire and consternation was afoot.

Black, ever the serene one, said, "We would consider it a great favor if you would give him over to us, Jose."

Favor, huh? But I did have enough sense to keep my mouth shut. Black was better at tiptoeing around the injured feelings of deadly and touchy crime lords than I. Oh, yeah.

"Of course, Nicky. Whatever you and Claire think is best."

Carlos sagged in relief. I think he'd been holding his breath.

Jose said, "Felipe will stay with you, of course, but would you like a couple of my men to tag along, just to make sure he doesn't cause you trouble?"

Yeah, like I'd like two holes in my head. "No, sir, Mr. Rangos, I can handle him. I've been trained to bring in bad guys." Once again, I smiled engagingly. Yes, I can do that, on occasion, rarely, of course, but it is possible. "I think he's learned his lesson about attacking out-of-state law enforcement officers."

Jose Rangos laughed merrily, mightily tickled by me, I guess. "I hope you will visit again soon with Nicky and do me the honor of being my guest here at my compound. It would be my great privilege."

Just what I always wanted, to go on holiday in a house

with a handy Inquisition-equipped torture chamber in the garage. "That sounds lovely." I lie sometimes, too.

We took our leave. Needless to say, conversation was stilted on the way to the Ocean Club. The three of us found we had little to chat about. Apparently, Foxy Felipe wasn't much for casual verbiage, either, though purportedly adequate with wire garrotes and weighted saps. As it turned out, Carlos's alibi was pretty rock solid. He could not have gotten to Missouri and back, not with twenty witnesses saying otherwise, their abs still sore from the crunches and lunges he forced them to do. I decided not to take him down to the Miami PD since most undercover snitches don't like to hang around with the cops employing them, so we cut him loose back at the Ocean Club and left him to lick his wounds, and I do mean that literally.

It was well after midnight when we drove back to the Hotel Imperial and our superluxurious penthouse, and I tried not to notice just how buddy-buddy Black was with Felipe, our bodyguard/assassin/chauffeur. I was not in a good mood. Actually, it was as black as it could get. I'm talking India ink and road tar, here. I did not like Black's underworld friends or being dragged into their houses to rescue police informants. Once in the penthouse, Black surprised me with a fancy midnight dinner with candles and champagne and lobster and caviar and roses, you know, the ultimate romantic works.

Smiling, he said, "I thought we'd get back earlier, but they've kept the food nice and warm for us."

"I'm not very hungry." My remark sounded more like I was allergic to foodstuffs for the rest of eternity.

Black ignored my less-than-friendly tone. "You should probably try to eat something. I suspect you haven't had a bite all day."

I hadn't, but so what? I was pissed. But he had gone to a

lot of trouble, and I tried to soothe my ruffled feathers enough to pretend to enjoy his surprise. Surprise, surprise, I hated surprises, and he knew it. The table was set out on the terrace, facing the ocean with vanilla candles everywhere, all sensual and dreamy. I sure as hell wasn't in the mood for casual chatter or a leap into the big bed just behind the white linen curtains wafting around all over the place in the cool ocean breeze.

I picked at my food. Black ate like there was no tomorrow. He was not upset by my silence, and that upset me further.

"You feel all right?" he asked after about fifteen minutes of stilted silence.

"I'm fine. "

Ten more minutes passed, and then I'd had enough sitting around doing nothing.

"I've gotta go over a file. Thanks for dinner."

I stood up and moved into the living room. I got the Esteban Rangos murder file and sat down in a chair in front of the cocktail table. Black followed, poured himself a drink at the bar, chose a novel from the bookcase, relaxed down into a brown leather chair nearby, and began to read. Probably *The Godfather* or the true life story of *Donnie Brasco*. He didn't seem too perturbed by my cold shoulder. Frigid shoulder, actually. The same thing had happened before when I was forced to clink goblets with his underworld buds, and I did remind myself that I *had* gotten the Vasquez interview because of Black's unsavory connection with Rangos. But I was still ticked and didn't feel up to hiding it.

More time passed in sullen silence. The interior of the room soon frosted up to about the same centigrade of a Siberian Christmas Eve. Frostier and frostier, I checked my nose for icicles as Black sat unperturbed and absorbed in his book. I tried to see what he was reading. It was a Michael

Connelly, but I couldn't see the title. I was not happy, and the more I thought about Black dragging me out to visit Mr. Miami Scarface, the more resentful I became.

I stared at the report that laid out the circumstances of finding Esteban Rangos's body. Some guy going fishing one morning saw the cadaver floating faceup, snagged in some underwater reeds. I tried to think about the words I was reading, considered asking Black what he knew about this kid's gory death, but didn't. For some reason the angry bonfire blazing inside my head acted to impede my concentration, but I finally pinned down what was bugging me the most. I felt betrayed.

Black should have told me about his shady associations in Miami before I accepted the flight down with him. I had made it clear I could have no part in his brother's trade. I had overlooked those kind of connections once when we'd first met, but now here we were stuck again with a bunch of smiling, helpful goodfellas smack dab in the middle of my investigation.

"Want to tell me what's eating you?"

I looked up. Black studied me calmly, then took a sip of his Chivas. I guess he'd gotten to a boring part of the book. Now he sat, looking relaxed and confident, propping the short glass of whiskey atop his crossed knee, a habit of his. He stared straight at me and smiled, all dimpled up and sexy. I tried hard not to jump up and throttle him. This was a serious matter, one I couldn't tolerate, and something for a change that we couldn't solve by jumping into the sack.

"I don't like being blindsided like this. I told you I cannot have any perceived association with your brother's business or any other criminals. I thought I made that clear."

Black locked gazes with me, calm as a tranquilized cat. "I understand that, and I'm sorry this happened. But these people are like family to me, especially Jose. You knew about my brother's dealings almost from the beginning. It's never been a secret between us."

"You didn't tell me about it before we landed in Miami. I cannot involve myself with these kinds of people, not while I'm wearing this badge. Not ever."

Black's voice remained quiet. "I'm not a criminal, Claire. I've worked hard for everything I've got. I was never a part of Jacques's business and I'm not a part of Jose's, either. I left all that behind at eighteen when I joined the army, and I've never had anything to do with it since that day. They've accepted and respected my decision. I visit them now and then because they are family, that's the extent of it. Jacques is my brother and I love him. Jose is my godfather, and I care about him, too. I've never asked them to do any kind of favors for me, and they haven't asked me to compromise myself, either. I'm sorry this puts you in an uncomfortable position, but I'm not going to turn my back on either of them. Not for you or anyone else."

"One more thing, Black, guess you didn't happen to tell Jose how Hilde was mutilated, did you?"

Black's frown was quick, so was his anger. "Hell, no. You know better than that."

"Just wanted to make sure."

"You know you can trust me."

I did know, and I did feel ashamed to have accused him, but I said nothing, just returned my attention to the Esteban Rangos police reports. I clutched the paper, but couldn't concentrate enough to read it. I didn't want to talk about any of this right now because I was pretty sure there wasn't a good solution. But the truth was, he should never have asked me to go into the Rangos compound, much less taken me there. By now, probably every law officer in town knew I'd been out there cozying up with the local mob.

Black wasn't ready to let the subject drop. "I don't want

to discuss this any more than you do, Claire, but it's not going to do us any good to ignore it and hope it goes away."

"I'm not ignoring it. As far as I can see, we've got a big problem. And to be honest, I'm not so sure it's one that we can get past."

Black's azure blue eyes held me, intense, unblinking, questioning. Okay, I had his undivided attention and here we were. Now what? Black carefully placed his drink on the table beside him. He was furious. I could tell. He wasn't one to show emotions, but he always flexed his jaw when he was angry and the flexing going on now looked like he was about to grind his molars off at the gum. He stood up and his movements got really slow, deliberate, deadly. He did that when he was ticked off, too. All coiled and ready, like some kind of big panther.

"Maybe it's not my family that's really bothering you, Claire. Maybe it's the fact that we've been together for quite a while now. Maybe you know it's time for you to make some kind of commitment or we should go our separate ways. Maybe you just don't want to face that little problem."

I frowned, irked somehow. What did this have to do with Rangos? "I never made you any promises, Black."

"Yes. And that very well could be the problem."

I didn't like where this was going. One minute we were talking about his family, then all of a sudden it was do or die. "Look, let's talk about this some other time. I've got to read through this file and see if I can find a lead. Our personal relationship will have to wait."

Black nodded. "There you go, and well do I know where your priorities lie. You haven't had much of a personal life in the past, and now I think you're finding that having one cramps your style."

"Would you please stop with the analyzing crap?"

"No, I think it's time we had this discussion. I have a few

gripes myself, and I think it's time we laid them out on the table."

That surprised me, yes, it did, he was usually fairly complimentary about me. I looked at him, not sure what was coming and not particularly wanting to hear it. We hadn't had many fights since we'd met, but I had a feeling we were about to have one helluva doozy, ooh yeah.

"Okay, Black, whatever you say. Number One for me. I don't like you dragging me as a sworn law enforcement officer into meetings with known criminals. How do I annoy you? Hit me."

"First off, it annoys me that you sometimes go off half-cocked without waiting for backup and almost get yourself killed. Yeah, you bet that annoys me. Second, it annoys me that you take chances you shouldn't, that you're reckless as hell, and that your luck's going to run out one of these days and you're going to end up dead. I don't want to see that happen. I don't like having to dread a phone call telling me to pick you up at the morgue."

I laughed, and yes, it sounded scornful as hell. "Get real, Black. I'm a cop. I have a dangerous job, and I'm damn good at it. If you want a housewife type who bakes you chocolate chip cookies and irons your top-of-the-line silk shirts, I'm sure women from here to Alaska will line up for the honor."

At my outburst, Black became utterly still and lapsed full force into his shrink persona. "What are you really saying?"

I jumped up, big time agitated. "I'm saying exactly what I'm saying, and if you'd listen to me for a change and quit parsing and analyzing every freakin' word I say, you might actually hear me."

Man, that got to him. Black's jaw was working down underneath his tanned skin, but he was definitely under steely control. He was always under control. "Okay, let me put this plainly so we'll both understand. I want a commitment from you, Claire.

I'm tired of running over to your house whenever you snap your fingers. I want you to move in with me so we can have at least the semblance of a normal life and actually spend time together like a regular couple. I've changed my schedule and put aside work to suit yours, time after time, but when have you ever done the same for me? I don't want a casual affair with you anymore. I want more than that. What do you want?"

I didn't know what to say. I didn't know what to do, either. I didn't know what I wanted. I didn't like this conversation, and I certainly didn't want to talk about commitment. Lots of didn'ts going on here. I turned away from his unwavering stare and copped out. "I like things the way they are now."

"Could've fooled me."

I turned around and looked at him. I could be calm, if he could. "You're turning this around on me. I don't like my professional integrity being compromised by your friends. That's what this is about right here and now, and you ought to understand that. This has nothing to do with commitment. I haven't been with anybody else since we met, and I don't intend to. I don't want to."

"Well, I want more than that. You need to decide if you do, too."

"I need space to breathe. I don't like being smothered."

"Is that what you feel like I'm doing? Smothering you?"

I didn't want to say it, but I did feel that way occasionally, as ugly as it sounded. "Sometimes, yes."

Again, dueling eyeballs. Flexing jaws. Black was not in the mood to back down. Neither was I.

"I want a commitment, right now. I want you to move into my place, where I know you'll be safe when I'm not around."

"I can take care of myself."

"For God's sake, Claire, how many times have you been in the hospital since I met you?"

"I said, I can take care of myself. I'm still breathing, aren't

I? Maybe if you're so unhappy with things the way they are, we ought to part ways for a while. See if that suits you better."

My ultimatum hung in the air, and I knew I regretted saying it before the words died away, but couldn't seem to take them back. I waited, angry at him for forcing all this when it was unnecessary, but somehow relieved that it was all out, too.

"Is that what you want to do? Part ways?"

"Oh, come on, Black. You know how I feel about you, but I'm not ready to move in at your place. I like my house. I like my privacy, and peace and quiet, and you never have either one around you, not with your employees always hanging around like some kind of damn entourage."

At first, Black said nothing. Quite eloquently, too. Then he nodded. "Okay, so be it. Maybe a little break from each other will help us sort things out."

Black walked away from me and down the hall into the master suite. He shut the door, and a few minutes later I faintly heard his voice, talking on the phone. Probably calling Felipe to put a hit out on me. I sat back down and stared at the file in front of me, not sure how I felt. Stunned, maybe, at how fast all this had come down. A little abandoned, too, I guess. But I knew what I needed to do. I needed to forget Black for a while and think about Hilde's murder before the killer struck again. My job had to take priority at the moment, and maybe putting some distance between Black and me would help give momentum to the case. Besides, I didn't like ultimatums any more than he did.

That was fine and dandy for a while. I kept thinking about him in the other room, sulking, no doubt, but I forced myself to think about the case. When I was finally able to concentrate on the lead detective's progress reports on the Esteban Rangos investigation, I found they hadn't turned up much. Without cooperation from the Rangos family, it had been pretty much a dead-end case from the start. No forensic evidence found, of course, not after so much time in the water.

My phone started its song, and I glanced at the clock over the fireplace. It was almost three o'clock in the morning. This would not be good news.

"Yeah, this is Morgan."

"It's me. Ortega."

I tried to figure in a hurry how I was gonna break it to him that I'd already interviewed Carlos Vasquez and without Ortega standing in for the MPD as previously agreed upon. So I said, "You found Vasquez, I take it."

"Yeah, I found him. Attacked and left for dead."

Rarely ever am I speechless. This time I was.

Black must've heard my phone ring because he came into the room, saw the expression on my face, and said. "What now?"

I said to Ortega. "He's not dead?"

"Not yet. But he's in real bad shape. I found him at his apartment."

"Who's not dead?" said Black. He frowned when I ignored him.

"You sure it's Vasquez?" I said to Ortega.

"Oh, yeah. I called 'cause I thought you might wanna know somebody knocked him out, tied him up, then hacked off his mouth."

"Oh, my God. Like the other two?"

"Yep. I must've gotten there pretty quick after it happened. He was bleedin' like hell from the mouth and just comin' to. I got paramedics out there in about five minutes. They found the lips, believe it or not, and the doctors sewed 'em back on, but he lost so much blood that he's not doing so hot. Surgeon said he might be able to talk some in recovery so I thought you might wanna be there and ask him a few questions."

"Where are you?"

"Sittin' in front of your hotel in my Jeep."

"I'll be right down."

I flipped the phone shut and looked at Black. "Somebody tried to kill Vasquez tonight by cutting off his lips and leaving him to bleed to death. Might've even been your friend, Felipe. So much for your so-called godfather's word of honor."

"If Jose told me he wasn't going to kill him, he didn't have anything to do with it. He's never lied to me."

"Yeah, right. He's a regular Billy Graham, isn't he? Well, I'm gonna need a lot more reassurance than your vouching for Rangos's word."

I picked up my purse and headed for the door.

"Where are you going?"

"Ortega's waiting outside. We're going to the hospital and see if Vasquez can identify his attacker."

"I'll go with you."

"I don't think so. And I don't know when I'll be back. If you need to fly home, feel free. I can catch a regular flight out of Miami International."

"I'll wait."

"Go on back and take care of the pageant. You don't need to get any more involved in this Carlos Vasquez thing than you already are."

"I'm not involved in Carlos's attack, other than when I was with you. And like I said, I'll wait for you. Right here. We'll fly home when you're done."

We left it at that, and I grit my teeth in frustration as I rode down in the elevator. Rangos was the obvious choice for best suspect at the moment, but why would he order the mouth severed? I'd turned up no connection between Rangos and Hilde, other than she'd dated Vasquez, but Vasquez had said they were asking him about her. Or maybe another crime syndicate was out for revenge for some kind of slight? The Rangos did that cute earlobe thing; maybe their counterparts did lips. Still, it just didn't add up. And why didn't the perp just kill Carlos Vasquez and be done with it? They sure as hell hadn't left the other two vics alive to finger the assailant. I just hoped Carlos didn't succumb to his injuries before I got to him.

Vasquez was out of recovery and in critical care by the time Ortega and I arrived at the hospital. The attending surgeon met us at the swinging door to the CCU and reluctantly gave us permission to enter and ask a few questions, but only under his personal supervision. We followed him inside and past several other glassed-in areas where seriously ill patients suffered and moaned. Vasquez was lying in bed, hooked up to all kinds of monitors and tubes. They were giving him blood. I thought of Bud and how he'd looked when he'd almost died, of Harve in his hospital bed, of lots of people who barely made it, and then I shoved those thoughts out of my head and concentrated on the task at hand.

Carlos Vasquez was not a pretty sight. The surgeon had sutured his lips, but they were swollen and purple and sickening to look at. But he was breathing. That's more than Hilde could say. He was half conscious and heavily drugged, but the doctor said he could understand me if I talked to him. He told me to have Vasquez nod or shake his head instead of talking. I leaned down close to his face and could smell the antiseptic and his foul breath. His sutured mouth was covered with some kind of shiny Vaseline-type ointment.

"Carlos? Can you hear me?"

Vasquez opened his eyes and stared blearily up at my face. I could tell he was in terrible pain.

"Nod if you can hear me, Carlos."

He gave a little nod, and Ortega and I looked at each other. We just might get lucky right here, right now.

"Do you know who I am?"

Again, he nodded.

"Can you tell me who did this to you?"

He didn't move, shut his eyes.

"Was it a Rangos hit, Carlos?"

He shook his head and I breathed a sigh of relief. Black had been right, thank God for that much.

"Did you see who did it?"

He shook his head and tried to talk, managed thick, slurred speech. "Jumped me . . . dark . . ."

"How do you know it wasn't Rangos?"

"Voice . . . the voice . . ."

Ortega said, "Give us his name, Vasquez. We'll go get him."

Vasquez shook his head slightly. Tried to lick his bruised, engorged lips. Big black stitches were visible, and he ran his tongue over them as if they were foreign objects he didn't recognize. I glanced at the heart monitor. His pulse rate was rising fast, and the doctor was reading the monitor and frowning. He wasn't going to give us much time. I had to get more out of Vasquez.

"Try to tell us whose voice it was. You don't know his name? How do you know him then?"

"Hilde . . ." he breathed out.

"It was a man? A friend of hers?"

He nodded, and then his lips moved again. "He . . . scared her . . . he . . ."

"Is he an ex-boyfriend?"

His eyes were closed but he shrugged a little.

"Did he say anything? Talk to you when he did this?"

Carlos jerked a little, nodded some, but seemed more agitated and fearful. The doctor put his hand on my shoulder and tried to urge me away.

"Detective, you need to go now. You're endangering his recovery."

"Please, Doctor, just a couple more minutes. It's important."

The doctor didn't like it but he nodded. "Hurry it up, he needs to calm down."

I leaned in close again. "What'd he say, Carlos? Please, try to tell me. We wanna get this guy for what he did to you."

Carlos's tongue was licking at his butchered mouth again, but his glazed eyes were latched on my face. His words came out hoarse and ragged. "Said . . . I'd . . . die . . . smiling . . ."

Then he began to cry, tears leaking out his swollen eyes and rolling down between the stitches. The doctor pushed us both away from the bed, and we walked out into the corridor, both of us pretty shaken up.

"Well, we know it's a male and a friend of Hilde's for sure," I said. "That's better than nothing. I'd call that a lead, wouldn't you?

"Why do you think this guy went after Carlos?"

I shook my head. "I don't know. Could be he was jealous of him, or thought Carlos knew something on him, could finger him for something incriminating. His voice must be distinctive if Carlos recognized it. Man, this is bad, and getting worse."

"I gotta have some coffee. Want some?"

"Yeah. Make mine black."

While Ortega headed for the vending machines at the far end of the corridor, I pulled out my cell phone and poked in Bud's cell. He picked up quickly, but his voice was groggy. Wonder why? It was just two forty-five a.m. his time. He said, "Claire? You back yet?"

"No, but soon. You still tailing Costin?"

"Yeah, but he's walking the straight and narrow. Goes to work, then back home in the morning to sleep, then drives down to Springfield in the p.m. for classes. I came home to get some sleep. I'll pick him up again when he heads back to Missouri State for classes."

"You think he made you?"

"Are you kiddin'? I'm the best. He doesn't know I'm anywhere around."

I smiled. Now he sounded more like my Bud. "Anything else going on since I've been gone?"

"No, it's pretty quiet. Bri's still all weirded out, sayin' she's gotta go away for a while. Try to come to terms with everything that's happened."

Maybe I'm pessimistic, but that sounded a lot like a breakup in the works to me. I waited for him to confirm that, but he remained silent. "What about you and her?"

"She said she loves me, but maybe she needs a little time to think things through, now that Hilde's gone. She said alone time might help her cope."

Uh-oh, not good. "Well, if it makes you feel better, Black and I just went down the same road."

"No way. You broke it off with the guru?"

"Sort of. I don't know. It was our first fight, so I don't know if he meant it or not, but let's talk about that later. Know that guy Hilde lived with down here?"

"Carlos Vasquez? You find him?"

"Oh, yeah, and not all in one piece, either. Somebody showed up at his place tonight, cut off his lips, and left him for dead, just like Hilde, but without the strangulation and posed crime scene. He was damn lucky a detective outta the MPD found him before he bled to death."

Bud gave a low whistle. "So you didn't get to interview him?"

"Yeah, earlier tonight. His alibi held up, big-time, so I cut him loose. Apparently, when he got home, the guy was waiting for him, scissors in hand."

"Did he know who cut him?"

"Not by name, but he got out that it was some friend of Hilde's, a man. He recognized his voice."

"He give you a name?"

"Nope. He's still pretty groggy. Just talked about the voice. That trigger anything for you?"

"Costin?"

"Yep. Darth Vader himself."

"But Carlos didn't get a look at him?"

"Uh-uh. Said it was too dark, but hey, a lead's a lead.

We'll have to check out her prior boyfriends and if Vasquez makes it, and they think he will, maybe he can identify his assailant. At least that'll give us an idea who to investigate. We ought to be able to get a recording of Costin's voice for him to listen to, identify him that way."

"Yeah. When you coming back?"

"In the morning, probably. I'm still at the hospital, but Black's waiting for me at the hotel. I left my car at Cedar Bend, so that's where I'll go first."

"I'll meet you there before I pick up the tail on Costin again."

"See you later."

We hung up, and I checked with the doctors one last time before Ortega and I took off. They said Vasquez was sedated and holding his own at the moment. They seemed pretty sure he was going to survive. At the hotel, Ortega said he'd continue to investigate the attempted murder and keep me posted, that maybe Vasquez would remember something else once some of the anesthesia wore off.

Upstairs in the penthouse suite, Black was sitting in the living room, waiting. He was fully dressed and by the frown he greeted me with, he was still hot under the collar. I wasn't used to seeing him so un-glad to see me. Didn't like it much, either.

He said, "You ready to go now?"

I said, "Yes."

He said, "Then pack up. I'll call for the limo."

I packed up. He called for the limo. We rode in abject silence to the airport. We flew in abject silence to Missouri. Fun, fun, and more fun. Man, alive. In other words, the whole world sucks.

Sisterly Love

After that day, the older one concentrated on making a new life for herself and forgetting the boy and Sissy and all the others. The only one she ever missed was Bubby, and sometimes, she did break down and call him on the phone. He always said he was okay and that everybody was treating him all right, but she sometimes wondered if the boy was still playing the game and making the others do his evil bidding.

The boy himself called often and left messages, and Sissy called once and said she was sorry and that the boy had made her his slave and that she had to do what he said and then she cried very hard and pitiably, but the older one was not moved and did not believe her. She wanted nothing to do with them, not even when the boy moved down to Florida for college and came to see her.

By then, her real daddy had returned home to Europe with his wife and son, but she had already started college and didn't want to go live with them again until after she graduated. She stayed behind in their house and began to compete in beauty pageants again and was doing very well. She was happy and content and had met a transfer student at the university that she liked a lot. He was handsome and sexy and they dated for a long time before she asked him to move into her place.

Then one day the boy showed up when her new boyfriend was in class and told her how sorry he was, how much he still loved her, and she told him that it was over and had been for a very long time. She told him that she was happy in her new life and to leave her alone.

"Don't say that," the boy said and pulled out a big sharp knife.

"I'm not afraid of you," she said to him.

"You should be," he said to her.

"Go ahead, kill me then," she said, because she knew he couldn't do it, that he loved her too much.

Then he laughed and it was an evil laugh, one she remembered from the night they ran down the girl in the stolen car. "Oh, I'll never hurt you, darlin', and you know that, don't you? I'll hurt that guy you're living with, and I've still got all my little minions to help me. Or maybe, I'll just cut up Bubby a little bit. Maybe I'll cut off his nose, or better yet, his lips and send them to you, all gift wrapped up, nice and pretty."

The older one's blood ran cold because she knew he would do it, that there was nothing she could do to stop him. "I'll call the police. I'll tell them everything I know about you. You'll never get away with it."

"Go ahead. And I'll show them the video I have of you and Sissy and Bubby killing your daddy. Poor things, you'll all go to jail forever."

"And so will you."

"Maybe, or maybe not. I never said a word the entire time I was filming you smothering the poor guy. I'll tell them I found the tape hidden in Bubby's room."

The older one knew he was telling the truth, and she knew

he'd do it and enjoy it, too. And he was so smart, he'd figure out a fail-safe way to put all of them into jail without serving time himself.

"We were children. They won't charge us because he was abusing us."

"You can take that chance, if you want, but all of you will wind up in jail, trust me."

"What do you want from me?"

"I want you to kick that bastard the fuck out of this house, and then you're moving in with me. And then it's gonna be just like it used to be before you decided I wasn't good enough for you anymore. So, we got that straight? Now get your clothes off. I'm gonna fuck you raw, and then you're gonna beg me to do it again. You're mine now, just like you used to be, but now you're gonna be my sex slave like Sissy and you're gonna like it, or Bubby's gonna pay the price. Remember my favorite quote, 'Smile, and smile, and be a villain'?" Any of you ever betray me, you'll smile and smile, all right. You'll die smiling 'cause I'll cut off your lips and stuff them down your throats. And you know I'll do it, don't you, darlin'?"

The older one stared at him because she knew he *would* do it. He was capable of that and a lot worse. He came toward her with the big knife. He smiled as he stuck it down between her breasts and jerked it hard through her blouse. He ripped it off then cut off her bra and flung it away. Tears rolled down her cheeks when he pushed her down on the bed and began to unfasten his belt. He smiled. "Don't worry, things are going to be just like they used to be between us. You'll see."

He knelt on the bed beside her, the knife pressed against her upper lip. "What's a matter, baby, you're not smiling any more? You know how much I love that smile of yours. Maybe I ought to cut off your lips right now and make that smile permanent. How does that sound, huh? Just remember that nobody betrays me and gets away with it, nobody. Especially you. You damn well better remember that, too."

As the point of the knife pierced the skin above her mouth just enough to draw blood, she forced her trembling lips into the smile he said he loved and lay unresisting as he raped her.

Sixteen

As promised, Bud was waiting for me on the marina dock when we landed at the Cedar Bend heliport the next day. We'd gotten some sleep on the plane, but not much. We showered and put on clean clothes but not together this time. Neither of us were in a particularly chipper mood, and that was putting it mildly. I was glad to see Bud, glad to get away from Black's cold, controlled anger for a while. It appeared Black shared the sentiment. He nodded stiffly to Bud, then walked off ahead of us at a fast clip and headed toward the private elevator to his apartment.

"Black doesn't look so happy. What the hell happened?"

"Don't ask."

"Hey, before you take off, I want you to talk to Brianna, and then Charlie said he wants us both down at the station, pronto."

"What's he want?"

"Didn't say. Just said to get the fudge down there."

Bud grinned, and I had to smile, too, despite my horrible mood. "Why'd you want me to talk to Brianna?"

Bud shook his head. "I can't get through to her. Maybe you can."

Me? I don't think so. "Well, it's understandable she's screwed up, Bud. My God, she's been through a lot."

"Just do me a favor, okay? Come inside and talk to her. She's in the ballroom."

We started walking toward the hotel proper. "Why's she out here?"

"That's what I'm talkin' about. Now she's decided she's gonna take Hilde's place in the competition. And the director, that Cardamon lady, said she could."

"No way. Why?"

"Says Hilde would've wanted her to. I'm telling you she's messed up in the head. Acts like a different person. I hardly know her anymore."

When we got to the ballroom, it was readily apparent that Bud was right on the money with his take on said girlfriend. The dress rehearsal was going on, and Brianna was the next contestant to make her way down the stroll. When she walked through the curtain, she wore a 1,000-watt smile and a tiny black bikini that would probably fit comfortably into a demitasse cup. She waved cheerfully when she saw me and Bud.

Bud said, "See what I'm talkin' about? It's like she's forgotten all about burying her sister a few days ago."

"Yeah. Maybe Black ought to be the one to have a sit-down with her. He's the shrink, not me."

"You think he would?"

I nodded but I wasn't sure what Black would do anymore, especially for friends of mine. We stood silently as Brianna exited the stage and headed straight for us. The hotel busboys setting up tables and chairs stopped working and watched with dropped jaws as she sauntered past them, a regular Girl from Ipanema. I suddenly wished I had a terry cloth robe to throw over her exposed flesh.

"Hi, Claire. I'm glad you're back. I didn't want you to miss the pageant. Did Bud tell you I'm going to take Hilde's place?"

She beamed, the wattage still turned to high, and I checked her pupils to see how dilated they were. They looked abnormal, all right, not to mention that crazy little light in them. If she wasn't high on her meds, she needed to be.

I smiled back, but remained wary. "Are you sure that's a good idea, Bri?"

"Of course, I am. Hilde would've wanted me to do this. The idea just came to me yesterday when I was trying to sleep and I realized what a fitting memorial this would be to her, especially if I win. I'm so excited I could just die."

I cringed inside. Bud looked aghast. Brianna's insensitive remark, however, obviously went right over her drugged-up head. I decided then and there Black had better find time for a get-down-and-serious, heart-to-heart session with this woman, and quick, too.

My cell rang and I walked a few steps away and saw on Caller ID that it was Charlie. I wasn't ready for the onslaught, but I didn't have the guts not to pick up.

"Yes, sir."

"Where the devil are you?"

"Cedar Bend Lodge. We just landed a few minutes ago."

"Get the hell down here right now. I already told Bud to report in and to bring you with him. I don't know where the hell he is."

"Yes, sir, he's here, too, but . . ."

Click. And that was that. Charlie wasn't always the most polite of chatterers.

"Let's go, Bud. Charlie wants us downtown, and I mean, yesterday."

We left in a big hurry, and I rode with Bud in his Bronco. He was coming back later to get Brianna and I'd pick up my

Explorer then, too. I filled him in on the details of what had gone down in Florida, even the part about Rangos and his merry band of henchmen.

"Not good, Claire. Charlie will flay you alive if he finds out you went into the Rangos compound to interrogate Vasquez."

"Yeah, tell me about it."

"That what's wrong between you and Black, I take it?"

"Yep."

We rode in silence after that, and once we arrived in the office, it didn't take us long to find out what was the matter. Charlie looked ready to blow a trunk full of gaskets.

"Sit down and look at this."

We sat down and looked at the dark TV screen while he shoved a videocassette tape in and hit play. Static. And then a picture of a semidark room and two people going at it in a big way. In other words, having wild and uninhibited sex. I made sure it wasn't me and Black, then sat back and waited for the punch line. After a few minutes of some impressive huffing and puffing and orgiastic groaning on screen, I said, "Sheriff, uh . . ."

"Just wait a minute, damn it."

Bud and I shifted uneasily in our chairs, never having watched porn together before, and I hoped to the devil that Mrs. Ramsay didn't show up with Charlie's preacher man again. No wonder Charlie had locked the door and drawn the shades.

About that time a loud knock occurred in the delightful skin flick that was making all of our faces tomato-red and warm to the touch, and on the tape was frightened whispering and a scrambling and frantic grabbing of clothes.

"Who's there?" the man of the hour cried in a gravelly, disturbed voice, jerking his shirt over his head. He turned to look back at the woman and put a finger to his lips to keep her quiet, but I'd recognized him the minute he'd opened his mouth. It was Walter Costin, the negligent night watchman at Lohman's Funeral Home and now primary suspect in the attack on Vasquez.

I froze when I heard the next voice. It said clearly and distinguishably. "It's Johnny. Let me in, and hurry it up."

Bud said, "Oh, shit."

Charlie said, "Both of you, shut up and listen."

We watched Walter Costin move out of the room into the hallway and open an outside door. He remained in view as Shaggy Becker came in, glanced in the room where the girl was hiding offscreen, briefly, but long enough for us to see his face. Then the two of them moved off camera and had some kind of inaudible but heated argument. After about ten minutes, Costin appeared in the doorway again and said softly, "It's okay, Pam, he didn't see you." Then he walked across the room to the camera and shut it off.

Charlie clicked off the television set and glared at us.

I said, "I interviewed Shaggy about this, sheriff, and he swore he wasn't there that night."

"Yeah? Well, guess what, he lied. That's why the two of you are going to interrogate him again, and you're going to do it right this time."

Crap. I could not believe this was happening. Why would Shaggy want to lie to me? I said, "Yes sir. You want us to pick him up and bring him in now?"

"He's already here. Interview Room Two. So is Walter Costin. He's in one. They haven't talked to each other, and they're not going to. Get down there and find out what the hell is going on. Buck's mad as hell and Shaggy's already offered to hand in his resignation. And guess what? Costin said he's already released this tape to the local press. It's gonna air at six o'clock on Channel 7. He's also sent a tape to Steve Grant at KY3 in Springfield. He says it's the only way to convince the police he was telling the truth because we were protecting one of our own in the coroner's office."

I began to get that little sick sensation in the pit of my

belly that never boded well for me, and by the look on Bud's face, he needed to fizz a couple of Alka-Seltzers himself. We decided to take on Costin first. We entered and found him sitting at the table, legs crossed, arms crossed, and I hoped his fingers weren't crossed, too.

"Hello, Mr. Costin," I said politely.

"Hello, Detectives." He smiled. I frowned because I noticed his gravelly voice and how distinctive it was. Carlos's attacker had a distinctive voice. That could not be a coincidence. Bud sat down at the table. I leaned against the wall and dug out the small tape recorder I carried in my leather bag. I set it atop the table. I could play it over the phone to Carlos. Maybe he could identify it. It was a long shot, but one worth taking.

"You don't mind if we tape your interview, do you, Costin?"

"Well, actually, I do. Just don't trust those things. You know, tapes can be doctored to make people look guilty when they're as innocent as driven snow."

"Driven snow, huh?" That was Bud. "Or maybe if they are guilty as hell."

"No, sir. I am not guilty, but that's why I brought a copy of that video down here to Sheriff Ramsay. I heard that Johnny Becker was telling you he wasn't there that night, and I knew I could prove different. I'm not taking the rap for messing with that lady's body, not with visual proof in my hands."

"What were you and Shaggy arguing about when he got there that night?"

"What'd you think? I was having sex with my girlfriend. He disturbed us."

Bud said, "Rocked the coffin, huh?"

I said, "We might want to come to your place and check out your sewing kit for needles and thread, maybe a sharp pair of manicure scissors. You wouldn't mind that, would you?"

"Sure, but you won't find anything. I'm not into needlework. I'm a history buff."

"Oh, yeah, now I remember, ancient Troy and all those cool swastikas you like to wear."

Bud said, "Where'd you say you lived?"

"I didn't yet, but you oughta know. You've been following me all week."

Bud looked pissed that he'd been made, but I decided Costin was no fool. Something about his calm demeanor and those still, still eyes. He was just a little bit too smooth for a funeral parlor's night watchman. My hunch was that he was just chock-full of secrets.

"Look, I haven't done a damn thing and you're treating me like some kind of hatchet murderer."

Bud and I looked at each other. We'd had some experience with hatchets and cleavers, especially me. Wasn't a good memory, either. I wondered if Costin knew about it and that's why he brought it up.

Costin went on. "I have nothing to hide. You guys ought to bring in your good buddy, ol' Shaggy, and interrogate him. If I didn't bother that girl's body, and I didn't, he's the only one left who could've done it. Guess you'd rather sweat me than put a friend of yours under the microscope."

"You accusing us of collusion, Costin?" Bud asked.

Costin shrugged. "I think you two are the ones doing the accusing, not me. I'm just trying to prove to you that I'm innocent and had nothing to do with messing with that body. I'd never do that. Working there gave me the creeps anyway. It was hard enough just to know there were dead bodies in those coffins."

"Not a fan of Stephen King, I take it."

"I only read history books."

Bud said, "That sounds boring as hell."

"Not as boring as this," said Costin.

The two exchanged death glares. But hey, Costin was grating on my nerves, too.

I said, "So you're okay with us coming out to look around."

"Not at all, but I don't have much choice, do I? Just don't expect me to bake a cake."

"Ha ha," said Bud.

More glares, but Costin didn't seem overly averse to our home visit. And he was right. We didn't want to interview Shaggy. We wanted Costin to just admit he did it so Shaggy'd be off the hook. Who could blame us? Shaggy was a cool guy. Costin was a creep.

Bud said, "Why'd you think it necessary to give the tape to the media, Costin? That's just gonna cause a big shitstorm that'll complicate this case."

"Not for me, it won't. It's gonna show everybody exactly what I was doing that night and with whom, and it sure as hell wasn't attaching some lips to a dead broad."

Bud said, "Yeah, you showed what you did that night, all right, in a triple X-rated porno. I'm surprised they can even show it on TV."

I said, "Dead broad? That's real respectful. Mr. Lohman must be proud to call you an employee."

"I'm not going back there. Suddenly living around here doesn't appeal to me. Almost seems hazardous to my health."

Bud said, "Yeah, especially after everybody in the county's seen you getting it on like a porn stud."

I said, and yes, it was tinged with sarcasm. "Oh, please, don't leave town, Costin. We'd miss you too much."

"Yeah, right."

I was more specific. "Don't leave town, Costin, not until this investigation is over. Got it?"

"Sure. But step it up, would you? I've got a dig in Athens planned for early summer."

Bud said, "We'll do our best. We're pretty good, you know. We might even nail you if you're guilty."

I said, "Yeah, we'll be in touch, Costin, trust me. Keep your phone close by."

He grinned snidely but didn't reply.

When Bud and I left the room, we both had sour tastes in our mouths and frowns on our faces. And it was only going to get worse. We dragged our feet all the way next door to Interview Two and Shaggy, and then entered like convicted felons into a gas chamber. Nothing was worse than shaking down and grilling a good friend. Even Costin knew that.

Shaggy sat at the table, looking haggard and wan and like he wasn't over the flu yet. He looked up at us. He grinned a little, and said, "Hi, guys."

Hi, guys? We sat down across from him, and I took a deep breath. "You're in deep shit, Shaggy. No mistake about it."

"Yeah, tell me something I don't know."

"Why'd you lie to me?"

"Why do you think?"

Bud was not in a patient mood. "Quit bullshittin' us, Shag. You're in big trouble here, and we have you on tape in the funeral parlor the night Hilde Swensen's body was tampered with. We got two eyewitnesses, too. What the hell were you doing there?"

"It was stupid. I should never have done it, but how was I supposed to know somebody was gonna open the casket again?"

"Oh, God, Shaggy, why'd you go there and get yourself mixed up in all this? You gotta tell us why you wanted to go and mess with that girl's body. You gotta tell us what you did that night." I waited, but I wasn't sure I wanted to hear his explanation. That X-rated videotape had been disturbing enough.

Shaggy caught my drift real fast, and said, "Get real, Claire, I'm no pervert."

"Call me old-fashioned, but it seems a little perverted to

secretly visit an embalmed body in its casket at the stroke of midnight."

"I meant well."

"You meant well?" That was Bud. He had turned on the contempt; his words dripped it. "Well, now, that makes everything all hunky dory, now doesn't it? What the hell were you doin' there, Shaggy? And stop lyin' or you're gonna to find yourself in jail for criminal desecration of a corpse."

"I didn't desecrate her. I tried to help her, and that's all."

I said, "Tell us what happened, Shaggy. From the beginning. You're our friend. We want to help you if we can. But you're not making it easy for us."

For a long time, he just sat there and said nothing. Not Mahatma Gandhi when it came to patience, Bud got mad and stalked outside. He slammed the door. I knew he was upset because he liked Shaggy as much as I did. The three of us were good friends, more than good. We had pretty much assumed that the perp had tampered with the body, but I didn't believe for a moment that Shaggy had killed Hilde, much less cut up her mouth. Now, however, it was pretty damn apparent that he was somehow involved. Why else would he go there and why would he get in an argument with Costin, a man he said he hardly knew?

"Shaggy. Look at me."

Shaggy looked up, then avoided my gaze. Not a great sign, that.

"C'mon, man, what's up with this? You can talk to me."

"You came to my house and accused me of killing her. Why should I trust you?"

"Because we've been good friends for years, maybe? Because we like each other, trust each other?"

"I meant well."

I felt my nails biting into my palms. I wanted to jump across the table and jerk his dreadlocks until he told me the truth. He looked up again when Bud reentered the room, calmer now and holding a can of Mountain Dew and a package of barbequed Fritos. Oh, sweet, a peace offering. Bud was an even closer friend to Shaggy than I was, and they'd known each other longer, too. They'd even flown out to Las Vegas on vacation together a couple of times. This had to be killing Bud. Bud was getting hit from all sides on this case.

We sat again in silence and watched our friend drink his soda and crunch his way through the pack of Fritos. It was a few minutes past six now. The sex tape had run on the news, and we were in for a helluva long week.

"You know me, Shag. I'll sit here for a month, if I have to." My threat didn't seem to faze him. We sat some more. Shaggy finished the Fritos and wadded up the package.

"I meant well."

"Maybe so, but it didn't turn out that way. You got caught. Why the interest in this dead girl, that's what I want to know."

"Buck told me about the murder when I called in sick, and it bothered me a lot. You know, what he did to her, so I went down to the morgue to look at the body."

Bud and I didn't move. He was ready to talk, and we weren't going to do anything to trip him up. We remained silent.

"She was just so beautiful. I guess I kind of felt like I had to be with her one more time before they buried her."

"Oh, God, no," Bud said.

Shaggy jumped up really fast and started pacing around the small room, rubbing his palms together and shaking his dreadlocks. "I know what you're thinking, Bud, and it's not like that, so quit thinkin' it. I felt sorry for her, real sorry, to have her mouth cut off like that. God. It wasn't fair. It was terrible, awful. It made me wanna puke. I went back home, but it was all I could think about, the way that son of a bitch had cut off her lips and left her that way for everybody to see. I hated it, that's all, it was. I really did. I wanted to do something to make it better, to make her look better."

I looked at Bud. He looked as perplexed as I felt. He took over the questioning.

"So you went to the funeral parlor. Then what happened? What exactly did you do to the body?"

"I didn't do anything gross to her! What'd you think I am, some kind of freak pervert? I can't believe you'd think I'd do something like that."

"Why do anything? Hilde Swensen's a complete stranger to you, right? Why'd you take it upon yourself to screw around with her corpse and put your job in jeopardy?"

"I just wanted her to look better at the funeral. That's all. I swear to God."

I said, "It was a closed casket, Shaggy. Nobody was gonna see her, anyway. You risked going to jail for nothing."

Bud said, "Look better for the funeral? That's all you have to say?"

"That's right. And your girl, Brianna, she ended up seeing her, didn't she? So I did the right thing sewin' her up. So, there you go, there it is, and that's all there is to it."

Bud repeated wonderingly, "You went there and sewed some lips back on a woman you'd never met before because you thought she was pretty and that somebody might decide to open the coffin, even though it was designated closed casket. That it?"

"Yeah, that's it. Why's that so hard to believe?"

I began to feel like I was caught in one of my more unpleasant nightmares, the ones about plummeting down into hell. "How could you even do that? What did you use for lips?"

"I used her lips, that's what. Buck was gonna keep them as a tissue sample. So I went down to the ME's office and took them out of the evidence refrigerator, and then I brought them over there and sewed them back on her. I did a good job, too, didn't I? You saw. I bet you could hardly see those tiny little stitches I made, and then I covered them with mortician's makeup so she could be buried looking pretty."

I couldn't believe my ears. He was proud of this, wanted us to admire his work. "Are you freakin' serious?"

"Yes! You gotta believe me. It wasn't right to go ahead and bury her like that, with part of her missing. But that's all I did to her, you gotta believe me. I'd never dishonor her by doing anything else."

"Dishonor her?"

I stared at Shaggy, disbelieving he'd get himself into this much trouble for something this moronic. Bud got up again and walked out. His patience level was wearing thin again, tell me about it. I sat back and shook my head. I needed sleep. I needed a nerve pill. I needed a new profession.

"Shaggy, do you have any idea how much trouble you're in?"

"Yeah, sure, I'm not stupid."

"Buck's probably going to fire you flat out now that you've admitted you stole evidence out of his office and tampered with a body. Charlie's gonna have to charge you with something. Hell if I know what it'll be."

"I'm sorry. It's like I told you. I heard about the closed casket and didn't think anybody would ever find out. I just had to do it. I can't explain why. Him cuttin' off her lips just ate at me. I couldn't stand to think about it."

"And you didn't move the body or do anything else to it?"

"No, damn it." He looked highly offended. "You know me better than that. I wouldn't ever do that."

"I didn't think you'd do something like this, either, Shaggy." I took a deep, cleansing breath that didn't make me feel the least bit better.

Bud returned, stone-faced, and said, "What about Costin? What's your connection with that guy? He's a jerk."

"Yeah, he is. I already told Claire all that. I just met him a couple of times."

"What were you arguing about when you got there that night?"

"He didn't want me to come in because he had his girlfriend in there."

"Okay, this has gotta be Charlie's call. Just sit tight while he decides what he's gonna do with you."

After a long and profane tirade, Charlie got the prosecutor to charge Shaggy with tampering with evidence and hold him as long as he could in the county jail until the press frenzy over the murder died down. I left with Bud as soon as we could get free, wanting to get the hell out of there. I was saying uncle. I'd had more than enough for one day.

Outside in the back parking lot, I was more than surprised to find Black waiting for me, more than pleased, too, I must say. He was leaning against the front fender of his giant black-and-chrome Humvee. I was so glad to see him there, so glad he'd made the first move at reconciliation, that I felt stupid and emotional and like I was gonna tear up.

Bud said, "Your ride's here and doesn't looked nearly as pissed as he did last time I saw him. I guess I'll see you tomorrow at the pageant."

"Okay."

I walked over to the Humvee. Black said, "You want to drive?"

Feeling magnanimous and ultra relieved to see him, I said, "You can."

I climbed into the passenger's seat and watched him get in, turn the ignition, and fire the engine. He stared straight ahead for a moment, then leaned against the steering wheel and looked across the seat at me.

"I thought I'd stay at your house tonight, if you don't mind."

Wanting to meet him half, even three-quarters of the way, I said, "No, you always have to come over to my house. I'd be thrilled to come to your place, if you'd rather. Maybe I could learn how to make chocolate chip cookies real fast and bring those, too."

Black grinned, showing all those damn dimples that turn me on so much. I smiled back, indeed turned on and rather giddy, too, I fear, and that was that. Fight over. No problem, unless and until he was visited by more hoodlum cohorts. I felt relief flooding over me sort of like warm vanilla cream and wondered just how far gone I was on this guy.

"You may want to reconsider that offer," he said. "Jude's back in town for tomorrow's pageant, and I sure as hell am not in the mood to entertain my ex-wife tonight."

"So the truth's out. That's the real reason you're here, olive branches be damned."

"Yeah. It's just gonna kill me to have to sleep in your bed again."

I laughed, and he shifted into gear and took off. I considered telling him how glad I was to see him and how glad I was that he came to find me because I was feeling pretty low about Shaggy, and the case in general, and a hundred other things, but couldn't quite bring myself to be that vulnerable. He'd be okay. He was used to me. I knew his close familial associations with known criminals and my unwillingness to commit to what he wanted was still there between us, like some kind of thick glass wall, that we'd have to discuss it and work it out, break it down someday somehow, but I didn't want to do it now. We'd hash that big question mark out some other day when everything else in my little world wasn't going to hell in a handbasket like it was today. He didn't broach the subject, either. Apparently, he was willing to wait a spell, too.

So we drove in companionable silence for a few minutes before Black said, "I caught Costin's sex tape on Channel 7. Pretty risqué stuff. They had to blur out most of it and cut the feed, but Shaggy showed up clear enough at the end. Want to talk about it?"

I declare, he does have such a nice shrinkish way of broaching subjects. "Nice, right? Real Paris Hilton kinda stuff."

"What's Shaggy have to say now?"

I told him about Shaggy sewing on the lips and how Bri was acting like she'd lost her mind. Just the usual pleasantries between a man and his gal pal.

"Hasn't exactly been great for you the last few days, has it, Claire?"

"Nope. Not even close"

"Let's stop and get a Big Mac. That oughta make you feel better."

I nodded and relaxed even more. Black knew my comfort foods, but truth be told, I already felt better because we'd patched things up, at least for the moment, and I didn't have to go home alone. He was a good sounding board with good insight, and a nice strong, hard body to snuggle into at night, and that's exactly what I needed.

We took a sack of fast food to my place, and I told him everything that went down in the hospital with Carlos Vasquez and today with Shaggy and Costin. I asked him what he knew about Esteban Rangos's murder, and he told me that the boy had been Jose's favorite nephew and protégé and was murdered several years ago by unknown assailants. He said Rangos was heartbroken and had vowed to find the killer. But Black stopped short of revealing whether or not Rangos had put out an open-ended hit on the killer. I didn't ask for any more details, either, and he didn't offer them. We let it drop, and he sat and listened silently while I paced back and forth in front of him. After a while he stood up.

"Okay, let's work out together. Maybe you'll work off some of this tension and dare I say it, aggression. That's what I did when I got off the plane this morning. It cleared my mind."

We headed for the backyard, and he held my punching bag while I absolutely beat the ever-living hell out of it for about fifteen minutes. After a while, though, I collapsed on the mat, breathing hard and red faced, my upper arm aching, sweating with exertion. Black dropped down beside me and propped his head in his palm.

"Feel better, sweetheart?"

"No."

"You will after we soak in the hot tub and massage each other for a couple of hours."

"Sounds like a plan."

He leaned down and kissed me, then murmured against my ear. "You'll get him, whoever the hell he is. He'll slip up and you'll find him."

"You're right on there. But this case is going absolutely nowhere. Nothing makes sense and nothing connects. Lots of bizarre goings-on here, everywhere I turn. We're missing something. Something significant. It's right there in front of me, I sense that, but I just can't put it together."

"You need more time, that's all. It's just been a few days. What about tomorrow? I take it that Charlie is ordering surveillance at the pageant?"

"We're gonna watch the audience. See if anything seems suspicious. It's a long shot but stranger things have happened. We're filming it, too, in case we miss something."

"Good idea."

Staring at me with his famous, lightning-charged, I'm-coming-now-to-jump-your-bones-ready-or-not look, Black stood up and pulled me to my feet. I followed him inside and let him strip off my clothes, and then lowered myself into the hot foaming water and watched with not a little enjoyment as he did the same. He was a well-honed specimen of virile, rock-muscled manhood, make no mistake about it. He submerged himself to midchest, still smiling that killer smile of his, and I headed straight for him, our flesh sliding together like two parts of a sensual puzzle, yin and yang, I tell you, slick and wet and over-the-top carnal sensation, and I shut my eyes and felt myself loosen up and my body go limp under his warm mouth and gentle fingers and probing tongue, but my last thoughts before I let the magic take me was that I wasn't so sure anything was going to look better tomorrow. In fact, I had a real strong intuition that something really bad was going to happen.

Seventeen

I have this thing about kiddie beauty pageants. Truthfully? I hate them worse than a weeklong bout of food poisoning. I think they are stupid, wrong, exploitive, child abusive, should be against the laws of God and humanity, near felonies, but that's just my humble opinion. So I am not particularly enjoying myself at the moment. I'm standing at the back wall of Black's biggest, glitziest ballroom watching garishly painted-up moms parade garishly painted-up little girls around like prize ponies with flower wreaths around their necks.

Just outside the door, and unfortunately near enough for me to overhear, a wacko mother is telling her baby to shut up and smile, that she needs to win because they need the cash for rent. I restrain myself from attacking A-hole Mommy, but her comments remind me of the note attached to poor Hilde and her dreadful death mask, not to mention the Esteban Rangos autopsy pictures and Vasquez's black-stitched, grotesquely swollen mouth, all of which are reasons why I am forced to endure this ridiculous sideshow. The children are now performing their so-called talents, and not very well, but the parents are oohing and aahing to beat the band. I just wish it was over.

Bud is covering the excitement going on near the stage and probably enjoying it to the same sublevel extent as myself. And yes, Brianna is still set on competing as a contestant, but hadn't made her appearance yet. Across the room, my lone female colleague in the department, Connie O'Hara, was busy filming the goings-on. She'd had her own baby two months ago, and this was her first day back on duty. I wondered if they held beauty contests for two-month-old infants? Probably did, their talent being burping and messing their diapers.

Eric Dixson was also busy, shooting pictures as fast as humanly possible, too, at the end of the runway where he could get better close-ups for the girls' portfolios. My new good friend, Jude, was sitting among the other judges, probably waiting with bated breath for Black to get here so she could pretend she didn't like him anymore.

Star magazine was probably lurking around, too, looking for the scoop on the famous duo's reconciliation. They'd probably already made up some asinine nickname for them like they did for *Brangelina* and *Bennifer*. Let's see, Nick and Jude together, yeah, the morons would probably coin them as *Nude.* And as for Black and me, Claire and Nick would no doubt become *Click.* I could see the headline heralding the return of the super couple now: "Nude Back Together at Last. Poor Click Casualty of Love."

I watched the people. My gut told me that the perpetrator had an intense interest in beauty pageants, maybe this one in particular, maybe not. He was probably here, plotting, or maybe it was a she, all decked out in her sparkling gown or skimpy bathing suit, now in position to win the coveted crown. Killing a competitor for a rhinestone tiara seemed a bit farfetched, but then again, a lot of murder motives were.

There was the usual assortment of obsessive people and

crazy mothers, I would say, not that I'd attended many such events. The ballroom was full, everyone craning their necks and flashbulbs popping all over the place as their favorite contestant walked out from behind the curtains. I scanned each row, looking for something, anything that tweaked my suspicions, or a familiar face, or a guilty one. Mostly families grouped together, some with a father and an older bored sibling or two of Mama's precious little princess, but most were strident stage moms, with maternal aunts and grandmas in tow, faces stiff with tension that filtered down to their child and no doubt made them feel like crap if they didn't win.

Then I saw somebody I recognized, Joe the Psychic McKay. He waltzed in the door beside me, and I cringed, hoping he wasn't here to put Lizzie through the toddler hellfire of kiddie pageants. He was searching the room and when he turned in my direction and saw me, it was pretty obvious he'd come here just to seek me out, which couldn't be good.

"Hey, there, Detective, thought you might be hanging around in here."

"Hey. Why'd you think that? Vision?"

"Nope. Nick Black told me."

"So? What's up?"

"Nothin' in particular, just checkin' on you."

I glanced back at the stage as a little girl froze up at the sight of the gawking audience, reversed herself back through the curtains, and refused to come out. Her mother was crying louder than she was. "Please, McKay, tell me you're not here because you entered Lizzie in this stupid circus."

"Hell, no, but she'd win, hands down, not that I'm prejudiced, or anything. Fact is, she's upstairs right now spendin' a little time with your favorite head examiner. I dropped by to tell him she wasn't sleepin' so good, see if he had any ideas to fix that, and he said he had an hour he could spend with her before he had to show up down here as a judge. I left the two of 'em in his office, playin' Barbies and building towers outta blocks. He's gonna do it pro bono, too. Said he owed me since I helped you get outta that nasty little situation last winter. Nice guy, bad as I hate to admit it."

"Yes, he is." Except for his tommy-gun-toting, Top Ten Most Wanted secret relatives. I looked back to the runway where a toddler in a cowgirl outfit was skipping her way down the runway and singing a majorly off-key rendition of "Home on the Range." "So Lizzie's not sleeping, huh?"

"Not much. She wakes up a lot screamin' until I can get to her and calm her down. She's takin' to Nick a little, though, maybe, we'll see if it lasts. I've gotta get back up there, but I had to talk to you first."

"Why?"

We had a mutual gazing contest then, for just a little too long but he seemed reluctant to spill the beans, which made me reluctant to dump them out, either. I finally got tired of waiting for him to lay it out in black and white, because it was probably a lot more black than white. "Okay, give it to me straight, McKay. You got another terrifying nightmare starring me, right?"

"As a matter of fact, yes."

"Oh, great, tell me. How bloody's this one?"

"It's the same old story, Detective. I feel you're in danger. I've been getting flashes of little girls, like those up there"—he gestured at the stage, where the children were all lined up for the crowning—"all dressed up in these frilly petticoats and stuff, but the clothes looked sorta retro, two of 'em, girls that look sort of alike."

"You're seeing me with little girls in kiddie pageants?"

"Yep. Not sure why, either, but you're right there in the middle of 'em, too. Got any ideas why I'm gettin' this stuff?"

"For Pete's sake, McKay, why can't you be as good a psychic as John Edward? It would make my job a heck of a lot easier. He'd just say, there's a little girl to your side with a bowie knife in her hand. Take care 'cuz she's gonna stab you in your bathroom on May first. Something like that."

McKay grinned, dimpled impressively. What was it with me and dimply men? Seemed my goose bumps just couldn't get enough of them. "Yeah, that'd be nice. I'd be a helluva lot richer, too. Can't control what I see, comes in snatches, and it's not cooperatin' this time the way I'd like it to. I also see Bud sometimes, with you, but there's something between you. Some kind of bars or barrier, that make any sense?"

"Nope. Bud's right over there. He's working this case, too."

McKay followed my gaze to where Bud slouched against the far wall, watching the girls on stage and looking bored as hell. "Maybe if you gave me something personal of the victim's to hold, or let me go look at the murder scene like last time? That might help me get a bead on."

"Maybe you need to find some psychic good enough to get his own TV show and take some lessons."

"Maybe I will. Maybe I'll make a profession outta this and get richer than Nick."

Nobody's richer than Nick, I thought, except maybe J. K. Rowling and the queen of England. "I'll see what Charlie says. It can't hurt, and he was all for it last time. Maybe tomorrow? That be good for you?"

"Just give me a call and tell me when and where."

The runner-ups were being announced by a guy rated on the cheesy scale just under David Hasselhoff, and one beautiful little girl beamed a painfully fake smile at being selected third runner-up, and the second runner-up collapsed in her petticoats, bawling like a hungry calf. These things oughta be outlawed, I'm telling you. Apparently McKay felt the same way, because he frowned and didn't hang around.

He said, "Better go. Lizzie might get scared if I'm outta sight too long. We're gonna rent a movie tonight. *Shrek*. I'd ask you to come over and watch it with us, but know you won't. If I pick up on anything else, I'll drop by your place and tell you."

"Thanks. I mean it, McKay."

After he left, I stood alone and hoped that Black could do something to help Lizzie survive her horrific ordeal; she was definitely lost in her own little monster-inhabited world. I watched in agony as the pageant dragged its way through all the age groups, exploiting elementary schoolchildren, then junior high, then high school, and then the big event itself was heralded at the microphone by Mr. Cheese Whiz.

Connie O'Hara edged over to me and lowered the camcorder for a moment. "You having as much fun as I am?"

"Oh, yeah, I just love to watch smiling pretty girls strut their stuff around. How's the baby?"

"Oh, he's fine. Thanks for that little sleeper with the Cardinals' logo. You need to come over sometime and see him in it. Mom's moved down to Osage Beach, so she can keep him for me while I'm on duty. She never liked Kansas City anyway. She's a small-town gal like me."

"That's good. Having somebody you can trust to keep him safe."

I thought of my Zach and how he'd been staying with a trusted relative the night he died, but it didn't do him any good. I really didn't want to talk about her baby, or any baby, for that matter, so I changed the subject. "Was it hard to get back into the grind?

"No. I missed working more than I thought I would. Didn't think my first assignment would be filming a stupid beauty contest, though."

"My sentiments exactly, believe you me."

"Well, here comes the next lovely, so back to work. See you later."

I watched her move away, and the lights dimmed as the main event began. I was still having trouble believing that

Brianna was actually taking Hilde's place in this ridiculous show, but I tended to think the poor girl was having some kind of post-traumatic stress syndrome. I hoped she would agree to go into therapy with Black, too, and sooner rather than later. Wouldn't be long at this rate before he'd be analyzing everybody I knew at Lake of the Ozarks. What does that say about my friends and neighbors? I searched the crowd, saw no one acting strangely or eyeing anybody's lips with scissors in his hand. I glanced at my watch, wondering if the stupid thing was ever going to get over. The pageant was well run, though, so I guess old Pattycakes Cardamon knew what she was doing.

I knew Brianna was last, and she walked down the runway with long easy strides and that odd hip walk beanpole models always slink around with. She was smiling, easy, relaxed, and I wondered how in the world she could put on that kind of calm face, after all she'd been through the past few days. I guess they learned to look beautiful, serene, and unneurotic at beauty pageant school. Couldn't be good for their mental health, if you ask me.

Brianna won the thing and was crowned Miss Spring Dogwood, and should have, I guess, and then she gave this soft-spoken, breathy thank-you speech in a voice that didn't sound anything like her, talking about her sister and how she accepted the crown in honor of her precious memory. The crowd was appreciative and hushed, and I knew then I had to be in the outer chambers of the *Twilight Zone* with a bunch of mist around me, or even purgatory, maybe. After the victory ramp strut, the curtains came down, everybody got up, packed their duds, and headed to the next pageant, weeping kids in tow.

After a while, Bud and Brianna came out from backstage, and I saw Eric Dixson approach them for the winner pictures. Some newspaper photographers hovered around, too, waiting their turns. Bud left Brianna posing on her throne with her giant tiara and roses and walked over to me. He didn't look particularly happy that she won. I tried not to think how much she looked like dead Hilde sitting in that bleached-out shower stall.

"See anything?" he asked me.

"Nope. Just the regular beauty-obsessed folks."

"Me, either. Nothing happened backstage that amounted to anything. I thought the guy might try to pull something dramatic."

"Maybe he was here." I heard my phone go off and Caller ID lit up with Miami Police Department. "Hold on, Bud, it's Ortega, he must've got something."

I answered in a hurry. "Yeah? Ortega?"

He said, "Vasquez's is talking some. Said he remembered something else about the perp."

"Hit me with it."

"Said the guy was wearing a swastika on a chain around his neck. That ring any bells at your end?"

My heart leapt. "Oh, yeah, you bet it does. We gotta a suspect up here that knows all about swastikas. And guess what? He's got a real distinctive voice, too."

"Think it's him?"

"I'm gonna find out. How's Carlos? He gonna make it?"

"Yeah. They said he's gonna have to have some plastic surgery to repair his mouth, skin grafts, stuff like that. But he's doing better than they expected after losing all that blood. But now for the interestin' part. Get this. A coupla guys from the Rangos's organization paid him a visit at CCU and made sure he knew it wasn't them that hit him, said they thought the same guy did Carlos's nephew. Problem is, he told them he thinks it's that friend of Hilde Swensen's he saw that time, told them about the voice, too, everything he told us. So now we gotta worry about them finding the guy first."

"Well, that's not good news. But if it is Costin, there's no way they can get to him first. We'll go pick him up right now, see what he has to say."

"Keep me posted."

"You bet. Thanks, Ortega."

I dropped the phone back into my purse. "Okay, Bud, we got something good here. Carlos Vasquez said his assailant had a swastika hanging around his neck. Sound familiar?"

"Costin? Shit, let's go get him. Let me tell Bri. She's got to hang around here a couple of hours anyway for a press conference and photos. I'll pick her up later."

He headed toward her, and I headed for Black, who was introducing Brianna to the gaggle of reporters. I stopped outside the pack of jackals and motioned that I'd see him later. We had our own secret signals, you see, for that and for other stuff, too. He didn't look particularly happy I was taking off without him but who would with the press idiots yelling demands at him. Jude, who was getting her fair share of the shutterbugs, smiled and waved at me, used to the adoring melee, I guess. I ducked behind a pillar before the media saw me and took chase.

Bud was back and ready to roll, as eager as I was. Ten minutes later we were in Bud's SUV and I had Charlie on the telephone.

"We think it's Costin, sheriff. We need a warrant to search his place."

"What do you have on him?"

"According to the Miami PD, the Florida perp had on a swastika necklace and so did Costin when I first interviewed him. That can't be a coincidence. The vic identified the perp as having a distinctive voice so that matches, too. And he's the one who let Shaggy in at the funeral home. That should be enough for probable cause."

"Okay, you got your warrant. I'll get it signed and over to you. Where's he live?"

I got the address from Bud and repeated it to him, then Bud stomped the accelerator for Walter Costin's place, not bothering to adhere to the speed limit. He said nothing, just drove hard, but his jaw was flexing with anger and I knew his too-close association with the case was taking a toll on his impartiality. I thought of McKay's prediction and that maybe those bars he saw between Bud and me was Bud in jail for murdering Walter Costin with his bare hands. Maybe Charlie shouldn't have put him back on the case. He didn't appear to be particularly objective at the moment. I decided to rein him in a bit before we caught up with our suspect. You know, small talk to calm the savage beast within; it couldn't hurt. "Brianna's pleased she won, I guess? For Hilde's sake, and all that."

Bud kept his eyes on the road. "She's actin' like nothing happened, happy almost. Maybe doin' it was good for her, who knows? It seems to me like she's puttin' on a big act."

"Why would she do that?"

"Who knows?"

"I don't see how she got through it without breaking down."

"Everybody grieves differently, right?"

Right. And did I ever know it. Brianna took the cake, if you asked me, but Bud didn't ask me so I kept my mouth shut.

Walter Costin lived in a fairly new apartment complex in Camdenton, one by the name of Berkshire Gardens, and one that had tennis courts, a swimming pool, and a little picturesque residential lake with a jogging path around it, not to mention lots of serpentine lanes through well-lit parking lots and flower beds full of red tulips and yellow daffodils. Seemed a little on the pricey side for a student/funeral parlor night man, now didn't it?

We got there a few minutes later. Bud didn't want to wait in the car for the warrant to show up, and neither did I. Costin had a first-floor unit, all dark and unwelcoming, and we approached it, guns drawn, as if Osama bin Laden was holed up inside. No car, nobody answered the door, but a few of the neighbors were peeking out their windows, finger hovering over 911, no doubt.

Bud took off to the manager's office to flash his credentials, and I stayed with weapon trained on the door in case Walter threw it open and invited me in for tea and Nazi pastries. By the time, Bud got back with the manager, our colleague Doug Obion had shown up, signed warrant in hand. Charlie can move fast when the case demands it. I told Obion to stick around outside for backup, then handed the manager the official papers. He unlocked the door and flipped on the light, and Bud and I entered, weapons galore and wary as hell.

The place checked out clear, so we left Obion outside watching the parking lot for Walter's arrival and began our search. It looked like Costin didn't have a lot of furniture, or many other possessions, for that matter, or else he'd cleaned out the place after our little interview downtown. I had a sneaking suspicion, however, that he lived somewhere else and used this address to con unsuspecting employers and law enforcement officers. He was a pretty smart cookie if he managed to get down to Florida, slice up Vasquez's face, and leave him for dead, then beat it back here in time for that interview we had with him. But he could've done it; he'd had enough time.

I told Obion to get hold of Lohman's Funeral Home and find out if Costin had quit his job or not. I had a feeling he was long gone by now. Obion was back quick enough with the news that Costin had stopped showing up a couple of days ago. Lohman didn't know where he was. Bud was tossing the kitchen cabinets, taking out his frustration on some unfortunate brass hinges, but I headed for the telephone answering machine, which was my investigatory wont. Glad to see it had both Caller ID and an answering machine with three messages blinking, I pressed the button. The first one came up, a hang up, and I had a feeling they all would be hang ups. I was proved wrong, however, when the second one was his stripper girlfriend's whiny voice wanting to know where he was and why he'd stood her up. Number three, however, hit the jackpot.

"We gotta talk. You know where. We'll both be there."

That was it, but funniest thing, it was Shaggy Becker's voice, clear as day. Bud and I looked at each other, and then I punched back through the ID listings. "He called from the jail."

Bud slammed a cabinet door. "C'mon, let's go. Shaggy knows a helluva lot more than he's sayin', and he's going to tell us the truth this time, if I have to beat it outta him. Look, I gotta go back to the Lodge and pick up Bri. I'll run her home and meet you downtown."

"Okay. I'll nose around here some more. Shaggy's not going anywhere."

I watched Bud get out his cell and dial up Brianna. But see what I mean about Bud's mood? Temper, temper, my, my, and I thought I was bad about that sort of thing.

Sisterly Love

The older one did as the boy said, although her new boyfriend tried to talk her out of breaking it off with him, even refused to leave when she asked him to. He didn't understand, and she was afraid to tell him the truth, afraid of what the boy would do. And her fears were well founded. One day her boyfriend just went missing and no one knew where he was. He simply disappeared. And she knew, she knew the boy had killed him, even before the day the present was left at her front door.

It was a pretty pink gift bag with three long-stemmed carnations decorating the front, and as she pushed aside the crumpled white tissue paper, she was filled with cold dread. When she saw the blood and severed lips lying in the bottom, she ran to the bathroom and vomited. She burned the bag with the lips inside, and when her new boyfriend's family came around looking for him, she told them that he had just not shown up one day, that she didn't know where he was, that she feared for his life, and they believed her. Then his body was discovered, and even when it was, the police didn't come around to question her. They had no leads, no idea who could've done such a terrible thing. The older one knew, she knew in her heart that the boy had killed him, but there wasn't anything she could do about it, not with his threats to harm Bubby and her. He had proved himself capable of cold-blooded murder more than once. He'd kill them both in the blink of an eye. He had no conscience, no sense of right and wrong. He had become the personification of evil.

That's when she made the decision. She had to get away and take Bubby with her. They had to flee the boy's evil influence and go into hiding. But she told the boy that she realized how much she loved him now and told him everything was back the same between them, just the way he wanted, but all the while she suffered his attentions, she planned her getaway. Sissy moved into her house, too, but she didn't tell Sissy because Sissy was loyal to the boy, in love with him. Sissy would still do anything for him; Sissy would probably like it when the older one was gone and no longer competition for his affections. Then Sissy would have him to herself, and eventually, Sissy would probably die.

Bubby had just turned eighteen and was thinking of going to college. He was ready to move out of their adoptive parents' house, anyway, because the two doctors wanted to move their practices to Seattle and settle there with the twins. All their older children already were out on their own, but they truly loved Bubby and begged him to go along. Once she'd made her escape plan, the older one talked privately to Bubby and told him that she was going to disappear and that he needed to do the same. She told him about her boyfriend and that she would send him enough money to find a safe place where he could go to school and make a new life. He refused at first, but she told him that once he was settled somewhere, she would escape and join him and they could be together. Then they would be safe from the boy and try to forget all the terrible things that had happened in their childhood.

Bubby agreed to go, and one day he just left home and told the parents that he was going off to travel the world and decide what he wanted to do and not to worry, that he would be all right. Nobody knew where he went. The older one pretended that she was as shocked as Sissy and the boy at his decision, but inside she felt nothing but relief. Bubby was out of danger, out of the boy's evil clutches, and soon she would be, too. So began her own secret plan to escape. She bided her time, thought out everything in detail, planned for every contingency, and made sure the boy and Sissy had no idea what she had in mind.

But she hated the boy now, hated him for all the things he'd done, for killing her boyfriend, who'd done nothing but love her. She hated looking at him, hating it when he forced her into his bed, but she smiled and pretended she loved him again. She continued with school, as if nothing happened, got her degree and made some money, and all the while she kept in touch with Bubby on the sly.

Then the day came. Bubby had prepared the way, and he'd chosen a wonderful place, a place she knew a little bit about, but where nobody would think to look for them. He was happy there, had a good job, one he loved and was very good at. She waited until the boy and Sissy went out clubbing one night, and then she left everything as it was and walked out the door forever.

Eighteen

I poked around the apartment for a while and found a few things, one of which was an old photograph of some kids, two boys and four girls. I recognized Walter as the oldest in the group right off the bat. They were standing in front of what looked like an indoor swimming pool. The other boy in the picture looked a hell of a lot like a miniature Shaggy Becker. One more good reason to sweat Shaggy in his cell, I must say. As much as I didn't like the idea, Shaggy was shaping up as a suspect or accomplice or person of interest, at the very least.

I nosed through some books and notebooks, found nothing, except that Walter Costin liked Shakespeare, which fit rather nicely with our Smiley Villain quote. I pulled the mattress off the bed and almost missed the piece of clear tape that blended into the white mattress pad. I ripped it off and found that somebody had cut away about a four-by-six-inch square of padding. I lifted it out and found three videotapes secreted inside. I smiled, pleased as punch, and pulled them out. Plain VHS tapes, no writing, no labels, but highly suspicious.

I searched the apartment for a cassette player, found none, but was pretty sure we would find whatever Costin was hiding in his bed interesting, to say the least. Then again, he filmed himself and his girlfriend having sex at the funeral home and didn't mind showing it on TV so maybe he made a habit of videotaping unsuspecting women. If so, we'd nail him for that, too.

After about an hour, I tried to put in a call to Bud and tell him about the tapes but found my cell on low charge. I took Obion's car with a promise to have it returned as soon as I reached the sheriff's office, then I left him on guard at the Berkshire Gardens, in case Walter Costin was stupid enough to show up there, which I was pretty sure he wasn't unless the videotapes meant something special and/or incriminating to him. I plugged my cell phone in the car charger and drove downtown, wondering if I really wanted to know how much Shaggy was involved in this case. He just wasn't the type to kill somebody, nobody could make me believe that, and I never pegged him as the type to protect a guilty party, either. Especially a killer like Costin, if indeed, Costin was the killer. But we were getting close now, to some piece of the puzzle that would hopefully ignite a lightbulb inside my head and I could say, "You're busted, freakshow."

The sheriff's office was pretty much deserted this late at night. Just a couple of dispatchers at the duty desk and the jailors downstairs. Charlie hadn't come in, must've made his call to the judge from home. I made sure Obion's squad car got back to him, and then I went upstairs and plugged in the VCR in our conference room. I chucked in the first tape and found it was another porno, all right. This one wasn't semi-dark like the one Charlie had shown us. This one had lights set up all around. This one was of Hilde Swensen and Walter Costin getting into some serious S and M stuff, with whips and belts and black leather restraints. Enough to bring blood, but they were both enjoying it, no doubt about it. The tape went to static for about ten seconds, then I put in the second tape.

Another sex scene began, but this time it was Brianna and Walter Costin. Good God, what the hell's going on with these people? This one was much more tender, a couple in a hayloft, and they were really young, too, not much more than teenagers, it looked like. They kept saying how much they loved each other, but I'd seen enough to get the drift. I punched Eject and pushed in number three, wondering who Walter's next lover would be. This time it was a darkened bedroom with a large man lying on a bed snoring, but it wasn't Walter.

There was some low whispering in the background, and then the light on the camera came on and focused on the man. Three children appeared around the bed, but their faces were partially shadowed and I couldn't tell for sure who they were but my skin crawled because the tallest one looked a whole helluva lot like Brianna Swensen. She picked up a pillow and put it over the man's face. The other two leaned on it and helped her press it down, then all three calmly looked into the camera lens and smothered the guy until he was dead. The tape went to static, and shocked, I stared at it until the tape hit the end and began to rewind.

I had just witnessed a snuff film and/or an actual murder, and a cold-blooded, deliberate one, at that, one perpetrated by a bunch of kids. I frowned, tried to think how all this fit together. Was the other girl Hilde? The boy, Shaggy? That didn't make a lick of sense, but everything pointed to it. Still I couldn't believe any of them would kill somebody like that, not now, much less when they were children.

Frowning, I took the three tapes and headed down the steps to the county jail, in too much a hurry to use the prisoner elevator. A deputy let me in the heavy steel door, and then led me back to Shaggy's cell block. Surprisingly, Bud was already there. I thought it'd take him more time to get Brianna home and tranquilized. Shaggy was lying in his bunk fully clothed, a little odd in itself, but who knows, maybe Shaggy always slept in his clothes. After all, it was Shaggy I was talking about.

Bud stood outside the bars. He didn't mince words. "Okay, Shaggy, I've had enough of this shit. We served a warrant on Walter Costin's place and found your message on his answering machine. What's going on between you and him? Where were you plannin' to meet him?"

Shaggy didn't looked surprised by the news, which surprised me. Something was wrong with this whole scenario, something I couldn't put my finger on, but made me damn nervous. He just stared at me, then looked at the tapes I was holding. He said, "What're those tapes? You find those at Costin's house?"

"Yeah. Why?"

"Just curious."

"I found them hidden in Costin's mattress, as a matter of fact. You know anything about them?"

He sat up quickly. "You watch them?"

"I sure did. You in one of them, Shaggy?"

"What tapes?" That was Bud.

"There's a couple of sex tapes, one with Costin and Hilde, and I'm sorry, Bud, but one's of Costin and Brianna, when they were really young."

"What the hell?" said Bud.

"And one looks suspiciously like a snuff film. But since it's three juves smothering a guy, I think it's probably some kind of homemade horror movie they did for laughs."

"What the hell?" Bud said again.

Shaggy went white and retreated to the corner of his cell, as far away from us as he could get.

"Are you the little boy in it, Shaggy? Or is that Walter Costin?"

Shaggy put his hands over his face and began to rock back and forth. Bud and I looked at each other, and then Bud grabbed hold of the bars, his voice tight but controlled.

"Shaggy, you gotta stop this and be up front with us. We're tryin' to find out what went down. We know you're involved with Costin. He's the perp, isn't he? He killed Hilde, didn't he? Why are you protectin' him?"

"I don't know anything."

"Bullshit." That was me. Very pissed, to be sure.

Maybe Bud and I should play some good cop/bad cop like in all the movies. Problem was, Shaggy knew us both too well not to see through that bluff. And at the moment, we'd both be the bad cop, anyway.

Bud said, "Where's Costin now? You gotta tell us."

"Why should I?"

I had to admit; this innocent act of Shag's was wearing pretty damn thin.

"Let me have him alone for a minute," Bud said, not looking at me.

I'd never seen Bud act like this before. He wasn't even trying to be impartial anymore. He needed to be taken off the case, oh, yeah.

"What're you gonna do, Bud? Beat him with a rubber hose?" I laughed. Ha ha, but I sure as hell hoped not.

Bud gave me a look that told me to get real. I believed it and decided that maybe he had some kind of trick up his sleeve that would entice Shaggy to spill his guts. It went against my grain to walk out, even for a few minutes, but I played along. Bud was pretty good at stuff like this, even when he was enraged. He had calmed considerably now, though. His teeth weren't even gritted.

"Okay, I'm gonna go upstairs and get us some coffee and check in with Obion at Costin's apartment. See if he's seen anything. Play nice, the two of you. Remember, we're all friends here."

Or used to be.

I went for the coffee, called Obion, and found out that all was quiet at the Berkshire Gardens, which was about what I expected. Walter Costin had been smart enough to fly the coop, and all we had to do now was get Shaggy to tell us where he was supposed to meet him. And why. And when. And who had killed who in that snuff tape.

Afraid to leave them alone too long, I waited five more minutes and then entered the cell block again. Bud had the keys from the jailor and was unlocking Shaggy's cell. That didn't appear a good idea to me.

"What the hell are you doing, Bud?"

"He's gonna show us where Costin's holed up."

"You got the sheriff's okay on this, I take it?"

"Yeah."

"Like hell you do."

The jailor was sitting in the next room, ignoring us, reading a *Hotrod* magazine. I could see him through the observation window. He didn't seem to notice that Bud had the keys and was unlocking his prisoner. I frowned.

"Bud, this is a stupid idea."

Now he was inside the cell, snapping handcuffs on Shaggy's wrists. "He won't tell me here, but he said he'll show me."

Shaggy said, "I'll tell you everything I know, but only if I go along for the ride. You couldn't find the place, anyway. It's way out in the sticks."

I hesitated. "We need Charlie's permission to do something like this."

"He's gonna show us where Costin's supposed to meet him, Claire. What's the matter with you?"

"What's the matter with you? This is throwing procedure to hell. We can get our badges pulled for this. I'm not willing to do that."

"Then you stay here. I think that's a better idea anyway. But I'm taking him out and I'm gonna finish my interrogation while I've got him. Then he can show me where the perp is, or soon will be. It's not exactly unheard of. Hell, Claire, we've done stuff like this before."

I wavered, because we had done similar things in the past on multiple occasions, but my instincts were screaming that this was all going to go very bad very quick. "I'm not staying here. And I'm not going without Charlie's say-so."

"Okay, damn it, I'll call him."

Bud pulled out his phone, and I immediately felt a wash of relief. Lynch mobs went against my grain, even if it was a mob of one pissed, out-of-control detective. He punched in the sheriff's number and instantly turned into Mr. Calm and Pleasant. Well, that was unsettling. "Sheriff, sorry to disturb you again, but I'd like permission to take Shaggy out of his cell. He thinks he knows where Costin might be holed up, says he can't tell us, but has to show us or we'd never find it."

As he listened to Charlie, he stared poisoned arrows at me, not so Mr. Calm and Pleasant where I was concerned. "Yes sir." Pause. "Yes sir, she's right here."

He handed the phone to me.

I took it. "Yes sir."

"Is this on the up and up, Detective?"

"It seems to be, sir. He's not talking unless we take him with us."

"What's Shaggy's connection with Walter Costin?"

"I'm not sure. We're trying to find out. It's definitely there, sir. I think they've all known each other since they were kids, and that includes Brianna. I found some tapes at Costin's house that seem to prove it. I just don't know exactly how it all fits together yet." I hesitated, not wanting to tell him, but I did. "One appears to be a snuff tape, but I think it's probably just a homemade movie somebody made. I'm not sure, though."

"Are you shittin' me? You're not sure?" Lots of low swearing, muffled, then, "Then take him out, if you have to. But put him in cuffs, you hear me. And don't screw this up or I'll throw all three of you in jail."

Maybe that's where McKay's Bud-Behind-Bars vision came in, but we now had Charlie's permission. The truth was, of course, I couldn't see Shaggy giving us any trouble or trying to make a run for it. He was just in lockup temporarily, anyway, for Pete's sake. As far as I knew, Charlie couldn't hold him much longer, probably until tomorrow morning. Now, though, his involvement had deepened to possible homicide charges, or accessory to murder charges, which made him dangerous, even to Bud and me.

"Okay," I said. "Let's go."

Bud didn't waste time, but gripped Shaggy's arm and pulled him outside. We signed him out at the desk and said it wouldn't take long. We placed Shaggy in the front seat of Bud's SUV. Bud drove. I sat in back behind Shaggy, in case he did try something. But what the heck was I going to do if he jumped out and ran? Shoot him in the back? That was laughable. I could never shoot Shaggy. But Shaggy wouldn't do that to us; he wouldn't run. Nobody could make me believe that.

Shaggy told Bud to head to I-44. We did. We rode in silence until I'd heard enough of it.

"Okay, Shag, it's time to talk. What's going on with you and Costin? Who's the man on the bed in that film? Did those kids kill him or was it just an amateur movie?"

"Christ," said Bud.

Shaggy stared straight ahead, at our headlight beams flashing past the thick tracts of trees on either side of the road. "We gotta go to Springfield."

"Springfield!" I said. "That's an hour and a half from here."

"That's where he'll go, sooner or later."

Springfield was the third largest city in Missouri, a city of about a hundred and fifty thousand people. "Shaggy, there's no way we're driving all the way to Springfield unless you tell us why."

Shaggy didn't appear to like that idea.

"Okay, Bud, turn the car around. I've had enough of this crap. He can rot in jail, for all I care."

Bud braked and hit the turn signal.

Shaggy said, "Walter Costin's my stepbrother."

"Shit." That was Bud but I thought the same thing.

"Okay. Let's hear it all."

"There isn't any more."

"Shag, I'm warning you."

"He did that to Hilde, cut her. I can't prove it but I know he did."

"Why's he's in Springfield?"

"That's where we grew up. It's out in the outskirts. On a kinda farm."

Bud was letting me handle this, and I was glad of it. He took Highway 5 south to Lebanon and kept driving, eyes glued on the road, fingers clenched in a stranglehold grip around the steering wheel.

"Why would your stepbrother want to mutilate and murder Hilde?"

"I'm not sure. I just know he's capable of it."

"Why? Has he done it before?"

"I don't know what all he's done. We got away from him for a while, then he found us."

I said, "Who's we?"

Bud said, "Come on, Shaggy, don't sandbag us. You got out your relationship with Costin. Why are you protectin' him?"

"I don't know, maybe I am, but not why you think."

"Well, enlighten me."

Shaggy got mad. "I don't know. He's bad, real bad, sometimes. He made me do things I didn't want to do. He scares me. You should be scared of him, too."

Shaggy sounded scared. Bud lapsed into silence again. My turn.

"Tell me why he scares you?"

"Why do you think?"

"Did he hurt you?"

"He hurt lots of people. He gets off on it, always has."

"Are you saying he's murdered people and you knew it?"

"I can't say any more. He'll kill me. He'll kill you. He'll kill Brianna. He'll kill all of us. And he'll get by with it. He always does, always, every single time."

"If you're taking us to arrest him, how can he kill you?"

"He just can. He's smart. He's so smart you wouldn't believe it. He figures out everything, manipulates everything and everybody. Everything's a game with him. He likes to play cat and mouse, trip people up, catch them in traps."

"Nobody's that smart." But truth be told, I was beginning to get a little edgy myself. "Is he gonna be at this place outside Springfield? Would he try to ambush us? Are we gonna need backup?"

"Maybe. I don't know for sure where he is. But he'll go back there. He always goes back home. And that's where we're supposed to meet, early tomorrow morning after I got outta jail."

"Is that where he's been living?"

"No, I drove up there and checked a few days ago. We still own it, but he's been living down in Florida some. He didn't know where I was until he followed Hilde and she led him straight to me at the lake. She didn't know he was followin' her. I didn't know he was here until I found out he was working at Lohman's, then it was too late."

"Why Hilde, Shaggy? How does she fit into this?"

"Just get him and lock him up so we'll all be safe."

"I know you know more than you're telling us."

"Okay, okay, it's the smile thing, that quote he left on her.

I've heard him say that a thousand times. That's why I think he did it. But that doesn't prove he did."

Shaggy wasn't making a whole lot of sense and I knew good and well there was plenty more to this bizarre tale. He seemed genuinely afraid of his stepbrother, if Costin truly was his stepbrother. But I had a feeling we weren't going to get much more out of him.

"Were he and Hilde lovers? Was it a jealousy thing?"

"I guess so. I moved away 'cause I know what he's capable of. I'm warnin' you, Claire, we can't mess this up. He's too dangerous, he's cunning and savage. He's evil."

"Evil, you say. Your stepbrother is evil."

"Yeah, that's exactly what I said, yeah." Shaggy turned to Bud. "Take I-44, our place is just off it. It's way out on the north edge of the city."

"Right."

I pressed for more, but couldn't get anything else out of Shaggy. It looked like his stepbrother was going to have to be the one we forced the answers out of. I was sort of relieved that Shaggy had been protecting a family member rather than being a part of the murder himself. I still didn't think he had it in him to hurt anybody. All of it was weird, though, and not quite kosher. I checked both my weapons, made sure they were loaded and handy, my cell phone charged up to the max, just in case I was wrong and ended up with a pillow over my face.

We made the drive in record time. Bud has a heavy foot, when need be. The farm was isolated, all right. We left the interstate and bumped down a rural gravel road with houses showing up every hundred yards or so, and then about a mile farther up Shaggy pointed out an overgrown lane leading up to a farmhouse. As Bud turned in, our headlights flashed on the front of the house. It was two stories, and I could see a barn roof behind the house.

"Doesn't look like anybody's home," Bud said. "No cars. No lights. You sure he's comin' back here?"

"Yeah, positive. In the morning between eight and ten. He was giving me time to get outta jail and make it up here. Park out behind the barn. You don't want him to see your car or he'll take off."

I looked around at the dark house and overgrown yard, the sheer isolation of the place. "I think we better get some backup out here, Bud. I can call the Springfield PD. This place gives me the creeps."

"Not yet. Let's go inside and see what we can find. There might be proof of what he's been doing. Is that right, Shaggy? Is this his lair?"

Shaggy stared at the house. "Yeah. It's his lair, all right."

Bud and I got out. I said, "Man, I don't like this, Bud. Something's not right. Can't you feel it?"

"Let's get inside and call from there. If we can surprise him in the morning, it'll be easier to take him down. We get a bunch of uniforms out here, he won't get within a mile of this place."

Bud opened the door and helped Shaggy get out. The cuffs stayed on. Shaggy looked straight at me, and I didn't like the expression on his face, either. He looked scared and guilty and nervous.

We moved around the side of the barn, Bud and Shaggy in front. I followed, my Glock held down beside my leg, my finger alongside the trigger. There was no sound except for some insect mating shrieks, and it was pitch black except for some moonlight filtering through the tree branches. The house was dark and silent, seemingly deserted.

"You got the key, Shaggy?" I asked.

"It's not locked."

"That's not much of a lair."

Bud said, "C'mon, let's get inside in case he shows up early."

We climbed the back steps and Bud tried the door handle. It opened easily, just like Shaggy said it would.

"The electricity isn't on, but there's a kerosene lamp on the kitchen counter. Matches, too."

Bud moved through the darkness to the counter and fumbled a second or two then I heard the scratch of a match. The kerosene lantern flared, and I gasped and raised my weapon as the kitchen door swung inward. My aim faltered as Brianna appeared in the doorway. I watched her run into Bud's arms. He held her, his eyes locked on mine.

"Oh, thank God, you're here," she was saying. "I've been so scared he'd come before you got here."

Confused, wary, not liking any of this, not one bit, I held the three of them in my gun sight, not sure what to think. "Okay, Bri, stand back away from Bud. I mean it, Bri."

I watched her back away. I looked at Shaggy. He smiled. Can't say I liked that, either. "Put down your gun, Claire. You're not gonna shoot us, and you know it."

I said, "Bud, what the hell's going on here?"

I turned to him and saw he had his weapon out now. Problem was, though, he had it pointed at me. "Bud? My God, what'd you think you're doing?"

Bud said, "I'm sorry, Claire, I really am, I tried to get you to stay behind at the jail, but right now you're gonna have to put your weapon down on the floor and let me handle this my way. I don't want you to get hurt, I swear to God. I don't want you to compromise your principles or lose your badge over this, but I can't let you stop me from doin' what has to be done. Just cooperate, just until we take Costin down, then you can take me in, if you want. You can take all of us in."

I tried to think what the devil was going down here, get my mind around the fact that the three of them were in this together. Against me. My three good and loyal friends had lured me out here, tricked me like I was some kind of colossal chump. I held my Glock steady on Brianna. She didn't look so beautiful anymore, not now, holding her own gun leveled at my head.

I said, "I guess we're at a bit of a stand-off then, aren't we, fellas?"

"Be reasonable, Claire," said Shaggy from beside me. "You don't have to get hurt. I don't wanna hurt you. I don't wanna hurt anybody. You wouldn't be involved tonight at all if Ortega hadn't put you on to Walter at the last minute. Bud was gonna get me out before you got to the jail. You just showed up too soon and forced us to bring you along."

"What are you planning to do? Gun Costin down in cold blood?"

"Yes." Shaggy, calmly, unequivocably.

"Are you crazy?"

"We have to, it's the only way out. He always finds us. He killed Hilde as a warning to us. So we're gonna kill him first, Brianna and I together. When Bud picked up Brianna tonight, she explained everything to him, how Walter showed up and made her take Hilde's place in the pageant, made her promise to leave Bud and go off with him. And once he heard what all Walter did to us when we were little kids, the terrible things he made us do, he said he wouldn't stop us, that he'd help us cover it up."

"My God? You've lost your freakin' minds. Listen to yourselves. You can't be serious. Bud? Think, think. You can't do this."

I kept shaking my head, hoping I was dreaming, and trying to figure how I could stop them from getting themselves locked up for the rest of their lives, but while I was working on Bud's conscience, Shaggy darted at me suddenly and caught me off guard. He hit me from the side, and then Bud had my gun arm up, twisting the Glock out of my hand before I knew what hit me. He stuck the Glock in his waistband, then pulled the .38 out of my ankle holster and the cell phone off my belt while Shaggy held me still. He tossed Brianna the keys to the handcuffs.

"Unlock Shaggy. Then put the cuffs on Claire."

"What the hell's the matter with you, Bud? I thought you had more sense than this. You're a good cop. You'll never get away with this. And for what? We can take him down in a matter of hours. Legally, put him away for good. We've got the jump on him. He doesn't know we're here waiting. We can arrest him and none of you will have to go to jail for it."

Brianna knelt down in front of me and locked my hands together, apologizing to beat the band. She began to cry a little. "I'm so sorry, Claire, I know you've been trying to help me, but you can't do it, don't you see, you can't stop him. Nobody can stop him. You think we haven't tried? All my life I've been trying to get away from him. He finds me every time. He killed Hilde because she knew where I was and didn't tell him. He followed her here. He cut off her lips as a warning to me. To make me go back with him. He's obsessed with me."

Shaggy frowned, made sure the cuffs were tight enough on my wrists. "You don't know Walter like we do, Claire. He's been killin' people for years. It's a game to him, and he's made us his accomplices ever since we were little. Hilde didn't mean to, but she led him straight to us. He kills anybody that looks at Brianna. He wants Bud dead. He was shooting at Bud that day at the Royal Condos, not you. You just got in his way."

I said, "Let me handle this. I can get more officers here right now. We'll surround the place and arrest him when he shows up. Bud, you're ruining your life. You're kissing your career good-bye and you're gonna rot in prison for this."

"No, no . . ." Brianna was sobbing. "You just don't understand what all he's done to us. But we can't prove it. There's no way we can prove anything he did. He'll go free."

Shaggy said, "Hilde was our sister. We called her Sissy. That's why I wanted to fix her mouth for the memorial service, you know, to make her look better because I knew Bri was gonna put that heart necklace on her at the funeral." He choked up but quickly shook it off and grabbed me by the arm. "We're gonna have to put you where you'll be safe until this is over, where nobody can ever say you were involved in it. We aren't gonna hurt you, if that's what you're thinkin'. We'd never do that. We love you, all of us do. You just got in the way at the last minute and we can't let you stop us."

I looked at Bud and held up my shackled wrists. He had the decency to look ashamed. "How long've you been planning this, Bud? Seems you're a pretty fair actor."

"I didn't know the whole story until tonight. Like Shag said, Brianna told me when I went back to pick her up. That's when I decided to take Shaggy out of jail so he could meet Costin like they planned. I knew Bri and Shaggy couldn't handle him alone. They can't do this alone, so I'm gonna help them."

"You're signing your own death warrant."

They all three looked guilty, but not enough to stop them from herding me outside the house, across the backyard, and into the old barn. Brianna and Bud stood back with the lantern and watched Shaggy wrangle me up the steps to a hayloft. Our elongated shadows flitted in the dancing lamplight, chasing dark patterns up the walls, but gave me a dim overview of the barn. I saw some kind of box sitting in one corner, one with a barred door on the front. I was prodded inside. The door shut behind me, a padlock set with a final click. It was big enough for me to sit up with my knees bent, but not enough to stand.

"Okay, Claire, hold your hands out through the bars and

I'll uncuff you. No need to be uncomfortable till we get back. This's gonna go down in the morning. Then we'll get you out."

I held up my hands. He removed the cuffs. Brianna and Bud were waiting at the base of the steps. I could see the lantern flame leaping, and I could hear Brianna crying and talking to me.

"Claire, listen, please, please forgive us for this. I brought Bud into this tonight when I told him the truth, but I don't want him to get hurt. I just told him because Walter is going to kill him. He had to know that, so he'd be careful. I told him I'd go back with Walter so he'd leave Bud alone, but Bud wouldn't let me. And I don't want to be with Walter. I won't. I'd rather be in jail for killing him than to have to live with him and do the awful things he makes me do."

I felt a terrible, unwelcome wave of resignation roll over me. "You'll never get away with this. You'll all be as bad as Costin. You'll be murderers. Bud, wake up, stop this before it's too late."

Bud's voice came then, angry, forceful. "You saw that tape, right, Claire? The way Costin manipulated those children to kill Bri's stepdad. He was older; they looked up to him, trusted him. And now he's been holding that tape over their heads for years, making them do whatever he wanted. He'll end up killing them all, just like he did Hilde. Cutting off her lips was a warning to them. Bri and Shaggy have gone through hell since they were little kids because of him. I'm going to help them stop him once and for all."

"You're not thinking straight. Don't do it."

But then they were gone and I was left locked up and helpless in the pitch-black barn. I couldn't see my hand in front of my face, so examined the box with my fingers, found it old but sturdy. Maybe I'd get lucky and the wood would splinter at the hinges if I kicked the door hard enough. There wasn't much else to do. I couldn't believe Bud got himself in this mess. And Shaggy and Brianna, murderers? Never. Even as bad as Costin was. I lay down on my back, doubled my knees, and kicked the door with both feet as hard as I could. If I could break out of this damn cage, I could still stop them.

Sisterly Love

The older one left the barn and walked alongside the man she loved. No one spoke, all of them thinking about the friend they'd just locked up in their old punishment box. Bud had betrayed his own partner, and she knew it was killing him. And it was her fault, every bit of it; it was all her fault. She shouldn't have ever told him the truth when he picked her up after she'd won the pageant. She had gotten so emotional and frightened and had wept and spilled out the whole story, from the very beginning, the day when she'd met the boy under the bleachers.

Bud had been incensed that Walter had put her and Bubby through so much hell and he had wanted to help them. He was the one who sent her here ahead of him while he got Bubby out of jail, and she had been so relieved that he didn't hate her, that somebody like him, who knew how to use a gun, somebody tough and experienced and good would help them face the boy. But she should never have involved him in this. It would ruin his career as a homicide detective, and worse, it would destroy Claire's trust in him.

She waited until they were inside the house, in the living

room, and then she said, "Bud, I'm so sorry all this happened. I know it's killing you to do this to Claire."

Bud stared into her eyes. His face was strained, serious, tortured. He glanced over at Bubby, then paced a few steps across the room before he turned and looked back at them. He shook his head.

"Bri, I just can't do it. I thought I could, but there's no way I can let you and Shag kill him in cold blood. As bad as he is, I just can't do it. Claire's right about everything. He'll be dead, true, but all of us will be, too, because we aren't like him and we can't live with something like this. She's right, right about everything. You both know it, too, don't you? I know you do."

The older one nodded because what he said was the truth. She turned to Bubby, tears in her eyes. All this had been his idea, thought up while he sat in his jail cell. He had planned the ambush, originally just the two of them, Bubby, who had hated the violence and murder they were subjected to as children more than any of them.

She said, "Johnny, we can't. Bud's right. We'll all end up in jail for the rest of our lives."

Shaggy stood silently. "We gotta kill him before he kills us." His voice broke. "Like he killed Sissy."

Bud said, "We can still take him down. Just the way we planned, but we'll subdue him and make him confess to Hilde's murder. He has no way of knowing I'm here. He expects you and Bri to be alone. And he thinks he's getting her back. We can put him away for life."

Brianna said, "He'll find a way to get away. He always finds a way."

"Not this time. All you have to do, Bri, is sit down here in the livin' room and wait for him. I don't want you hurt. Tell him Shaggy's not here yet. Just stay here long enough to get him inside. I can hide at the top of the stairs until I can get the jump on him. Then we'll cuff him, force him to confess, and take him in. It's our word against his. If you both testify against him, tell the prosecuting attorney everything you know, we can put him away. Shaggy, you hide in the dinin' room with the shotgun. Once he gets inside, I'll come out on one side of him and you on the other. With both of our weapons on him, he won't try anything stupid."

The older one and Bubby listened to Bud's plan and followed his directions. But when their eyes met, they knew Bud's plan wouldn't work. The boy would try something, and it would work. He would get away free and clear. That's the way it always had been and that's the way it always would be.

Nineteen

"Kicking like that's not gonna do you a bit of good, Detective."

The voice floated out of the darkness of the loft, close by, as icy calm and terrifying as if the grim reaper had materialized out of thin air. And I knew who it was only too well. Walter Costin. A grim reaper of his own sort. I recognized the voice, just as Carlos Vasquez had identified it before his lips were hacked off. I froze, muscles rock-rigid with dread. I strained to find him out in the inky black. An intense white light flared suddenly and slammed into my face. Momentarily blinded, I shut my eyes and shielded them with my hands.

Boards creaked as he moved closer, and then I heard him laugh, softly with no amusement. "Wanna know why you can't get outta there? I reinforced that box when I had to lock dear little Hilde inside it for a few days. She was havin' a little problem remembering to obey me, the little stinker. But it didn't do me much good. I found out later she'd been sneakin' up here to Missouri behind my back and visitin' Johnny and Brianna, all the while lying to me like a damn dog. Swore to me she didn't have a clue where they were, put her hand on the Bible, even, said she sure wished she could find them. On and on, you know the story, she missed them so much and sure hoped they both were okay. All lies, because the truth is, she was a lying, betraying little bitch."

Now he was near enough for me to see him, but only a vague form looming behind the powerful flashlight beam. He kept up the chitchat, seemed almost pleased to tell me his story, lonely, I guess. Too bad I didn't have a tape recorder. Problem was, he no doubt thought he could spill his guts like I was Oprah Winfrey because he knew I didn't have a chance in hell of getting out of this box alive.

"I gotta admit they covered their tracks pretty well. Managed to throw me off the scent for a long time, which I never would've believed possible. None of the darlings are exactly Einstein material. Except for Johnny, he's fairly bright, I'll give him that. But then I finally woke up and got a tad suspicious of Hilde's odd little out-of-town jaunts back here to Missouri. So I asked myself? Why, indeed? Our family's long gone, nobody around here anymore. So why's she signing on for this little hick contest at your boyfriend's hotel? So I decided to follow her and see what she was up to. Imagine my surprise when I saw Brianna drive up and get out of her car. And who shows up a minute later. Little Bubby himself, but that's right, you call him Shaggy, don't you? All three of them together conspiring against me. The rest is history, as they say. Especially for Hilde." His voice had grown increasingly cold, hard, and angry.

I sat very still, said nothing, and tried to think through my options. I had no weapons, no phone, and was locked up helplessly inside a very sturdy box. That was pretty much it. There were no options this time. Maybe I could scream, try to give Bud a warning. But that was about it.

Apparently, Costin was thinking along the same lines. "Don't waste your breath tryin' to scream. Nobody's gonna hear you. They're hiding inside the house, the Three Stooges, planning a killer surprise party for me. Even your partner jumped in on the deal, all his scruples suddenly shot to hell. That's the effect Bri's got on men. Most of 'em end up doing just about anything she asks them to. Even murder, like poor Bud. Not that I don't know how it feels to be under her spell. She got me in her web when I was just a kid, long before she got as beautiful as she is now. Difference is, I found I rather enjoyed killing people for her. I doubt if Bud's going to like it much, though."

Okay, if this freak wanted to be chatty, that was fine by me. Maybe it'd buy me time to think my way out of this mess. "So tell me this, Walter. Why'd you go after Carlos Vasquez? That seems a bit unnecessary. Overkill, even."

"C'mon, Detective, Carlos saw me at Hilde's house, met me, in fact, could describe me to you. I knew you'd go down there sooner or later to check him out as a suspect and he'd tell you Hilde was deathly afraid of me. I had to shut him up and do it fast, but you still managed to get to him faster than I did. I cut him so you'd have a distraction to worry about. Figured it'd keep you down in the Sunshine State lookin' for the murderer."

"Yeah? Only one thing went wrong."

"Oh, yeah? What would that be?"

"Carlos Vasquez didn't die. In fact, he put us straight onto you. Detective Ortega in Miami and Sheriff Ramsay both know you cut him up. They're both out looking for you right now for murder one, not to mention that attempted murder. Don't think you're getting away with this, Costin. You're not as smart as everybody else seems to think."

He laughed some more, this time sounded genuinely amused. Jolly as Old Saint Nick, he was. "Know what? I've gotten away with every single, goddamn thing I've done my entire life, good and bad. Brianna and Johnny know that only too well. That's why they're in the house waitin' to gun me down. Problem is, they're not as smart as I am, and neither are you, judging by where you're sittin' right now. You did give me a run for my money there for a few days, I've gotta say. Luckily, the Three Stooges saw fit to lock you up, so now I don't have to worry about you. And they're in for a very big surprise, because guess what? I bugged that house out there years ago. I knew I couldn't trust them anymore. Hilde stood with me for a long time, then she betrayed me worse than any of them when she went over to their side."

"My advice, Costin? Get outta here while you still can. I already called in for backup from Springfield PD. They'll be out here any minute."

"Yeah? You call them before your friends locked you in this box and took your phone, or after?"

I was silent, but I was in one helluva bad fix. I tried to think how I could warn Bud but didn't have long to worry about it.

"Okey-doke, Detective. Time to have that surprise party but it's gonna have a real surprising twist. And you're gonna help me." He knelt down in front of the box, the bright light still trained on my face. I heard a key scrape, and the door swung outward. I lunged out and head-butted him in the legs, but he evaded me and the arc of the light beam slashed downward and got the top of my head. The heavy Maglite cracked against my skull and I went down face forward. Stunned a little, I felt him grab my arms and bind my wrists behind my back with some kind of rope. I tensed my arms, hoping to create some slack in the knots, but he turned me over, jerked a gag tight around my mouth, and hauled me up by the back of my shirt. He shoved a gun barrel into my right ear.

"Okay, I enjoyed all that bravado, you're quite the girl, but that's enough outta you for the moment. I've read all about how gutsy you are, but I don't particularly want to kill you yet because you're my ticket inside that house. But I'll slit your throat, if need be, right here and now, if you try anything else stupid like that. You really need to understand that I won't hesitate to do it. Then I'll cut off your mouth and leave you bleedin', just like Hilde and Carlos, and anybody else who ever crossed me."

Still a little dizzy, I staggered alongside him as he gripped the back of my shirt and half lowered me down the steps. Then he just let go and I dropped like a sack of cement and hit the floor hard. Grunting, I rolled with the fall and desperately tried to regain my feet. But he was down the steps way too fast and had me again, one fist gripping my hair. He put his mouth very close to my ear, made his voice husky, low.

"Now you be real quiet, got it? We gotta surprise our good friends over there hidin' in the house."

He made his way around the edge of the yard, dragging me along with him. It was still dark outside, and Costin's car was not in the driveway. Nobody's car was in the driveway. All hidden; everybody playing cat and mouse. Unfortunately, Costin was Sylvester and I was Tweety's unlucky cousin. He'd been here the whole time, watching and listening, playing us for fools. I just hoped Bud and the others were inside that house, armed to the teeth, on guard and waiting for Costin to show up. He pushed me in front of him around back behind the barn. I stumbled once and almost fell, but he jerked me upright and forced me out into some trees edging the property. He brought me out of the woods at the far side of the house. It was all dark, quiet, but I know nobody inside could hear us. He shoved me to my knees while he threw a latch on a cellar door, lifted it up, and then took me down some steps to another door. He opened that one and pushed me inside.

"Okay, Detective, listen good. Bri's waitin' for me up there in the living room, all ready to pretend she's going away with me. Isn't that the sweetest thing? Johnny and Bud are lurkin' around, too, ready to shoot me in the back, blow me away like some kind of stray dog. Not exactly brilliant or creative, but then again, they didn't have me around this time to plan it out for them. So let's go, you're gonna be my human shield. None of them will risk puttin' a bullet in you."

We moved up the steps that led into the house, me in front but in his grip, and then out into a dark, chilly hall off the back porch. I could see a dim light in the living room and tried to yell a muffled warning until Costin put his arm around my neck and squeezed my throat shut with his forearm. The sound dried up. Then he walked me to the open archway that led into the living room. Brianna was sitting in a rocking chair beside a cold fireplace.

"Hello, sweetheart, look who I've brought along to see you."

Brianna hadn't seen us yet, and the sound of Costin's voice brought her up out of the chair and on her feet. Her face twisted with fear, and her eyes became enormous and glittered in the light from the kerosene lamp on the table beside her. "Don't hurt Claire. Walter, please, please. I'll do whatever you say. I swear I will."

"Okay, that's cool. Tell Bubby and Bud to scoot on out here with their hands up, or I'll blow her fuckin' brains out."

I stood silently in front of him, his hand still fisted in my hair, his other hand holding a gun to my temple. I hoped to God Bud had the guts to open up on him. If they didn't gun him down first, we were all dead.

"Bud, Bud, he's got a gun to Claire's head," Brianna cried out. "He'll do it, Bud, he'll do it!"

Silence, maybe ten seconds worth, then my eyes caught a movement on the staircase leading to the second floor. Bud appeared on the landing. He had his arms straight out, his .45 up and targeted on Walter's head. Shaggy suddenly loomed out from behind the dining room wall. He had already lowered his weapon.

"Well, isn't this nice? The whole family right here waitin' on me to show up. That's true family loyalty."

Bud didn't move, didn't react, kept his weapon sighted on

Walter's face. Walter's breathing didn't alter. He was as calm as ice on a pond. "Go ahead, shoot me, Detective Davis, kill me, if you like, but your partner's gonna be dead, too, before she hits the floor."

I saw Bud's eyes shift toward me, just barely, and I shook my head. "Shoot him, shoot him," I cried out underneath the gag but my words were muffled and my heart dropped when I caught Bud's first hesitation. I knew then we were all goners.

"Okay, Costin, we'll put the guns down. Don't hurt her."

Walter said, "You, too, Bubby boy, then get down on the ground on your stomachs, both of you."

Squeezing my eyes shut, I tried to figure out what I could do next as the two men slowly put their weapons aside and lowered themselves to the floor. They shouldn't have done it, no, no, don't do it, I thought frantically. He's gonna kill you, all of us, that's why he's here.

"Brianna, baby doll, you'll find some rope under the couch. Get it out and tie them to those dining room chairs over there. And make it good and tight. Don't give me a reason to shoot the detective here."

"Please, Walter, listen to me. If you love me, truly love me, you won't hurt anybody. I said I'd go with you, be with you from now on. That's all you said you wanted. I'll never run away from you again, I swear to God, I won't."

"Now that, my dear, is music to my ears. Tie them up like I said and we'll get the hell out of here."

Brianna quickly obeyed, and Walter pushed me down on the floor and held the gun pointed at the top of my head. My mind raced, but it didn't go anywhere that had an answer to this dilemma. I couldn't see any way out this time. Maybe he was telling the truth, maybe all he wanted was to kidnap Brianna and force her to go with him. But who was I kidding? This guy cut off people's lips with scissors. You think he'd leave three witnesses alive to finger him? Huh-uh. We were dead.

After Bud and Shaggy were tied to chairs, Costin jerked me up into a third one and bound me tightly.

"Okay, now I feel a bit more secure about my odds. Come over here, Brianna, give me a kiss."

Brianna went to him and pressed her body up tightly against him. He hugged her close, the gun dangling loosely behind her back. They kissed long and hard, brutally, and I watched Bud struggling desperately to get loose. Shaggy looked petrified.

Costin stepped away, smiled down at Bri's upturned face, then backhanded her so hard with the pistol butt that it knocked her completely off her feet. She fell hard on her back and lay still, bleeding from the mouth. Both Bud and Shaggy went berserk, trying to tear their arms loose. I continued to work the ropes tying my wrists. It was my only hope.

"Brianna, Brianna, you really think you're gonna get by with this shit? Leavin' me without a word and making me worry about you all these years. And now, here you are, plottin' with these two losers to gun me down. I mean, I'm an easygoing guy, but really . . ."

Brianna came to enough to try to scramble away from him, but Costin was on her again, grabbing her up, then slapping her face hard enough to knock her down again. The knot I was working with my fingers gave slightly, and I frantically kept at it as Brianna tried to crawl away on her hands and knees. Now she was bleeding profusely from both the nose and mouth. Blood was pouring down her blouse and onto the floor. Bud was yelling curses, threats, and fighting desperately against his bindings, almost hysterical.

Bud and I both went stone still, though, when Costin pulled out a pair of scissors from his jacket, jerked her head back by the hair, fisted it, and held the point to the hollow of her throat. "You're gonna die smilin', too, baby, just like little

Sissy did in that shower stall, but you're gonna have a audience around to watch you die."

Brianna was crying and begging for her life as he pushed her into a chair across from me, then secured her there with more of the rope. I watched, terrified, but finally wiggled a couple more knots loose. Eyes locked on Costin, I fumbled clumsily with the last knot, desperate to stop him, then tensed all over when Costin squatted down in front of Brianna and gently fingered loose strands of blood-soaked hair behind her ears.

Oh God, I knew then what he was going to do. He was going to hack off her lips, just like he did to Hilde. I knew it, knew it in my soul, and I fought the bindings behind my back. I had to get loose!

Horrified, I watched him take his left thumb and forefinger and pull out her lower lip, then he opened the scissors and began to cut through the soft flesh, hacking at her lip like a piece of steak he was in a hurry to eat. Brianna screamed, shrill, heartrending, agonizing, as more blood gushed out of her mutilated mouth and slowly soaked through her white cotton blouse. Walter was smiling. "Now your fuckin' detective boyfriend's not gonna like you so much, is he, Bri? Now you're not gonna be so enticing to the opposite sex. Maybe that'll keep you with me for good this time since you're such a lyin' whore. Or maybe, I won't want you anymore, either, now that you're all cut up and ugly. I do have my standards."

My right hand suddenly came free as he put the scissors to her mouth again, and I thrust myself hard to the left, throwing myself and the chair to the floor, then shoving it frantically toward Brianna's chair and the table holding the kerosene lamp. The whole thing crashed over and hit the floor with a crash and tinkling of glass. The room went black for an instant, and then the kerosene ignited and whooshed into a fiery blaze so quickly that Costin and Brianna had no time to get out of the way. It caught Costin's pants and Brianna's skirt, and I could heard Brianna screaming.

I scrambled and shoved myself toward the spot where Bud had given up his .45. I grabbed it, swung toward Costin, and fired off five quick rounds at Costin, but he'd seen me and dived behind the couch, his pant leg still on fire. Brianna lay still, blood pumping from her face, her skirt on fire. Bud was trying to get to her, lying on the floor on his side, still tied to the chair, but struggling his way to her. I could hear Costin behind the couch, rolling to put out his burning clothes. I took quick aim, fired through the sofa back three more times, but he'd already darted out toward Shaggy's shotgun. He got it and sprinted for the hall and front door, and I fired again and thought I hit him this time in the leg by the way he went down. But he twisted on the floor and sprayed us all with a single blast from Shaggy's gunshot. I felt the sting of birdshot hit my foot and ducked behind a chair for cover, pressing the trigger and unloading on the bastard, blam after blam that filled the room with noise and smoke, and the caustic smell of cordite.

Then all went quiet except for Brianna's shrieks of pain and horror, Bud and Shaggy's screams of rage, and the crackling of flames as the sofa caught fire. Smoke filled the room in a gray haze, and I crawled to the wall and kept my back against it while I reloaded. I could hear Costin now, his footsteps running across the front porch and down the steps to the yard. He was getting away, damn it, and everything in me said to go after him, stop him, but I knew Brianna was bleeding heavily, her skirt still on fire, and Bud and Shaggy were helpless to reach her.

I pulled myself to Brianna and smothered the flames with an afghan off the couch, and then I got the scissors and cut the bindings on Bud. He scrabbled on all fours to Brianna, jerked off his shirt, and held it against her butchered mouth.

Then he cradled her in his arms, groaning with despair. I cut Shaggy loose, but found he was hit, too, in the chest and arm, and having trouble breathing. I stamped out the small blaze still burning on the carpet and sofa, then found my cell phone still in Shaggy's pocket where he'd stowed it earlier. I punched in 911, requested police, the fire department, and multiple ambulances, and then did my best to remember how to direct them to the house.

Twenty

It took the Springfield police about ten minutes to reach us, with the ambulances and fire department right behind them. The fire damage was minimal, but the scene was grisly and surreal, smoky, blood spattered and horrific, all of us injured or shot up in one way or another. Brianna was the worst off, by far. The paramedics managed to staunch the bleeding on her mouth and even locate the severed tissue and get it on ice for possible reattachment at the hospital. I tried to reassure Bud with an account of Carlos Vasquez's successful surgery. He just stared blankly at me, so I shut up.

Shaggy was stabilized and loaded onto a gurney. They weren't sure yet but didn't think his internal organs had been damaged, except maybe for his lungs. Bud was hit, too, not bad, but he paid little attention to his own wounds, more concerned with getting Brianna the medical attention she needed so desperately. He looked in shock. I was in shock.

Walter Costin had gotten away clean, just like he said he would, just like Bri and Shaggy said he would, slick as an eel, he is. I put out a statewide, all points on him as soon as I could but wasn't sure what car he was in, so I had no way of identifying the make. Chances were slim he'd get picked up. That's what I was thinking about, that, and how to explain the whole sordid mess to Charlie, without incriminating Bud and Shaggy for locking me up, much less their discarded and ineffective plan to murder Costin. Not exactly the thing you wanted your detectives and criminalists to be doing in their off time.

I couldn't say I blamed them, not now, not after witnessing what Costin was capable of, what he'd done to Brianna in front of my eyes, the woman he purported to love, at that. I shared their eagerness to hasten his demise, actually, because if anybody on this green earth needed a bullet between the eyes, it was one Walter Costin. I wouldn't mind being the one to do it, either, in fact, relished the idea, was now fantasizing about it most of the time, but I had to take succor in the fact that I'd hit him. I was almost positive he was wounded. Maybe it'd be fatal, and he'd crawl off to some dark hole to bleed to death and we could have a job-well-done party.

Brianna and Bud were rushed away together in the first ambulance. Bud holding her hand. Shaggy and I shared number two. He was unconscious now, and the EMTs took my vitals and examined my foot and said I'd been damn lucky, a damn sight luckier than everybody else. Yep, lucky me—the wound in my instep barely even hurt. Sirens blaring, they sped us all to the St. John's Regional Health Center just off National Avenue in Springfield, where I sat quietly in a green-draped cubicle in the ER while a young doctor named Marta Barnes put a couple of stitches in the instep of my left foot, all neat and even like a real Betsy Ross. But I could handle stitches, hell, I should buy my own needle and thread and carry them with me, for injurious days. I didn't even limp too badly. Yeah, one out of four of us had been quite the lucky duck. Only bad thing, Costin had put some holes in my brand-new black hightops.

Black called me up about the time Dr. Marta finished winding gauze around my foot.

"Where are you? I've been waiting an hour at your place for you to show up. Food's getting cold."

"St. John's Regional Health Center."

"In Springfield? Oh, God. What happened? Are you okay?"

"I'm okay, so are Bud and Shaggy. Brianna's not." I told him the gory details then, and it sounded even worse when I said it out loud. I wish I didn't have to listen to myself when I talked like this. I finally dwindled off with the story, and so did my spirits.

"You're lucky to be alive."

Black was beginning to say that a lot. Almost like a mantra. But he sounded really worried, which was nice, I guess.

"The helicopter's in Kansas City picking up a patient, but I'll come get you in the Lear."

I thought that sounded pretty good. I was tired and wanted to sleep, somewhere safe and without scissors, maybe with Black there, armed with a loaded pistol and standing guard. "Thanks. I'd really appreciate it if you would do that."

We hung up, and I knew Charlie was next on my list to be apprised of the situation. I didn't want to make that call, uh-uh, no sir. Maybe I'd just let Bud do it, let him explain how this hellish catastrophe managed to transpire. Better yet, maybe Bud and I needed to sit a spell and get our stories straight before we contacted anybody who had the power to fire us. Even more than that, I wanted to make sure Bud was all right. I couldn't forget the terrible, stricken, horrified expression on his face when Brianna was being mutilated. One that never faded off to his regular expression. The senseless brutality had affected me big time, too, and I couldn't even let myself think about her flawless, beautiful face or how it must look now or the way Walter Costin had just scissored off her bottom lip like he was cutting a tag off a pillow.

Nope, emotionally, Bud probably wasn't doing so well,

and since it was going to take Black a while to get to Springfield, anyway, I decided to hobble upstairs and check on my partner. I did swallow down the pain pills they gave me and found out Bud had been admitted with minor gunshot wounds down the left side of his body. Brianna and Shaggy were both still in surgery.

The early morning shift was just coming on duty, and I meandered my way through a relatively deserted emergency room now that our little bloody band had been triaged and admitted, and into one of the main hospital corridors, where I found a gaggle of nurses in a rainbow-hued variety of uniforms chatting together and drinking Starbucks coffee. I asked at the desk where they'd taken Bud.

According to her name plate, the receptionist's name was Cassandra Case, and she was wearing the coolest turquoise suede boots with fringe on them I'd ever seen. I usually preferred black police-issue combat boots, but these looked great on her legs. She had a nice smile and friendly manner and was gorgeous enough even to work at Black's hotel. The way she had her stuff arranged on her desk, all in right angles, even her ballpoint pen, told me she just might be a bit on the anal side, too. She directed me to a semiprivate room on the second floor west.

The halls were whispery quiet, most patients asleep and dreaming in darkened semiprivate rooms. When I pushed Bud's door open, I heard snoring, which I figured was a good, positive sign that they'd given him a potent sedative to calm him down and take away that horrible expression imprinted on his face. It would be better for him if his mind was completely numb, just sitting there, sterile, convoluted gray matter, with no thoughts of Bri's mouth streaming blood. But when I pulled back the curtain, it was a young boy who looked about eighteen, snoring happily, mouth open, one leg suspended in traction.

I limped past the first patient and pulled aside the privacy curtain. The other bed was empty, white sheets thrown back, IV needle on the floor, its bag still half full of fluid.

I left there in a hurry and asked at the nearest nurses' station if Bud Davis had been released. He hadn't. They'd last checked on him about an hour ago. My concern mounted, and I took the elevator down, my gut all twisted up. I dialed his cell number but didn't know if he even had it with him or if it was ringing endlessly somewhere in that blood-splattered farmhouse from hell. He wasn't waiting in the surgery wing, either, and Brianna wasn't out of the OR yet, so where the hell had he gone? Then it dawned on me where he'd gone. He'd gone after Walter Costin.

My alarm bells really started to go crazy. I called the Canton County Sheriff's Department and filled in the duty officer on the status of the case, then asked if he'd seen Bud. He said nobody had seen him and to try his cell phone. I headed back upstairs again, punching in Bud's number again. I let it ring the whole time I walked down the corridor to the recovery room. Shaggy was now out of surgery and I wanted to talk to him. I flashed my badge, and the nurse let me in, but said I could stay only a few minutes. I was getting a lot of practice visiting recovery rooms since I'd gotten this case.

Shaggy was still pretty out of it, but he recognized me when I leaned down close and put my hand on his forehead. He felt feverish.

"How you doing, Shag?"

"Not so hot."

"They say you're gonna be okay."

"Doesn't feel like it. Bri okay?"

"She's in surgery. It sounds pretty good. They can do wonders now." Well, that was a big lie but he didn't need to hear the other, less rosy side of the coin. He shut his eyes and didn't question me. When he opened them again, it took a second for him to focus, then he said, "I'm sorry. We shouldn't've ever locked you up. We should've let you get him. You would've done it right."

I glanced over at the nurse who was tending to another patient, one who was sick from the anesthetic he'd been given. I blocked out the gagging sounds he was making. "Listen, Shag, you gotta tell me where you think Costin might go."

"I dunno."

"I think Bud's gone after him. Did Brianna tell him where Walter might hole up if things went wrong?"

Shaggy was so groggy that he had to struggle to stay with me. "We talked about gettin' him in Florida, if he didn't show up at the farm. He's gotta house down the beach from Bri and Hilde's. Hilde said he bought it after Bri took off. He watched their place all the time to see if she ever came back."

That surprised me. I wondered if he'd been there, watching me chase Carlos up the beach the day Ortega tackled me. "You gotta tell me exactly where it is. I think Bud's gonna try to take him down by himself."

Shaggy's eyes were bleary, nearly closed, almost done with me, and he shook his head slightly, slurring now. "Walter's too smart. Bud'll never get him. He'll kill Bud. You saw. You saw how he is."

"I think I winged him. You really think he'll go back to Florida and hide out?"

He nodded. "For a while, maybe. He probably thinks nobody but Hilde knows he's got that place."

Shaggy managed to get out that Costin's house was the last one on Hilde's beach cove heading south, that it was another old place with a detached garage in the backyard, weathered gray and more rundown than hers. He said it had a swing on a screened-in front porch and a big Chinese wind chime. Shaggy didn't last much longer after that and he dozed off. That's when the nurse told me to leave. Still Shaggy'd given me enough. I remembered seeing pictures in Hilde's scrapbooks, with her sitting on a porch swing. Yeah, that's exactly where he'd go, especially if he thought we didn't know about it. He'd think himself safe for a couple of days, then he'd get a flight straight to Bolivia if he was smart. And he was.

I dragged myself down the hall to an empty waiting room overlooking the front of the hospital. I didn't see any long black limos roaring into the parking lot to save me, so I took a deep breath and punched in Charlie's number. He answered on the second ring and sounded his usual pissed self. I filled him in on what had happened and he was silent then said, "So everybody's gonna be all right."

I said, "Yeah, but we gotta big problem and not much time to take care of it. I'm pretty sure Bud's gone after Walter Costin, and if he has, he's probably in trouble. I need your permission to go after him."

"Where'd he go?"

I hesitated. "Florida. He probably thinks Costin will head down there."

"You bet that's a problem. We have no jurisdiction there. Call Ortega and let him handle it."

I lied. "Well, I'm not a hundred percent sure Bud's heading there, but I know he's injured and emotional, not thinking clearly. I doubt if he can find Costin before I intercept him, but if he does, I think he's gonna get hurt before he can bring him back. I gotta get down there, Sheriff."

"Let Miami handle it."

"He cut off her lip right in front of us, Charlie, while she was alive and begging. That's why Bud's wants to get Costin himself."

"You're talking about another damn jurisdiction, Claire."

"Sheriff, we can put down at an airstrip up around Hollywood, where Costin's purported to have a house. That's where I think Bud's headed. I'll call Ortega and have him check the passenger lists and wait for Bud at Miami International. One of us is bound to intercept him."

"I can't give you permission to do this, and you know it."

I cursed under my breath, furious at the time we were wasting. "Then I'm requesting a leave of absence, sir, for personal reasons."

More silence. Then Charlie said, "Granted."

"Thank you, sir."

"Make sure you make that call to Ortega when you land, I mean it, Claire. And be careful, goddamn it."

That's the first time I ever heard Charlie use the Lord's name in vain, but I forgave him. I clicked him off and punched in Black on speed dial. He answered quickly.

"We're approaching the Springfield-Branson Airport. We'll set down there in a few minutes."

"I need you to get me to Miami, and fast."

"What? Why?"

"I think Bud's gone down there after Costin, and we're wasting time."

"Damn it, Claire." Silence. "All right, I'll have my pilot work up a flight plan. Where are you now?"

"I'm still at the hospital. I'll get a cab and meet you at the airport. It'll be faster."

We hung up, and a mere twenty minutes later we were in the air. I filled in Black on the details, and he frowned a lot, but he listened until I was finished. Then he said, "This is not a good idea. In fact, it's stupid as hell. We're talking about trying to apprehend a killer outside your jurisdiction."

"No. We're just gonna go pick up Bud. We're stopping him from doing something stupid."

"You're headed for trouble, Claire."

"Bud's caught up in some kind of blinding bloodlust thing and I'm afraid he'll get hurt." That wasn't all I was afraid of, but I didn't say it. "I can't let it happen."

"Well, hell, I'd say Bud has good enough reason to be out for blood. I'd like to kill that son of a bitch, too, for what he did to you."

"Just get the pilot to land as close as he can get to Hollywood, Florida. That's all I'm asking. I can talk Bud down from this, make him see reason. I know I can."

Black was not happy. I could tell by his massive frown and the way he was pacing the floor and shaking his head and making disapproving growls. "Only if you check your weapons with airport security like you did last time. God, I can't believe I'm letting you talk me into this."

I left him to talk to the pilot and arrange permission to land, and then I punched in Mario Ortega's number.

He answered and said, "You get him?"

"Not exactly." I explained what went down in Springfield and what was going down now.

He said, "Holy shit."

I agreed. Same phrase, too.

He said, "When's your partner setting down out at MI?"

"I don't know. How about checking out the passenger lists for me? He'd fly out of either St. Louis, Kansas City, or Springfield, Missouri. Would you be willing to find out and pick him up when he gets off the plane? We're gonna land up the coast near Hollywood, then drive down to Costin's place. Can you find out if he's on a flight anywhere in to south Florida?"

"Yeah. Won't be easy, but I'll get it done."

"How about getting me permission to carry instate when I land?"

"Yeah, I'll arrange it. Just don't shoot anybody."

We hung up and I felt distinctly relieved. So would Charlie. So would Bud when he came to his senses. And then, hooray, all our troubles would be over.

We ended up landing at the Fort Lauderdale–Hollywood International Airport, where Black had a rental car lined up and waiting. I still hadn't heard from Ortega. In the misty morning light, we took the coast highway south, Black driving because of my stupid foot, and it took us almost twenty minutes to reach the road that turned off the highway and led us to Hilde's beach. When I thought we were close to the house Shaggy had described, we pulled off the side of the road and stared at the rental car parked on the opposite shoulder. Bud had beat us there, after all. How, I couldn't figure. Or maybe it was Costin's. Whoever the car belonged to, the driver had obviously wanted to sneak in to the beach house from the back, probably on foot. We climbed a low hill and got our first look at Costin's hideout. It was pretty much as Shaggy had described it. Quiet and deserted. Gray, weathered, the ocean swelling and ebbing in front of it, the roar loud and foreboding. A green Concorde was parked at the rear of the house. I got a really, really bad feeling in the pit of my stomach.

That sensation increased when I saw that the back door stood open. Black and I approached, weapons out and ready. Yeah, he had one, too, just like last time. I didn't like this, not at all. We stood on either side of the door. I peeked around the door. It led into some kind of laundry room. No sound inside. Nothing looked disturbed. No sign of human habitation, except for the two cars.

So in we went, me first. We performed the same wary dance outside the door to the kitchen. I darted a look around the door frame and saw a kitchen table and two chairs. There was one plate sitting on top. Half-eaten macaroni and cheese. A glass was overturned, milk pooled on the table. Lots of white gauze bandages and antiseptic burn ointments lying around. One of my slugs had hit Costin. Broken dishes littered the floor and crunched under our feet. Through the living room, we saw that the front door was open, too. It looked like either Bud had dragged Costin out the back or vice versa. Knowing Bud had the element of surprise, I had a feeling it was the former. *Oh, God.*

Outside, we again met with ocean roar. Wind in the sea grasses. No one to be seen.

Black looked at the old garage. "They've got to be in there."

We headed for it, gained the door, and stood on each side, guns ready. We were getting good at this team thing. I pushed it open with my left hand. At the creak it made, Bud spun around to face us. He was sitting in a chair. His face was ashen. He gripped his .45 in one hand, but had it lying atop his lap. He didn't say anything.

Costin was taped to a chair a few feet in front of Bud, ankles, arms, forehead. He had tape over his mouth. His eyes were open and staring. He had a bullet hole between his eyes.

I said, "Oh, God, Bud, what'd you do?"

Bud stared at me. He seemed slightly stunned, but dead calm. Black and I moved forward, but my heart was in my throat. If Bud had lost control and murdered Costin, he was finished in law enforcement, finished period. He was going to prison for a very, very long time.

Bud said, "He was dead when I got here."

"Bud, that's not gonna wash. Charlie knows you came down here. Ortega knows. How could you do this?"

"I didn't do it."

Black had gone straight to the body. He squatted down in front of Costin but didn't touch him. "Claire, look at this."

I joined him and stared at the corpse and knew then Bud hadn't done it. Both Costin's earlobes were gone, neatly sliced away, blood coagulated on the straight edge. Relief flooded me.

"Cutting off the earlobes is the Rangos trademark," Black told me, "This is their hit, no question about it."

Black waited for me to argue, but I only nodded. I already knew whose calling card it was. Ortega told me what the Rangos did to their victims when I was at the station going over Esteban Rangos's file.

When I didn't speak, Black raised both hands, as if to

ward me off. "I had absolutely nothing to do with this," he said. "I swear to God. I haven't spoken to Jose since we saw him at the compound."

I believed him, of course. "I know you didn't. They found out Costin killed Esteban, that's why they did him. Ortega said Vasquez told them it was Costin who cut his mouth when they came to the hospital."

"How'd they know where to find him?"

That was a good question, so I shrugged.

Black answered it himself. "Doesn't matter. Jose has his ways."

I nodded, sure that was true, but I was so glad that Costin was dead and so damn relieved that Bud hadn't done it, I didn't really care who had. Just so Bud didn't have to rot in some stinking jail cell for murdering this piece of garbage. That's all that mattered to me.

Bud was staring at the body now, and I had a feeling he was a little disoriented. "I was gonna kill him. I wanted to kill him. I couldn't stop thinkin' about it, couldn't stop thinkin' about what he did to Bri."

I put my hand on his shoulder. "Well, you didn't, thank God. And you probably couldn't have, any more than you could go through with it in Springfield."

"I wanted to kill him. I wanted to shoot him."

I had to snap Bud out of his fog, and do it fast, because I had to get Ortega on the phone and report this crime right now. But that didn't mean Bud had to hang around and get involved.

"You gotta get outta here, Bud. Now. I'm calling Miami PD in on this, and they'll alert Hollywood authorities, and you're in no shape to be interrogated. It's better if they don't know you were ever here."

Black nodded. He said, "Let's go, Bud, you need to get your car and drive up to the airport. My plane's here, waiting for us, refueled and ready. Get on it and stay out of sight."

"You don't understand. I wanted to murder him." Bud looked lost and bewildered, bandaged arm and leg, bloodshot haunted eyes. He hadn't slept; none of us had. We were all operating on anger and adrenaline. Under his windbreaker, Bud wore the clothes he'd worn the night before. Brianna's blood crusted his sneakers.

"You're gonna have to snap out of it, Bud, now. Do what we say. Brianna needs you. She's barely out of surgery, and you're not there. How's that gonna make her feel?"

"Oh, my God, poor Bri."

Tears welled up in Bud's eyes, making them shine in the dim light. His features twisted with utter agony, and he sobbed, totally out of it, bleary with fatigue and grief. "You saw what he did to her. You know how she suffered. I can't get it outta my mind. I can't stop thinkin' about it . . ."

Black took hold of Bud's arm and pulled him to his feet. "Okay, Bud. Let's go. I'll drive you to the airport in your car. Claire can handle this on her own until Ortega and the local authorities take over. You need some rest, that's all. I've got something on the plane that'll make you relax and sleep."

Like a sleepwalker, Bud moved obediently to the door and stood there waiting, his eyes latched on Walter Costin's corpse.

Black turned to me. "You *will* be all right here alone, won't you?"

"Yeah, I'll turn this over to Ortega and then I'll meet you at the airport."

"Well, don't forget, and don't get caught up in something else in the meantime. And don't worry. Bud'll be fine. I'll talk to him, give him a sedative."

I looked up at him. "That's a lot of don'ts there, Black."

"I know you."

I smiled. "Know what, Black? You're not so bad to have around."

Black smiled. Whoohoo, I do like that sexy smile he's got.

"Remember it. The truth is, I don't need to be found at the scene of a Rangos hit, either. So why don't I get Bud out of here so you can hand this thing over and we can get the hell out of here? I've had enough for one night."

I watched Black leave with Bud in tow, then I flipped open my cell phone and called Mario Ortega. When he answered, I said, "It's Claire Morgan, Ortega. You better sit down."

I told him everything and gave him directions to the crime scene, then I glanced one last time at Walter Costin, who had ended up exactly the way he deserved. I wasted no pity on him. His deadly games were over for good. He would never hurt anybody, ever again. I walked outside and sat down in the shade of a palm tree and looked out over the ocean. I did so love the ocean. In time, I heard the wail of lots of police sirens.

Epilogue

Charlie didn't ask too many questions, thank God, but the ones he did ask were punctuated with lots of fudge references. Bud took some time off, but he was all right after he spent a couple of days sedated in a hospital bed. He thanked us for what we'd done and told us he must've lost his mind for a little while, did things he wasn't proud of, that he'd never have done if he was thinking straight. I believed that.

Brianna got better, at least physically. Black flew in the finest plastic surgeons in the country to reconstruct her mouth, and they were as successful as anybody could be. But she couldn't bear the terrible memories of the lake and all that had happened there, so she left for her beach house in Florida to rest and recuperate. Bud let her go, but they kept in touch. He was struggling to forgive himself for what he might have done if the Rangos family hadn't struck first.

Shaggy was reinstated at the coroner's office, but on probation, and I didn't tell anybody what Shaggy, Bud, and Brianna had planned to do. Their plot had failed, so no harm, no foul. Well, that wasn't exactly true, but at least Walter Costin was rotting in his grave. Truth was, Jose Rangos had just as much reason to want Costin dead as the rest of us, and he didn't have any pesky law-and-order issues to deter him. I didn't exactly condone the hit, but I wasn't going to cry myself to sleep over it, either. Too bad he couldn't whack all my other recurring, disturbing nightmares, too. Then all really would be well.

Black came out smelling like a rose, of course, and I agreed to spend more time at his place if not completely move in with him, at least when he was in residence here at the lake. I felt like I owed him, you see, plus they did have some pretty awesome perks at Cedar Bend Lodge—room service and free housekeeping and a way cool weight room, to be exact. But I still liked my cabin by the lake, that was my home, and I still lived there, too, when Black jetted off on his ever-present, ever-important business trips, which was often, or whenever I felt I needed space and some time alone.

Black backed off and hasn't pressured me for a commitment, thank goodness, but that's what he wanted and now we both knew it. I'll make that decision later. I was enjoying some downtime while my foot healed and went fishing with Harve, now that he was back home from Michigan, not to mention having some quiet, intimate dinners with Black aboard his sleek motor yacht out in the middle of the lake where I was at the moment. These peaceful, halcyon days were well appreciated by Black and me, let me tell you, but they'd only last unless and until somebody else decided to kill their victim on my turf. And that would be a big mistake on their part, believe you me.

I could see Black now, where he stood inside the big plate-glass windows of the main salon. He was talking business on the phone, but he only had on a pair of khaki shorts and no shirt, so I got to enjoy looking at all those hard, tanned muscles and ripped six-pack, remembering how good all that felt rubbing up against me. I did so with a great deal of appreciation and lascivious inner enjoyment. Yep, Black looked good, all right. Actually, he brought to mind one of my old college posters, you know the one all girls have tacked up in their rooms at one time or another, the one that says "a hard man is good to find."

When he saw me watching him, our eyes locked and some pretty strong sexual currents went crackling back and forth. I knew the minute he decided it was time to put down the phone and ring some erotic bells. I know that intense look he gets, that little pleased smile, that air of sensual anticipation. How do I know? Because I look pretty much the same way at the moment. So, so long, I'm heading inside and see what happens. Truth is, I know a good thing when I see it. And believe me, I've seen it.